ON VERITY'S ACCOUNT

A NOVEL

by

Valerie Hansard

Grosvenor House
Publishing Limited

The right of Valerie Hansard to be identified as the author of this
work has been asserted in accordance with Section 78
of the Copyright, Designs and Patents Act 1988

The book cover is copyright to Valerie Hansard
Book cover design by Bella Hansard

This book is published by
Grosvenor House Publishing Ltd
Link House
140 The Broadway, Tolworth, Surrey, KT6 7HT.
www.grosvenorhousepublishing.co.uk

This book is a work of fiction. Any resemblance to
people or events, past or present, is purely coincidental.

A CIP record for this book
is available from the British Library

ISBN 978-1-83975-091-5

Chapter One

'You could just try it, Mother, and see how you like it. Treat it like a holiday. You haven't had a holiday in years.'

Verity Davis looked across at her daughter and was reminded of herself at the same age. Petite and slim, with hardly enough flesh to cover her light bones, Alison Hobbs looked older than her fifty-two years. Her finely chiselled face was more deeply lined than most of her contemporaries and her greying hair, scraped back into a bun at the nape of her neck, made her look rather severe. But her face lit up when she smiled, genuine warmth flowing forth. As always, she was well turned out, and today she looked immaculate in an oyster-white lambs-wool sweater and well-cut black trousers. She wore practically no make-up and her only jewellery was the gold Cartier watch her husband, Steven, had given her for her fortieth birthday in more prosperous times. Verity stirred her tea carefully and broke her Marie biscuit in half. She didn't really like Marie biscuits. She preferred chocolate digestives. Hobnobs were the best. She had asked Mr Jones several times to keep a stock of Hobnobs especially for her: 'milk chocolate please, Mr Jones. I don't like that dark bitter chocolate.' But Mr Jones kept forgetting. She had bought out his supply of milk chocolate digestives only the other day, so this morning there were only Marie biscuits left. And they had seen fresher days. That was the trouble with corner shops. They hardly ever had what you wanted and when they did it was very often stale. Verity would much rather have done her shopping at Safeway, as she always used to when Hal was alive. But the branch in Wanstead High Street had closed down several years ago, as it was too small with insufficient car parking. The nearest supermarket was Sainsbury's in South Woodford, but that was too far to walk. Now aged seventy-nine, Verity had given up driving, so the large Sainsbury's in Barkingside was also out of the question. Alison had offered to drive her, or even do her weekly shopping for her. 'I'll take on your shopping, Mother, with pleasure.' But it was the emphasis that Alison had given to the word 'pleasure' that made her feel the extra burden of her shopping would give her daughter anything but pleasure.

Besides, Verity somehow had to fill the hours in the day. She got up as late as possible and was generally in bed before nine pm, unless there was something interesting on the television. But that was rare. And there was a limit as to how much she was able to sleep at night. Particularly as she seemed to doze off during the day almost every time she sat down. Then there was the question of her independence. She felt proud that she was still able to do her own shopping, her own cooking, laundry and housework. It made her feel free. Alive. Still a person in her own right. And now her daughter, Alison, was planning to take away her freedom.

'Going into a retirement home is not really the same thing as going on a holiday.' Verity dipped half the Marie biscuit in her tea, lost it and tried to fish it out with a teaspoon.

'It depends how you look at it,' said Alison.

'How should I look at it?' Verity felt the biscuit against the side of the cup, soggy and unresponsive, so she decided to leave it where it was.

'Think of it as an adventure.'

'An adventure into increasing old age?'

'No, Mother. Of course not. No one is younger than you are for their age.'

'Then why should I go into a retirement home?'

'For more comfort and security. To lessen the drudgery of daily chores. To be pandered to. For a change of scene.'

'But I have plenty of comfort and security here. I quite enjoy doing my daily chores and I don't particularly want a change of scene.'

Alison was beginning to realise that her plan to install her mother in a retirement home was going to be far more difficult than she had envisaged. She would have to work hard to find good reasons why Verity should move out of the comfortable granny flat. It was pointless explaining that she and Steven needed the rent. Verity saw no reason why she should pay rent. She had bailed them out ten years ago and now she owned the flat. She owned the house and the travel business as well. In fact, Verity owned everything she and Steven possessed except the clothes they stood up in. The only possible solution to their continuing financial problems was to get Verity settled in a suitable retirement home and then find a tenant who would pay a substantial rent.

'Would you like to have a look at it, Mother?'

'Just a look?' Verity felt sure there was a trap some-where.

'Well, yes. I thought this afternoon might...'

'You mean you've already arranged it?'

'It can always be rearranged.'

'We'll go this afternoon,' Verity conceded. 'I've nothing else pressing to do.'

It wasn't far to Oaklands. The area was full of retirement homes and Alison had seen most of them. Many were dingy with untended front gardens, peeling paint and grimy net curtains at the windows. The accommodation was often cramped, with two or three residents sharing a bedroom. Alison knew there was no question of suggesting such depressing places to her mother. After all, it would be a move for life. There would be no question of her ever returning to the granny flat or even moving on anywhere else. Wherever she went to live next, Verity would undoubtedly end her days. Alison had been consumed with guilt as she had toured these dismally depressing places. Even though she now had Steven on her back, pressing for immediate action as the bills poured in and their debts mounted, she felt, that for all her shortcomings, Verity merited better treatment than to be incarcerated in one of those prison-like retreats for the rest of her life.

Then one day, driving down a wide, pleasant tree-lined street on the way to Wanstead Cemetery for the funeral of her best friend's mother, Alison had seen a discreet notice on a large house opposite a deconsecrated church, saying: 'Oaklands - Retirement Home - Vacancies.' By then she had all but given up hope of finding suitable accommodation for her mother, thinking that Verity's next move in ten years' time or more would be into the cemetery itself. After the funeral she returned to have another look at Oaklands. The front garden was neatly kept; and although it was still only February, new spring shoots were already peeping through the well-manicured soil. The house had been newly painted and freshly laundered, tastefully plain net curtains hung behind gleaming white window frames. The front door was a glossy deep red. Alison parked her car opposite, walked up the short drive way and rang the front door bell.

'Oh, they're nearly all reluctant, Mrs Hobbs. That's quite usual. A little top-up?'

'Thank you.' Alison passed her cup to be refilled.

'Have another scone? They're homemade. Cook's speciality. She used to be a pastry chef. Most elderly people have a sweet tooth, don't you find?'

Pamela Price adjusted the hairgrips in her snow-white stiffly starched cap and smoothed down the equally well-starched dark blue skirt of her nursing sister's uniform. She always wore her uniform while on duty. As owner of the retirement home, it gave her status. And status gave her confidence.

'Certainly,' agreed Alison. 'My mother's tooth is notoriously sweet.'

Things were going better than she had ever dared hope. She had been given a full tour of the home. Almost every resident had their own bedroom and some had private bathrooms. The communal rooms appeared to be light, airy and spacious, even though the patterned walls and carpets did seem a little garish. Many of the residents were playing cards or board games. Others were chatting amongst themselves. Only those most advanced in years were slumped, silent and inert, in their easy chairs. An attractive nurse in her early twenties was moving between the groups, passing out cups of tea and biscuits. Alison had accepted an invitation from Miss Price to join her for tea in her private room.

'So you say that your mother is suffering from severe memory lapses, Mrs Hobbs?'

'Oh, yes. Quite severe.' Alison's heart skipped a beat. How did she dare to lie so blatantly? But this was just the beginning. Fortunately no one would ever know. It was her word against Verity's.

'My mother thinks she is at the peak of health and totally in control.'

'Oh, yes, they all do.' Pamela Price had plenty of experience with this kind of situation.

'You see,' continued Alison, warming to her theme, 'my mother goes out shopping and forgets where she is. Several times in the last couple of months she has been brought home by complete strangers. Once it was even the police!'

Alison wondered if she had gone too far. The police could always be checked up on.

'Oh, yes, I hear these stories constantly. They're what I call "the beginning of the end." The onset of old age begins with confusion and ends up in a home like this one. But that's what we're here for, Mrs Hobbs. We're here to ease the confusion, comfort the elderly and free their relatives from further worry.'

Alison felt a warm glow flowing through her veins. 'It sounds too good to be true.'

'Of course the problem will be to persuade your mother to move in here.'

'That will certainly be a problem,' said Alison with some feeling.

'Does your mother have many friends, Mrs Hobbs? We always encourage our residents to receive as many visitors as they wish. It helps them to keep in touch. Though sadly many have no friends left.'

'I can imagine.' Alison thought how few friends her mother had had, even in her younger days.

'And we do suggest, in the case of the most reluctant prospective residents, that they pay us a social visit before definitely deciding to move in. Say, calling in for tea one day. Does your mother have a favourite tea-time food?'

'Hobnobs.'

'Hobnobs? How interesting. That's quite a new name to me. As Cook bakes all our cakes, I find I'm a little out of touch. Is it a type of cake or…?'

'No. It's a biscuit. A chocolate biscuit. The milk variety. My mother dislikes plain dark chocolate.'

'I see.' Miss Price made a note on the pad on the table beside her. *Mrs Davis likes Hobnobs. A type of biscuit. Milk chocolate only.*

'And now, Mrs Hobbs, much as I hate to talk about money. If your mother should decide to come and join us, and I do hope that you will be able to persuade her to do so - if she does come to live here, I shall need to know whether her application will have the backing of council funds or whether…'

'You needn't worry, Miss Price. My mother will be able to pay your fee without any problem.'

Pamela's eyebrows shot up. Any admission of wealth was most unusual. It so often sent the wrong signals.

'Would she have sufficient funds to cover a steep rise in the charges if, say we were to have rampant inflation and she were to live to an extreme old age?'

'I would have thought so.'

Wealthy residents were worth their weight in gold. Pamela had far too many residents who were supported by the council. Mrs Hobbs and Mrs Davis were certainly worth working on.

At first Verity refused to get out of the car.

'Take me home please, Alison.'

'But Mother, just a quick look. We've been invited to tea. We can't just not turn up. It wouldn't be polite, would it?'

'It's only tea. There'll be plenty of other people to drink it.'

But she was a little stung by her daughter's accusation that not turning up would be impolite.

'Look, Mother, how clean and bright the house looks. It's recently been painted. And the front garden is immaculate. Already full of little green shoots.'

Very reluctantly, Verity agreed to take a look at the front garden. Alison felt a surge of relief as she helped her mother out of the car and across the road. They were admiring the brightly coloured crocuses and the strong green daffodil shoots when the front door opened. Miss Price had been watching them sitting in the car from her front window. She suspected that Alison was having difficulty in getting her mother to visit Oaklands. The garden was a good ruse. She felt that she and Mrs Hobbs would get on well together.

Miss Price extended her hand. 'I'm sure you must be Mrs Davis. Your daughter has told me all about you. Welcome to Oaklands. Do come in.' She hoped her voice sounded warm and friendly.

It was already getting dark when Verity and Alison took their leave. Verity was the first to extend her hand.

'Thank you so much for your hospitality, Miss Price. It's been such an interesting tour, hasn't it Alison? It's given us a lot to think about. But I'm sure you'll agree it would be unwise for us to come to any hasty decision.'

Alison and Pamela exchanged despairing glances.

'I'll let you know as soon as possible,' said Alison. Thank you for the tea. Come along, Mother.'

Pamela Price stood on the front doorstep watching Alison slowly shepherding her mother across the road to the car. As she installed Verity in the front passenger seat, Alison raised her hand in a final farewell. As she returned the wave, Pamela heard soft footsteps coming from the side entrance towards the front of the house. She hesitated, but before she had time to go in and close the front door, a male figure appeared out of the deepening gloom and a familiar voice said: 'Miss Price?'

Miss Price gave a nervous little laugh. 'That you, Ken?'

'Yes. I've brought the stuff. Shall I put it in the garidge?'

Miss Price thought quickly. No one was likely to go into the garage before the morning.

'Well, yes. Why not? Will you be back in the morning to deal with it?'

'Yes. I'll be back in the morning. Goodnight, Pamela.'

'Good. Goodnight, Mr Spooner.'

Chapter Two

'Bugger off, you monster!' Kelsey screamed as Nigel held onto her too tightly.

'Language! Language! And you're drunk again.'

'Do you blame me, living with a scum-bag like you?' Kelsey tried to free herself from Nigel's arm-lock.

'Maybe the feeling is reciprocated. Hence my own inebriation,' said Nigel loftily.

'Stop spewing your highfaluting legal-speak at me.'

'You're just too thick to understand English that isn't written by a tabloid journalist.'

'Shut your mouth. Ow! Let go of my arm, you shit!'

'You're just half a person. The dumb half.'

'Nigel! That's a cruel vicious thing to say!'

'It's true! You still can't function on your own. You're always looking over your shoulder, expecting her to be there to help you out.'

'How dare you say that!'

'You won't face up to the fact she isn't there any more and she won't be coming back.'

'You brute! You pig! I told you before never to mention her again. You're a vile cruel bastard and I hate you!'

Kelsey twisted herself around and bit Nigel's ear hard. Her front teeth were sharp and slightly serrated and Nigel gave a yelp of pain as blood poured down the side of his face.

'You tart! You toad! You witch!'

'I'm glad it hurt. It was meant to.'

'Hurt! It's bloody agony!'

Nigel put his hand up to his ear and felt a piece of flabby flesh hanging loose. 'You've taken a bite out of my ear! You cow! You filthy bitch! I'll sue you for assault!'

'Sue away! You won't get anywhere. Even with your superior legal knowledge. I'll sue you for mental and physical cruelty.'

'I'm not cruel. You're too sensitive.'

'You are cruel. You're a cruel cheat and a lazy drunkard to boot. I'm sick of pretending we're happily married. I'm sick of pretending I've got a kind, caring, hard-working husband with a brilliant legal career in prospect, who's about to become the greatest barrister ever. When in fact you spend the entire day in your chambers humping your secretary...'

'Only once, Kel. Just that once. And Susie was very provocative.'

'That's no excuse. You should have enough self-control to leave her alone. You could have thought of me. We've only been married three years and you're already screwing your goddamn secretary.'

'It won't happen again, Kel. I promise.'

'Hurrugh! How do I know it won't? Not content with screwing your secretary you come home and say cruel things to me to remind me of the loss of my twin sister...'

'I didn't mean it, Kelsey. Honestly I didn't. It just slipped out.'

'Remarks like that shouldn't just slip out. You're thoughtless and insensitive.'

'I've said I didn't mean it.'

'It's too late now. And you were drunk at lunchtime.'

'Not completely…'

'So you live the life of Reilly, getting drunk at lunchtime and humping your goddamn secretary, while I go out to work all day, to earn the money that you should be making. Then all you do when you come home is shout abuse at me for not having your dinner ready on time and berate me for being only half a person. Then you lounge about the flat all evening doing bugger all except getting drunk and talking to your precious secretary on the phone. I'm just bloody sick of you, Nigel Potter! I'm going to pack my things and go and live somewhere else!'

Kelsey walked towards the bedroom door. Nigel grabbed her arm and held it, more gently this time. He began to cry.

'Please Kel! Don't go! I'm sorry! Ever so sorry! I love you! Honest. I promise not to say things like that again and I swear there's nobody else but you now…'

'Now!'

'Susie was only a one-off. An aberration. A stupid mistake that shouldn't have happened, but she was very persuasive. Come on, let's sit down and talk about it. Please!'

He felt Kelsey falter for a second. 'Please, Kel. Let's sit over there on the sofa we had such fun choosing. How long ago was that? Two years ago? We've barely been married three years. Let's put our past behind us…'

'Our past! Who's talking? You're the one with the past. Not me. I married you in good faith. Until death do us part.'

'For better or worse.'

'It couldn't be worse.'

'Well, now it can only get better.'

'When is it going to start?'

Nigel felt her weakening again. 'Now. Right now. Let's go to bed.' He put his hand inside her blouse and felt her bra strap.

'No! Nigel, no!' Kelsey tried to push him away.

'Why not? I want you. I love you.'

'You're not very good at showing it.'

'But I shall. I'm going to. I want to start right now. I want to have you right here on the floor, in front of the sofa we chose together.'

'Who was the last woman you had right here in front of the sofa while I was out at work earning the money to pay for it?'

'No one, Kel. Honest. You've got to believe me.'

As he rolled her nipple between his finger and thumb, he felt her shudder. He knew how to arouse her. Then he laid her on the floor in front of the sofa and slipped off his jeans.

'A little more meat, Nigel?'

'Yes please, Alison. It's quite delicious. Even my mother doesn't get pork crackling quite as crispy as you do.'

Alison laughed. 'I must say I can't think of a greater compliment from my son-in-law.'

'Kelsey, darling? Another potato, or a sprout or two?'

'No, thanks, Mum.'

'You're not eating enough, dear.'

'She hardly eats anything,' said Nigel. 'She's afraid of getting fat.'

'I eat plenty,' Kelsey said loftily, 'and I like being thin.'

Steven got up to refill Nigel's wine glass. 'I'm glad to see that you appreciate *Chateauneuf du Pape*, Nigel. Some people find it rather heavy, but it's always been a great favourite of mine.'

'And a great favourite of mine, too, Steven. Thank you.'

'Nigel likes any wine. He's not very discriminating. He prefers quantity to quality,' said Kelsey sweetly.

Nigel glared at her.

Just as he sat down Steven noticed the large plaster on Nigel's ear. 'Tried to shave your ear off, old chap?' he enquired jovially.

'Nigel bumped into a door,' said Kelsey, too quickly to be convincing.

'It must have been quite a hard door,' said Alison.

'Oh, yes.' Kelsey stepped into the breach again, as quick as a flash. 'Those doors in chambers, you know, they're terribly hard. It's to teach the barristers self-discipline, isn't it, Nigel?'

'Always ready for a witticism is our Kelsey.'

'Oh, yes,' said Alison. 'Kelsey has always been reno-wned for her sparkling sense of humour.'

'Who'd have believed it?' murmured Nigel.

'Any interesting cases coming up shortly?' enquired Steven conversationally.

'Oh, yes. Plenty of interesting things in the pipe-line.'

'They're always just around the corner,' said Kelsey. 'Aren't they, Nigel? There's always something around the corner.'

'Well, isn't that nice?' said Alison. 'It's always good to have things in prospect.'

Ignoring this remark, Nigel asked: 'how is your mother, Alison? Such a wonderful old lady. Quite indomitable.

She'll probably go on forever. You've got it so well arranged, letting her have that lovely little flat so that she has her independence but you're within call if she should need you. Marvellous planning, if I may say so.'

Alison and Steven exchanged glances.

'Thank you, Nigel, murmured Alison. 'Now if everyone has finished the first course perhaps you could help me clear away the plates, Kelsey darling, and I'll bring in the pudding.'

Kelsey sat at her dressing table brushing her glossy, wavy dark hair. She went on brushing hard, thumping her head and pretending it was Nigel. She was trying to punish him but only succeeded in giving herself a headache. If only she had the courage to leave him. But she had no money and nowhere to go. Above all, she couldn't face telling her family that she had married a complete shit. If only Kirsty... But it was pointless thinking about it. Kirsty was dead and the dead could never return. Should she try telling her mother that her marriage was in ruins and she was planning to sue for divorce? The answer was 'no.' Alison was too absorbed in trying to make ends meet and keeping her father off the bottle. What about Grandma? Kelsey was fond of her grandmother. She admired her pride and her fierce independence, living alone in her elegant granny flat and cooking for herself, even though Alison lived next door. Alison was always so absorbed in her own affairs that she never even offered to go shopping for her own mother. Of course Grandma had plenty of money. Life was much easier if one had money, and far more pleasant. Kelsey remembered, with a mixture of plea-sure and pain, the relatively opulent days of her own childhood, not so long ago, when she and Kirsty were given almost everything they wanted. Kelsey wondered what her grandmother did with all her money. She knew she had bailed out her father's travel business and was probably paying an enormous rent for the granny flat. But she lived simply and never seemed to buy anything new. So there must be plenty of money to spare. But for whom?

Would her mother, Aunt Julia and Uncle Russell benefit from a healthy inheritance? Or would - preposterous thought - the bulk of it go to charity? Was it possible that the old lady could be persuaded to part with some now? If her grandmother were to give her, or even lend her, five thousand pounds, she could leave Nigel and start her own business. She might even go to college. She had six GCSE's with B grades and two with C. It was worth a try. A visit to her grandmother was overdue. She might pop around on Sunday. But perhaps a call to Aunt Julia first would be a good idea. Aunt Julia saw things in a different way to her own mother. She was more observant and less immersed in her own problems. Big, over-weight Aunt Julia married to boring Uncle Graham. If over-eating was a symptom of stress, it could surely also be caused by boredom. Kelsey under-stood the stress symptoms only too well. After Kristy's death she had binged on chocolate for more than a year. But now Kelsey had found the solution to controlling her weight. It was ludicrously simple. No one else knew. It was one of her secrets.

Kelsey finished brushing her hair and banging her head. She put the hairbrush down on her dressing table, opened the centre drawer and took out her make-up pouch. She applied some foundation to her pretty oval face, covering the freckles on her small upturned nose. She dusted her face lightly with powder. Then she replaced the foundation and the powder compact in the make-up pouch and took out three cases of lipstick. She tested each one on her hand before making her choice, selecting a bright vermillion, which she thought would be more noticeable than her usual pale peach. She applied the lipstick with care, drawing a firm line around her shapely top lip. Who knew whom she might meet in Wanstead High Street on her way to work in Sun Med, her father's travel agency. She put the vermillion lipstick in her handbag and the other two into the make-up pouch, replacing the pouch in the dressing-table drawer. She stood up and walked to the other side of the room to inspect herself in the full-length mirror. She noted with approval the small firm breasts just discernible under the thin diaphanous blouse, the slim waist pinched in with a wide belt and the long shapely legs appearing under the shortest of mini-skirts. One could never tell what kind of punters would come in to book their holidays with Sun Med.

After all, that was how she had met Nigel.

'But, Aunt Julia, I always feel that you get on best with Grandma.'

'What makes you think that, Kelsey?'

'Well, you know how Mum is inclined to make heavy weather of things.'

'She does have Grandma living next door. In fact she's practically living in her house.'

Julia felt she ought to defend her sister, whom she always felt had shouldered most of the burden of their mother's widowhood.

'And Russell, well, being like Uncle Russell means one must have a different view of the world to other people.'

'Russell's okay. He does his bit too. He visits Grandma occasionally. She enjoys that.'

'But I see you as being in the middle, Aunt Julia.'

'Which, of course, I am.'

'I didn't mean as regards age. I meant more in attitude. You don't live next door to Grandma like Mum does, and but you're not like Uncle Russell either.'

'No, hardly,' said Julia. 'What is it exactly that you want, Kelsey?'

Kelsey wondered for a split second whether she couldn't just say 'money' and be done with it. But it didn't seem a very subtle approach, or very loyal to Nigel either. A few weeks ago she wouldn't have considered loyalty to Nigel, but now things were going better. Nigel had sacked Susie, his provocative secretary and engaged a plain, middle-aged old bag aptly named Miss Prim. He had cut down dramatically on his drinking and had started to bring her presents of flowers and chocolates. He had been given a couple of low profile briefs, so the money was beginning to trickle in at last. Even so, they never seemed to keep abreast of their numerous financial commitments.

'I was just wondering if you thought Grandma would lend us a little money.' Kelsey felt her heart beating faster. 'Just until Nigel gets on his feet. A barrister's career seems very slow to get started.'

'Yes. That's well known. But he'll win through in the end. You'll see. Why don't you drop round and ask Grandma yourself? She'd love to see you and hear all your news. Nigel could go with you. Grandma's so fond of Nigel. She was only saying the other day that she was thrilled when you married a barrister. She said: "at last we have someone in the family who is a professional; not just a businessman trying to make money." '

'I don't know what Grandma meant by that, I'm sure,' said Kelsey in some desperation. 'Nigel is in it for the money, but there just doesn't seem to be any around, that's all.'

'Go and see Grandma, Kelsey. I'm sure she'll help you all she can.'

'Thanks a bundle, Aunt Julia.'

Julia put down the phone down. Graham lowered his paper. 'And what was all that about?'

'Kelsey.'

'So I gathered. What did she want?'

'Money from Mother.'

'Oh! Well I hope she's more successful than the rest of us.'

Graham returned to his newspaper.

Chapter Three

'I've got a lunch date.'

'Oh! Super! Would I fancy him?'

Russell Davis stroked the back of his head in a characteristic gesture, smoothing down his carefully-styled thick, slightly greying mane of dark hair.

'I wouldn't have thought so. He's more my sort than yours.'

'Shame. Haven't you sold that old rocker yet, Russell? It's been outside your shop for months.'

'Yes, darling. Six months. And not a teeny-weeny peep out of it. Would it go better outside your shop, perhaps? You know how a change of position can improve even the slowest-moving item. And this is no rubbish, as you can see.'

Russell laid his well-manicured hand carefully along the back of the chair. Vicki bent down to inspect it, her long dark bob falling over her face.

'Lovely, isn't it, darling? Such a shame I can't sell it.'

'How much are you asking?' enquired the ever-practical Vicki.

'Six hundred.' Russell patted the back of his head again.

'What!' gasped Vicki. 'That's a monstrous price! You'll never get that. How much did you pay for it?'

Russell leant his tall, slight body towards her and lowered his voice. 'Two. But I'm not telling anyone else.'

'Russell! That's a two hundred per cent mark up! No one tries that!'

'But darling, these days things just aren't moving. You know how desperate business is. I've only sold two items all week and those were vastly under-priced. I don't know how people manage.'

Vicki was examining the chair with an expert eye. 'It is a lovely piece,' she acknowledged. 'Beautiful carving and such elegantly turned legs. Pity about the white calico. It's so dirty and not at all Victorian. I wonder who put that on?'

'I did.'

'Really? Why white?'

'I thought it would be neutral and appeal to all tastes.'

'And so in the end it's appealed to none. Look, Russell, I'll take it for a week and if I sell it we'll go halves, okay?'

'Halves! Darling, I can't afford to part with half my profit!'

'Half or nothing,' said Vicki firmly.

'Oh, all right, then.' Russell gripped the back of the chair hard so that his knuckles showed white. 'Only if you swap it for one of your beaded footstools.'

Vicki laughed. 'I'll consider it. Here's your dashing young dark friend about to waft you away to lunch. I'll be back later. Maybe even with a footstool. Hello, Sudip. Come to take Russell to Frederick's for lunch?'

Sudip smiled, his even teeth gleaming whitely in his dark face. 'Hello, Vicki. Lunch, yes; Frederick's, no.'

'I'm off then,' said Vicki with a wave. ' See you later, Russell. Have a good lunch.'

'Bye,' said Russell. 'Enjoy your date.'

Tall, slight and elegantly dressed in a beige Paul Smith suit, Sudip nodded goodbye to Vicki and placed his arm lightly on Russell's shoulder in a public apology for a hug.

'You okay?'

'In the pink, darling.'

'No movement on the rocker?'

'None at all. Unless you count a sideways move next door.'

'Which side?'

'Vicki's.'

'You mean she's bought it?'

'Oh, no, darling. But she's going to help me to try and sell it.'

'Professional solidarity?'

'Exactly.'

'I hope it works.'

'So do I, dear. I'm desperate.'

'I'll take you to lunch. But not Frederick's.'

Russell laughed, as they began to carry the items usually left on the pavement during opening hours into the small, crowded shop. 'Frederick's is only for the most special celebrations.'

Sudip picked up a Windsor chair. 'This is nice.'

'Yes. The yew ones are quite rare. Yours for eight hundred pounds.'

Sudip laughed. 'That's a bit steep. Then I wouldn't be able to afford to treat you to lunch.'

'But if you bought it then I could afford the lunch.'

'And dinner too.'

'For at least a week.'

They both laughed. With everything stacked away inside the shop, Russell closed the door and locked it. 'Hungry?' He smiled at his friend.

'Always,' replied Sudip.

'Where'll we go?'

'The Camden Head or Café Flo?'

'The Camden Head. We went to the Café Flo last time. The Camden Head does a nice salad.'

The two men wandered slowly along the Camden Passage, a well-established antique market just off Upper Street in Islington. It was a Tuesday and quiet. Wednesdays and Saturdays were the main market days when the bric-a-brac stalls were set up in Pierrepoint Row and along the pavements. It was late February, dry and bright, and the sun was already high enough to appear in the wider streets. A chilly wind whipped across from the northerly direction of The Business Centre on the opposite side of Upper Street. As they crossed the top of Charlton Place, Russell greeted friends as they passed.

'Hello, Maggie, darling. Chilly wind, isn't it? Morning, Eustace, I see you still haven't moved the bureau.'

When they opened the door of the pub, Sudip's glasses misted over as the warm air blew into their faces. They found a table in the far corner, hung up their coats on the Victorian coat stand and sat down to order their food. Russell sat hunched up for several minutes, saying nothing. Sudip looked at his friend with some concern and put his hand on his knee.

'What's the matter, old chap?'

'Business.'

'Bad?'

'Very bad.'

'Nothing moving?'

'Nothing at all.'

'Not even within the trade?'

'Nope. Everyone's suffering from the strong pound. It's driving away all the overseas buyers and the British punters are too lily-livered to buy anything at all for fear of another recession. It's a stalemate.'

'Any ideas?'

'Sell up.'

'Russell! You can't! Not after twenty years! You'd miss the business terribly. And the Passage just wouldn't be the same without you.'

'I know.'

'And what would you do?'

'I don't know. That's the problem. It's a catch 22 situation. I can't live by doing it and I can't live without it.'

'Tried a bank loan?'

'Oh, yes.'

'No joy?'

'None.'

'Rich relatives?'

'Mother.'

'Worth a touch?'

'As tight as a fish's arsehole.'

Sudip laughed in spite of the gravity of the situation. 'Another of your poetic English expressions!'

'I don't know about poetic, but it's certainly descriptive.'

'How old is she?'

'Nearly eighty.'

'Sound of mind?'

'Alarmingly so.'

'Where does she live?'

'In a granny flat in my sister's house in Wanstead.'

'Wanstead? Where's that?'

'East.'

'East London?'

'East of East London.'

'Sounds dreadful.'

'It is.'

'Why do they live there?'

'That's where we originated.'

'Really! You as well?'

'Me as well. I was born there.'

'You never told me.'

'I hadn't got around to it yet. We've only known each other just a few weeks.'

'True.'

'And I didn't think it was essential to our relationship.'

'No. Maybe not. But it's extremely interesting.'

'Interesting?'

'Everything about you interests me, Russell. No. Fascinates me. Your quintessential Englishness. Your upper-classiness.'

'I'm not at all upper-class,' replied Russell, still unsure of how much he should reveal. 'My grandfather was a costermonger in Petticoat Lane.'

'And he made good?'

'Very good indeed. He died a millionaire.'

'Which your father inherited?'

'Yes. In the form of several shops, I believe.'

'And he did even better than your grandfather?'

'He died a multi-millionaire.'

'How long ago?'

'It must be at least five years ago now.'

'And the money?'

'My mother has it.'

'All of it?'

'Yes.'

'Then why don't we pay her a visit?'

'We?'

'Why not?'

'She might be shocked.'

'That you have a boy friend?'

'Well, yes.'

'But surely she must know by now that you're gay?'

'I don't see her that often.'

'But your sister. Wouldn't she have said something?'

'I've no idea. I don't see that much of my sisters either.'

'Sisters! How many?'

'Two.'

'You are a dark horse!'

'Well...it didn't seem necessary... '

'No, okay. What are your sisters called?'

'Alison and Julia.'

'Alison. Julia.' Sudip rolled the names round his tongue like a piece of butterscotch. 'Nice. Very nice.'

'What?'

'The names. Alison and Julia. I like the sound of those names.'

'Haven't you heard them before?'

'Possibly. But one forgets. I don't see a lot of women.'

'What about your students?'

'They're different.'

'How?'

Sudip smiled. 'I'll tell you another time. Let's get back to your mother.'

'And her money?'

'Yes. Do you think she'd like to meet me?'

'I really have no idea.'

'Do you think she's ever met an Indian before?'

'I can't answer that question either.'

'Russell, I don't think I've ever met anyone who knows less about their immediate family than you do.'

'No?'

'No. And I think you should start finding out more about them right now. You might find that strengthening your family ties could have all sorts of benefits.'

'Of a financial nature?'

'Particularly of a financial nature.'

'And you wish to be included?' asked Russell teasingly.

'Only on the social side, of course. And possibly on the educational side too. Perhaps your mother would like to hear a little about India, first-hand.'

'Perhaps she would,' said Russell laughing. 'I'll give her a bell this evening.'

'And will you have an arranged marriage in India, Mr Banjaree?'

'Please call me Sudip, Mrs Davis.' Sudip's eyes were huge and serious. 'Like pools of deepest darkest water,' Russell had said the first time they had made love.

'I shall be delighted, Sudip. Any friend of Russell's is a friend of mine. And now, while Russell goes to the kitchen for the sherry bottle and the glasses, I want you to tell me all about India. But maybe you would prefer whisky? I believe a lot of whisky is drunk in India. Among the upper classes, of course.'

'Whisky would be excellent, thank you.'

'Would you bring in the whisky as well, please, Russell? While Sudip tells me all about this beautiful girl he is about to marry.'

'Of course,' said Russell, obligingly going out to the kitchen.

'Have you met her yet, Sudip?'

'No. Not yet.'

'So when are you planning to visit India for this most important occasion?'

Sudip realised he would have to be a little bit inventive, and above all, not let Russell down.

'As a matter of fact, Russell and I were discussing the possibility of a trip to India just the other day.'

'Oh, but how wonderful of you to include Russell in your matrimonial plans! I see you two are good friends. Will Russell be the best man at your wedding? Or perhaps you don't go in for that sort of thing in India?'

'No. In India there is really no best man. Everyone is best. The extended family and many friends participate in the ceremony, which at a Hindu wedding, can last for several days.'

'And are you a Hindu, Sudip?'

'Yes, I am a Hindu. But not always a very seriously practising one. I don't go to the temple as often as I should.'

'But of course your wedding will take place in the temple?'

Russell returned from the kitchen with three bottles and three glasses on a tray.

'Still on weddings, are we, Mother?'

Sudip threw him a despairing glance.

'It's so interesting to find out about marriage customs in other countries, dear,' said Verity innocently.

'Yes, of course,' said Russell. 'Where shall I put the tray?'

Verity patted her fine grey hair, looped up in a bun at the back of her head in a style very similar to her daughter's. She looked short-sightedly around the room.

'How about on that little table by the sofa, dear? Then we can all be quite comfortable while we sip our drinks and continue with our cosy little chat.'

'Good idea.' Russell put down the tray carefully on the side table and drew up an armchair. 'Will you sit here, Mother, and dispense the liquor, or would you prefer me to do it?'

'Oh, you do it, dear. I love being waited on, don't you Sudip?'

'Oh, yes, very much indeed.' Sudip stood up and helped Verity out of her chair, offering her his arm as she walked slowly across to the armchair on the other side of the room. She looks elegant in her long grey dress with a smart patent leather belt adorning her still slim waist, thought Sudip. But she looks frail too. I wonder how long she'll manage here on her own? As he settled her in the armchair, Verity flashed him a warm smile.

'You've brought three bottles, Russell. What's the third one?'

'A bottle of Burgundy I found in your cupboard.'

'Oh, really! And what is it?'

'It's a *Chassagne Montrachet*. I thought perhaps if Sudip - rather than whisky...'

'An excellent idea,' replied Sudip, who was enjoying improving his knowledge of wine since he had come to live in London nearly three years ago. 'Provided Mrs Davis...'

'Whatever you young men wish, I'm happy to go along with.' Verity settled herself comfortably in the armchair, wrapping her long grey skirt more tightly around her ankles.

'You know, Sudip, I think the family have abandoned all hope of marriage for Russell. He's dated a great number of pretty girls over the years, haven't you, dear? Whether he dropped them or the other way round, I don't really know. And of course it's not my place to ask,' she finished primly.

'Well, marriage isn't for everyone, Mrs Davis.'

'Indeed not,' said Russell with feeling, wondering how they could get off the subject without making it appear too obvious. 'Has Sudip told you that he's planning to take me on a tour of India next Christmas?'

'Yes. Sudip mentioned that he was hoping you would go along with him to help choose his bride.'

'No. Not exactly to choose his bride. Not this time. This time we shall go on a sightseeing trip, just the two of us.'

'But that sounds delightful!' Verity clapped her dry bony hands and gave a cackle of laughter. 'Just the two of you! How romantic! A sightseeing trip before any serious decisions are made. Now I'm all for a bit of pleasure before the real things start. And how long will you go for?'

'About six weeks.'

'Six weeks! That is a long time. You'll certainly see a great deal of India in six weeks. But what about your jobs? You haven't told me yet what you do, Sudip.'

'I'm a lecturer in mathematics at the LSE.'

'LSE?'

'London School of Economics.'

'They teach mathematics?'

'They offer a wide range of courses, Mother. Not just economics.'

'I see. That must be very interesting, rewarding work.'

'It is.'

'And is your degree from a university in India?'

'My BA is from Mumbai and my PhD is from Cambridge,' explained Sudip.

'Very impressive. And can you take six weeks away from your lectures?'

'The vacation is four weeks. I can arrange the rest.'

'Shall I open the *Montrachet*, Mother?'

'Yes, dear. Please do.'

Russell opened the bottle, poured the top into his own glass, poured a fresh half-glass and handed it to Verity. 'Will you taste it?'

'Oh, no. Please give that honour to Sudip.'

Russell handed the glass to his friend, looking deeply into his eyes. Sudip smiled his thanks and held up the glass expertly to the light, examining the colour. He savoured the bouquet, twirled the liquid around in the glass and took a sip.

'Delicious,' he pronounced at last. 'A bottle of supreme eminence. I congratulate you on a splendid purchase, Mrs Davis.'

Russell filled Verity's glass and poured his own.

Verity laughed. 'Oh, I'm sure I didn't buy it. It must have lain in the kitchen cupboard for a long time. My husband probably bought it. Hal, my husband...' She leant confidentially closer to Sudip, 'Hal had a splendid knowledge of wine. We always drank fine wines with dinner every evening when Hal was alive. But he could afford it, you know. It's different now that I'm a widow. A widow has many hidden expenses. The money doesn't seem to go nearly so far as it did when Hal was alive.'

She stared down into her glass, seemingly miles away. Russell and Sudip exchanged glances again. The silence continued for a few moments.

'May I propose a toast, Mother?'

'Of course, dear.'

Russell raised his glass. 'To India.'

'To India,' repeated Verity and Sudip.

'And what will you do with your shop, Russell, when you go off to India?' enquired Verity.

Russell took a deep breath. This was it. It was now or never. This was the whole reason for the little tea party in the first place. The tedium of his mother's stewed Red Label tea, the sandy Madeira cake and the stale milk chocolate Hobnobs, had all been endured for the sake of asking one simple question: 'Mother, please could you lend me some money?'

Against Russell's better judgement, Sudip had persuaded him that they should pay the visit together. But up until now Sudip had been proved right. So far the visit was turning out to be a huge success. Sudip had gone down a treat with Verity. Russell had never known his mother take so readily to anyone of his generation. She had treated Sudip almost like a member of the family right from the word go. Russell stole another glance at his friend, sitting calmly and relaxed beside him on the sofa, legs elegantly crossed, glass held loosely. As always he was immaculately dressed in grey flannels, navy blazer and a pale apricot Saville Row shirt, which enhanced his dark complexion. Sudip had dressed with great care in order to impress Verity. Russell took a sip of wine and felt a warm glow suffuse his body. Sudip's proximity added to the warmth and for a brief moment Russell wished they were alone. In a short six weeks Sudip had become part of his life, part of his being. Russell had never met anyone quite like Sudip and he often prayed they would never be parted.

'I have two choices, Mother.' Russell tried to keep his tone light and deliver his statement like a throw-away line in a play. 'I can get in a manager for the six weeks we're away, or I can sell up.'

There was another awkward pause as Sudip gave his friend a sympathetic glance. Verity looked straight ahead.

After what seemed an age, Verity asked: 'And what is your preferred choice, dear?'

'To get in a manager.'

'Then that's what you should do,' replied Verity.

'It's not as simple as that.'

'It looks quite straightforward to me. What's the problem?'

Russell decided to shoot from the hip. 'Money.'

'Money?' Verity's fine eyebrows went up a little. But I thought you were making plenty of money, Russell, dear?'

'I was. Until just over two years ago.'

'Then what happened?'

'The great financial crash. Don't you remember, Mother?

Verity looked at Russell with a vague expression. 'I remember something of that sort. Remind me, please, Russell.'

Russell's heart missed a beat. Surely his mother, with so much money of her own, would remember the huge world bank crash in 2008. After all, it was only just over two years ago. But hopefully, Verity's money was not invested in banks. The bank investments appeared to be the major problem to those who were made bankrupt. The more sensible investors, those who had put their money into more reliable companies, had been left largely unscathed, even though the value had more than halved.

'Well, in 2008, a very well-established bank in America, called Lehman Brothers collapsed, leaving a huge number of investors completely bankrupt...'

'But how could the collapse of an American bank affect your sales in that antique market place, Russell?'

Russell felt increasingly helpless. 'The collapse affected the whole world, Mother. Except, of course, the lucky few who had invested safely, out of banks.' He almost said: 'the lucky few like you,' but thought it would be too direct. 'It's a question of the right amount of money not being available...'

'To buy old furniture, which is not necessarily of vital importance to many people.'

'Well, that's one way of looking at it, of course... But I've always enjoyed handling antique furniture, especially English antiques, which foreigners have always been interested in buying.'

'And what did the foreigners do with the English furniture?'

'They took it home with them.'

'But that's rather a shame, isn't it? Surely it would be much better if our English furniture stayed here, where it belongs. I remember once there was a great fuss about the Greeks wanting their marbles back. Apparently the marbles were in some Englishman's collection and the Greeks demanded them back because they had originally come from Greece. I'm all for that. I do think things should go back to where they belong.'

Russell sighed. They were getting off the track again. Nevertheless, he couldn't resist asking: 'what about the Mona Lisa, Mother? Do you think it should go back to Italy?'

'Where is it now?'

'In the Louvre, in Paris.'

'That would mean sending it from one foreign place to another, wouldn't it? I don't see that would make any difference.'

Sudip struggled to keep a straight face. Russell's mother was certainly an interesting mixture of tolerance and narrow-mindedness. But the reason for their visit had not yet been achieved.

Russell refilled their glasses and tried again.

'To return to what we were discussing earlier...'

'Yes, dear. What was that?'

'Sudip's and my projected visit to India.'

'Of course! To choose a beautiful bride for Sudip.'

'Well, not right away.'

'No. But eventually.'

'Eventually. But the more immediate question is how I should finance my share of the trip.'

'Finance? Money?'

'Yes, Mother.'

'Ah, yes. I remember you were saying earlier that you were having a problem selling your furniture to foreigners.'

'That's right.'

'So maybe you should try selling it to English people instead?'

'Yes. But due to the financial crash, English buyers are also short of the ready.'

'So what you are angling at is a loan from me. A small sum just to tide you over while you romp off to India for six weeks?'

'Well, I wasn't sure if I could state it so directly, but that is indeed correct.'

Verity picked up her glass and took another sip, looking long and hard at her son.

'I'll have to give this matter very careful thought. After all, your father helped to set you up in business. Whether that's a reason for me to continue to do so, or whether it's the reason that you should have learnt to manage on your own, I can't really decide in a hurry. And now, dear, I'm beginning to feel a little sleepy. Perhaps it's the wine at my age.'

'Of course.'

The two men stood up to take their leave. Russell leant over Verity and gave her a kiss on each cheek. 'Goodbye, Mother.'

'Goodbye, dear. It was nice of you to call.'

Sudip extended his hand.' Goodbye, Mrs Davis. And thank you. It's been delightful meeting you.'

'And I, too, have had an equally delightful experience. Goodbye, Sudip. Please forgive me for not getting up.'

Chapter Four

'I don't quite follow these figures, Ken.' Graham scra-
tched his head, feeling rather bewildered.

'It's like what I said, Mr Brookes. The little bit extra
in the wage packet comes from what we hasn't declared
on the VAT.'

'But there wasn't meant to be a little extra in the wage
packets.'

'Only ever so little, Mr Brookes. Just to keep the boys
sweet, like.'

'Yes. I understand the point of keeping the key men
sweet. Without the carpenters, electricians and plumbers
we wouldn't have a workforce at all. But I see no reason
to reward the labourers as well.'

'I wouldn't like to think of it as a reward, Mr Brookes.
Just a little extra, like I said.'

'But if we give all the men a little extra, as you put it,
it negates what we've gained by not paying the VAT.
After all, if we'd continued to pay the normal price for
everything, including the VAT, we would have got some
of the VAT back from the government anyway.'

'Eventually, Mr Brookes. Eventually.' Ken Spooner
took off his steel-rimmed spectacles, laid them on the
desk and rubbed his rheumy shortsighted eyes. 'But we
would have paid a lot more for the materials.'

Graham looked hard at his manager, disliking what he saw. He wondered what lack of judgement had led him to employ this shifty-looking man with the close-set glassy blue eyes, protruding lower jaw and hair dyed jet black, plastered down with Brylcreem? What had persuaded him to follow this creep's crackpot advice and start cheating the government, just so he would pay a little less for his materials? The answer, of course, was quite simple. Business was bad and he needed to save money. But he should never have agreed to Ken's illegal suggestion.

'I don't see why the entire workforce needs a little extra, as you call it. Why not just reward the key men and leave it at that?'

'It's not as simple as that, Mr Brooks.' Ken Spooner rubbed his thin hands together in an action that reminded Graham of Uriah Heap. 'Not simple at all.'

'Perhaps you would enlighten me, Mr Spooner? Allow me to follow the intricate workings of your complex mind.' Graham thought that if he sounded sarcastic it would help make him appear superior. All he thought was: you're up to something I haven't quite cottoned on to yet, you scheming, evil bastard.

'It's like this, see, Mr Brookes.' Ken made himself more comfortable by placing his left ankle across his right thigh, almost kicking Graham in the process. 'The bank crash over two years ago was a great shock and affected everyone. And we knew things wasn't going to get better in a hurry either. Not the way the recession was going, like it was beginning to affect the toffs and the middle classes like yourself. So you comes to me, Mr Brookes, it must 'a been a good two years or so back - and you says to me, asking my opinion like: we need to make a few economies somewhere, Ken, if we's going to keep the same number of men on the payroll and still stay in business.'

'I'm totally aware of that. But we're talking about a payroll of fifteen men at the most! The rest are all casual labourers! They're paid by the day, some even by the hour. They could be laid off at any time.'

'Of course, Mr Brookes. But we wouldn't want to have to lay off men unnecessarily, would we?'

Why does he say 'we?' thought Graham angrily. I'm the boss. He's merely the employee, much as he wants to be one of us. But all he said was: 'nobody wants to lay off men. Of course not. The casual labourers have families and goods on tick just as much as the permanent workforce.'

'Or even the toffs,' interjected Ken.

'Yes, even the toffs,' Graham agreed. 'But if the work isn't there - if we're not getting the contracts because the bank loans aren't available for building or renovating, or even just for a little bit of decorating, then we can't keep employing men we don't need.'

'But that's where my little economies come in,' said Ken craftily. 'The sparks on the site up at Trapps Hill, Loughton, told me his brother-in-law knew of a chap what sold good materials, no rubbish, mind, good stuff, but cheap, and you don't pay no VAT neither. So I bought a little load as an experiment, like, and it seemed like real good stuff. But when the lads saw the lorry didn't come from Travis Perkins, as per usual, they wanted to know why. So I explained I was doing the boss a favour and getting the stuff on the cheap, without VAT. And the word went around that sparks was getting his cut, his little bonus is what I mean, and the lads guessed that I'd be getting one too, so of course they all wanted to be in on it. Sounds to reason, eh, Mr Brookes?'

'But this is preposterous! You can't go on like this! Your little economies haven't saved me a penny!'

'You agreed in the beginning, Mr Brookes.'

Graham felt a noose tightening around his neck.

'I only agreed to a few items being purchased more cheaply, to economise a little. I had no idea that it would involve avoiding payment of VAT and bribing my entire workforce into the bargain. I'm supposed to be running a building business, not a protection racket.'

He immediately regretted his choice of words.

'That's just what it's become, Mr Brooks: a protection racket.'

'Well, It's got to stop at once.'

'Can't stop it now.'

'Why not?'

'It's gone too far.'

'What do you mean?'

'There are too many people in the know.'

Graham felt his blood run cold. He wanted to sack Spooner for his outrageously illegal behaviour, but he realised as soon as he opened his mouth to do so, he would eventually be held to account.

'Just leave it all to me, Mr Brookes. I have everything under control - and I have you over a barrel.'

Still smarting from his unpleasant experience with Ken Spooner, Graham made a thorough inspection of the site. Brookes Builders Ltd had nearly finished building four three-bedroom bungalows intended for retired people near the railway line in Woodford. They had been originally advertised as a 'luxury development,' but thanks to the slow progress of the casual labour force, costs had escalated to such a degree during construction that Graham had been forced to extend and increase his bank loan. It was now a question of cutting out as much luxury as possible to avoid an even bigger loan. Graham went into one of the bungalows and chatted with the carpenter, Mick Kelly, one of his longest serving employees, a reliable and highly skilled man. They discussed finishing details; small points noticeable just to the discerning eye; but details that could make an enormous difference to the overall impression of the property: a difference that might be worth several thousand pounds in the selling price. As Graham bid his carpenter farewell, he couldn't help wondering how much he knew about Ken's financial machinations - and how much he stood to gain personally.

His tour of inspection over, Graham walked back to his car. He consulted his watch. Twenty minutes to four. Plenty of time to inspect the renovations at the Queen Anne house near Roydon, off the Epping Road and still make it back to Wanstead for five o'clock tea. In late February there was still daylight until nearly six. He had plenty of time. He slightly regretted having promised Julia he would be back for tea. Graham considered afternoon tea rather unnecessary, a non-event for people who didn't work and were addicted to cream cakes. People like Julia. For some reason William was coming to tea with his new girlfriend and Julia was keen for him to meet her. Graham liked to try to please Julia, if her demands didn't interfere too much with his work. However, if he were delayed, he could always phone her from his mobile.

Something made Graham go around to the back of the first bungalow to the temporary accommodation where Ken had his office. It wasn't that he actually planned to spy on Ken, he merely wanted to see what his manager was up to; which probably amounted to the same thing. As he approached the hut, the noise of hammering and drilling came from the third bungalow a little further on. Graham smiled at the thought of Mick, the chippie, putting the finishing touches with his usual devotion and expertise. Arriving at the back of the hut, he was surprised to find the door not only closed, but locked. What was Ken up to now? Hoping to find another, more tangible reason for sacking his maverick manager, Graham peered in through the window, shielding his eyes from the low afternoon sun. Everything was scrupulously tidy. The telephone stood squarely on the table beside a pile of telephone directories and the fax machine. The computer stood next to it, its screen a dark blank. Plans of several building sites were stacked in a neat pile beside the computer. Beside it lay Graham's mobile phone. Damn, thought Graham, that's blown it. I must have left it there by mistake, so I can't ring Julia if I'm delayed. I'd better get a move on.

At first he was puzzled that the pile of buff pay packets that he had brought Ken over an hour earlier were missing, but he quickly realised why. Today was Thursday. Payday. Payday had always traditionally been a Friday but a few years ago Graham had readily agreed to Ken's suggestion that it should be changed to a Thursday. 'Less people with thousands of pounds rushing around the countryside,' he had pointed out. Ken, as manager and responsible for handing out the pay packets on all of Brookes building sites, was obviously fulfilling his duties at this very moment.

Graham now realised that not only would he probably run into Ken Spooner later in the afternoon, but he would also have to organise the rest of the day without his mobile phone. He walked slowly to the first bungalow, where he had parked his sleek, dark green BMW in the driveway. He took off his navy Aquascutum overcoat and laid it carefully on the back seat. Opening the door, he slid his long, thin body into the driver's seat, shut the door and studied his face in the rear mirror. Aged fifty-two his fair hair was thinning a little on top and greying at the sides. His face was lined, but still handsome and he was proud of the fact that he had no need to wear glasses, either for reading or driving. He straightened his tie and smoothed back his hair. He liked to keep up his smart appearance, even in the car. He switched on the ignition, reversed into the road and drove off in the direction of Epping High Road. He always enjoyed the drive out to Epping. The road through the Forest was narrow but straight, and the traffic was seldom heavy. It gave Graham time to think.

At first he let his mind remain a pleasant blank as he admired the pale yellow primroses and the darker-hued celandines nestling in the banks along the road. There were catkins on the hazelnut bushes, buds already bursting forth on the trees and in places the occasional green shoots were peeping through. Slowly his thoughts turned to the present and his unpleasant meeting with Ken Spooner. He didn't doubt he was being held to ransom. The question was: what should he do about it? If Ken were sacked, he would certainly inform the VAT office and the Inland Revenue of dubious dealings at Brookes

Builders Ltd. Then the fat would be in the fire. The answer lay in putting his financial affairs in order first and then sacking his manager. He had to sort out his VAT, work out more satisfactory income tax returns and lay off his surplus workforce. It all boiled down to money. He needed money right away - several thousand pounds. There was one quick, possible solution: Verity. Graham didn't really like Verity. He respected her and admired her for coping so well with the practicalities of life on her own at the age of nearly eighty. Of course life was always easier if one were as rich as Verity. Enormously rich and extremely mean. A few years ago Julia had asked Verity, at his request, for an interest free loan but Verity's only response was: 'I helped Hal to set Graham up in business. Now it's up to him.'

Just one more try, thought Graham. One more request. He wondered what Verity actually did with all her money. As far as he could gather from Alison and Steven, Verity neither entertained nor went out much. She had few friends and no interest whatsoever in cultural activities. She ate frugally, drank little, didn't smoke and rarely bought anything new. The flat was over furnished, containing as much furniture and memorabilia as could possibly be squeezed into the confined space, when she moved from her spacious house. Graham imagined that Verity's money was in a vast investment portfolio, making hundreds of thousands of pounds a day. He began to wonder, not for the first time, who eventually was going to inherit Verity's money. Alison, Julia and Russell? Or would the bequests extend to Kelsey, William and Samantha as well? Would he and Steven receive a legacy each or would their portion just be absorbed in their wives' share? How long before

Verity pegs out? he mused. People don't go on living indefinitely. Even healthy bodies eventually wear out. Verity appeared in the best of health. But could something be done to - well - speed up the disintegration process, as it were? Were there any foods that might - Good God, he thought. Whatever has got into me...?

He turned left off the Epping Road towards Roydon. The road was narrower here and full of twists and turns. The area contained many old properties, particularly cottages clad in Essex weather-boarding. But despite being almost in the country there was a distinct aura of suburbia, no doubt due to the brand new housing developments of semis and 'luxury bungalows' of the type that he himself was responsible for building. Graham had nothing against new housing. On the contrary, he couldn't live without it, but his personal preference was for old houses and he was particularly enjoying supervising the renovations of the beautiful Queen Anne property near Roydon. Looking in his rear mirror he noticed that the same car, which had joined the Epping Road at the Robin Hood Roundabout, was still behind him. The car was a bright red Ford Sierra and for some reason it looked vaguely familiar. Changing down into third gear before a steep bend, he heard the car behind revving up as the driver also changed down. Rounding the bend he realised that the driver was very close behind him, flashing his headlights.

'Stupid fool,' muttered Graham. He put his foot on the accelerator and pulled away a little. But the other driver accelerated too, coming so close that his front bumper almost touched the rear bumper of the BMW. Graham's mouth started to go dry and the palms of his hands were sweating. He glanced quickly in his rear mirror to see if he could find out what sort of a maniac was following him. But the low sun shining directly through the rear window blinded his vision. The cars raced through the hamlet of Roydon, happily deserted. Then Graham saw a new housing estate on the left with a large roundabout. Perhaps he could surprise his pursuer by turning off suddenly. He took the turn sharply, hoping the red Ford Sierra would react too slowly and continue to drive straight on ahead. But the red Ford seemed to have anticipated his move. The driver took the sharp left turn, followed him around the roundabout and back onto the country road. Graham was becoming nervous. What was the driver doing? What was this mad chase in aid of? Should he stop, get out of the car and confront the motorist face-to-face? Or should he just drive on and try to shake him off? Any confrontation with such a madman might only lead to something worse. Another roundabout loomed ahead. Graham planned to take the second exit rather than go straight on. He drove around it once, and then, without thinking, he went around a second time. The red car was out of sight now. The Ford hadn't managed to keep up with his superior BMW, so hopefully Graham was beginning to shake it off. He had just reached the second exit for the second time when, to his horror, a car came around the roundabout in the opposite direction. It wasn't the red Ford Sierra, but a small white Peugeot with a French number plate. Graham braked as hard as he could, but his car went out of control and skidded across the road. It hit the Peugeot a hard blow on the driver's side before it ended upside down in the ditch. Then Graham blacked out.

A few seconds later the red Ford Sierra arrived on the scene. The driver got out and surveyed the carnage. He walked up to the BMW and then went over to the Peugeot. Both drivers were groaning loudly, so he reckoned they must still be alive. He went back to his red Ford, reached inside and picked up a phone on the passenger seat. Although it was Graham's mobile phone, he dialled 999 for the emergency services.

Chapter Five

'Yes, madam?'

Julia Brookes felt her excitement mounting as she heaved her great bulk towards the large glass display counter. Since entering the bakery she hadn't taken her eyes off the tempting array of cream cakes. The queue seemed endless and the waiting time was much longer than usual. Strange, as it was only Thursday. Usually there were only long queues on Fridays and Saturdays. Perhaps the cream cake obsession was beginning to afflict increasing numbers of Wanstead residents? Julia hoped not. She couldn't bear the thought of supplies of butter, sugar and cream running low. Nor did she like the idea of being in competition with other pastry addicts. Julia didn't enjoy competition. She preferred an easy life with everything handed to her on a plate: preferably a plate of cream cakes.

The assistant stood behind the counter with her tongs poised over the cake tray. Ready for her. For Julia. The assistant was short and plump, her cotton gingham dress almost bursting at the seams, her floury pink apron secured at her bulging waist by a huge safety pin. She knew Julia by sight, of course. She knew all her customers by sight, but she didn't address anyone by name. She didn't believe in fraternising. She thought it was undignified. She felt it would undermine her authority and weaken the natural boundary between her and the customers, well established by the large shop counter. She believed in boundaries in her shop. She needed them, as they helped her to feel important. Julia shuffled her cumbersome weight from one foot to the other, hesitating over her choice. There were three cream cornets left and five cream doughnuts. William was coming to tea with his new girl friend, Sandra. Julia had only met Sandra once and had no idea of her tastes in food. But her son, aged twenty-one, had a formidable appetite and shared his mother's passion for cream cornets. Graham would be there too. Although he tried to maintain an indifference to sweet things in general, he always seemed to manage to select the largest and the most delectable pastry on offer.

'No, go on, Julia, darling,' he would encourage his wife. 'You have the cream cornet. I'll be quite happy with the plain jam doughnut.'

But Julia knew he wouldn't be and her inbuilt instinct to subordinate herself to the male sex in general and her husband in particular, meant she always gave him the best of everything. So she usually missed out, unless she made contingency plans.

'Yes, madam?' repeated the assistant, clicking the tongs impatiently. The queue was well out of the door by now, twenty deep.

Julia pulled down the capacious navy and white-striped over-shirt, which hid her bulging waistband, in a habitual gesture. She was still hesitating. The logical choice would be four cream doughnuts so everyone could be offered the same. And a cream cornet for her, to be consumed as soon as possible. But that would deprive all of them, including herself, of enjoying a cream cornet this afternoon. Her eye travelled to the second tray of cakes. There were still two chocolate éclairs left. Perhaps she should buy two cakes for everyone? If she were to buy four cream doughnuts, two éclairs and three cream cornets there would be a certain amount of choice for everyone this afternoon and she would have the pleasure of consuming an extra cream cornet this morning. All on her own. In just a few minutes.

This was the best and most expensive bakery in Wanstead, so the cakes didn't come cheap. Graham might make some adverse remark about unseemly extravagance, which would embarrass William in front of Sandra. Julia knew Graham's business was recently not doing as well as he wished and money was a bit tight. No. Two cakes each was out of the question. The tongs were clicking away now and some of the other customers were becoming restless. Decision time was overdue.

'I'll take four cream doughnuts, one cream cornet, please and one chocolate éclair,' said Julia, her mouth watering as she watched the assistant put down the tongs, select a flat piece of cardboard, white on one side, gold on the other, and form it expertly into a neat box. Then the tongs were poised once more over the cake tray.

'Four cream doughnuts, madam?'

'Yes, please. And would it be possible - do you think you could put the other two cakes into a separate box? You see, they're for someone else,' finished Julia lamely.

'Yes, madam. Of course. Anything to oblige our customers.' The assistant clucked in disapproval as she created a smaller box with equal skill. 'What was it, madam?' The tongs hovered again. 'Two chocolate éclairs, or two cream cornets?'

Julia hesitated again. 'I think - make it one of each please.'

'Very well, madam.' Julia's selection was finally made. The cream cornet and the chocolate éclair were carefully placed in the second box and both boxes were tied up with gold ribbon, expertly finished with a flamboyant bow.

'That'll be nine pounds and ninety pence, please.'

'Oh, goodness me, that is a lot.' Julia felt herself blushing, struggling with her change purse, as the assistant silently held out her hand.

Julia left the shop with her purchases feeling considerably poorer. Ten pence change from a ten pound note! Goodness me, life is expensive! But she cheered up as she thought about her purchases and her mouth began to water again. Two cream cakes just for her! To eat now! Should she eat them in the car or in the little park by the church? She would have more privacy in the car, but more comfort in the park.

It was a brisk day in late February, and although there was a nippy wind, there was already slight warmth in the sun. Julia walked slowly along the pavement towards the small park by the church, carrying her two boxes. She had already done the rest of her shopping and put it in the car, parked around the corner. The gate to the park was open and Julia walked down the main path towards the church looking for a seat in the sun. She had plenty of choice, for the small park was completely deserted. She put the two boxes down on a bench and sat down beside them. She picked up the smaller box, slid off the gold ribbon, and opened it. Inside nestled the chocolate éclair and the cream cornet. Which should she eat first? The cream cornet was her favourite, so logically it should be kept until last. On the other hand, there was nothing more satisfying than the first bite of a favourite delicacy to take the edge off one's hunger after a - well - fairly modest breakfast of five pieces of liberally buttered toast and honey.

Carefully, almost with reverence, Julia lifted the cornet out of the box, her taste buds salivating. She took her first bite from the wider end. Cream squished out over her face and a dollop of jam went up her nose. She sucked gently at the feather-light pastry, spreading the cream around her mouth with her tongue. Then she paused for a moment in appreciation before she took a second bite. The cornet was a little narrower at this point, so almost all the jam and cream went into her mouth. She spread the filling around again with her tongue, making a satisfying suck-ing noise. Scrumptious. Only one mouthful remained. Julia demolished it quickly without a pause, feeling slightly regretful when the cornet was finished.

Fortunately the chocolate éclair still remained in the box, nestling in its stiff white paper cup, the moist chocolate gleaming darkly on top. Julia picked it up, turning it around with both hands. Yes, one end was slightly thicker than the other one. She held the thicker end in her right hand and took a bite. A little cream joined the jam on the bridge of her nose. She took another bite, more gingerly this time, so as not to waste any of the cream. The third bite finished that off too. Delicious.

Now Julia was filled not only with regret, but also with a desire for more. The cream cornet and the éclair had merely whetted her appetite. She flattened the smaller of the boxes, folded it up and placed it neatly on the bench beside her. She hesitated for a moment before opening the second box. What about tea this afternoon? Would the family be expecting cream cakes? Would they enquire if there were any? She could say she had thought about buying some, but had dismissed the idea. Or she could say that the bakery had sold out. Or she could just eat one more herself now and refuse anything at teatime, saying that she had finally decided to go on a diet. Graham might even be pleased by the prospect of her losing some weight.

Finally desire overwhelmed her and all her self-control vanished. She opened the box and took out the first cream doughnut. It felt soft and squidgy. She took a large bite amid a shower of sugar. She took another, and then reached for the second doughnut. She demolished this in two bites and bit into the third one without a moment's hesitation. She was gobbling now, in a frenzy, in a frantic orgy of creamy food. She felt she couldn't get enough. She felt elated. She wanted to demolish boxes and boxes of cream cornets, doughnuts, éclairs, *mille-feuilles* and cream sponge. She wanted... she wanted to go back to the bakery to buy them out. She wanted to come here every day and just gorge herself on cream cakes. She leant back against the hard slats of the bench feeling exhausted. Two teen-age girls came into the park and walked past her. Julia heard one of them say: 'oh, do look at that fat lady, Sharon! Doesn't she look a scream with that fluffy white stuff all over her face? I wonder what it is?'

'Looks like funny foam to me. Maybe she's just been to the circus.'

'More likely she's polished off two boxes of cream cakes. Which wouldn't be surprising, given her size and the empty boxes beside her.'

Julia waited until the two girls had left the park. Then she picked up the second box, folded it neatly and got up to put both boxes in the litterbin. The sudden movement jolted her stomach and made her feel queasy. Still holding onto the boxes, she was violently sick all over the path, the vomit splashing up over her shoes. Julia found another bench and sat for a while to recover. I've been bingeing, she thought. That's what it's called: bingeing and then throwing up afterwards. She'd read about it in magazines. Adolescents did it, especially girls. They gorged on food and then deliberately made themselves sick afterwards so they wouldn't get fat. There was a special word for it, which she couldn't rightly remember. Except she hadn't made herself sick deliberately. It had just happened.

'More tea, anyone?' There was a general shaking of heads. 'Anything more to eat?'

'No, thanks, Mum.'

'Thanks ever so much, Mrs Brookes, that were real nice.'

Sandra stretched out her long thin legs, which seemed to start at her armpits. They were clad in satin-finish tights and she wore a bright purple low-cut velour top with the shortest mini-skirt Julia had ever seen. Studying her angular body, Julia couldn't help wondering how Sandra managed to eat so much and remain so thin. She hadn't really taken to Sandra and was relieved when she and William took their leave.

'Goodbye, Mum, and thanks for the really nice tea.' William, fair haired, tall and gangling like his father, bent down and kissed his mother on each cheek. 'Take care and say "hello" to Dad for me. I'm sorry we missed him. Sandra was looking forward to meeting him, weren't you, love?'

'Oh, yes.' Sandra giggled nervously. 'I really were an' all.'

'But there's bound to be a next time though, isn't there, Mum?' said William, well aware that his new girl friend hadn't gone down too well.

'Of course, dear. I look forward to seeing you both again, very soon.'

Julia closed the front door and went back into the spacious living room, which ran along one side of the house. The front window overlooked the curved drive-way with parking space for three cars, and from the picture window at the back there was a sweeping view of the well-kept garden, with a trim lawn sloping down to a large ornamental pond at the bottom. The substantial house, with three reception rooms, five bedrooms and three bathrooms had been built in mock Tudor style in the 1930s. When Graham and Julia had bought it in 1987, just over twenty-three years ago, money had been tight. In fact, it had cost far more than they had planned to spend. But they had fallen in love with it, seduced by its spaciousness and aura of grandeur. The house had style and class, and now, with the phenomenal rise in house prices during the 1980s, it seemed to them that they had bought it for a song.

Julia sat down on the large, soft, comfortable sofa and surveyed the remains of the tea. Here there was no destruction or debris; rather an orderly assortment of not-yet-consumed sandwiches and biscuits, still attractively displayed on matching plates, each adorned with a paper doily. Barely hesitating, Julia popped a wafer-thin cucumber sandwich into her mouth and lifted the lid off the teapot. Only tea leaves remained. Lamenting the absence of any cream cakes, Julia slowly worked her way through the rest of the sandwiches: three more cucumber and five egg mayonnaise. Then she turned her attention to the remaining selection of biscuits and cakes. There were three chocolate biscuits, four short-bread slices and one ginger nut, a piece of fruit cake and two slices of Swiss jam roll. Julia picked up a slice of shortbread and devoured it in two mouthfuls. Now she was beginning to wonder where Graham was. He had said he would drop in for tea. Although this was rare, particularly mid-week, Graham was always a man of his word. In fact, mid-week afternoon tea was a rarity in the Brookes' household unless Julia felt obliged to invite her mother. Now and again Julia felt guilty that her sister, Alison, two years her senior, took more care of their mother than she did. Of course, she told herself, it's much easier for Alison to be on hand than for me. After all, Mother practically lives in her house: in that marve-llous granny annexe, as Alison used to call it while the extension was under construction. So well appointed, with a fridge-freezer, dishwasher, washing machine, split-level cooker and microwave. It was built with no expense spared, aimed at the top end of the rental market. The granny annexe label had only been a sop to placate Verity and Hal, who were at the time still living in their enormous Victorian mansion. 'Just in case you need somewhere smaller one day, Mother.' Alison had laugh-ed her high tinkling laugh and put the flat on the market at an exorbitant rent.

Julia and Graham were surprised that Alison and Steven had sufficient funds to be able to afford such a luxurious and expensive extension, even with a serious commercial goal in mind. But the two couples rarely discussed business plans or financial problems. Steven and Graham had never had much in common except that they had married two sisters. The fact that both men had been set up in business by their father-in-law was never alluded to.

Without any doubt, Steven and Graham were grateful to Hal Davis's money. Neither had any money of their own, nor was there any to speak of in their families. Neither had shone academically at school, nor did they possess much entrepreneurial flair. Each had their own particular brand of charm and attraction and each had married one of Hal's daughters. That was enough for Hal Davis. He had plenty of money to spare and was quite happy to give it to a good cause. What better cause than to further his daughters' happiness?

Originally it had been Alison's idea that Steven should start up a travel business. When they were married twenty-five years ago 'package deal' holidays were all the rage and demand totally exceeded supply. Steven had cashed in on a rapidly expanding market and for fifteen years had done extremely well. When Julia met Graham, he had already started up a modest painting and decorating business. When Hal Davis led his younger daughter up the aisle almost two years to the day after that first happy occasion, he had already bought his prospective son-in-law a substantial builders' yard with room for expansion, in Buckhurst Hill, Essex. Hal had planned that Brookes Builders Ltd would rebuild and repair most of Essex, East and North East London. For more than twenty years Brookes Builders prospered. Then something started to go wrong. Julia was never sure exactly what it was. As her husband never discussed financial matters with his brother-in-law, nor did he discuss much with his wife. Both Steven and Graham came from a world where the men ran the business and the women ran the home. In the early days of marriage both women were busy bringing up children. As the children became more independent, Alison took up golf and Julia took up bridge - and the serious consumption of cream cakes.

Later, as Steven became too submerged in financial problems to cope, Alison took charge. Graham's financial difficulties happened more slowly. At the start, he let the odd hint drop that small businesses were beginning to be affected by the recession. But as Julia couldn't see any tangible change in their life style, she took little notice. William had already left school and had gone to Salford University to read business studies. Samantha, their daughter, showing little academic ability, had left school at sixteen and in two years had become a top model. The days of school fees were happily over and as her house-keeping allowance continued to rise in line with inflation, Julia saw no cause for concern.

She had fallen asleep on the sofa. Eating often made her feel sleepy, especially eating of the over-indulgent kind. A shrill ring at the front door jolted her fully awake. She looked at her watch. Ten minutes past seven! Goodness gracious! She must have slept for over an hour! And where was Graham? That must be him now, she thought, swinging her heavy legs off the sofa and onto the floor with considerable difficulty. Not like him to forget his house key. She walked unsteadily into the hall, feeling slightly drugged. She paused to look at herself in the hall mirror.

'Good God! I look a right mess!' she said out loud and went into the cloakroom to tidy her hair and fix up her face. But she had barely got her handbag out of the cupboard and taken out her make-up pouch, when the doorbell rang again, more insistently this time. She hurried across the hall as fast as her great bulk would allow, calling: 'Graham, darling! I'm coming! There you are at last!' She opened the front door with a flourish, but stopped dead when she saw that it was not Graham on the doorstep, but a policewoman.

'Mrs Brookes? Mrs Julia Brookes?'

'Y-yes.'

'May I come in please, Mrs Brookes?'

'Why, yes, of course.' The two women stood in the hall, the policewoman nervously fingering her hat; Julia holding on to the shelf above a radiator, as if trying to support her vast bulk.

'Mrs Brookes, I'm afraid your husband has been hurt in a road accident out near Roydon. He's in St Margaret's Hospital, Epping. I think I should take you there straight away.'

Chapter Six

Kelsey lay on the bed feeling limp and weak. She had been sick again. Not deliberately this time. She hadn't had to force it. It had just happened. She had barely made it to the loo in time. Normally when she forced herself to throw up it was all under control. Carefully planned and calmly executed with great precision. First the binge - she preferred the phrase 'eat-in' - then the regurgitation. All done in private and total secrecy. No one in the whole world knew that she, Kelsey Potter, aged twenty-four, was a bulimic. She had only recently learnt the word herself. She had read an article in a magazine she had picked up at the hairdresser's about anorexia. She already knew what that was. The victim (it was described as a psychosomatic illness) had such a fear of becoming fat that he or she almost starved themselves to death. The victim was invariably a 'she.' To Kelsey this made complete sense. Neither men nor boys had any need to half-starve themselves in order to find an attractive mate. They had the choice of all the women in the world without making the slightest bit of effort to improve their bodies. Okay, there were some ugly blokes around whom the prettier girls passed over. But most men found a mate in the end, even if it was only someone as ugly as they were. But a good-looking man, a really handsome man, often looked even more attractive and desirable if he were well padded. Several well-built male bodies floated through Kelsey's mind's eye, as if to prove the point to herself.

But well padded women! Perish the thought! Women only looked good when they were really thin. Every picture in every newspaper or magazine, on TV or on the cinema screen, showed thin women. Women, that is, who were attractive, desirable and glamorous. It was interesting, the magazine article stated, that such a large proportion of these 'victims' were young people with middle-class backgrounds.

Of course there were fat women who managed to look elegant. Women who looked as if they had been born fat. Women like Aunt Julia, who were neither ugly nor stupid. In fact, Kelsey had long suspected that Aunt Julia was a great deal cleverer than she let on. Kelsey had the feeling that Aunt Julia tried to pretend she wasn't that bright, so she wouldn't eclipse Uncle Graham, who, Kelsey felt, was struggling to keep up with the complexities of life. Despite being so fat, Aunt Julia always looked well turned out. She never slouched or slumped as she walked, but floated along like a well-proportioned balloon. Kelsey knew Julia consumed a great quantity of cream cakes - everyone knew - but as Aunt Julia had been fat ever since Kelsey could remember, she reckoned that she would be fat anyway, with or without the cream cakes.

It was curious that neither William nor Samantha were in the least bit fat. They obviously took after their father, Uncle Graham. Sam, in particular, was like the proverbial beanpole. With no brains and little personality, she made the perfect clothes-horse. Kelsey secretly envied her cousin's figure. If only she could be born again, that is how she would like to look.

It was the wedding preparations that had started it all. Kelsey, then twenty-one years old, with long, dark wavy hair, hazel eyes, five feet four with a nicely rounded shapely figure, had nearly died of shame when the fitter in the wedding gown department at Selfridges's had called out her measurements to the entire floor.

'Thirty-six, twenty-five, thirty-seven.' She started measuring again, pulling in the tape a little. 'Will you be going on a bit of a diet before the great day?'

Another tug on the tape. Kelsey winced.

'You'll want to look your best, won't you, dear? All young brides want to look their best.'

'Oh, yes,' said Kelsey, helplessly.

'Take an inch off all round, Mabel,' said the fitter to her assistant.

'An inch everywhere, Mrs Cohen? Don't you think that might just be a little - er - extreme?'

'Well,' conceded Mrs Cohen, 'keep the bust measurement as it is. Quick diets don't usually have much effect on the bust. That'll make the young lady thirty-six, twenty-four, thirty-six. Nice round numbers that will look good in the order book.'

Perhaps good in an order book, but not so good on a body unaccustomed to being squeezed into too small a garment. Kelsey had felt miserably uncomfortable on her wedding day and she wept over the photos. To her, the dress made her look *a really fat person*. Something had to be done. So in less than a year she had gone from an attractively rounded nine and a quarter stone to a scrawny, scraggy, stick insect weighing just over seven stone. Her hazel eyes had lost their sparkle, her hair had lost its lustre, her skin had become dry and pallid and her periods became irregular. Her family and friends all remarked on her weight loss. Some people were complimentary, others less so. Her mother was worried.

'Have you been to see your doctor, Kelsey, darling?' enquired Alison.

'No, Mum,' replied Kelsey. 'Why? I'm not ill.'

'But you're so thin! You were never thin.' Alison was beginning to fear that her daughter was suffering from some wasting disease. Having lost one child, she couldn't bear the thought of losing her only remaining one.

'Mum, I was fat,' said Kelsey with emphasis, 'and now, happily, I'm thin.'

'Are you still dieting?'

'Yes.'

'A sensible diet, I hope?'

Kelsey said nothing. She was as chuffed as hell that she had managed to lose more than two stone in under a year and now she had reduced from a size twelve to a size eight and her vital statistics now read: thirty-four, twenty-two, thirty-four. But having starved herself for so long she was now beginning to *crave food*. Having denied herself proper nourishment and the pleasure of eating, she now began to dream about food. Then she gave in and began to eat more normally.

Nigel noticed. 'Thank goodness you've eaten a normal amount,' he remarked one day at supper.

'I was hungry. Anyway, what's normal? What's right for one person is not necessarily right for another.'

In bed, Nigel had also remarked. 'You're too thin,' he said, caressing her rib cage. 'A woman should have a bit of flesh.'

'But not too much. I was fat! Remember those awful wedding photos?'

'The dress was too tight.'

'Because I was too fat.'

'Nonsense. They should have made it larger.'

'Then it would have been outsize.'

'Rubbish. You looked beautiful.'

'Not any more?'

'Of course you do. Very beautiful and very desirable - but too thin,'

So Kelsey started eating properly again. Cautiously at first, then more recklessly. Then she began to eat the wrong sort of food; food she knew her body didn't need and wouldn't be able to absorb without her getting fat: cakes, biscuits, chocolate and sweets. All the hitherto forbidden foods she had successfully managed to avoid for almost a year. She was sure she must be getting fat again. She felt her thighs: they seemed a little more rounded than they were a few weeks ago. She took off all her clothes and stood naked in front of the mirror in the bedroom. She studied herself sideways. She definitely appeared fatter. Her stomach seemed more rounded too. In horror she rushed to the bathroom and stood on the scales. Eight stone two! In six weeks she had gained over a stone! What could she do? It was plain that if she were to enjoy her food she would no longer remain thin. So she cut out all the junk food, weighed herself daily and lost half a stone in two weeks. But then the craving for junk food really began in earnest. She couldn't seem to handle life without chocolate, cake, or a couple of biscuits. She became cross and tetchy. People began to notice; even the customers in the travel agency.

One night she and Nigel were driving home quite late after a party. While they waited at a red light, a drunk swayed across the road and threw up on the traffic island.

Nigel laughed. 'That poor geyser's had more than is good for him.'

'And so he's got rid of it,' said Kelsey. 'What a good idea.'

What a good idea! What a laughingly simple solution! You eat as much as you want and then you vomit afterwards. That way you can have your cake and eat it.

At first Kelsey found it difficult to be sick deliberately. But gradually she got the hang of putting her finger, or even a spoon or her toothbrush down her throat and hey presto! She brought up the entire contents of her stomach with ease. For five months Kelsey enjoyed her secret. She could eat exactly what she wanted, throw it up and remain thin.

Kelsey turned on her side and looked at the clock on the bedside table. Twenty past five. More than an hour before Nigel would be home. She had left work early because she wasn't feeling well. Maybe a sleep would make her feel better? She sat up gingerly, undressed and slipped on her nightie. She plumped up the pillow, got underneath the duvet and promptly fell into a heavy, troubled sleep, haunted by dreams.

She was swimming strong rhythmic strokes up and down the pool. Up and down, up and down. She was eleven years old. Too young yet to realise how boring it was to swim up and down, with an instructor screaming at her like a maniac. Kirsty, Kelsey's identical twin sister, was also swimming up and down. There were four other girls of the same age in the class too, but Kirsty and Kelsey were by far and away the best swimmers. They were so alike that even their mother, Alison, couldn't always tell them apart and their father invariably got them mixed up. The twins were an attractive, vivacious, fun-loving pair. They had pale, almost translucent skin, mid-length dark, wavy hair and sparkling hazel eyes. They were still quite small for their age and their rounded, soft, curvaceous pre-pubescent bodies had that little extra amount of flesh that was a vital protection against the chilly water, as they swam relentlessly up and down the pool during their seemingly endless training sessions. Their coach, Tim Roche, frequently told their parents that Kelsey and Kirsty were two of the most talented swimmers he had ever had the pleasure of coaching.

'Kirsty just has the edge on Kelsey,' he would explain. 'It's being that fraction taller that gives her the extra advantage with the first dive in. But they're both growing every day, so Kelsey might even overtake Kirsty in the end. You've a grand pair of swimmers there, Mrs Hobbs. They'll do you proud one day. They'll win Olympic Golds, I shouldn't wonder.'

Alison and Steven were flattered and excited by the excellent progress of their talented daughters. At first Alison wondered how on earth Tim Roche could tell the two girls apart. But then she realised that the coach must have noticed the mole on Kelsey's thigh. A pretty mole, just in the right place. As the weeks wore on Tim Roche found it more and more difficult to keep his eyes off the mole on Kelsey's thigh. And the more he looked at the mole, the more difficult he found it not to let his glance travel upwards and imagine what attractions might lie above it, higher up her thigh, in the private area just concealed by the smooth, sleek Olympic-style black swim-suit.

The two girls were extremely competitive and made sure that one of them always beat all the other girls taking part in the training sessions. But as Tim Roche began to pay more attention to Kelsey, Kirsty grew jealous and a fierce rivalry developed between them. Gradually, in whatever concerned Kelsey, Tim Roche's guidance took a more physical form. Before he had merely demonstrated and explained the points verbally. Now he made the most of every opportunity to touch Kelsey's arm or leg, especially the thigh with the mole.

The twins were now twelve, sprouting little breasts, on the threshold of womanhood. Kelsey was flattered by her coach's advances. He was a bronzed and handsome twenty-eight year old with a lean muscular body and wore Brut For Men.

'I think Tim-boy fancies me,' she remarked gloatingly to her sister one day.

'You can have him. I don't want him,' was Kristy's retort. But she became insanely jealous of the extra attention that Kelsey was receiving and tried to show her superiority in every other way. A rift began to develop between them.

One evening Tim Roche came into the changing room while Kelsey was naked in the shower. He came over and stood close by, wearing only his swimming trunks.

'Hello,' he said.

'Hello,' said Kelsey innocently, as she went on soaping herself. She rinsed off the soap, turned off the shower and stepped out. Tim Roche just stood there, watching her. Kelsey took two steps towards him, one arm outstretched to retrieve her towel, hanging on a hook just behind him. They were less than a foot apart, and as Tim Roche watched Kelsey, glistening with moisture, take her towel off the hook, he became insane with desire.

'You're beautiful,' he gasped, his hands cupping her small breasts.

Kelsey went rigid. She could neither move nor call out to Kirsty, who was dressing in one of the curtained cubicles nearby. Tim Roche began to stroke her body, savouring her smooth skin. Kelsey screamed and fled into one of the curtained cubicles, sobbing and trembling. Tim Roche hurriedly left the changing room.

Kirsty came out of her cubicle, fully dressed.

'What's up, Kel?'

'It's him. He's a pervert.' Tears were pouring down her cheeks.

'Course he's not.'

'He is.'

'What did he do?'

'He touched me where he shouldn't have.'

'Rubbish!' Kirsty was scornful. 'You imagined it.'

'I didn't.'

'Anyway, you lusted after him.'

'Only a little.'

'You wanted him!'

'Not any more. I hate him and I'm going to tell Mum.'

'No, you're not.'

'Yes, I am. And I'm not going swimming any more either.'

'Yes, you are. Because I want to. We're twins. We're in it together. We're good and we're going to be famous. If you back out, you'll let me down too.'

Kelsey started to cry and thrash around in the bed. It was dark in the room and she felt frightened and confused. She couldn't remember where she was or even how old she was. Then the telephone rang harshly in her ear. She rolled over onto her side and lifted up the receiver.

'Hello?'

'Kelsey?'

'Oh, hello, Dad.'

'Are you okay? Emma said you left the shop early.'

'Yes, I felt ill. I've been throwing up.'

'I'm sorry to hear that. Something you ate?'

'Probably.' It always was.

'Is Nigel home?'

'No. Not yet.'

'I'm sorry to give you bad news when you're on your own and not feeling well.'

Kelsey felt alarmed. 'What is it, Dad?'

'It's Uncle Graham. He's been badly injured in a road accident and he's in hospital. That's all I know at the moment.'

'How terrible!' said Kelsey, shocked and unnerved. How could Uncle Graham have been involved in a car accident? How badly was he hurt? Which hospital was he in? Another accident in the family, which had already been devastated by her sister's accident. Kelsey put the down phone and started to sob uncontrollably. Her vivid dream had brought back memories of Kirsty, for whose death she still felt largely responsible.

Chapter Seven

Verity Davis reached out a skinny, desiccated arm and switched off the alarm just before it went off. Five minutes to nine. She had been awake since seven am, lying warm and comfortable in bed. But she felt she shouldn't spend the whole day in bed, so she usually set the alarm for nine o'clock, in case she went back to sleep again. There wasn't any point in getting up too early. The granny flat was so well appointed with labour-saving gadgets that there was hardly anything left for her to do. Steven and Alison had spared no expense when they had it built more than six years ago. Verity appreciated living in a nice flat, but she also felt the flat was her due. After all, she had bailed out her son-in-law's business, so to her it seemed perfectly just and fair that she should own, not only the flat, but the house and the business as well. Of course her daughter, Alison, was trying to evict her by subtle means. Oh yes, Verity saw through Alison's ruses. She was doing her utmost to pronounce Verity unfit and incapable, so she would agree to go into a retirement home, and then she and Steven would be able to let the flat at an exorbitant rent. Although her joints ached, she was going a little deaf and had become increasingly shortsighted, Verity felt reasonably fit and capable. She was still able to shop and cook for herself and do light domestic chores.

Most housework beyond the reach of the machines was done by Alison's cleaner, Lill, who came in three times a week. Alison did all her personal washing in the machine and the household linen went to the laundry. There was no garden, only a small balcony where Verity tended her potted plants. Even though, at the age of seventy-nine, she felt she deserved a little peace and quiet, Verity found that time often hung heavily on her hands. But was peace and quiet really what she wanted? Quite often she thought that peace and quiet had become synonymous with boredom and emptiness.

She got out of bed slowly, took a shower and dressed with care in a well-cut, calf-length, moss-green wool skirt and mustard-gold silk blouse. She sat down at her dressing table and laboriously fixed her fine shoulder-length grey hair into its customary severe bun. This operation usually took some time for she wasn't always successful at first. But it all helped to fill in the day. She made up her face, lightly and carefully, and finally exchanged her battered comfortable bedroom slippers for a pair of beige Ferragamo shoes. She was now ready to face whatever might turn up.

It was already a quarter to ten when she went into the hall and retrieved two letters and *The Daily Telegraph* from the doormat, bending down and straightening up again with difficulty. She glanced at the two letters. One was from *British Telecom*, the other was a pale mauve envelope addressed in bold, rather flowery handwriting, which looked extremely familiar.

She went into the well-appointed kitchen and put the newspaper and the letters on the table already laid for breakfast with blue-and-white floral china. Laying it in the evening filled in a little spare time before bedtime, although sometimes the following morning she regretted her foresight. She pulled up the blue-and-white-striped blind, switched on the coffee percolator and took the fruit juice, bread and milk out of the fridge. She sat down at the table and poured herself a glass of orange juice. Slowly sipping the juice, she wondered whether to open the letters first or make the toast.

Having finished the orange juice, she decided to open her letters. As the phone bill was paid quarterly by direct debit, the letter from *British Telecom* would merely be a statement and was of little interest. She put it aside and picked up the mauve envelope, which looked far more interesting. She slit open the envelope with the silver Victorian paper knife lying parallel with her place mat. She kept all her personal letters in boxes, still in their envelopes, so it was important that all the envelopes had neatly cut edges. She slid out the letter, a smell of perfume gently wafting into the air as she opened it. She wasn't surprised to read the address:

24 Sudeley Street, Islington, London N1.

'Dearest Mother,

Sudip and I so much enjoyed our visit to you last Sunday. Sudip took to you instantly and speaks constantly of you: of your elegance, your charm and your famed generosity. His dearest wish is to see you again very soon. We have frequent discussions about our projected trip to India. Although it is planned for next November, (which might seem a long way off as we are not yet into March,) there are many issues to consider, the main one being, of course, money. As I explained to you last Sunday, business is bleak at the moment so, dear

Mother, I shall come to the point quickly and ask you if you would be able, generous as I know you are, to lend me £10,000 interest free for two years. I promise to repay all the money within this period. I know you will consider my request very seriously and I am sure you will do everything within your power to help me.

I await your reply with keenest anticipation and remain your very loving son, Russell.'

Verity pursed up her lips, slid the letter carefully back into its envelope, pressed down the lever on the toaster and poured her coffee.

A pale sun was shining as Verity pushed her shopping cart past the closed garage doors, across the front of the house and down the driveway. She thought she had heard Alison drive out earlier and felt a little hurt that her daughter had neither popped in, nor called to say she was going shopping. To think that Alison went shopping in her car while she, Verity, only had a cart! She was sure Alison had gone to the Sainsbury's in Barkingside, where the choice was much greater and the prices far lower than in the local shops in Wanstead High Street. Although Verity knew she needed daily projects and she enjoyed buying her food in a proper shop and chatting to the shop assistants, she still harboured resentment that her daughter, living in the same house, rarely offered her any help.

Verity walked slowly, sometimes pushing the cart in front of her and sometimes trundling it along behind, depending on the state of the pavements. Never a person to let her mind remain blank for long, her thoughts soon turned to Russell's letter. £10,000 was lot of money!

Curious that Julia had recently asked her to lend Graham the same amount. Interest free too, of course. She was now awaiting the same request from Alison. It was strange that neither her son nor sons-in-law had much business acumen. You would have thought that Russell might have inherited his father's flair for making money. On the other hand, his grandfather was the first one in the family to become a millionaire, so maybe the talent was just skipping a generation.

Should I lend, or even give them all some money? Verity asked herself. I shouldn't miss £30,000, even with the loss of interest. The gesture would certainly be much appreciated. But would it be wise? Russell, Steven and Graham had all received very substantial help from Hal in the past. They shouldn't really need more. It might be spoiling them and leaving herself open to more possible demands in the future. They would get a great deal more than £30,000 on her death. Why not let them wait until then? They would get the bulk of her fortune too, as she had arranged an insurance policy to take care of the inheritance tax.

Then there were her grandchildren to consider. Would it be fair to give large sums of money to her sons-in-law and nothing to her grandchildren? But did they need it? Samantha, the youngest, seemed to be earning a fortune rushing around the world being photographed in outrageous outfits. Whoever would imagine there was so much money to be made in being photographed in outlandish clothes, which no normal person would ever consider wearing? Verity sincerely hoped that her granddaughter was getting good investment advice while her luck lasted. After all, one or two wrinkles or half a stone around the midriff could kill her career stone dead.

William, a student, was still living on other peoples' money. Probably a mixture of Graham and the state, thought Verity. But he seemed a bright young man, who had done very well in most of his examinations so far. Verity was optimistic about William's future. She felt confident that her grandson had inherited some of his grandfather's and great-grandfather's abilities.

That left Kelsey. Dear little Kelsey. The twins had always been Verity's favourite grandchildren. It had taken her a long time to recover from the shock of Kirsty's death. And poor Kelsey! Coping with life on her own without her other half, her identical twin. The more dominant half, Verity had always thought. Kirsty had always entered a room first, spoken first and had seemed to take the lead in their joint decisions. For several years after her sister's death Kelsey seemed to regress, to shrink and shy away from almost everything. She gave up swimming immediately after Kristy's accident. She stopped concentrating and did badly at school. She sat her GCSEs, but had to retake nearly half of them. She continued to gain weight, bingeing on chocolate to comfort herself. There were times when Verity worried that Kelsey would end up a bloated balloon like her Aunt Julia. She tried saying something to Alison.

'Don't you think, dear, that Kelsey is in need of some professional help?'

Alison had stiffened, as she always did, if anyone made a suggestion or tried to interfere with the way she ran her life.

'Professional help? I don't know what you mean, Mother. Why should Kelsey need help?'

'Well,' said Verity trying to tread gently, realising she was on dangerous ground. 'She has recently lost her twin sister...'

'And I've lost my daughter.' Alison pursed up her lips and spoke in her typically tight, strangled voice.

'But Kelsey has lost a twin! You've still got a daughter left.'

'Then I'll decide what's best for her,' Alison had replied tartly.

And so the matter was closed.

Verity continued to watch Kelsey growing up with considerable anxiety. She watched her become fatter and fatter, but Alison did nothing. Kelsey left school at sixteen with no plans or prospects. She dabbled and drifted for almost a year. Then, nearly seventeen, she enrolled at Loughton Sixth Form College to study for A Levels in English, psychology and business studies. Everyone was delighted, particularly Verity and her parents.

Kelsey enjoyed the first year. 'Much more fun than school,' she had confided in Verity one day. 'It's much freer and we can study whatever we like.'

She worked hard during the first term and got high grades in the pre-Christmas exams. She was eating more sensibly and losing weight. She was beginning to blossom into a very pretty, sexually attractive young girl. She met new people. She went to parties. She became aware of men for the first time. She dated. Sometimes she went out with boys in a mixed group from the college. Sometimes she went out on a double date.

Then Kelsey met Nigel at the Sun Med travel agency, where she was working for her father. Steven was employing Kelsey for a great deal less than he had paid his previous assistant. He needed to save as much money as possible so he could buy back his business, his house and his flat from his parsimonious mother-in-law. He eased his conscience by trying to convince himself that he had also helped his daughter to find a much-needed job. At the time Nigel was already engaged to a tarty-looking redhead called Joanne and he came into Sun Med to book a holiday for them both in Torremolinos. Sadly, Nigel and Joanne split up in Torremolinos and a few weeks later Nigel returned to Sun Med to book another holiday to help him get over his broken engagement. This time he noticed Kelsey and was charmed by what he saw. Kelsey took to Nigel right away. Aged twenty-four he seemed enormously mature and sophisticated. She had never before met a law student and the prospect of Nigel in court wearing a wig quite took her breath away.

Nigel was tall, dark and good-looking. He was considerate and had beautiful manners. He didn't rush into sex, which was a great relief. But when it finally happened, on the sofa in Nigel's flat, Kelsey was amazed and touched by the tender and skilful way in which he managed to arouse her. And when it was over, she felt an enormous surge of relief and happiness and assumed she must be madly in love. When they married three years later Nigel had already started on his slow, tentative career as a barrister, and his not so slow, far less tentative succession of women, of whom Kelsey was as yet blissfully unaware.

Verity was delighted with Kelsey's marriage to Nigel. A barrister! The first member of the family to number among the professional classes. So beautifully mannered and well educated. And with such sound financial prospects too. She was sure Kelsey and Nigel would be blissfully happy and have no financial worries. It was a great relief that her favourite member of the family was so happily and suitably settled.

Verity slid the shopping cart gently down the pavement slope, constructed by the council expressly for the purpose of easing the passage of carts, prams and wheelchairs. She crossed the last side road, easing the shopping cart up onto the pavement on the other side. It had taken her more than twenty minutes to walk down Orchid Avenue, and as she turned the corner into Wanstead High Street it started spitting with rain. Oh dear, she thought, who would have imagined it was going to rain? It was sunny when I left the flat, so I never thought of taking an umbrella. But it's too far to go back now, so I suppose I'll just have to get wet. A chilly February wind blew down the main street. Verity shivered, and pulling her scarf more tightly around her neck, she turned up her coat collar. I hope I've remembered the shopping list, she thought. She took off her glove, reached into the pocket of her overcoat and felt a piece of paper. 'Good,' she said aloud to the empty street, 'that must be it.'

First she went to Dewhurst, the butcher. The queue was eight deep, so she was forced to stand outside for ten minutes in the now quite heavy rain. At last she reached the counter.

'Good morning, Mrs Davis, and how can I help you?'

The butcher, in a navy-and-white-striped apron and straw boater, was ready to serve her. His friendly voice lifted Verity's now flagging spirits.

'Good morning, Mr Tooley, and a raw one too, isn't it?'

'It certainly is. I always say February is the worst month, what with Christmas well behind us and Easter a good way off yet. But we're nearly in March. It'll be spring in no time.'

'I hope you're right, Mr Tooley.'

'And what can I tempt you with today?'

'I'll have two lamb chops, a slice of liver and a pound of lean mince, please.'

The butcher selected two of the choicest chops, a juicy slice of liver and weighed out the mince. He wrapped each item separately in greaseproof paper and then made one parcel of the whole lot, expertly folding it in a large sheet of wrapping paper. He handed the package to Verity over the counter.

'There you are, madam.'

'Thank you *very* much,' replied Verity, as if she had just been given a present.

The butcher waited patiently while Verity rummaged in her large handbag for her purse. She dropped a glove on the ground and the other one fell into her shopping cart. I wonder why elderly people can't have their money ready in advance, mused Mr Tooley, not for the first time. The queue had piled up again and was now well out of the door. A toddler pulled at Verity's shopping cart, shaking it. His mother grabbed his hand away and picked up Verity's glove.

'Oh, thank you,' said Verity, beaming as she struggled with the zip on her purse. 'Oh dear, I don't seem to have any change,' she said, handing over a £20 note.

'No problem,' said Mr Tooley, taking the note and giving her the change. 'Soon goes, don't it?'

'Thank you *so* much,' said Verity again, as if she had received another present. 'It doesn't last long, does it? I don't seem to have enough hands,' she murmured, grappling with her glove, the meat parcel and her change. The toddler, curious, opened the flap of Verity's shopping cart.

'Don't touch the lady's shopping, Jack,' remonstrated his harassed mother.

'I'm sure he's just trying to help,' said Verity gratefully, dropping the parcel, glove and the change into the bottom of the cart. 'Goodbye dear, goodbye Jack. Goodbye Mr Tooley - and thank you!'

Verity walked slowly out of the shop into the damp gloomy High Street.

'Yes, dear?' said the butcher to Jack's mother. 'How can I help?'

'Looks as if that old dear needs more help than what I do. I'll take a shoulder of lamb and two pounds of stewing steak, please.'

'Done in a jiffy, love,' said the butcher.

Suddenly Verity felt very tired. She realised she had dropped her purse and her glove into the shopping cart, and wondered if she would be able to straighten up again if she bent down to retrieve them. Better not try such a complicated manoeuvre on the wet pavement with shoppers pushing by, she thought. The rain has almost stopped so I'll go into that nice little park by the church and get everything sorted out. Then I can pop into the baker on the corner and buy something special, like a cream doughnut. She walked on slowly to the pedestrian crossing with its flashing orange beacon. The cars stopped straight away, and crossing with care, she continued to walk the two hundred yards to the park and went in. Feeling exhausted, she sat down on the nearest bench, pulling the shopping cart up beside her. As she lifted the lid to retrieve her glove and her purse, she noticed a large heap of vomit on the path, too substantial to have been washed away by the light fine rain.

'How disgusting!' she said out loud. 'Why can't people be sick in the lavatory instead of fouling up a public park?' She got up, her stomach churning, wondering whether she could face the sight of an array of rich cream cakes in the bakery. It was hardly the place for a friendly chat either. The shop assistant barely said 'hello,' but merely took the money and handed over the goods. However, the bakery was just across a small side road; so near it was a pity not to look in the window. Verity walked out of the park, trundling the shopping cart behind her. The cart seemed a dead weight, and it was practically empty. She hadn't been to the greengrocer yet, so the heaviest shopping was still to come. Her legs felt like lead and she was feeling light-headed. I really ought to go home and lie down, she thought. But she had reached the end of the footpath already and the bakery was just across the road, no distance away. By now the rain had eased off, but there were several small puddles on the pavement and the surface was slippery.

At the next corner there was no pedestrian crossing. Despite the fact that buses used it, the council had apparently felt it was an unnecessary expense. Verity stood on the kerb, her head throbbing and her breath coming in short little gasps. She looked both ways as a car came around the corner quite fast. She waited, looking both ways again. The road seemed clear, but as she stepped off the kerb she seemed to lose her balance and everything started to swing round. At the same moment a bicycle shot around the corner silently, the cyclist carrying a long pole over his shoulder with a bucket at one end. The bucket caught Verity on the back of the head with a resounding crack. She fell onto the road and lay in a crumpled heap as the cyclist fell on top of her. A bus followed hard on the heels of the cyclist, revving up to cross the High Street in front of an oncoming lorry. The bus driver pulled up sharply with a screech of brakes when he saw the tangled heap lying in the road. The lorry, too heavy to stop suddenly, ran into the back of the bus.

Then all hell broke loose.

Chapter Eight

Alison arrived home shortly after midnight. Steven was away, so the house was dark and deserted. She had been to visit an old school friend, who lived in Chelmsford. Although inseparable from their early school days, the two women now saw little of each other, their visits being generally restricted to the temporary absence of one or other of their husbands. On this particular occasion the visit had been arranged at short notice. Steven had told Alison only two days ago that he was off to Minorca to inspect some new hotels, which might, hopefully, be ready for occupation the following season. Alison was tired after the drive and relaxed after a few glasses of wine and as soon as her head touched the pillow she fell into a deep sleep. The following morning she overslept the alarm, had to forgo breakfast and rushed out to work without noticing that nothing was stirring in the granny annexe. Returning home from work at about four thirty, Alison still noticed nothing amiss next door. She made herself a cup of tea, read the paper and decided she would call in on her mother. She didn't visit Verity every day. She felt that would be spoiling, which was against her principles. The meaner side of Alison felt that Verity was quite spoilt enough already. The fact that her mother, with untold wealth, lived rent free in such a beautiful flat that by rights belonged to her and Steven was often more than she could bear. She took her finished cup of tea into the kitchen and was putting it in the dishwasher when the phone rang. It was Julia.

'Oh, Ali,' she said, and burst into tears.

'Whatever's the matter?' asked Alison, alarmed. She couldn't remember when she had last heard her sister cry.

'It's Graham! He's had the most dreadful accident! His injuries are appalling…' Julia was sobbing hysterically now.

'Where is he? Where are you?'

'I'm at St Margaret's Hospital Epping, where Graham's in intensive care…'

'Okay, Julie. I'll be there as soon as I can.

When Alison arrived at St Margaret's Hospital Epping, she was deeply shocked by the appalling state of her brother-in-law's injuries. Privately she thought he didn't have much chance of survival. As she was comforting her sister, Julia, the telephone rang in her house, almost non-stop. It was late in the evening when she returned home and the telephone rang again.

'Mrs Hobbs?'

'Speaking.'

'This is Sister O'Reilly from Maple Ward at Whipps Cross Hospital. Your mother, Mrs Davis, was admitted yesterday at midday. She was knocked down by a cyclist in Wanstead High Street. It appears she had a stroke and fell into the road. She only regained consciousness late last night. We had no means of identifying her, otherwise we would have let you know earlier.'

'Oh, my God!' said Alison. 'I'll be there right away.'

When Graham woke up he saw a policeman sitting at the end of his bed.

'Oh, God,' he said, and closed his eyes.

The next time he woke up Julia was sitting in the same chair.

'Thank God you're not a policeman,' he said, and closed his eyes again.

This little charade was repeated several times. 'I dreamt you were a policeman,' he said to Julia. Julia laughed with relief. 'Do you feel like talking to the police now, darling?' she asked one day when her husband appeared to be a little more lively and coherent.

'What about?'

'The accident, of course.'

'The accident? What accident?'

'The road accident. Don't you remember? It's the reason you're in hospital. Would you like to tell me something about it?'

At first Graham could remember nothing at all. He had suffered severe head injuries, two cracked ribs, a broken leg, a dislocated hip and extensive bruising. He had now been in hospital for five weeks, three of which had been spent in intensive care. At first his condition had been so critical that the doctors feared he wouldn't make a full recovery. Julia was distraught. Nothing the policewoman had said on the evening of the accident when she took Julia to St Margaret's Hospital in Epping, had prepared her for the shock of seeing Graham in such an appalling state. He was unconscious and covered in blood from head to toe. His clothes were in shreds, his body crumpled and broken. There was a huge lump on the back of his head and a long gash down the right-hand side of his face. Julia thought afterwards that he looked as though he had been put through a mincer. For the first two weeks she slept at the hospital in a small side ward next to the intensive care unit. Graham underwent brain surgery to remove fragments of metal and shards of glass that had lodged at the base of his neck, which if left there, would probably have caused permanent paralysis from the neck down. By comparison, his other injuries were less serious. His lower right leg had been broken in two places and his right hip was badly dislocated, though not fractured. Both his leg and his hip were set in plaster and Graham spent nearly two months in traction. The cracked ribs were left to heal by themselves and the severe bruising was left to fade on its own. He was in constant pain and given regular doses of morphine. As he recovered from brain surgery, the pain eased, the morphine doses were decreased and Graham's mind slowly began to function again. Gradually a picture of the accident was built up after questioning by Julia and the police. Because his injuries were so severe, the doctors would only allow Graham to be questioned for short periods at a time.

'So what were you doing near Roydon, sir?'

'I was on my way to inspect a property that my firm, Brookes Builders, is renovating out there.'

'The Queen Anne House?'

'Yes. That's the one.'

'Beautiful property, if I may say so, sir.'

'Yes, it certainly is.'

'Did you visit the property? On this particular occasion, I mean?'

As the time and place of events had become temporarily confused, this question posed Graham some problems. At first he was sure he had visited the Queen Anne house on that fateful day; that he had seen Ken Spooner and had had a progress discussion with his carpenter, Mick Kelly. But when Mick Kelly was questioned about this discussion he assured the police that he had not been working at the Queen Anne house at the time.

'I'm on the Queen Anne house now, Inspector,' explained Mick. 'Mr Spooner, the manager, who's been running the business since Mr Brookes's accident, transferred me there only last week. But on the day of the accident I was working in them cosy little bungalows near the railway line in Woodford. I remember the day only too well, Inspector. As usual Mr Brookes was most complimentary about my work and he asked my advice on several points. I remember after our chat he went back to Mr Spooner's office and I saw him looking in the window. The office was locked so Mr Spooner must have already gone off somewhere.'

'What time would that have been?'

'Around three o'clock, I'd say.'

'Did Mr Spooner tell you he was leaving, or mention where he was going?'

'No, Inspector. But he didn't need to. After all, he's the manager. I'm only the carpenter, if you get my drift.'

'Yes, of course.'

'Mr Brookes, how long has your carpenter, Mick Kelly, been working for your firm?'

Graham had to think hard; his thought processes were still slow.

'Could be eighteen years. Maybe even longer.'

'And you have every confidence in his workmanship - and his integrity?'

'Oh yes, indeed. Every confidence, Inspector.'

'So when Kelly says he was working on the bungalows in Woodford on the day of the accident, not at the Queen Anne property, you would have no reason to disbelieve or mistrust his information?'

'None whatsoever.'

'In your opinion, is his word as reliable as his workmanship?'

'Absolutely.'

'On that afternoon, before you set off for Roydon to visit the Queen Anne house, did you speak to Mr Spooner in his office at the bungalow site in Woodford?'

'Yes, of course. Spooner is my manager. We always have things to discuss whenever our paths cross.'

'Paths cross, Mr Brookes? What exactly do you mean by that?'

'Well, if Spooner happens to be on a site that I'm visiting I would naturally want to have a word with him.'

'As haphazardly as that? You didn't have regular weekly or twice weekly discussions?'

'Not on any regular basis that I can remember.'

'Even though he's your manager?'

'Even though he's the manager, I'm the boss. I make all the important decisions.'

'But you wouldn't necessarily inform him of those decisions?'

Graham closed his eyes. He was feeling tired and confused. The inspector took his leave.

'Mr Spooner, where did you last see Mr Brookes on the day of his road accident?'

'I last saw him in my office on the bungalow site by the railway line in Woodford.'

'Did he seem quite his normal self? Not upset or unduly agitated about anything?'

'Not that I can remember.'

'Think hard, Mr Spooner. Did you and Mr Brookes have any discussions of an acrimonious nature?'

'No, I don't think so.'

'When Mr Brookes left your office he went to see the carpenter, Mick Kelly in' – referring to his notes the inspector continued - 'in bungalow No 3. Kelly states that before Mr Brookes drove off in his car, he went back to your office hoping to have another word with you. But, according to Kelly, the office was locked and Mr Brookes had to content himself with looking in through the window. Obviously, you had gone out. Where did you go on that afternoon?'

Spooner moved uneasily in his seat. 'It were a Thursday, weren't it? Thursday's payday. One of my duties is to give the men their pay packets.'

'So you went round all the building sites and paid all the men?'

'That's right, Inspector.'

'Kelly says he saw Mr Brookes looking in through your empty office window at about half past three. Can you remember what time Mr Brookes left your office to see Kelly and also what time you left to go on your pay round?'

'Mr Brookes would have left about three. And I suppose I would have left after I'd tidied up, about ten or fifteen minutes later.'

The inspector referred to his notes again. 'Would this have given you sufficient time to visit all nine sites, before the men knocked off at five o'clock? It appears rather an ambitious schedule to me.'

'No. I didn't have time to visit all the sites on that particular afternoon.'

'Which sites did you visit?'

'Woodford Green, Buckhurst Hill, Trapps Hill, Loughton, Theydon Bois...'

'The Queen Anne property at Roydon?'

'No. Not that afternoon. I knew I wouldn't make it before five o'clock, so I returned home after I'd paid the men at both Theydon Bois sites.'

'And you live in Wanstead?'

'Yes. That's correct.'

'That'll be all for the moment, thank you Mr Spooner.'

'But darling, your mobile phone was found in your car!'

'In my car?' Graham felt confused. 'But I'd left it in Spooner's office on the bungalow site. I remember quite clearly looking in through the window. Spooner had left the whole place spotlessly tidy, so it was easy to spot my phone lying on his desk beside the computer. I really cursed my forgetfulness, I can tell you. I hadn't forgotten the tea with William and the girl - what's her name...?'

'It doesn't matter now. William's dropped her, thank goodness.'

'So I won't ever meet her?'

'Unlikely. But you've missed nothing. Could we get back to the mobile?'

'Found in my car?'

'Yes.'

'In the wreckage?'

'Well, lying on the inside of the roof. The car had turned upside down.'

'Yes, of course. But if it was on the roof it must have fallen off one of the seats at the time of the crash.'

'I suppose so,' said Julia doubtfully, not quite seeing what Graham was driving at.

'But I never left it on the seat. I always put it in the glove compartment for safety. It couldn't have landed on the roof. The police said the glove compartment was jammed shut on the impact of the car hitting the ditch.'

'That's right, sir. The glove compartment was jammed shut. Later the police forced it open to look for car papers and identification. There was no one at the scene when the police ambulance arrived except for yourself and the occupant of the other vehicle involved.'

'How did the police know there had been an accident?'

'There was a phone call from the scene, sir. A mobile phone was found on the upturned roof inside your car.'

'My mobile?'

'The police at the scene assumed it was. They assumed you had made the call before you passed out.'

'But I didn't have my phone with me. I'd left it in Spooner's office at - at the bungalow site.' Graham was feeling tired and confused.

The inspector got up to leave. 'I'll come back tomorrow, Mr Brookes.'

'Just before you go, Inspector. What happened to the driver of the other vehicle? I remember it was a small white car.'

'Yes. A small white car. It was French. So was the driver.'

'What happened to him?'

'I'm sorry to say he was pronounced dead on arrival at the hospital.'

'I'm very sorry to hear that. So there were no witnesses at the scene of the accident?'

'That's the theory at the moment, sir,' said the inspector, taking a step towards the door.

Graham fell into a restless exhausted sleep and dreamt that he was in his car being chased down a narrow lane by a scruffy-looking red car.

Chapter Nine

'But, Mother, you won't be able to look after yourself properly now.'

'Why not? I did before.'

Alison sighed and moved back a little in the wooden fold-up hospital chair, trying in vain to get more comfortable.

'But this is after. Things were different before. You hadn't suffered a stroke and a broken hip.'

'A mild stroke, Dr Walker said.'

'Mild or severe - it was still a stroke.'

'From which I've happily made a very full recovery. The physiotherapist says I'm one of the best patients she's ever had.'

Alison smiled in spite of herself and patted Verity's hand. 'Yes, I know, Mother. You keep saying that. Everyone in the hospital thinks you've made an extraordinarily good recovery for your age.'

'I wish you wouldn't keep referring to my age. I'm only seventy-nine.'

'Eighty in December. In a few months' time.'

'I don't see what the number of years has to do with it. You're as young as you feel. And I feel - and appear - a great deal younger than most of the decrepit old wrecks in here, I can tell you.'

'It's much easier to feel younger when everyone else around you looks much older. Also, everything's being done for you in here. Absolutely everything. If you go back to the flat you'll have to cook your own meals and wash up. You'll have to tidy up and make the bed. You'll have to sort out things for the laundry. You can't walk without your Zimmer frame yet! You've no idea how difficult and exhausting it would be to try to cope on your own.'

'But you'd be next door.'

'Not all the time. Only in the evenings and at weekends.'

'You could always give up your job,' suggested Verity daringly.'

'Oh, no I couldn't,' said Alison quickly. 'It's not just any job. I virtually run St Mary's School. I've been the secretary there for nearly fourteen years. I'm part of the fabric. The place would fall down if I left. Besides, we need the money. Steven's trying hard to turn the company around...'

'So he can buy it back from me?'

'Well - yes. That was always the intention.'

'So with me incarcerated in a home, you'll be able to rent the granny annexe for an enormous sum and buy back Sun Med even sooner than you had imagined. My accident has really played into your hands, hasn't it, Alison?'

Alison sighed. 'I wish you wouldn't look at it that way, Mother.'

'And how do you expect me to look at it?'

'A new phase in life - an adventure.'

'An adventure into old age? You said that last time, when you were trying to persuade me to go into the home before the accident. I think I ought to try going back to the flat just for a short while and see how I get on. After all, you've agreed to do my shopping; which is very kind and generous of you. The hospital social worker said 'Meals on Wheels' would bring my lunch every day including the weekends. I can surely manage to get myself some bread and cheese in the evenings. Perhaps at first Lill could help me with the laundry. So I'll hardly have anything to do at all!'

'But, Mother, you'll be alone all day. You might have another stroke! It was the stroke that caused the accident. You had a stroke on the edge of the pavement and then you fell into the road. That's how you broke your hip.'

'But I won't be crossing the road. I'll stay in the flat all the time unless one of the family takes me out.'

'Mother! It just isn't possible for you to stay in that flat all day by yourself!'

Alison was beginning to feel really desperate when she heard a small commotion at the far end of the ward. A murmur of voices; the clink of metal objects on a tin tray; the swish of curtain rings going across the rail; occasional subdued laughter.

Alison glanced down the long ward. 'That's quite a procession down there.'

'That'll be Dr Walker and his troop,' said Verity, unable to look around from where she sat.

'They've never been this late before. I thought hospital rounds always took place early in the morning before there were too many visitors.'

'Hospital consultants have no regular hours for visiting their patients,' explained Verity. 'Sometimes they come quite late at night. I suppose it depends on who's just been admitted and who's going to be operated on.'

'The operating theatres must be very busy.'

'Sister says they're in use around the clock.'

The little troop was working its way steadily nearer.

'Maybe you ought to leave now, dear,' suggested Verity slyly.

'Leave! I wouldn't dream of it. I haven't seen Dr Walker for weeks! I want to ask his opinion of your chances of survival in the flat on your own.'

The group reached Verity's bed.

'Good evening, Dr Walker,' said Verity. 'Do you remember my daughter, Alison Hobbs?'

'Indeed I do, Mrs Hobbs,' said Dr Walker, turning back immediately to his patient. 'And how are we today, Mrs Davis? Ready to face the big wide world in a few days time? Have we got some suitable accommodation lined up?'

There was a clatter as James Parker gathered all the dominoes into a heap and turned them face downwards.

'My turn to deal, ladies?' he enquired.

'Yes, go on, James,' said Gladys Bates, fumbling in her handbag.

'I thought James dealt the last round,' objected Brenda Barnes.

'You can never agree with the majority decision, can you dear?' said Mabel Cooke, straightening up her orange wig, which had gone slightly askew in the excitement of winning the last round.

'I didn't think we'd come to any decision, majority or otherwise,' said Brenda, taking off her horn-rimmed glasses and polishing them on the tablecloth. 'James runs the domino group whether we agree or not.'

'No, I don't,' said James. 'But someone has to orga-nise it or we won't get in seven games before tea.'

'Does it have to be seven?'

'We've always played seven ever since we started.'

'Yes, we have, so we may as well stick to our original plan.'

Gladys was emptying her handbag onto the table, slowly extracting various unsavoury objects: a filthy pale blue comb, a brush full of hairs, a very dirty white handkerchief and a wallet almost in shreds.

'Lost something, dear?' enquired Mabel, wrinkling up her already very wrinkled nose, expecting the con-tents of Gladys's handbag to smell.

'The little book,' replied Gladys, putting a bag of congealed boiled sweets on the table beside the other dubious objects and sweeping the whole lot into a pile in the corner. 'Sweetie, anyone?'

There was a faint murmur of 'no thank you.'

'What little book?' asked Brenda, replacing her glasses, still not satisfied that she was able to see any better.

'The book with the winners in it,' said Gladys with some agitation.

'Don't worry, love.' James tried to sound soothing. 'We've only had three games so far this afternoon. First round to Brenda, second to me, third to Mabel.'

'That's right,' said Mabel, bouncing up and down so that her wig fell forward again. 'Three games and three different winners. I'll write it down on this scrap of paper.'

'Then let's get on with it. Turn up your pieces, ladies,' said James, impatient to get on. 'Who has the double six? Mabel? Okay. Your go. We must try and get through all the games before tea. You know old Pricey doesn't approve of us playing games for money.'

'Did you know we have a new resident?' asked Brenda, finishing a good run in which she managed to get rid of four pieces.

'Today?'

'Yes. In Rosie's old room.'

'Poor Rosie. I miss old Rose.'

'I do too.'

'She *was* ninety-eight.'

'Two more years to go before she would have got her telegram from the Queen.'

'The Queen doesn't send telegrams any more. There aren't any now.'

'No need for them with all those fax machines.'

'And emails.'

'Who'd have thought of all that sixty years ago?'

'My round,' said Gladys with satisfaction, gathering up the pieces with a clatter. 'One each. I'll deal.'

'Okay,' said James. 'Who's the new resident, Brenda? Have you met her?'

'No. I haven't met her. I just saw her go down the corridor with Pricey to Rosie's old room. I felt she shouldn't have been going in there, and with a Zimmer frame and all - just like poor Rosie.'

'Is she old then?'

'Hard to tell from the back.'

The rattle of china and cutlery on a metal tray could be heard in the corridor. The noise became louder as the door of the sitting room was opened abruptly.

'Here's the tea,' said Gladys, gathering up the grimy contents of her handbag that were still left on the table and hastily stuffing them back into her bag again. The nurses took a poor view of any unnecessary mess around at mealtimes.

Mary Mulloy, the pretty young red-haired Irish nurse, neat and trim in her uniform, pushed the trolley into the centre of the room and began to pour out the tea. She took the first two cups over to the table where the domino players sat, the dominoes still piled up untidily in the centre of the table.

'Haven't you a box to put those things in while you have your tea, Mr Parker?' she asked firmly, albeit with some humour.

'Oh, yes,' replied James, fumbling under the table. 'The box is right here.'

As he replaced the dominoes in the box, a familiar click-clack of metal heels echoed down the corridor.

'Just in time,' murmured James as the clip of heels became louder and Miss Price swept into the room, her stiffly starched uniform rustling. She was followed slowly by Verity pushing her Zimmer frame.

'Good afternoon, everyone. I hope you're all enjoying your tea. I'd like to take this opportunity to introduce our new resident, Mrs Verity Davis.'

Chapter Ten

'How's your mother settling into the retirement home?'

'With difficulty, according to my sister.'

'Another cup?' enquired Sudip, holding the teapot aloft.

'No thanks, darling,' replied Russell, securing the cord on his dressing gown, as they sat at the kitchen table having tea. 'I must leave room for dinner. Today is a special day. Our three-month anniversary. Where'll we go to celebrate?'

Sudip laughed, flashing his beautifully even white teeth. 'Frederick's?'

'A bit pricey, isn't it? Shouldn't we go somewhere a bit more restrained?'

'Restrained! I love that from you! You're the least restrained person I've ever met!'

'Only with you, darling.'

'Not just with me. You're totally unrestrained! In your manner, your expressions, your clothes, your opinions. It wouldn't do for us to celebrate anywhere restrained.'

'So it's Frederick's, then.' Russell got up and started to clear away the tea things.

'I don't see why not as it's such a special occasion.'

'Better book it,' said Russell, getting out his mobile.

'You think so? Even on a Thursday?'

'Best to book any day at Frederick's. Besides, it's always better to book at any restaurant. You get a better reception and usually a better table.'

Russell pushed open the swing door to the elegant restaurant in the Camden Passage.

'Good evening, sir. Do you have a reservation?'

'Yes. Davis. Russell Davis. A table for two near the garden.'

The manager made a tick in the order book. 'Of course, sir. No problem. Will you have a drink at the bar, or go straight to the table?'

Russell turned to Sudip. 'A drink at the bar or at the table?'

'Oh, let's have it at the table. Then we're settled.'

'Exactly.'

Looking smart and feeling confident in a well-cut Austin Reed suit, Russell followed the manager down the wide shallow steps to the dining area where the tables, covered in snow-white napery, were set pleasantly far apart amid a profusion of house plants and indoor trees. The manager indicated a table, partly obscured by a large palm tree, which had a splendid view of the sheltered walled garden.

'Will this be suitable, sir?' he enquired, holding back one of the chairs.

'Perfectly, thank you,' said Russell, indicating to Sudip that he should take the seat by the wall, with a better view of the restaurant. Russell ordered two *Kirs Royales*.

'Here's to a special occasion,' said Sudip, smiling.

'Indeed. And to many more.'

They clinked glasses and then got down to the serious study of the menu and discussion of the wine list. The white-aproned wine waiter hovered nearer and Russell ordered a bottle of *Chablis Premier Cru.*

'Just for starters. We can have a bottle of red with the main course if we wish. After all, we're walking home.'

'Perfect.' Sudip smiled across the table. Russell thought how handsome he looked in a pale mauve shirt and matching tie.

The wine waiter returned with a bottle. 'Would you care to taste the wine, sir?'

'No. Please give my friend that privilege,' replied Russell. 'His palate is much finer than mine.'

The waiter moved round to Sudip's side of the table and showed him the bottle, glistening coldly.

'A *Chablis 2006*, sir? *Premier Cru.*'

Sudip inspected the bottle. 'Yes, fine, thank you.'

Sudip drained the remains of his *Kir Royale.* The waiter removed the empty glass and poured a little *Chablis* into one of the remaining three glasses on the table, his left arm held neatly behind his back, toes slightly apart and heels together. Sudip picked up the glass and went through his customary ritual of swilling and sniffing before finally tasting.

'Yes, it's delicious. Thank you.'

He looked up at the waiter and gave him one of his beautiful, dazzling smiles. The waiter melted.

'Thank you, sir.' He placed the bottle in an ice bucket at the side of the table and backed away, his eyes still on Sudip. The head waiter arrived and Russell ordered their meal. As he left he asked: 'how did you manage in India without wine?'

'Before I came to live in London I was unaware of its seductive delights. But now that I've discovered them I intend to continue my indulgence for as long as possible.'

Russell laughed. 'Excellent! Let's drink to that. To wine!'

'To wine, and to us!' replied Sudip, raising his glass. 'And to better business and greater cash flow.'

'Thank you.'

'Isn't it time we paid your mother another visit?'

'In the retirement home?'

'Well, yes. Isn't that where she is?'

'So I believe.'

'You gave me the impression she'd be there for ever.' Sudip took another delicate sip of *Chablis*.

'Did I? I don't know if Mother would like the prospect of being in a retirement home forever. It sounds so fatalistic. But she's certainly going to be there for some time. She still walks around with a frame thing.'

'What about her lovely flat? Has your sister let it?'

'Oh, yes. For a simply huge amount, I believe.'

'Did she tell you how much?'

'No. But I heard through my niece.'

'The thin one?'

'That's right. Far too thin.'

'But very pretty.'

'Quite enchanting, if you happen to be that way inclined.'

'Most men are.'

'Luckily for women.'

'Yes. So your mother's flat has now been rented.'

'For the foreseeable future.'

'So it looks as if she'll stay in the retirement home for the foreseeable future.'

'It does, doesn't it? I don't think Steven and Alison will be prepared to forgo their rent in a hurry.'

'No? Even though your mother owns the flat?'

'That was in exchange for a massive loan she gave them about five years ago.'

'That must rankle.'

'It does. These tiger prawns are quite delicious. Such light filo. Hope your avocado and crab mousse is as good?'

'Mm. Delicious,' mumbled Sudip with his mouth full.

'So you see, it's completely in Alison and Steven's interest for Mother to stay in the retirement home for ever.'

'I see. Poor Mrs Davis.'

'But not so poor - financially.'

'But I imagine she now has to pay for her accommodation in the home?'

'Oh, yes. I'm sure she does.'

'Those places can be extremely expensive.'

'Unless the local council pays.'

'But surely your mother wouldn't need any financial help from the council?'

'I wouldn't have thought so for a moment.'

Their conversation ceased as the waiters cleared away their empty plates and served the main course.

'My, this looks delicious, doesn't it!' exclaimed Russell, admiring his portion of roast duck in a glazed honey sauce. I think this calls for a bottle of red, don't you, darling?'

'Absolutely,' said Sudip, waving a languid hand in the direction of the wine waiter, still hovering near their table, his eyes constantly on Sudip's handsome dark face.

He was by Sudip's side in a moment. 'Sir, how can I help?'

'May I see the wine list, please?'

'Of course, sir,' said the waiter, producing it instantly.

'Shall I...?' Sudip looked up at his friend.

'Of course. Please go ahead.'

'A bottle of *Rully 2004*, please.' Sudip flashed the waiter another dazzling smile.

'Certainly, sir.'

'How will the cost of the retirement home affect your chances of getting a loan?'

'I'm not sure yet. Everything is a little uncertain at the moment. Mother's accident set things back quite a bit.'

'Yes, of course. Most understandable.'

'And then there was my brother-in-law's accident too. On the same day!'

'Yes. Appalling! Who would have believed it? Two members of the same family in near-fatal accidents on the same day.'

'Graham was extremely lucky. It's amazing he wasn't killed. I reckon the soft verge of the ditch saved him. You remember how it never stopped raining in the two months after Christmas? The ground was very soft.'

'But the road was wet. That probably caused him to skid.'

'Possibly. But the accident was caused by an idiot Frenchie coming round the roundabout in the wrong direction. The two cars collided head on.'

'What happened to the Frenchman?'

'He died on the way to hospital.'

'Oh, God! How awful! Did your brother-in-law realise? At the time, I mean.'

'I don't think so. He blacked out after he had phoned the emergency services on his mobile.'

'That showed great presence of mind.'

'It did, didn't it?'

The waiter returned with the red wine and Sudip went through his tasting ritual once again. For a moment the two men enjoyed their meal in silence.

'Is your brother-in-law getting better? Is he still in hospital?'

'Yes. But I believe he's going to come out any day now.'

'That's good news. How mobile is he?'

'Not very, according to my sister, Julia.'

'So he'll be off work for some time yet?'

'Ye, I think so.'

'Who's running the business?'

'The manager. A chap called Ken Spooner.'

'Is he reliable?'

'Graham swears by him, so I'm led to believe. But then I don't know much about the affairs of my family - sexual, business or otherwise. We all lead very separate lives.'

'Yes. I remember when we first met how amazed I was that you knew so little about them.'

Russell laughed. 'I remember that too. You also couldn't believe that Mother didn't know I was gay.'

'It did strike me as strange. That wouldn't happen in most Indian families.'

'No?'

'No. Because the extended family lives in the same house. With so many people around all the time it's difficult to keep secrets or have any privacy.'

'How dreadful!'

'Not if one's brought up to it.'

'Were you brought up that way? I mean, did your extended family share your house?'

'Y-yes. I have quite a big family, but we lived in a large house so we did have some privacy. Perhaps more than the average Indian family.'

'So yours was not the average Indian family?'

'No. I'd say probably not,' said Sudip, sounding a little evasive.

'Come to think of it, you haven't told me a great deal about your family either.'

Sudip smiled. 'Have I not? Perhaps it's because they're so far away.'

'Out of sight out of mind?'

'No. Not completely. But they no longer belong to the immediate part of my life.'

'Like?'

'Like you do.'

Russell felt a warm glow steal over his body. 'Yes, I'm glad.' He took another mouthful of duck. 'And why is your family not the average Indian family?'

'Because of where we live - and how we live…'

'What does your father do?'

'I was just coming to that.'

'Yes. Sorry.'

'He works for the Indian Government.'

'A civil servant?'

'Well, yes. In a manner of speaking'

'So what is he exactly?'

'He's the Governor of a large province: the province of Rajasthan. The capital is the beautiful pink city of Jaipur.'

'Really! And you never told me!'

'Like you not telling me about your family. There didn't seem any urgency to tell you about people who live so far away. And it didn't seem relevant.'

'No. How did your father become the Governor of Rajasthan?'

'It was a return favour. My grandfather gave land and property to the government after independence. You could call it typical Indian graft, I suppose.'

Russell's eyebrows shot up. 'So your family owned a lot of land?'

'Yes. They still do; in spite of giving a substantial amount away.'

'So your family is wealthy?'

'Yes, in a way. But most of the money is tied up in land and property.'

Russell was fascinated. This was quite a new development.

'Which I suppose will be eventually divided among your extended family.'

Sudip laughed. 'Yes. Probably.'

'Do you miss India?'

'Yes, and no.'

'Would you want to live there again?'

'Not without you.' Sudip leant across the table and looked deeply into his friend's eyes. Russell felt his stomach turn over.

'Oh, good,' he said lightly. 'That settles that. Now let's settle the question of the dessert.'

The hovering waiter returned once more with the dessert menu and they made their selection. Sudip ordered two glasses of Sauternes.

Russell giggled. 'We'll have to be carried home.'

'In a rickshaw. Wouldn't that be splendid?'

'Marvellous.'

'Russell, I think we should plan on going to India in October.'

'Not before?'

'No. It's much too hot. You'd hate it. And I don't think I could stand the Indian summers either. October and November are the best months. The country is still green after the monsoon.'

'Then I'll seriously have to start raising some money. But first I'll go and visit my mother again.'

'I'll contribute what I can.'

'Nonsense. I wouldn't hear of it. Mother's loaded.'

'But as tight as a fish's arsehole.'

'Well remembered! Will you come with me to see Mother?'

'I don't see why not; if she'll allow me to see her.'

'Of course she will! She adored you at first sight.'

'Probably the only woman who ever did, apart from my own mother.'

Russell laughed and signalled to the waiter to bring the bill.

Chapter Eleven

'How are you, dear? Settling in all right?' Mabel Cooke straightened up her orange wig and gave Verity a friendly smile.

'Oh, yes thank you, I'm fine.' Verity came across the room slowly, placing the Zimmer frame in front of her before each step. As she reached the large sofa under the window, Mabel patted the seat beside her.

'Come and join me. Verity, isn't it?'

'Yes, that's right. Verity Davis. And you're...?'

'Mabel Cooke.'

'Pleased to meet you, Mabel.' Verity extended a thin, frail hand, the other one still holding onto the Zimmer frame as she cautiously lowered herself onto the sofa.

'Rather low down, isn't it?'

'It is a little.'

'I mightn't be able to get up again without a bit of help.'

'Don't worry, dear. Plenty of that around.'

'Oh, good.' Verity settled herself into the cushions.

'Hip, was it?'

'Yes.'

'Badly broken?'

'Bad enough.'

'Just the one place, or was it several?'

'Just one.'

'That's not so bad then. They'll soon have you running around like a spring chicken.'

'That would be nice.'

'How did it happen?'

'I fell crossing the road.'

'Just slipped?'

'Yes. It was raining, so I slipped.'

'It's a nuisance, dear, isn't it?'

'Falling over?'

'And growing old.'

'Yes. It's more than a nuisance. I'm nearly eighty,' said Verity in a sudden burst of confidence.

'I'm nearly eighty-five,' rejoined Mabel.

Verity looked around the room. She hadn't taken in much when Miss Price had introduced her to everyone almost a week ago. She had been so overwhelmed by the sea of new faces that she had insisted on meals alone in her own room. The décor wasn't what she would have chosen herself. Certainly not what Alison would describe as tasteful and restrained. The loud floral-patterned carpet clashed with the seventies geometric design of the curtains. The wallpaper went with neither. Mercifully the ceiling was white. Verity wondered if residents in retirement homes generally spent most of their time lying back in their armchairs, gazing at the ceiling. Perhaps it was something to be recommended in the present circumstances.

'Been at Oaklands long?' Verity felt that having been out of circulation for almost a week, an attempt at conversation was overdue.

'Nearly five years.'

'Any particular reason?'

'Why I'm in here?'

'Yes.'

'I'm too old to be anywhere else.'

'You didn't fall?'

'No, not yet. But it'll happen. It usually does. All old people fall, especially women. It's the weak bones. Osteoporosis, they call it.'

'True. But nowadays there are pills you can take to strengthen the bones.'

'Oh, yes?'

'Yes. It's called HRT. Both my daughters are on it. Do you have a family?'

'Three sons. Two in Australia and one in Brazil.'

'So you don't see much of them.'

'Haven't seen the family for years. That's another reason why I'm in here.'

'Do you like it?'

'It was difficult at first. But you get used to it. You have to when there's no choice.'

'I'll be out soon,' said Verity.

'You'll be lucky.'

'What do you mean?'

'No one's ever got out in the five years I've been in here except in a wooden box.'

'No? That makes it sound like a prison.'

'It is in the sense that no one ever leaves.'

'Except in a box.'

'Exactly.'

'I own a flat,' said Verity, in another burst of confidence.

'Oh, yes? So did I until I was forced to sell it to pay the fees in here. Astronomic, they are.'

'Yes. That's another reason to move out soon.'

'Yes. It certainly is, if you have somewhere else to go.'

Mabel wasn't quite sure if Verity was sound of mind. Verity wasn't sure about Mabel either. The room was filling up. A distant clinking of the tea trolley could be heard along the corridor. Gladys Bates came and sat on a hard chair by the sofa, clutching her large handbag. Mabel made the introductions.

'Gladys, this is Verity Davis, our new resident. Verity, this is Gladys Bates, also known as "handbag." '

'How-do-you-do,' said Verity.

'I'm doing fine,' said Gladys. 'How're you doing yourself? I'm pleased to meet you, I'm sure. Settling in all right, are you?'

'Oh, yes thank you. It takes a bit of time, of course. It's such a big change after my flat.'

'Yes,' said Gladys sympathetically. 'We all find it a big change. But you have to get used to it, if you've nowhere else to go.'

'I'll be moving out soon, back to my flat,' said Verity.

'Oh, really?' said Gladys, obviously not believing it.

'I have such a nice flat. All mod-cons.'

'Verity's recovering from a fall,' explained Mabel. 'She's only here temporarily.'

'I see,' said Gladys, thinking, they all say that in the beginning. 'Where did you fall?'

'In the street.'

'Just slipped?'

'No. I was knocked off the pavement into the road by a cyclist coming along just at that moment, carrying a bucket on a pole. The bucket hit my head and knocked me out.'

Gladys and Mabel roared with laughter.

'Oh, would you believe it!'

'I've never heard anything so funny!'

'I'm sorry, dear...'

'I didn't mean to be rude...'

Gladys, her eyes streaming, was rummaging in her capacious handbag looking for a handkerchief when James Parker came over to join them. He put his hand on Gladys's shoulder.

'All right, love?'

'Oh, yes. It's poor Mrs Davis. She was knocked into the road by a cyclist carrying a bucket on a pole.'

James's eyes widened. 'Well, I hope you sued him, dear? That's dangerous carry-on, that is.'

'Well,' said Verity, not quite sure how to handle the situation, 'in the end I decided I wouldn't. He was such a young chap you see...'

'Yes.'

'Quite right.'

'Absolutely.'

The murmur of asset continued as the tea trolley was wheeled noisily into the room by an attractive young nurse in uniform.

'That's Mary Mulloy,' Gladys said to Verity. 'She's the best there is.'

'I know...' began Verity when a tall, thin woman with a long grey bob came over to join them. She had pince-nez and a little black book each hanging on a separate ribbon around her neck. She drew up a chair to the end of the sofa where Verity sat.

'Hello, dear,' she said. 'You must be the new girl.'

Verity wasn't sure whether or not to feel flattered. 'New, yes. But hardly a girl.'

'Oh, we're all girls in here, dear. All girls at heart.' She looked round anxiously at the tea trolley and leant forward confidentially. 'I do hope the tea won't be late. I have an appointment.'

'An appointment?'

'A most important appointment.'

'With your doctor - or a visitor?'

The thin lady unclipped the small black book from the ribbon around her neck. Verity could see it was a diary.

'No. With one of the governors.'

'Governors?' Verity felt sure she'd missed something. Perhaps her hearing aid needed new batteries.

'Yes. The governors of my school. They're coming to see me today.'

'She thinks they're coming every day,' murmured Mabel. 'Verity, this is Miss Prescott. She used to be the headmistress of a school.'

'I *am* a headmistress, dear.'

'Of course,' said Verity. 'I'm Verity Davis. How-do-you-do.' She extended her hand and Miss Prescott held out hers. 'How-do-you-do.'

The nurse, pretty red-haired Mary Mulloy, was handing out cups of tea. 'Miss Prescott, Mr Parker, Mrs Davis. Nice to see you in here, Mrs Davis. I hope everyone is helping to make you feel at home.'

'Thank you, Mary.' Verity took the proffered cup. 'Everyone is most kind and welcoming, thank you, dear.'

Mabel slopped some of her tea into the saucer. 'Oh, dear, how clumsy of me. Another footbath.'

Mary handed her another saucer. 'Don't worry, Mrs Cooke. Here's a clean one.'

'A clean footbath, dear?'

'Yes, that's right.' Mary was handing out biscuits.

'Oh, should I really?' said Brenda Barnes, polishing her glasses on the trolley cloth. 'What about my figure?' She gave a little laugh.

'You do better than the rest of us, dear,' said Marjorie Grimes, a very stout lady in a bright floral-patterned blouse and sage-green home-knitted skirt. 'It was all them chocolates,' she explained to Verity. 'I packed chocolates for Cadbury's for forty-four years. I knew every chocolate. I could draw you the designs for each one. I swelled up like a balloon after one year in the factory. We could eat as many as we liked, of course. There'd be no point in rationing anyone, would there? It would have been impossible to keep track of all the missing ones. You should have seen the young girls when they came in first; some as pretty as a picture with figures like the models you see on them catwalks. Then a couple of years later they'd be enormous. A lot stopped eating after a few months. They realised the dangers and didn't ever touch them again. Some left to get married. Some just left. But for a few people, the hard-core, the chocolates were like the drink to an alcoholic. They turned into chocoholics. Unfortunately I was one of them. I never married either. I just stayed in the factory, packing and eating chocolates. And now I'm in here. But I don't touch chocolates no more.'

'I see. That's most interesting.' Realising she had been the only person listening to the little story, Verity wasn't sure what she should say.

Brenda Barnes got up and came over to say hello to Verity. She pulled up a chair and sat down next to her.

'Hello,' she said, extending her hand. 'I'm Brenda Barnes. You must be the new resident.'

'How-do-you-do,' said Verity, shaking hands.

Brenda took off her glasses and wiped them on her handkerchief. 'That's better,' she said, replacing them. 'Now I can see you better.'

'Glasses are a nuisance, aren't they?' said Verity sympathetically. 'But not as bad as these,' she said, tapping her hearing aid, almost hidden by her hair.

'You can hardly see it,' said Brenda, peering shortsightedly at Verity's ear. 'I used to be a hairdresser, so I got used to arranging the hair around those things.'

'I suppose you did.' Verity looked Brenda up and down. She was immaculately turned out in a well-cut beige dress, a navy scarf at her neck secured by a little gold pin and matching navy shoes. Alison would approve of what she called 'elegant understatement'. Verity felt more drawn to Brenda than to any of the other ladies.

'Been at Oaklands long?' she asked Brenda.

'Two years,' said Brenda.

'Well settled in then?'

'Well enough. But I'd rather be in my own home.'

'Wouldn't we all? I'm going home soon.'

'Oh, really?' Brenda raised her eyebrows and said nothing.

'Have you got a family, dear?' enquired Verity.

'Two sons and two daughters.'

'All married?'

'Yes. I have ten grandchildren and four greatgrandchildren,' said Brenda proudly. 'And what about you? Do you have a large family?'

'Not as large as yours. I have two married daughters, a son and three grandchildren.'

'Son not married? '

'No. Not yet.'

'How old is he?'

'Forty-seven.'

'Maybe he's gay. I have a grandson who's gay.'

'How nice. I do like people to be happy, don't you?'

Brenda gave Verity a strange look, but said nothing.

James Parker came over to join them. He wore his customary sports jacket and tie with well-pressed grey flannels. He was a well-built man of medium height, now grown a little portly. He had a good head of thick grey hair, a straight nose, a small moustache and clear, candid blue eyes. It was still apparent that he had been extremely good-looking as a young man. He held out his hand to Verity.

'You must be Mrs Davis. I'm James Parker. How-do-you-do?'

'How-do-you-do?' replied Verity, extending her hand. 'Please call me Verity.'

'I'd be delighted to.'

'I don't know if you play dominoes,' James began diffidently.

'Oh, I haven't played for years,' said Verity. 'But I believe it's quite a simple game to grasp.'

'Oh, quite simple,' said James.

'Except we have our own rules,' said Brenda. 'We play for money, you see.'

'Lot's of money?' Verity sounded surprised.

'It depends on what we agree in the beginning,' said James.

'James runs a gambling syndicate,' explained Brenda in a loud whisper.

'A syndicate?' Verity was rather mystified.

'Well, sort of. But it's not approved of in here.' Brenda took off her glasses again and polished them on the hem of her dress. 'Miss Price thinks we're too old to gamble.'

'Oh, really?' said Verity, beginning to think that Oaklands might be a great deal more interesting than she could ever have imagined.

Nurse Mary Mulloy came over to the little group around the sofa.

'Mrs Davis, you have two visitors.'

'Two visitors? What sort of visitors?'

'Two young men. One is very dark and extremely handsome.'

'Oh, that'll be my son and his friend.'

'Will you see them in here or shall I show them to your room?'

Verity looked around the sitting room with the garish decor. It was much noisier and livelier than she had ever expected an old peoples' home to be, but it would be more peaceful in her room.

'I'll go to my room, I think. Please help me up, Mary.'

Mary took one arm and James Parker took the other. As they eased her slowly off the sofa the door opened and Russell walked in, followed by Sudip.

'Hello, Mother,' said Russell.

Brenda Barnes looked up. I thought so, she said to herself.

Chapter Twelve

'We've got some bargains for Cyprus in June. Or there's Crete if you prefer? Full board in Hania for one week starting at £320.' Kelsey rustled through the pile of brochures on her desk, the telephone receiver held expertly under her chin.

'No? Not Crete. Nothing Greek. Right. You don't like the Greeks. Okay, sir, how about Turkey? Though Turkey does get quite hot in June. Let me see if we've got any attractive bargains on offer in Turkey. I beg your pardon, sir? Not Turkey! I thought you said you didn't like the Greeks, oh, or the Turks. Well, yes. North Africa? No, I certainly wouldn't advise Algeria and I don't think the Foreign Office would either. You're not British so it wouldn't matter? But Algeria's not a safe place to go to whatever nationality you are. It's not even safe for the Algerians at the moment. You like islands? How about Elba or Sardinia? No. They're not French. They're Italian. Corsica is French.' Kelsey sighed. 'Sir, might I suggest that the best thing for you to do would be to come in here and pick up some brochures. Yes, we are a proper travel agent, ABTA bonded, of course and we'd be delighted to give advice. That's what we're here for. No, I can only make suggestions. I can't choose your holiday for you. Exactly. Sun Med, Wanstead High

Street. Just opposite the park. You can't miss it. Yes. We're open until six pm, even on Thursdays.'

Kelsey replaced the receiver and burst into tears.

'Oh, hell's bells and shit-a-brick!'

Emma Unwin looked up in concern. 'Kel, what's wrong?'

'I'm fed up with these bloody punters who don't know what they want. Why can't he bloody well decide on his holiday by himself before trying to book it?'

Kelsey put her head on her arms on top of the desk and sobbed. Emma came over and put her hand on her colleague's shoulder.

'Kelsey! Don't worry about the bloody punters! You mustn't let them get you down.'

A man passed by the open street door, paused as if to go in, changed his mind and walked on. Emma got up, walked over to the door and locked it. She pulled down the blind and turned the 'Open' sign to 'Closed.' She returned to Kelsey's desk, pulled up a chair and sat down beside her.

'There,' she said, patting her friend's shoulder. 'That's settled the punters for a bit. Now let's get you sorted out.'

Kelsey looked up, smiled wanly and blew her nose loudly. 'If Dad comes along and finds we've locked the door, he'll go mad.'

'Don't you worry about your dad. I'll deal with him if necessary,' said Emma determinedly. 'I'll point out that his daughter is more important than the punters.'

'Thanks. You're a brick.' Kelsey sniffed loudly.

'As long as I'm not a shit-a-brick.'

Kelsey tried another wan smile. 'No. Of course not.'

'What's wrong, Kel? It's not just the punters, is it?'

'No.'

'Nigel?'

'Sometimes.'

'Meaning?'

'Sometimes I think he's still two-timing me.'

'I thought you'd got that straightened out?'

'So did I. But I can't change his nature.'

'What do you mean?'

'Even though he's sworn to be faithful, he can't help being what he is.'

'Which is?'

'A randy old bugger.'

'But aren't you giving him his oats? You've always said that was one of the best things between you and Nigel.'

'It is, and I do.'

'What makes you think he's still roaming?'

'Oh, all those little things. The way he's late home. The way he's not in his rooms when I phone. The way he once he smelt strongly of perfume.'

'How did he handle that one? Did he deny it?'

'No. He said a very rich client had worn very strong perfume. So there wasn't much I could say, was there?'

'Not really.'

'And he's being so nice lately. Always bringing me flowers and little gifts. Even chocolates.'

'I thought you didn't eat chocolates.'

'No. Mostly I don't.'

'What else is wrong?'

'Emma, I'm so tired. I wake up tired.'

'You need a holiday.'

'We can't afford a holiday. Especially not at the moment. Nigel's just beginning to get on his feet. You know so far he's been getting only a few low-profile briefs? Well, he's working on a big one at the moment. He's part of a team.'

'Oh, great!' Emma sounded really enthusiastic. 'Is it a murder trial at the Old Bailey?'

'Sorry. I'm not allowed to say anything yet. I'm sworn to secrecy.'

'Well, if it's a juicy murder, perhaps we could both go and sit in the public gallery?'

'I don't see why not.'

'Will there be money in it? For Nigel, I mean.'

'Could be. It's hard to say. This is just the beginning.' Kelsey stood up. 'I must go to the loo.'

She walked to the back of the room, glancing up longingly at all the posters of sun-drenched beaches fringed by palm trees.

'Better unlock the door and say we're open. Dad might come in at any moment,' she said, as she went through the door marked 'Private.'

'Yes, in a minute. I'll handle your dad if he comes in.'

The phone rang on Emma's desk and she went over to answer it.

'Yes, certainly. If you know the holiday number you can book it over the phone. What's the name of the tour operator? Thomson's? Excellent. If you wouldn't mind holding on a moment I'll go and get their brochure. Yes. Ready now. Fire away.'

Emma quickly took down the holiday details, filling in the boxes with neat pencilled ticks, to be inked over when the holiday was confirmed. 'Yes, yes, I've got all that. I'll just confirm with Thomson's and call you back, Mrs? Mrs Sidcup. Yes. As soon as I can.'

Emma got up, unlocked the door, raised the blind and turned the 'Closed' sign round to 'Open.' She returned to her desk just as Kelsey came back from the loo. She looked pale and wan and walked with her hands folded across her stomach. The pose jogged something in Emma's memory. Who was it she had seen walking like that within the last year or so? Of course! It was her older sister Lucy, in the early stages of pregnancy. She wondered if Kelsey could be pregnant? But if she were she would surely have told her. They had become close friends, working in the same small room for more than two years. Emma couldn't imagine that Kelsey wouldn't have told her such important news.

'Kelsey,' she began, 'is it possible...'

At that moment a customer walked in. As the door had been closed for nearly fifteen minutes Emma felt she couldn't let any more business slip away. The big question would have to wait.

Kelsey was late for work for the second time in a week. At least she could be sure she wouldn't get the sack. Her own father would hardly hand her a P45. Kelsey had a new problem: she couldn't find anything to wear that would fit. The bed was littered with clothes. Skirts, trousers, shirts, T-shirts and tank tops lay in mounds or cascaded onto the floor. They all seemed too small. The skirts and trousers were too tight in the waist, the shirts were straining at the buttons and her breasts bulged out of the T-shirts. Kelsey was puzzled. Of course she had been bingeing, but hardly any more than usual. Anyway, she always got rid of it, throwing it all up in the loo. But she had been eating a bit more than usual lately and often she hadn't had to force herself to throw up. It had happened quite naturally. Kelsey assumed that her daily vomits had become second nature; occurring without any effort at all on her part, usually quite soon after breakfast. Thinking about it made her feel queasy. She felt the bile rising up from her stomach and rushed off to the bathroom. She squatted on the floor by the loo, lifted the lid and the seat and vomited noisily into the bowl. What a relief! She was sweating and shaking as she flushed the lavatory. That was dinner and breakfast safely disposed of. She ran the cold tap in the basin, wiped her face with a flannel and rinsed out her mouth. Then she went back unsteadily to the bedroom, pushed the pile of clothes to one side, pulled back the duvet, got into bed and fell fast asleep.

The telephone woke her nearly two hours later. It was Emma from the travel agent.

'Kel! It's Em. Are you okay? It's twenty to eleven. I just wondered if there was anything the matter?'

'No. I'm okay. Nothing's really the matter. I was sick two hours ago. Throwing up, I mean. It must have been last night's Chinese take-away. But now it's in the sewer I feel a lot better. I'll be in soon. Is Dad there?'

'No. He's gone to Morocco.'

'Morocco? I didn't know Sun Med did any business in Morocco.'

'Well, perhaps your dad is opening it up. So you can take your time. See you later. Take care,' said Emma and rang off.

Kelsey got out of bed slowly, feeling a little the worse for wear. She sat, naked, on the side of the bed, looking with some disgust at the untidy heap of clothes strewn around. That's why I'm late for work she thought. I couldn't find anything to wear. Nothing seems to fit. I'm bingeing and getting fat again. But how could I be getting fat when I'm throwing it all up? By now I'm the expert bulimic - anything that goes down comes up.

She went back to bed and slept again for more than an hour. Finally she got up again for the third time that morning and surveyed the mess on the floor. Why didn't her clothes fit? There must be a reason. She returned the mirror to its original position between the two windows and stood in front of it. No doubt about it: her breasts had grown larger. She stood up straight and examined her whole body. Her skin glowed with a sheen that hadn't been there before. She looked at herself sideways. No doubt about that either: her stomach was protruding. It wasn't a soft, flabby fat like Aunt Julia's, but round, firm and hard. Then she knew: it hit her like a thunderbolt. She was pregnant.

That explained everything: the hunger, the craving for different foods and the throwing up so easily. Of course she'd missed a few periods but she'd been missing them anyway. The bodily abuse of drastic dieting and the bulimia had caused them to be irregular. She sat on the end of the bed. She was pregnant with Nigel's baby. For although Nigel had slept around, she certainly hadn't. She felt a chill of revulsion creep over her. She shivered violently and pulled the duvet around her. A baby. Nigel's baby. She felt stunned and numb. Her elation evaporated. She no longer felt independent and in control. She felt trapped. She didn't want a baby, anyone's baby, especially not Nigel's. She felt no urge to recreate herself. To her, motherhood was a ruse to keep women indoors, away from the exciting, important things in life. With the arrival of a baby all her freedom would vanish. She was already sharing her body with another human being who was tapping into her personal physical resources, living off her food supplies. When it was born it would be helpless and demanding, cry in the night and need constant attention every hour of the day. She would never be able to leave it on its own. She would be totally responsible for its well being, for its nourishment, its every action. She would be forced to give up her independence and surrender her identity to a baby she had neither planned nor wanted.

What should she do?

'You look tired, darling.'

'I am tired, Mum.'

Alison looked more closely at her daughter, noticing the rings under her eyes.

'I daresay you could do with a holiday.'

'I daresay I could.'

'Any chance of Nigel getting away for a week's break? He owes it to you.'

'I know he does, but it's difficult for him at the moment. There's an important case coming up soon.'

'Oh, good. I'm pleased about that. Perhaps when it's over you two can go off. You should be able to arrange something with all the information literally at your finger tips.'

'Yes, Mum. I know. But it's the money as well.'

'Surely you can find some good bargains?'

'Yes. There are bargains - but nothing is for free.'

'No. True.'

'And of course the fact that Sun Med is still in debt to Grandma doesn't help. It means I have to pay the full price of any bargain.'

Alison pursed her up lips and frowned. She didn't like anyone, particularly her own daughter, referring to

Steven's financial problems. But Kelsey looked peaky and in need of a holiday.

'Have you been to visit Grandma lately?' she enquired, partly as a way of changing the subject.

'In the home?' Kelsey sounded a little alarmed. 'With all those old people watching?'

'You needn't go into the communal sitting room where all the other people are. Grandma's got her own room. You could visit her in there and have a cosy chat. It's much nicer than the hospital and you were very good about visiting her in there.'

'But that was different,' objected Kelsey.

'What's different about it?'

'People in hospital need visiting. They're ill and they have nothing else to do except receive visitors.'

'There's not a great deal to do in a retirement home either.'

'But at least the people aren't ill.'

'No. Just frail, and maybe bored and looking forward to seeing someone from outside.'

'I don't have a lot of time, Mum, to go and visit old people in homes.'

'I don't have a great deal of time either, darling.'

'But Grandma's your mum. That's different.'

'She's your grandmother. What's different about it?'

Kelsey sighed. 'Is she going to be in Oaklands forever?'

' "Forever" is a big word, Kelsey. It's not quite clear yet how long she'll stay there.'

'Is she still walking with her frame thing?'

'She was the other day.'

'Is someone in the home helping her to walk without it?'

'Oh, I think so.'

'That's all right then. When she can walk without the frame she'll come out, won't she?'

'Possibly.'

'Then I can visit her next door.'

'That mightn't happen for months. Go and say hello to your grandma. She might even help towards your holiday. You never know.'

Chapter Thirteen

'I love this mash, don't you, James? It's so easy on the old teeth, isn't it?' said Marjorie Grimes, helping herself to a large second helping of mashed potatoes.

James Parker laughed, helped himself to a smaller portion and offered Marjorie the rest. 'Here you are, Marjorie, finish it. You need building up at your age. Especially since you no longer have all those chocolates to keep you going.'

'Too right I don't.' Marjorie scraped the serving spoon clean on her fork and licked it off. 'Mm. Delicious.'

'It is good, isn't it?' said Verity, surprised in spite of herself, how good the food tasted at Oaklands.

'That your granddaughter who came in this morning, Verity?' asked Mabel Cooke, pouring a large amount of gravy over her plate.

'Yes, it was,' said Verity. 'That was Kelsey. She's always been my favourite.'

'Pretty girl, isn't she?' remarked Gladys Bates, pushing the roast beef around her plate with a sprout at the end of her fork. She didn't care for beef very much. She found the stringy parts got stuck in her dentures. She much preferred mashed potato but Marjorie had got most of it this time. Maybe tomorrow she ought to try sitting at the other end of the table where the food arrived first.

'Yes, she is pretty,' said Verity, 'although I think she's too thin.'

'Baby'll take care of that, won't it,' remarked the ever observant Brenda Barnes.

'Baby!' said Verity in some surprise. 'No one mentioned anything about a baby!'

'No? I must be wrong then,' said Brenda smoothly. 'I just thought I saw a curve under her baggy shirt.' What an extraordinary family, she thought. Gay son, pregnant granddaughter and Verity doesn't seem to know anything about them at all.

'All the young wear those baggy shirts nowadays, don't they?' remarked Elsie Morrison, struggling to cut the stringy beef. Her knife slipped and the meat fell onto her lap, just missing her table napkin. It landed on her freshly laundered pale blue skirt, splashing gravy down the front of her white blouse, which although clean that morning still showed the faint dark stains of similar past accidents. The knife fell to the floor with a clatter.

'Oh, look what I've gone and done!' wailed poor Elsie. 'And I was all togged up and clean for my son and daughter-in-law coming in this afternoon!'

Good-natured Mary Mulloy got up from her end of the table, picked up the knife and handed Elsie another one.

'Don't worry about it, Mrs Morrison. If you like, I'll help you to pick out some clean clothes after lunch.'

Elsie flashed Mary a grateful smile. 'Thank you, Mary. You're kindness itself.'

'Not at all,' said Mary in her soft singsong West Cork accent. 'Sure I'm only doing me job.'

'And you do it beautifully,' said James, the admiration showing through in his voice. 'We'd all love to have your patience, wouldn't we, ladies?'

There were murmurs of assent around the table.

'The point about baggy clothes,' said Brenda, 'one of my granddaughters told me, is that they hide whatever's going on underneath.'

'Why should girls want to hide things underneath their shirts?' asked Marjorie, who, having no family, was not as well up to date with the latest fads and fashions as the other residents.

'Well, things such as gaining weight, losing weight and unwanted pregnancies,' said Brenda, rather regretting her last remark.

'I thought unwanted pregnancies no longer existed,' said Gladys, rummaging in her large handbag for a handkerchief.

'What do you mean?' asked Mabel. 'Not all babies are planned nowadays are they? Accidents do happen.'

'What I meant was,' said Gladys, finding her handkerchief after she had emptied half the contents of her handbag onto the table. 'What I meant was that there are all those pills and coils and things to stop conception; and, as a last resort, termination on the NHS.'

'You're very well up to date with your gynaecology, Gladys,' said Elsie censoriously.

'It pays to keep up with things, dear.' Gladys didn't care for Elsie, whom she thought often sounded superior.

'Well, I suppose not all contraception methods work,' said Mabel. 'Would you agree, Mary, as a member of the medical profession?'

'Ah, sure, I wouldn't have any truck with them kind of things at all,' said Mary, who was a devout Roman

Catholic. 'If its God's will, there'll be a baby. If it isn't, there won't.'

James looked across at Verity sitting directly opposite. He wondered why she had taken no part in the conversation. Usually she wasn't backward in voicing her opinions. He wondered if she was somehow protecting her granddaughter. Perhaps her pregnancy, if it existed, was being kept a secret? Although normally eager and ready to join in general discussions, James was beginning to discover that where her family was concerned, Verity could be extremely tight-lipped. There was the question of her son and his adoring handsome dark friend. It was obvious to James that the two men were deeply in love. Verity's son was quite obviously gay, but Verity had never mentioned it. Trust that forward, attention-seeking, trying-to-be-glamorous Brenda Barnes to put her foot in it again. James was beginning to find Brenda more and more irritating. Verity would never irritate him, he thought. She had a cool composure that was soothing and rather attractive.

'Pass to the end, please.' Mary's voice broke into James's thoughts. 'Pudding time.'

There was a general clatter as the plates were passed down to the end of the table near the door. A few items of cutlery fell on the floor, to be quickly retrieved by the ever-present Mary.

'What's the pudding, dear?' asked Gladys, looking down to the far end of the table where Hilda Haddock sat, staring down vacantly at her empty plate. Hilda wasn't quite with it. Of course all the residents had their little off-moments, their little foibles. Otherwise they wouldn't be in a retirement home. Except for James. Gladys still didn't understand why James needed to be in

Oaklands. Aged seventy-five he was much the youngest of them all and seemed surprisingly sprightly for his age. He always read a daily newspaper and watched the more interesting, mind-improving programmes on television. He still drove a car and often went out for a drive on his own in the afternoon, before they started on their domino games. Gladys wondered where James went in his car, and why he never invited anyone to go with him. Gladys would have liked to know more about James and perhaps be invited to go for a drive. In fact, she was beginning to fancy him, just a little.

But that Hilda Haddock was a bit strange, thought Gladys. She seemed to have little interest in anything and rarely joined in the conversation. She lacked concentration too. Nothing that was said to her seemed to register. She never mentioned her family and, as far as anyone knew, she received no visitors.

Then there was the affair of Mabel's brooch. A few weeks ago Mabel couldn't find her brooch. It was a particularly favourite piece of jewellery, which her husband had given her on the occasion of their fortieth wedding anniversary. Mabel had searched everywhere for it without success. Finally she had mentioned its disappearance to Gladys, who had helped her to search her room a second time. A few days later during tea in the sitting room, Mabel had gone up to where Hilda Haddock was sitting slumped in her chair, her face as usual quite expressionless.

'Like a scone, dear? Fresh today. Cook's best.' As she proffered the plate, Mabel noticed that Hilda was wearing a brooch identical to the one she had lost. She leant forward to take a better look. 'Pretty brooch, dear. Do you know, I have the identical one.'

'Really?' said Hilda, taking a scone. 'Well I never.'

Hilda continued to wear her brooch and Mabel's brooch never turned up.

Gladys was brought out of her reverie by the arrival of the dessert. Glancing down to the far end of the table again she noticed that Hilda's empty plate hadn't been removed. Realising that Mary was already busy serving, she decided to be helpful and remove Hilda's empty plate herself. It never occurred to her that Hilda should remove her own plate. Her subconscious told her that Hilda would probably be incapable of such an insignificant act.

'Finished, dear?' she asked Hilda. 'Lovely, wasn't it?'

As she bent over to pick up the plate, a bright object on Hilda's wrist caught her eye. 'That's a pretty bracelet!' she exclaimed, bending closer to get a better look. 'Goodness! I have one exactly the same! How extraordinary!'

'Really?' said Hilda, putting her hand over the bracelet. 'But this one's mine.'

Gladys picked up the used plate, carried it to the far end of the dining room and put it on the sideboard. Then she returned to her seat.

'Thank you, Mrs Bates,' said Mary. 'That was most thoughtful of you. The pudding's apple crumble. Would you like it with custard or ice-cream?'

'I'll have both, please. Thank you dear.'

Gladys ate her pudding in thoughtful silence.

As soon as lunch was finished and the plates were being cleared away, Gladys slipped off to her room. She went straight to her dressing table, opened the top right-hand drawer and took out her large jewellery box. She looked carefully at the top tray. It was all in order. She lifted off the tray, put it on top of the dressing table and inspected the contents of the bottom layer where she kept her best pieces. The bracelet was missing. She replaced the top tray, put the box carefully in the drawer, locked it and put the key in her capacious handbag.

As the domino group gathered for its first game later in the afternoon, Gladys managed to have a quiet word with Mabel. 'You know you thought that Hilda Haddock pinched your brooch? Well, she's taken my bracelet too. I think we've got a megalomaniac in our midst.'

Mabel laughed. 'Megalomaniac! Gladys, dear, I think you mean kleptomaniac.'

'Never mind which maniac. What's serious is that we've got a thief living here. What do you think we should do about it?'

Chapter Fourteen

Verity had finished tidying up her room. She always left it immaculate each morning, so when the maid came in all she only had to do was clean it and make the bed. Verity prided herself on her orderliness. She went to her dressing table and rearranged the photographs and her silver-backed brush and comb for at least the third time. She looked at her watch. One and a half hours until mid-morning coffee; then another hour and a half until lunch. How should she fill in the time? Should she tidy out her drawers and rearrange the clothes in her cupboard? She went over to the tallboy in the corner and opened the top drawer. Impeccable. There wasn't an object out of place. Verity opened each drawer in turn, surveying the orderly contents with a mixture of pride and a tinge of disappointment: disappointment because there was no reason for any rearrangement. She walked over to the hanging wardrobe on the other side of the room and slid open the door. Again, all was tidiness personified. Her winter clothes hung in plastic covers; her summer clothes, grouped in matching colours, were all readily available. Verity heaved a little sigh. It was all very well being so tidy and so well taken care of, but what was there to do all day? Even less than there had been in her flat.

The inspection of the drawers and the cupboard had taken ten minutes. Ten minutes less of the morning to fill in. At least something had been achieved. She wandered over to the window. Her room over-looked the garden, which in early June was beginning to look its best. The first rose blooms were appearing; the lilac and honey-suckle were out and only last week the gardener had planted masses of bright scarlet geraniums, in pots and in the flowerbeds. Craning her neck a little, Verity could see the pale lavender blue wisteria running riot on the back wall of the house. A stroll in the garden would be the perfect way to fill in - Verity glanced at her watch - the remaining hour and a quarter before mid-morning coffee. She looked down at her feet. She was wearing her beige Ferrogamo shoes, elegant and comfortable and toned so well with her mid-calf beige skirt. But stouter footwear might be more appropriate for a stroll in the garden, especially if she were tempted to walk on the grass. She went to the cupboard, selected a pair of sensible, lace-up walking shoes, sat down on a chair and put them on. She looked around the room for her stick (two weeks ago she had learnt to manage without the Zimmer frame), saw it by the door, picked it up on her way out and went slowly down the corridor to the garden door. The door was open and a light breeze blew in, bringing with it the rich intoxicating scent of summer flowers. Verity felt a little excited at the prospect of a garden stroll. It was the first time out on her own since the accident.

She negotiated the two shallow steps down to the garden path without difficulty, holding tightly onto the handrail strategically placed for those not too steady on their feet. Then she wandered down the central garden path, admiring the colours in the well-kept flowerbeds. She had decided her goal should be the bench at the far end of the path. At that moment a figure, whom she recognised as James Parker, also enjoying a morning stroll, approached from the other direction and sat down on the bench. James looked up as he saw Verity approaching.

'Verity! Good morning! How nice to see you out here on this beautiful day.' He stood up to greet her and indicated the seat beside him. 'Do come and join me.'

'Thank you. I'd like to.'

They sat down side by side on the bench.

'I haven't seen you out here before,' said James conversationally.

'No. It's my first time.'

'The first time since you've been at Oaklands?'

'Yes. I was a little nervous of going out on my own in case - you know - I tripped or something.'

'You only needed to say the word and I would have come with you anytime.'

'Thank you. I really appreciate that,' said Verity gratefully. 'But now I think I'll be able to manage on my own'

'The more's the pity. I like a bit of company.'

Verity didn't ask him why he hadn't suggested it before, or indeed, invited any of the other residents to take a garden stroll with him.

'Good to see you managing so well without the walking frame.'

'Yes, isn't it? I was determined to do without it as soon as I could. It's such an encumbrance - and so undignified.'

James laughed. 'Yes. I never thought of it as being undignified. I suppose you'll be going back to your flat soon now that you can walk without the frame?'

'I don't know about that. You see, my daughter and her husband are letting it at the moment at quite a high rent.'

'I see. And they need the money?'

'Yes, they do. But I miss my flat and my independence.'

'Perhaps you could pay them rent instead of the tenant? That way you'd have your flat and your independence and they'd get their money.'

'Yes. That's always a possibility. But I don't think Alison would consider that alternative at the moment.'

'Why not?'

'She lives in the house next door. She thinks I would be a liability living on my own so close by. She wants her freedom too, you see.'

'Freedom from you?'

'Yes. I suppose that's the direct way of putting it.'

'But you seem to be settling in very well here.'

Verity sighed. 'Oaklands is a very nice home and I like many of the other residents. But as well as missing my independence, I find I don't have enough to do.'

'Yes, that is a problem,' agreed James, thinking: I must find things for Verity to do. 'You've never joined us for dominoes, have you?'

'Nobody asked me,' said Verity, with disarming directness.

James smiled. 'I'm asking you now. Come and join us this afternoon.'

'Will the others mind?'

'I shouldn't think so. They generally agree to my suggestions.'

I suppose they would, thought Verity, as you're the only male resident.

'We play for money.'

'So you mentioned before. Much money?'

'It can be. It depends on what stakes are decided.'

'I don't know if I have much cash in my room at the moment.'

'Don't worry about that. During the game we play for match sticks and the winning amounts are written in a book.'

'Gladys's little book?'

'Yes.'

'I've seen her put a little book in her handbag.'

'That's the one. We make a note of all the winnings and settle up every Saturday after everyone has had a chance to get some money from the bank.'

'Do Mabel and Gladys go out to the bank?' asked Verity in considerable surprise.

'No. They rarely go out. Gladys's daughter gives her money every week and Mary Mulloy cashes cheques for Mabel.'

'I see. I could ask Alison to cash cheques for me.'

'Oh, good. So it's all settled then. A two thirty start in the sitting room. The table in the corner by the window.' James glanced at his watch. 'It's five to eleven. Let's go in for coffee, shall we?'

He stood up and offered Verity his arm.

'Doesn't the time pass quickly when one is in good company?' said Verity, without realising the significance of her remark.

'Ah, here she is,' said Mabel straightening her wig, as Verity made her way slowly to the corner table by the window.

'It'll be a bit of a squash with five,' complained Brenda Barnes, polishing her glasses.

'We'll manage,' said James. 'The enjoyment of having an extra player will more than compensate for a little lack of room. Verity will be a splendid addition to our group. Hello, Verity and welcome to the domino club.' He stood up and held out the chair next to him.

Verity sat down and smiled up at him gratefully. 'Thank you, James.'

James leant under the table and produced two boxes of dominoes.

'Does Verity know we play for money?' enquired Gladys.

'Oh, yes,' James replied.

'Does she know the rules?' asked Brenda

'Not yet,' said James. 'But they won't take long to explain. Ready, Verity?'

'Yes. I'm ready.'

'The pieces are dealt out,' explained James, 'and as there are five of us we use two sets.'

'So there are two of everything,' put in Brenda.

'So I gathered,' said Verity.

'The first person to realise they have a double six knocks twice on the table. Like this,' said James demonstrating.

'Must be twice?' asked Verity.

'Yes. Must be twice,' said James. 'Then before placing the double six on the table, they set the betting stake on any sum between £1 and £10.'

'Is that all?' Verity sounded disappointed.

The others laughed.

'You wait,' said James. 'It grows. Let's say the stake had been set at £5.'

'The winner wins £5,' said Verity.

'No, no. Not yet,' said James. 'We play seven games. There's no winner until we've played all seven games.'

'So what happens to the £5?' asked Verity.

'The winner decides whether the stake should remain or be doubled.'

'So if it's doubled the next stake is £10.'

'Exactly.'

'So if the stake is doubled each time, by the end of the seventh game it will be - let me see,' said Verity thinking hard, '£320.'

'Exactly,' said James. 'Very sharp, Verity. Shall we have a trial round?'

The trial round was played very quickly. Mabel declared her double six by knocking before Verity had realised what had happened and Gladys finally won the round.

'Good,' said James, collecting up the pieces. 'Now we'll go for the real thing.'

He mixed up the pieces thoroughly and dealt them out. They all stood their pieces up in front of them on the table.

Verity knocked first. 'I've got a double six,' she said, placing it on the table.

'Right,' said James. 'Now declare the stakes.'

'£10,' said Verity, without batting an eyelid.

'Oh, big ones,' said Mabel, putting down the next piece.

Brenda won. 'I'll double,' she said.

Mabel started the next game. James won it. 'Double,' he said.

Gladys won the fourth game and decided to stick.

'Still a £40 stake,' said James.

Verity won the fifth game. 'Double,' she said.

'Stakes at £80,' said James.

The adrenalin was flowing as they started the sixth game. James won again. 'Double,' he said. 'Stakes at £160'

The atmosphere grew tense. Brenda knocked first and placed her double six on the table. Mabel got rid of three pieces in a row. The turns followed in quick succession until they were all down to two pieces except Brenda and Verity, who only had one each. Mabel put down another piece. There were three front-runners. The tension became unbearable. It was Brenda's turn, but she couldn't go.

'Pass,' she said.

Everyone watched in suspense as Verity studied the curious domino layout on the table.

'Yes!' she cried, putting down her piece. 'I've won!'

'Well, done, Verity,' said James admiringly. 'Put it in the book, Gladys. Verity won £160'

'Congratulations, Verity,' said Mabel, not sure whether she really meant it or not.

'I hear the welcome rattle of the tea trolley,' said Brenda, with some relief.

'Very timely,' said James.' Another round tomorrow, ladies?'

'I wonder if you'd put a little money into the bank for me, Alison?' asked Verity a few days later.

'Of course, Mother. But I'm sure you mean out of the bank not into it.'

'Oh, no. I mean into the bank.'

'Where did you get it from?'

'I won it, dear.'

'You won it? How? On a horse?'

'No. Playing dominoes.'

'Dominoes? In here?'

'Yes. That's right. We play dominoes for money.'

'But that's gambling!' Alison sounded aghast.

'So? James Parker runs a syndicate.'

'A syndicate!'

'That's what he calls it.'

'A gambling syndicate in a retirement home!'

'Yes. Why not? We're old enough and there's not much else to do.'

'I see,' said Alison slowly. 'How much did you win?'

'£160.'

'Good Lord!'

'It could have been more. The maximum's £760.'

'£760! Are they all millionaires in here?'

'I've no idea. No one seemed too bothered by the amount.'

'Where does the money come from?'

'The kitty. We all pay £120 to join the domino club initially. Basically the money just circulates between all five of us.'

'Well I never. Perhaps you'd better keep it for next time.'

'I'd like you to bank £60 for me, please.'

'Yes. OK.'

'I'll get it while I think of it.'

Verity got up, went to her dressing table and opened the top drawer, feeling underneath her nighties where she had hidden the money the day before.

'Good grief! It's gone! It's true what Gladys said. There's a thief living at Oaklands!'

'You mean - someone has stolen money from your room?'

'Yes. Unfortunately.'

'Don't you have a key to lock the door?'

'No. No one does. They tried it - but several were lost. Most of the people living here can't handle keys.'

Chapter Fifteen

'Oh! You feel so smooth and silky!' Nigel's hand went gently down the slim body and stroked the hard firm stomach. At the same time he began to lick her ear, tonguing the orifice and taking the odd nibble of the soft, fleshy ear lobe.

'Do you know, Kelsey once bit my ear so hard I had to have stitches.'

'Really?' Susie put her hand to her ear lobe, feeling perhaps it might be in danger. She sat up in bed, propping up the pillow behind her so that she could see the whole of Nigel's face.

'Why did she do it?'

'She was in a temper.'

'Does she often have tempers?'

'Often enough.'

'What was that particular temper about? It must have been something quite bad to make her so violent.'

'Yes, it must have been, mustn't it?'

'Can you remember what it was about?'

Nigel looked thoughtful for a moment, unsure as to whether he should reveal his wife's secrets. 'I think it was about you,' he said at length.

'Me? You mean us?'

'Yes. It was about us. She suspected I was having it off with you.'

'Does she still suspect?'

'No. I don't think so. Otherwise she'd probably have bitten off the other ear by now.'

'I don't think I've ever been violent.' Susie started to stroke Nigel's breasts.

'Do you really love me, Nigel?'

'I love being in bed with you and making love to you.'

'That's not quite what I mean.'

'What do you mean?'

'I mean, do you love me enough to spend the rest of your life with me?'

'Spend the rest of my life with you?' Nigel was mystified and a little suspicious. 'What does that mean exactly?'

'Just that.'

'But you know I can't. I'm married to Kelsey.'

'Would you be prepared to leave Kelsey and spend the rest of your life with me?'

'I've never really thought about it.'

'Are you prepared to think about it - seriously, I mean?'

'You mean right now?'

'Well, sooner rather than later. After all, it seems that Kelsey is sometimes violent, which is something that can't be levelled at me.'

'No.' Nigel was beginning to wonder where the conversation was leading. 'Is there some particular reason why you're asking me all this?'

Susie took a deep breath. It was now or never.

'I'm pregnant,' she said, very quietly. 'With your baby.'

'Fucking hell and holy shit!' Nigel leapt out of bed, dragging all the covers onto the floor, leaving Susie completely naked. 'How could you do this to me?' He marched over to Susie's side of the bed and began to shake her violently.

'Why did you do it? You bitch! You cow! You viper! You trapped me! You planned it all along! You assured me you were on the pill and hadn't missed any periods.'

He shook her more violently, then picked her up and dropped her hard on the bed. Susie screamed and burst into tears.

'You bastard! You goddamn lousy bastard! You'll kill our baby!'

'I don't want our baby! You've no right to have a baby without my knowledge. It's a vile sneaky thing to do. You know perfectly well I'm married to Kelsey. She's the only one who has a right to have my baby. You'd better damn well get rid of it as soon as possible, unless you want to be an unmarried mother and face the future with a child all on your own. Because I'm going to clear out as soon as I'm dressed and hopefully never see you again!'

Now Susie was crying uncontrollably, clumsily trying to wrap the duvet around her vulnerable naked body. 'I thought you loved me! I thought you cared about me! I really thought you would be excited and proud if I had your baby. But you're a callous, uncaring scum-bag!' Susie's voice rose in a scream. 'You're utterly selfish! You take what you want from people and then drop them and trample on them. You're a violent repulsive shit! I hate you! Now get out!'

Susie rushed into the bathroom trailing the duvet after her. She slammed the door, locked it and sat down on the lavatory seat, sobbing hysterically. Nigel dressed as quickly as possible, took the keys of Susie's flat out of his pocket and put them on the dressing table where she would see them. Then he let himself out.

Kelsey looked at her watch and heaved a sigh of relief. Ten minutes to six. She was much too tired to carry on working even for another ten minutes. No one would know. Steven was still in Morocco and Emma had left the shop at one o'clock for her half day off. Kelsey went to the front door and locked it, turning the 'Open' sign to read 'Closed'. She went back to her desk, tidied up the pile of papers, arranged the brochures in a neat bundle and put them to one side. Then she sorted out the heap of lose papers, putting one pile in the tray marked 'Definite Bookings' and the other into the tray marked 'Probable Bookings.' She went to the back of the shop and into the room marked 'Private', used the loo and then studied her face in the mirror. Her mother had been right: she did look tired. On the other hand she looked well. Her hair shone as it had not done for a long time, her face had filled out a little and her skin had an almost translucent glow. She wondered if she looked pregnant. No one had remarked. Had anyone noticed? Should she tell someone? It was now definite. She had been to the doctor who had her confirmed suspicions. He had congratulated her, obviously thinking that she would be delighted.

'Congratulations, Mrs Potter! This is really splendid news.'

Although she had expected it, Kelsey found the news far from splendid. Could she tell anyone yet? Should she tell Nigel? What would his reaction be? Would he feel proud to have sired a child? Or would he feel trapped, cornered, burdened and deprived of his liberty? It was hard to tell. Kelsey regretted having married Nigel. He was unfaithful to her, so he was plainly untrustworthy. Any happily - well, fairly happily married man who slept around was a cheat. She couldn't trust a cheat. If Nigel cheated on her with other women, how else was he cheating her? And if he cheated on her, his chosen wife whom he had married presumably forever - would he not also cheat on their child? So if she wasn't going to tell Nigel about the baby, in whom could she confide? Her mother? Kelsey felt sure her mother would be delighted by the prospect of being a grandmother. But she would take charge completely for the whole nine months; supervise her antenatal appointments, buy the layette and even choose the baby's name. No. Kelsey wasn't sure she wanted Alison to have such a close involvement in her life any more. She was, after all, grown up and quite capable enough of organising her pregnancy on her own.

Could she tell Emma? Emma had become a good friend over the last two years. But Emma was bossy too. She could be overbearing and was inclined to be very effusive. She could hear Emma saying: 'Oh, Kelsey, darling! How absolutely fabulous! Lucky you!'

No. She couldn't tell Emma either.

Kelsey sighed. This was one of the many times when she missed her twin sister so much that it hurt. If only she had paid more attention to what Kirsty had been up to on that fateful day in the swimming pool. Tears came into her eyes and she felt a constriction at the back of her throat. But that was now all in the past. All the wishing in the world wouldn't bring Kirsty back now. Her life would have to go on without a sibling.

She finished making up her face, took her handbag out of the cupboard and went to the main shop, locking the door marked 'Private' behind her. She picked her jacket off the back of the chair and looked around to see that everything was in order. Then she unlocked the door to the street, went out, double locked it from the outside and set off on her way home.

It was a brisk twenty minute walk from the travel agency to their flat. In good weather Kelsey found it a pleasure. In bad weather Nigel gave her a lift on his way to work and her father dropped her home in the evening. The first ten minutes took her along Wanstead High Street, still busy with shoppers on a balmy evening in early June. Feeling extremely hungry, Kelsey couldn't remember if there was enough food in the house. First she stopped off at the local delicatessen called 'The Ham 'n Cheese' and bought a bagful of delicacies for dinner. Then she went into the greengrocer and bought four new season's peaches. As she passed the off licence, an advertisement for light summer white wine caught her eye, so she went in and bought a bottle of *Sancerre*, already chilled, shimmering with a cold bloom. Well laden with goodies, she walked slowly along the two leafy residential streets to where she and Nigel had bought their airy, spacious ground floor flat. She let herself in and was just about to call out: 'Ooho! Nigel! I'm home!' when she heard him talking on the telephone.

'I'll pay for it,' Nigel was saying. 'I'll pay for everything. It won't cost you a penny. But you can't keep it! It's impossible. You know it is. I'm married to Kelsey, not to you. And I don't want to think of my illegitimate offspring being brought up in a sleazy basement flat by an unmarried mother. Just the fact of having no father will be tremendous handicap for a child, however well the mother cares for it. You'll be handicapped too because you're a single mother. You won't be able to work. You'll have to get income support, which is worse than receiving charity. Susie! You can't go through with this! I beg you to consider an abortion! Please! Please! Please!'

Kelsey froze. Susie. Income support. Abortion. Susie was pregnant with Nigel's baby! She took off her shoes and crept noiselessly into the kitchen, standing frozen to the spot. Her worst fears were confirmed. Susie was expecting Nigel's baby. She was obviously planning to give birth to the baby and bring it up on her own, against Nigel's wishes. Nigel had obviously been screwing Susie until kingdom come, having all the pleasure and taking none of the responsibility. And now he was trapped. Was it a deliberate move on Susie's part? Or had it been an accident? Had Nigel tried to find out? On the other hand, did it matter whether it was an accident or not? What mattered was that now Nigel found himself in a compromising situation. Not only had he made his mistress pregnant, but she was also insisting on keeping the baby into the bargain. After all, Nigel wasn't married to Susie, but to Kelsey. So he had a great deal of explaining to do. And the baby would be an added financial burden, a burden that Nigel could well do without at this stage. Then there was the extra equation, as yet unknown to Nigel, that his wife was also expecting a baby.

Kelsey felt rage and frustration welling up inside her. How dare he! How dare he cheat on me like this, she thought. The bastard. Wait until I tell you what I think of you, Nigel Potter! She took a bag of tomatoes out of the plastic shopping bag and unwrapped the bottle of *Sancerre,* still glistening coldly. Carrying the bag of tomatoes in her left hand and the bottle of wine in her right, held like a club, she crept noiselessly towards the living room. Nigel was sitting in an armchair by the window, his stockinged feet on the coffee table, his back to the door. He was reading *The Evening Standard,* a glass of whisky on the table beside him. Kelsey slipped noiselessly into the room without Nigel noticing. She crept up behind him, and exploding with rage and humiliation, she brought the bottle down on the side of his head, grazing his damaged ear.

'You filthy bastard!'

Nigel leapt up in shock, putting his hand to his ear.

'You bitch! You monster! What on earth…?'

Blood trickled down the side of his head, dripping into his white shirt.

'You toad! I'll get you!' Kelsey started pelting him with tomatoes. Some of them reached their target; others fell on the floor with a squelch.

'You've gone out of your crazy little mind!'

'Oh, no, I haven't. You're a fucking cheat!'

Having run out of ammunition, Kelsey started to pummel him.

'Kel, what are you doing?'

'Hitting you.'

'What for?'

Kelsey went on hitting him. 'Because you're a cheating bastard.'

'Why? What have I done?'

'Screwed around.'

Nigel tried to push back the armchair, but Kelsey pushed it forward. Nigel tried moving the coffee table, but its legs stuck in the deep shaggy pile of the carpet, so he knocked it over.

'Kel! Stop fighting! Please!'

Nigel struggled around the side of the armchair and tried to grab Kelsey with the idea of trying to calm her down. But she twisted out of his way, grabbed a china table lamp and hurled it at his head. Nigel ducked and the lamp hit the television set, sending splinters of glass and china into the air.

'Kelsey! Stop it, will you! You're wrecking the place! What's got into you?'

'You know bloody well what's got into me. It's more a question of what you've got into Susie. You've got Susie pregnant with *your* baby!'

Nigel stood motionless in disbelief.

'You heard! You crafty little minx! You eavesdropped on my phone call! You crept in and spied on me!'

'That's a load of bullshit.' Kelsey stood still for a moment, panting and pushing her hair out of her eyes.

'You just listen to me this time, Nigel Potter. I've as much right in this flat as you have. I came home, in the normal manner, having bought food and a bottle of wine for your dinner on the way, and when I opened the front door, I heard you on the telephone and…'

'You sneak! You could have said something like "hello Nigel…"'

'I didn't want to interrupt your cosy little conversation…'

'Because you wanted to listen to what I was saying…'

'It didn't take long to find out…'

'That I was talking to Susie, who, if you remember, used to be my secretary…'

'What's that got to do with it?'

'It might have been legal business…'

'But it wasn't legal business, was it? It was pregnancy business. And you're the one who got her pregnant.'

'Now Kelsey, darling, you can't actually prove it…' Nigel tried the smooth, sweet approach.

'Don't you "Kelsey darling" me. Susie seems to think it's your baby and you obviously do too, otherwise you wouldn't have begged her to have an abortion.'

Nigel froze. 'So you heard the whole conversation?'

'Yes! I bloody well did!' Kelsey screamed at the top of her voice. 'Why do you think I'm so angry? You've been lying, cheating and screwing around the whole time since we've been married. I've suspected it all along. But now it's gone too far. I'm leaving you for good, Nigel Potter, and I'm going to sue you for divorce.'

'Kelsey, please...' Nigel felt the ground slipping from under him.

Kelsey came right up to him, taking him off his guard, and gave his face a stinging slap.

'Take that as my farewell present, you bastard. I'm leaving right now and I'm going to find a lawyer in the morning.'

Kelsey shot into the kitchen, picked up her jacket and her handbag and rushed out of the flat, slamming the door behind her.

Shocked and exhausted, Nigel threw himself onto the sofa. He surveyed the wrecked room in despair. He wouldn't even be able to watch television this evening to cheer himself up. He would have to buy another set tomorrow. He got up, went across to the drinks' cabinet, took out the whisky bottle and poured himself another tumbler. He took a large gulp and returned to sit on the sofa, placing the glass of whisky on the floor beside him. He picked up *The Evening Standard*, which lay on the floor just within reach. He tried to read, but found he couldn't concentrate. What a mess! What a bloody awful mess! He couldn't blame Kelsey for being so angry. On the other hand, she shouldn't have eavesdropped on his phone call. So it was really her fault. He was sure he could eventually have persuaded Susie to have an abortion, if he had offered her enough money. Perhaps that was his mistake. If he had offered her money right away perhaps she would have agreed to a termination. He could still try. Life would be easier and much more pleasant without the burden of an illegitimate child. Soon everyone in the family would know about it. Maybe even by tomorrow. He could imagine Kelsey telling everyone with a certain amount of self-satisfaction, tinged, of course, with self-pity.

'Nigel's been screwing around ever since our marriage. You didn't know? No? Oh, yes. I'd suspected it for some time. But now our Nige has really blown it. He's got his mistress pregnant! She wants to keep it, of course. Darling Nigel's precious baby. But Nigel is trying to persuade her to have an abortion. 'Amazing, isn't it?' And what am I going to do? Well, I'm planning to divorce him for a huge amount of money. Nigel has no money? Well, he'll just have to earn it then, won't he?'

Nigel wondered how Alison would react. Prim Alison, with her scrawny neck and pursed up lips, who found it difficult to react to anything, pleasant or unpleasant. Nigel mused, not for the first time, how dull life must be for Steven, living with Alison. Being in bed with her must be like sleeping with a bundle of sticks. But Alison would undoubtedly support her daughter and take Kelsey's side against him.

What would Steven think? Steven, always hearty and jovial, trying to be upper-class with his: 'Oh, well done, old boy,' and 'have some more *Châteauneuf*, old chap.' A bumbling drunkard who couldn't even run a business that had been entirely set up and financed for him. Nigel wondered how much sexual release Steven managed to find on his many trips abroad to inspect attractive holiday destinations. Was he cheating too?

But when it came to the question of his son-in-law cheating on his daughter, Nigel felt he wouldn't stand much chance of explaining his side of the story. And what about fat Aunt Julia, who insisted on being called Aunt by all the younger members of the family. Why was Aunt Julia so grossly, revoltingly fat? Genes, greed or an eating disorder? Nigel had wondered from time to time whether perhaps Kelsey suffered from an eating disorder too. The reverse of Aunt Julia's. Sometimes it had been on the tip of his tongue to enquire whether Kelsey took medication to keep her thin. On one occasion he had even searched the bathroom cupboard, but found nothing. Would Aunt Julia be horrified that he had cheated on her niece and got another woman pregnant? Nigel was sure she would be. Aunt Julia would certainly take Kelsey's side. There was no doubt whatsoever about that.

Then there was bumbling Uncle Graham. Well-preserved, but rather vain and too much under his wife's thumb. Nigel had little respect for hen-pecked husbands. He felt the man should always be in charge, especially in the home. Even so, he liked Graham probably the most of the whole hopeless family. Nigel had been genuinely upset when he heard about Graham's appalling accident and very relieved to learn of his good recovery. But Graham would undoubtedly be upset that his niece had been treated so badly and certainly take her side against him.

That left Verity, if one didn't count the cousins, and Nigel didn't. He found them a little beneath him, both socially and intellectually. Nigel's feelings towards Verity were mixed. He had always admired her independence and her strength of character. He thought it admirable that an old lady of seventy-nine was able to look after herself so well, with the minimum amount of help from her daughter, even though Alison lived next door. Now, of course, Verity was being fully taken care of in the retirement home, which had diminished her independence, but not her proud spirit or her regal bearing. But Verity had her mean streak. It was constantly alluded to by all the family, in a roundabout sort of way. So that it wouldn't sound like carping, but of course it was. Alison in particular would refer to Verity's frugal living habits.

'Mother eats little and buys even less,' she would remark. 'She spends next to nothing. I wonder what will happen to her money?'

Kelsey made similar remarks. 'Grandma's loaded. She's got nothing to spend her money on but she refuses to give it away to anyone.'

Even to Kelsey, who, Nigel had gathered in the early days of their courtship, was the favourite grandchild. Verity would defend Kelsey to the hilt. But Kelsey's family would certainly shun Nigel now. Very soon he would be an outcast. Beyond the pale. He finished his whisky and got up to pour himself another. He picked up the bottle, rejoicing that it was more than half full. He was admiring the golden liquid as it splashed soothingly into the glass, when the telephone rang. He put down his glass and went into the hall to answer it; slightly hopeful that it might be Kelsey to apologise for eavesdropping on his phone call and saying she was on her way home. But it was Alison.

'Hello, Nigel.'

'Oh, hello, Alison.'

'Is Kelsey there?'

'No. I'm afraid not. She's out.'

'At a quarter past ten?'

'Well, yes. She went out for the evening.'

'All on her own?'

'Well, no. I think she was going to meet a friend.'

'A friend? On her own? I didn't realise you both led separate social lives.'

'Well, no. Of course we don't. It was just an old friend, a school friend, Kelsey said. The friend called and suggested they go out for a walk together…'

'A walk in the dark? Nigel, you sound a little bit funny. Have you been drinking?'

'No. Not at all. Well, just a little. Tiring day.' Nigel realised he was slurring his words. 'Can I give Kelsey a message when she gets in?'

'Yes please. Ask her to give me a ring tomorrow to discuss Verity's eightieth birthday party.'

Nigel struggled to hold the telephone under his chin and write down the information.

'Of course, Alison, I've got that. Ring Alison about Verity's birthday party. Goodbye, Alison.'

Chapter Sixteen

Kelsey ran down the garden path, her hair flying. She opened the gate, slamming it shut behind her with a resounding bang. Despite her agitation, the evening air felt cool, so she struggled into her jacket as she raced along the pavement. 'The bastard,' she muttered to herself. 'The utterly vile bastard. Of course I knew he was screwing around. He's been screwing around almost ever since we returned from our honeymoon. The randy rat. Not only was he wearing me out but he was going hammer and tongs with Susie as well. But to get her pregnant on top of it all! That was the limit. Quite unbelievable. Totally unacceptable. Whether it was a deliberate plot on the part of Susie to trap him into marrying her was beside the point. Nigel shouldn't have gone to bed with Susie in the first place.'

Gradually Kelsey was forced to slow down. She was panting hard and felt a tight constriction in her chest. She had no idea where she was going. She felt rootless and rudderless. She sat down on a low front garden wall and tried to think. She had to make some sort of plan. She couldn't go on running, even walking, aimlessly all night. She had to decide where she was going to sleep. She looked at her watch. It was half past eight and it would be dark in an hour so she had to make a decision quickly. Tomorrow she would have to find a solicitor and somewhere to live. Those would be the biggest hurdles. But now night was already falling and she needed somewhere to sleep.

Could she go and stay with her parents? Most young married women who had been cheated on by their husbands would do so. But since Kirsty's death Kelsey had become gradually less close to her parents. It was as if losing Kirsty had divided her from her family. It was as if some of her love for her family had died with her sister. Kelsey felt it went both ways: that her family also loved her less since Kirsty's death. Although everyone had tried to convince her that she could never have prevented the accident, Kelsey always felt that her mother, in particular, held her responsible, which made her feel guilty and remorseful. Somehow her feelings towards all of her family seemed to have fused into the same bland emotion. She was no longer able to separate her love from her mother from what it had been before the accident: a more intense and possessive kind of love than she had had for Aunt Julia, Uncle Graham or Russell. Although she never quite saw Russell in the same light as either her father or Uncle Graham. She liked Russell, of course. He was very likeable and could be very amusing. But some years ago she had come to the conclusion that there was more to being gay than just having a male lover. Gay men had a different attitude of mind. Russell wouldn't understand her problems.

What about Samantha, her first cousin? Could she tell Samantha about Nigel's unfaithfulness? Kelsey dismissed the thought even before she had formed it. Samantha always looked gorgeous, but she had a birdbrain and was only really interested in being a thin, super-rich clotheshorse. Kelsey felt there was only one person she could talk to, and that was Emma. She and Emma had shared most things in the two years since they had worked together at her father's travel agency. Emma could sometimes be rather bossy and had a tendency to want to organise everything. But she had a great sense of humour and a heart of gold. And above all, she had a two-bedroom flat.

Emma lived on the far side of Wanstead, near the cemetery, not far from Oaklands Retirement Home. There was no direct bus route, so Kelsey decided she might as well walk. It would give her more time to think. Understandably, her thoughts focused on her pregnancy. At first she hadn't wanted the baby. She had been appalled by the idea that her body was playing host to another human being who was sharing her body and using its functions. A kind of parasite. But even worse, was that after the messy and painful birth, she would be physically and emotionally chained to a tiny helpless creature who would entirely take over her life. She would lose all her independence, maybe even her identity. Then, as the months passed, she had begun to get used to the idea of being a mother. Four and a half months was a long time to continue resenting her own developing flesh and blood. Slowly she had started to accept her condition and even look forward to motherhood. But this evening everything had changed. Her husband appeared to have sired two babies within a few weeks of each other. There would only be room for one. And Kelsey had already decided that it wasn't going to be hers.

By the time Kelsey reached Emma's flat it was after nine thirty and almost dark.

'All right, Kel?'

Emma came into her small, pleasantly furnished sitting room where Kelsey was lying on the sofa.

'No,' replied Kelsey miserably.

'Do you think you're going to be sick again?' Emma shot an anxious glance at her new pale beige carpet.

'No. I just feel awful.'

'I'll run the bath.'

'Very deep and very hot. Got the gin?'

'A big bottle. That should do the trick.' Emma picked a plastic carrier bag off the bookcase and took out a large bottle.'

'Oh, God! It's a litre!'

'You said a large one.'

'Yes. I just didn't think they came that big.'

'They do.'

'Do I have to drink all of it?'

'I suppose it depends how quickly it starts to work.'

'Before I'm sick.'

Emma left the room and went into the lavender-blue bathroom at the far end of the flat. She turned on the hot tap, sat on the edge of the bath and waited for it to fill up. Kelsey stared at the large bottle of gin as she listened to the sound of the bathwater running. Why gin? It was always gin. Mother's ruin. She felt miserable and guilty. She knew that what she was about to do was wrong - very wrong. And probably dangerous too. She wondered if she had asked her doctor straight out for an abortion whether he would have agreed.

'But Mrs Potter! I thought you were so pleased about it! A happily married young woman on the threshold of motherhood! Most people would envy your condition. Just think of all those couples that are unable to conceive!

I really do think, Mrs Potter, that you ought to reconsider your decision...'

Kelsey didn't want to reconsider her decision, but she wished whole-heartedly that she hadn't had to make it in the first place. Please God, let it work, she thought.

'Okay, Kel! Come on! Get in while it's hot. And bring the gin,' called Emma from the bathroom.

Slowly Kelsey dragged herself off the sofa, picked up the bottle of gin from the bookcase and went to the bathroom, where Emma was sitting on the stool with one hand behind her back.

'I'll stay here,' she said, 'in case.'

'In case?'

'It works.'

'Hopefully it will.' Kelsey placed the bottle of gin on the glass shelf above the hand basin, took off her dressing gown and hung it up behind the door. She tried the bath water with her toe.

'God, it's hot!'

'It's the only way.' Emma sounded as if she'd had previous experience.

Kelsey gave her friend a wan smile as she eased her slight frame into the steaming hot bath. Clothed, no sign of her pregnancy was visible. But now that she was naked, the slight bump showed quite clearly. She remained sitting for a few moments and then slowly leant back against the end of the bath. Emma put something on the floor with a faint clatter.

'What's that noise?' asked Kelsey in slight alarm.

'You'll know in a minute. Gin first.'

Emma poured the plastic tumbler full of gin and handed it to her friend. 'Drink as much as you can.'

Kelsey took a large gulp and gasped. 'It's ghastly!'

'I know.' Emma was sympathetic. 'One more gulp.'

Kelsey took another large mouthful.

'Now lie back.'

Obediently, Kelsey did as she was told. Emma bent and picked up the objects she had dropped on the floor: two metal knitting needles. She leant over the bath and handed one to Kelsey.

'Now try...

In a flash Kelsey understood what Emma meant.

'No! No! I can't! It's murder!' she screamed and burst into tears.

Kelsey was dreaming again. She was swimming up and down the pool with Kirsty, doing strong crawl strokes. One at a time her arms went up, over and in, up, over and in, with perfect synchronisation, the way she had been taught. At the same time her legs waved gently up and down, making no splash, just propelling her gently along. The twins' coach, Tim Roach, was shouting encouragement from the side. Tim Roach, the big he-man, smelling of nicotine and Brut for Men. Tim Roach, who had touched her up a few days before. Kelsey continued to swim, up and down, up and down, her arms and legs together in a perfect rhythm. But suddenly she was in trouble. Something had gone wrong. Her stroke was no longer smooth and co-ordinated. She was floundering. She was suffering from severe stomach cramp. She thrashed around in the water, shouting.

'Help! Help! Please help me! I'm drowning!'

Emma rushed into the room, pulling on her dressing gown, and switched on the light.

'Okay, Kel. Don't worry. Everything's going to be all right.'

She took one look at Kelsey's face, contorted in pain, and pulled back the duvet. The bed was a sea of blood. All the bedclothes were stained bright red. What hadn't been absorbed by the bedding was dripping inexorably onto the carpet. A thought flashed through Emma's mind: thank goodness this carpet isn't new. Immediately she felt ashamed at her self-absorption at such a critical time for her friend.

Kelsey's face was screwed up again with pain. 'Oh! O-oh!'

Emma held her hand tightly.

'Breathe deeply. Try and push.'

She pulled off the duvet and threw it on the floor.

'Raise your knees and push.'

Kelsey pushed, and screamed in pain. Emma looked down at the spot on the bed between her friend's raised legs, shocked and appalled by what she saw. Kelsey started to sob.

'Oh, no! Oh, no! I shouldn't have done it!'

It's too late now, thought Emma, kissing her friend and stroking her brow.

'I'll phone for an ambulance,' was all she said. 'You should be in hospital.'

Chapter Seventeen

'George?'

'Yeah. That you Eddie?'

'Yeah.'

'Got the stuff?'

'Yeah.'

'Where is it?'

'Outside in the van.'

'Where's the van?'

'Outside the 'ouse.'

'Full of stuff?'

'That's just what I said.'

'That's dangerous, that is.'

'What's dangerous?'

'Leaving a van full of stuff outside the 'ouse.'

'Where else'll I put it?'

'In the garidge.'

'I ain't got no garidge, you plonker.'

'I thought you said you 'ad a garidge.'

'No, I never. You must 'a been thinking of Vince. 'E's got a garidge.'

'Why didn't ya bleedin' put the stuff in Vince's garidge, for Christ's sake?'

'Vince weren't in.'

'You should 'a waited till he come home.'

'Naw. Too risky.'

'Why too risky?'

'Sitting outside someone else's garidge with a vanload of stuff.'

'No worse than a vanload of stuff outside your own 'ouse.'

'No problem. I can 'andle the Old Bill better on me own patch. It must be Bill-proof by now.'

'I sure 'ope so. When are we going to deliver the stuff?'

'Nine o'clock tonight.'

'Not dark enough.'

'At nine o'clock? Course it is.'

'No it ain't. It's almost June. It's not properly dark till ten.'

'Well, tough shit. I've arranged it now so you'd better be there or you won't get your cut.'

George sighed resignedly. 'Okay. I'll be there. Usual place?'

'Yeah. The Queen Anne pile out by Roydon.'

'Sure Mr Brookes won't be there?'

'Naw. How can 'e? 'E's just come out of 'ospital.'

'Out already, is 'e? We'd better get a move on then.'

'I'm ready to move when you are.'

'OK, Eddie. See you later.'

'Yeah. Bye.'

'Bye.'

George replaced the receiver and rubbed his chin reflectively. He wondered how long this business could continue. The money was good, but the risks were high.

'A delicious lunch, darling. Thank you. There's nothing like home cooking when you've spent three months on hospital swill. Lovely to have table napkins again too.'

Graham gave a deep sigh of contentment, and wiping his mouth carefully on his napkin, he looked around the dining room.

'House looks great. Nice to eat a good meal at a properly laid table. Did you eat in here on your own?'

'Oh, no. Only if William or Samantha came around for a meal.'

'And did they?'

'Oh, yes. Quite often for Sunday lunch.'

'I suppose they miss your home cooking too.'

'They probably do. Though Sam tries to eat as little as possible. She's terrified she'll get too fat for the cameras.'

I suppose a model's life isn't all glamour and large cheques.'

'It certainly isn't. And the duration of the work is strictly limited.'

'How long do you think she'll go on doing it? Another ten years?'

'She's - let's see - she's nineteen now so I'd say she's got at least another ten years to go.'

'At ten thousand pounds a week! Half a million a year! She'll be a multi-millionaire in ten years' time. She'll be able to bail us all out.'

'Not if she has to live on it for the rest of her life,' protested Julia. 'And hopefully nobody needs bailing out.'

'I'm not so sure.'

'What do you mean?'

'Well, I've been out of action for three months so I'm completely out of touch with my own business. Ken Spooner's being running it.'

Julia had started to clear away the plates, but stopped abruptly and sat down again. 'I thought you trusted him?'

'I did, until the day of the accident.'

'The day of the accident?' Julia's heart missed a beat as it usually did whenever the accident was mentioned. 'What happened to make you distrust him?'

'Well, it was just some small details we didn't agree on.' Graham wasn't sure how much he should reveal, even to his wife. 'There were some business matters I was planning to get sorted out as soon as possible. I didn't completely go along with Spooner's methods of ordering materials. He'd changed the builders' merchant without consulting me.'

'And as you're the boss, he clearly shouldn't have done. So I suppose you never had the chance to clear up the discrepancy because of the accident?'

'Precisely.'

'But now that you're getting your strength back, you'll soon be back at work again and able to straighten out everything.'

Graham looked gratefully at his wife. 'That's it,' he said, trying to keep his tone as light as possible.

Julia stood up and continued clearing away. 'And now perhaps a little rest?'

'Another rest? I never seem to stop resting. I've just had a three month rest. I need something to do.'

'You'll get plenty to do once you're back at work and the more you rest the quicker you'll be back.'

'All right, if you say so, I'll rest for one hour.'

'Excellent, dear. I do think that's sensible. Will you go up to bed?'

'Hardly worth it for an hour. I'll just put up my feet on the living room sofa.'

Graham groped for his stick under his chair and got up slowly from the table. Julia didn't offer him any help.

Graham had made it quite clear from his first day at home that he wished to be as independent as possible. 'Otherwise I'll never get going,' he had said.

Leaning heavily on his stick, he went to the far side of the table. 'I love you, darling,' he said, stroking his wife's cheek.

Julia gave a nervous little laugh. 'I love you too, darling. Now, off you go and have your hour's rest.'

Graham sat down on the chair next to his wife. 'I was wondering whether you would take me for a drive later this afternoon? After I've had my compulsory rest, of course.'

'A drive? Why not? Where would you like to go?'

'I was thinking of going out in the Roydon direction.'

'Roydon? Where the accident was?'

'Yes.'

'Would that be wise? I mean, to revisit the scene?'

'I think it's essential. The police have come up with nothing new.'

'Well, they say they don't have enough to go on.'

'I'd say they have plenty to go on. And they've had three months to work on it. Let's face it: a motorist was killed. I was almost killed and my car was a write-off. Deep in my subconscious I'm not sure there wasn't another car involved as well as the one that ran into me. And I feel Spooner must have seen something he hasn't admitted. You see no one has solved the problem of how my mobile turned up in my car, when I clearly remember leaving it in Spooner's office. Although he denies seeing it there and swears that when he locked his office it contained only his own stuff, I'm positive I did leave it in there. So it must have been Ken who put it in my car. When could he have done it?'

'While you were in one of the bungalows, talking to the carpenter?'

'No. I'd have seen it when I got back to the car.'

'Not if he'd put it in the glove compartment.'

'Julia, darling, that was the first place I would have looked. I always put it in the glove compartment. But it wasn't there. It was lying on Ken's desk after I came back from my visit to the carpenter in the bungalow. That's the one thing I'm really sure of.'

'I see. Is it possible that Ken Spooner could have seen your phone lying on his desk, realised how much you would miss it, driven after you in the hope of returning it and arrived at the scene of the accident just by chance? Then he would have seen the two mangled vehicles, reported the accident to the emergency services on your mobile and then driven off.'

'That could have happened.'

'But why would he have driven off? Isn't it against the law to leave the scene of a serious accident?'

'I would have thought so. But it is possible that he didn't actually see the accident happen...'

'But arrived just afterwards?'

'Yes. But even so he shouldn't have left the scene until the police arrived.'

'Have you told the police all this?'

'Oh, yes.'

'But they haven't found any finger prints on the phone?'

'No. None.'

'But there must have been another vehicle at the scene of the accident at some point, otherwise there would have been no call to the emergency services on your mobile. Can you remember if there was much traffic on the road?'

'Quite a bit on the Epping Road. But once I'd turned off there were no other vehicles on the road.'

'None at all? Are you sure?'

'Julia, darling, I'm *not* sure. That's the bit I'm not sure of. That's why I want to drive out there to jog my memory. I still don't seem to have got over the bump on my head. The details of that drive are still very hazy.'

'Right. You have your rest. I'll clear up lunch and then we'll drive out to Roydon by any route you wish.'

'Thank you, my darling.'

Graham got up and made his way slowly next door and settled down on the living room sofa. Julia went into the kitchen and opened the fridge. Carefully taking out several healthy food items such as skimmed milk, low-fat spread and low-calorie cream cheese, she reached right into the back and lifted up an innocent-looking paper bag, the two ends skilfully twirled around to form a loose closure. Supporting the weight underneath with one hand, she guided it gently out of the fridge between a carton of orange juice and a jar of low calorie mayonnaise and placed it on the draining board. She gave the bag a gentle pat, salivating in anticipation, and tiptoed to the kitchen door. She opened the door quietly, just a crack, and heard the sounds of contented snoring coming from the direction of the living room. Excellent, she thought. Hopefully, Graham will sleep for an hour. She closed the kitchen door silently, crept across the floor and surveyed the prize awaiting her on the draining board. Should she put the cornets on a plate or eat them right here out of the paper bag? Of course it would be more comfortable and more elegant to eat them off a plate. But concealment would be easier at the draining board. Concealment, that is, from Graham. Though why should she want to conceal the fact from her husband that she was about to demolish three cream cornets in as many minutes? It had something to do with guilt. Guilt because she was greedy, over-weight and addicted to fattening pasties. There were four more cream cakes in the fridge for tea. Two cream cornets and two chocolate éclairs. They had had rich delicacies for tea every day since Graham had arrived home. On the second day Graham had expressed surprise at their appearance.

'More cream cakes?'

'Yes,' said Julia. 'You need building up.'

'But surely not with so much cholesterol?'

'It won't hurt for a few days. After all, you've lost a lot of weight.'

'Yes,' was all Graham said, but Julia could imagine him thinking: Julia, my dear, you have not lost weight. You are becoming much too fat.

She decided it would be more prudent to eat the cakes at the draining board. If Graham were to appear un-expectedly early, she could pop the cornets under an upturned saucepan. He would never lift up a saucepan. He never did. With loving care Julia moved the paper bag containing the cornets onto the working top beside the draining board. Then she quickly washed up the two saucepans in which she had cooked lunch, squeezing in a few drops of Fairy Liquid and washing them under a running tap to save time. With both saucepans lying upside down on the draining board, she felt she had enough backup to conceal her feast if necessary. She wiped the excess moisture off the draining board with a sponge cloth and slid the bag gently across the work-ing top until it lay close beside one of the saucepans.

Quivering in anticipation, her heart beating a little faster, she untwisted the edges of the paper bag, and lifting up the end she saw the three cream cornets lying neatly side-by-side. She picked up the first one by the wide end and took a large bite, sucking hard so the cream would go into her mouth rather than splurging out everywhere. She spread the cream around her mouth with her tongue, feeling the lightness of the flaky pastry and savouring the taste of the jam. Another large bite finished it off. Reaching inside the bag for the second one, she thought she heard a noise in the hall. Thank goodness I'm not sitting at the table she thought, quickly folding the ends of the bag together and popping it under the saucepan. She slipped off her shoes and crept across to the kitchen door. She opened it noiselessly and listened, but all she could hear was the grandfather clock ticking in the hall and Graham's faint snores coming from the living room. She closed the door again and slid back across the smooth floor tiles to the two remaining cornets on the draining board. She took the saucepan off the paper bag and lifted out the second cornet, replacing the saucepan on the remaining one in the bag.

Knowing that Graham was still sound asleep made her feel a little more secure. She could take more time eating the second cornet. She bit slowly into the narrow end, taking a smaller bite this time. Delicious. The first bite was always the best. Three more bites and that cornet had also disappeared down Julia's throat and into her stomach to swell her massive body even more. One cornet left. Should she be a total glutton and eat that one too, or should she exercise a modicum of self-control and leave it until later? She could have her last feast of the day when she had washed up and Graham was already in bed. She was still deliberating when she heard the cloakroom door open and the lavatory being flushed. The door closed again and Graham's voice said: 'Ready whenever you are, my darling.'

Chapter Eighteen

Julia settled Graham into the front passenger seat of the sleek dark blue BMW, the glossy metallic finish gleaming in the warm late May sunshine. 'Comfy?'

Graham smiled gratefully up at his wife. 'Yes, thanks, darling.' He hated being helped, especially in such mundane matters as getting into a car, but in his present state he knew he had no option. Julia went around to the driver's side and opened the door. Flattening her voluminous navy skirt behind her, she slowly heaved her great bulk into the driving seat. Heaven's above, she thought, I'll have to start dieting or soon I won't fit behind the wheel.

'Lovely day for a drive, isn't it?' she remarked conversationally as she turned on the power, tapped in the security code, switched on the ignition and engaged the automatic gear lever into 'drive.'

'Yes, a beautiful day indeed,' returned Graham, wondering what the afternoon held in store.

It had been more than three months since the accident and still no one had any idea who the mysterious caller was who had phoned the emergency services on his mobile. It now seemed that the police were no longer interested either in the caller or how Graham's phone had turned up in his wrecked car. All that mattered to them was that the cause of the accident was quite clear.

Forgetting that Brits drive on the left, the Frenchman had careered the wrong way around the roundabout at high speed, smashed straight into Graham's car, and killed himself in the process. No witnesses were needed to hold an inquest. So it wasn't with any notion of helping the police that Graham felt compelled to revisit the scene of the accident. It had more to do with trying to find out whether Ken Spooner might have been involved.

Julia guided the car smoothly down several leafy residential side roads before edging out in a difficult right turn into Wanstead High Street. Graham lay back in the passenger seat feeling relaxed and a little indulged at being driven. Before the accident he had done all the driving, so it made a pleasant change to be a passenger. Concentrating on the traffic that was coming along the main road from the right, Julia waited for a car that turned into the road beside them at the last moment without signalling. It was a small car, the size of a Ford Fiesta, dark green with a metallic finish, and although it was probably five or six years old, it was clean and well kept. The driver was an elderly man with a good head of thick dark grey hair. The passenger was also elderly; a very well dressed lady with grey hair scraped into a bun behind her neck.

'Good God!' exclaimed Julia, braking so suddenly that the car stalled. Graham jumped, rudely shaken out of his pleasant reverie.

'What on earth's the matter?' he asked.

'Sorry,' said Julia lamely, restarting the engine. 'That was Mother.'

'Your *mother!*' Graham started to laugh. 'Out on a drive!'

'Why not? It's not exclusive to us.'

'No. I know. But even so, I thought your mother was in a home recovering from a hip fracture.'

'She is. But that doesn't stop her going for a drive.'

'No. I suppose not. Who was her companion? Did you see?'

'An elderly man who never learnt to give traffic signals.'

'Maybe he did learn, but he's forgotten.'

'He looked as if he wasn't sure where he was going.'

'Maybe he wasn't sure. Was he old?'

'Fairly old. But not as old as Mother.'

'Maybe we could find out who he was the next time we visit your mother. It could be quite interesting.'

'It could, couldn't it? We might call in on our way back,' suggested Julia. 'I haven't seen Mother for over a week. I wonder if Alison has told her about poor Kelsey?'

'I hope so,' said Graham fervently. 'It's not a task I'd wish on anyone.'

'No,' agreed Julia.

'Let's see how the afternoon goes, shall we? We don't know how it's going to turn out.'

'Good idea.'

They drove along Wanstead High Street in silence, stopping frequently in the heavy traffic. At the end of Wanstead High Street, by the Eagle Pub at the corner of Hollybush Hill, the traffic lights showed red. Signalling right, Julia slid into the right-hand lane and waited.

'Straight out on the Epping Road, isn't it?' she asked.

'Yes, replied Graham. 'Straight on for about ten miles.'

'On the day of the accident, did you start the drive from home and go directly to Roydon?'

'Oh, no. Don't you remember? First of all I went to Woodford where we were building those luxury bungalows for retired people by the railway line. That's where I had a meeting with Spooner in his office about…' Graham hesitated, not wanting to say too much… 'About the change of builder's merchant,' he ended lamely.

'Yes. I remember your saying that Spooner had changed to a different builder's merchant without consulting you.'

'That's right.'

'So you had your chat with Spooner and then drove out to Roydon?'

'Yes. But before I drove off I also had a chat with my carpenter, Mick Kelly, in bungalow No. 3.'

'An important discussion?'

'Very important, regarding the finishing details.'

'But not relevant to your discussion with Spooner.'

'No. The two weren't connected.'

'Before you drove off, did you speak to Spooner again?'

'I was planning to. I went back to his office, but he'd already left. So I looked in the window, just to check up on him really.'

'Because you didn't completely trust him?'

'Yes.'

'Was there another reason why you didn't trust him, as well as his having changed the builder's merchant without your knowledge?'

Graham hesitated. He knew he would have to confide in Julia some time. Perhaps better now than later. 'Well, the reason Spooner gave me for changing builder's merchant was that the supplies would be cheaper.'

'That seems a good enough reason.'

'It does on the face of it. But it didn't start off like that.'

'How did it start?'

Graham gave a deep sigh. 'After the bank crash in 2008, when the recession started to bite, I asked Ken if he had any suggestions as to how we might economise.'

'So the first suggestion came from you?'

'Yes.'

'So you could say that Spooner was only doing what he was told.'

'At the beginning.'

'Then he took it all a little further than you expected.'

'Yes, that's one way of putting it.'

'Right. So you asked Spooner for suggestions on how the company might economise and he suggested going to a cheaper builder's merchant.'

'Yes.'

'Which makes sense.'

'Yes.'

'But there must be more to it than that.'

'There is.'

Oh, my darling Julia, maybe you're too fat, but you're not stupid, thought Graham.

'Spooner knew of this cheaper builder's merchant through one of his mates. Not only were the materials cheaper, but the supplier didn't charge VAT.'

Julia couldn't help laughing. 'It sounds like a good deal.'

'Yes. It does, on the surface,' agreed Graham. 'But any reputable, registered company has to make tax returns: both to the Inland Revenue and the VAT office. Inspectors come round periodically to check up and God help the boss if the books aren't in order.'

'And have they been round?'

'Not yet, but I'm hoping to get the books in order before they do.'

'So at the moment the books are not in order.'

'No. 'They've been - let's say - adjusted.'

'By Spooner.'

'Exactly. Not only has he adjusted the books, but he's been paying his mates hush money with what he's saved Brookes Builders in cheaper materials and VAT payments.'

Julia was silent for a moment as she negotiated the roundabout by the Churchill statue. They drove on in silence until they arrived at a red traffic light by the Castle pub.

'So Spooner's mates are involved as well?'

'It appears so.'

'How long has this been going on?'

'About two years.'

'*Two years!* That *is* a long time. Did you realise from the beginning that Spooner had gone further than you intended?'

'No. Not for some time. Quite a long time, in fact.'

'So when you made your request for some economies, you had no idea that Spooner would eventually screw up your whole business.'

Graham sighed again. 'That sums it up perfectly. And I had no idea either that he would implicate most of my workforce into the bargain.'

The car stopped again at the traffic lights by the end of Whitehall Road. Through the large, impressive side gate Graham caught a glimpse of Bancroft's School through the trees: an imposing red Victorian Gothic building where he had once been a pupil.

'Your old school,' remarked Julia, reading his thoughts. 'Straight on towards Epping?'

'Yes. Straight on.'

Graham craned his head in order to get a better view of the front of the school, and as they drove on, his thoughts went back to his last journey along the same road. Three months ago it was early spring. He remembered admiring the yellow crocuses and celandines and noticing the delicate fronds of the catkins on the hazelnut bushes. Now it was almost high summer. All the trees were in full leaf, not fully darkened, but no longer the light pale spring green. Glinting in the slanting rays of the afternoon sunshine, the bluebells peeped shyly through the lush green grass in the ditch. Only two cars passed them on the long, straight stretch of road that led to the Robinhood Roundabout. As Julia approached the roundabout a small red car, coming from the direction of Theydon Bois, slipped in front of them.

'That's it!' shouted Graham, becoming excited. 'That's it! It looks like the same car that followed me all the way to Roydon. I first noticed it at this roundabout. It was red too, I swear to it.'

Julia felt her heart beating uncomfortably loudly. 'What do you want me to do?' she enquired.

'Just follow that car.'

'Wherever it goes?'

'Yes.'

'Even if it doesn't go to Roydon?'

'Yes. Just follow it.'

As the red car in front gathered speed, Julia put her foot down hard on the accelerator and kept as close as possible. She followed it as it sped along the Epping Road, the relatively light traffic making it easy to keep on its tail. Graham tried to see the driver, but without success. Just before the turn to Roydon the car slowed down, signalled and turned left. Graham was becoming more excited.

'I bet its Ken Spooner on his way to the Queen Anne House.'

'How far is that from here?'

'Not far. Three or four miles.'

'Shall I keep following him?'

'Yes. For the moment.'

'Is Brookes Builders still working on the Queen Anne House?'

'Yes. I imagine so. But I have been a bit out of touch for the last three months for some reason...'

'Yes. Obviously...'

'But if Spooner is going to the house then I would think Brookes Builders would still be working on it.'

'So his reason for going there could be quite legitimate?'

'It could.'

'On the day of your accident...' (Julia still had difficulty in forming the dreaded word without a shudder) 'On that day Spooner might also have been paying a perfectly legitimate visit to the house?'

'Possibly. But why did he keep on my tail when I made a detour around the first roundabout?'

'Maybe we'll never know.'

'Maybe. But I'm still curious to know who called the ambulance service on my mobile.'

'Of course.'

The red car slowed down and Julia also applied her brakes.

'We're nearly there,' said Graham, as large impressive wrought-iron gates, well set back from the road, came into view on a bend. One gate was wide open and the red car drove in with an assurance born of much practice.

'Would you stop for a moment, please?' asked Graham. 'I need to work out a plan of campaign.'

Julia obediently drew into the side of the curved entrance in front of the gates. Graham lay back in the passenger seat and closed his eyes for a moment. Julia felt a flicker of alarm.

'Okay?' she enquired.

'Fine. I think we should just drive straight on up to the house. After all, I am the managing director and the chairman of Brookes Builders. I have a right to visit my own building sites whenever I choose.'

'Quite right,' Julia agreed, and engaging the car in gear, she drove slowly through the massive wrought-iron gates and up the impressive drive, lined on both sides with magnificent horse chestnut trees.

'Is that the lot, Eddie?'

'Naw. Bit more still inside. I don't like this business. Shifting this shit in daylight.'

'Nor me neither. It were much safer in the dark.'

'Yeah. I think we should tell 'im.'

'Tell 'im what?'

'That we ain't going to shift no more stuff in the daytime.'

'Yeah.'

'I think he's diddling us too.'

George's eyes widened. 'What makes you think that?'

'Cos I think we ought to be getting a lot more dosh than we do.'

'What're you doing to do about it?'

'Ask him for more.'

'And if he doesn't play ball?'

'We'll rough him up a bit.'

George's eyes widened still further. 'Is that a good idea?'

'Can't do any harm - and we might get what we want.

'Which is more money.'

'And more say in how this operation's being handled.'

'Like...?'

'Who's in charge and how long it's going to go on.'

'Think old Brookes has an inkling he's being fleeced left, right and centre?'

'Naw. 'E's been too ill. Nearly died.'

'I heard he'd lost his memory.'

'Yeah. Just as well, ain't it?'

'Do you think it was done a purpose?'

'What?'

'The accident, you plonker!'

'Naw. I rec 'e just happened to be there at the time.'

'Was 'e trying to give Mr Brookes 'is mobile back?'

'Could 'a been.' Eddie leant nonchalantly against the side of the van they had been loading, getting oil on its spotless white surface. 'Where is the bloody geyser anyroad? 'E should be 'ere by now. This van don't 'alf look conspicuous with its name on the side for all to see.'

'Yeah. It don't 'alf.'

They both surveyed the smart white van with 'BROOKES BUILDERS BUCKHURST HILL ESSEX TEL 0181 504 9120' painted on both sides in smart black lettering.

'Let's get the rest of this shit in as quick as possible,' said Eddie, starting to walk up the elegant fan-shaped stone staircase to the front door of the house. George followed him inside to where the remainder of the stolen goods lay in a tidy pile on the floor of the magnificent drawing room. They picked up as much as they could carry, as the battered red Ford came up the drive and parked in front of the stone steps.

'There 'e is,' said Eddie, laying down his load. 'I'm gonna get my money before I load up any more of this shit, even if I 'ave to beat the bloody daylights out of him.'

The drive swung sharply around to the right, opening out into a graceful broad semi-circle with a weeping willow in the centre. Julia stopped short and gasped in amazement. This was the Queen Anne House that Graham had talked about so often and with so much enthusiasm.

'It's beautiful!' she exclaimed.

'Yes,' agreed Graham. 'It's considered one of the best examples of its period in the whole of southeast England. You see,' he continued knowledgably, pointing up at the house, 'it's completely symmetrical and built with local stone. Of course neither the roof nor the windows are original, but everything has been meticulously replaced in style.'

'I suppose it's listed?'

'Oh, yes. Grade One.'

'Does that pose problems?'

'It certainly does. Every bit of restoration and repair must be done strictly in the style of the period - both inside and out.'

'Do you have to use materials of the period?'

'Where possible, yes. But it isn't always possible.'

'Because they're no longer available?'

'Exactly. But certain modern materials are banned.'

'Such as?'

'MDF.'

'What on earth's that?'

'It stands for medium density fibre. It's compressed sawdust and wood shavings. Sort of leftovers. It's a cheap substitute for wood. Carpenters love it because it doesn't warp and there are no knots.'

'I see.' Julia was none the wiser. 'Do you want me to drive right up to the house?'

'I don't see why not.'

As Julia edged her way around the huge willow tree, the white van with BROOKES BUILDERS painted on it in black came into view, parked directly outside the front door.

'Your van,' remarked Julia.

'Yes. So I imagine the job is still in progress. Restoration of listed buildings can take a very long time.'

Beyond the van was the scruffy red Ford.

'There it is!' Graham shouted in excitement. 'That's Ken's car! 'He's here! I knew it! I bet he's up to no good.'

Julia felt her mouth go dry and her palms become sweaty.

'Shall I park here?' she asked nervously.

'Yes! Here! There! Anywhere! It doesn't matter!' Graham was becoming over-excited.

Julia parked rather awkwardly beside the red Ford, her heart thumping loudly. 'What are you going to do?'

'I'm going to go straight in there and find out what's going on. Please help me out of the car.'

Julia went around the car to the passenger side and opened the door. She handed Graham his stick and he got out of the car slowly and with difficulty. As he stood up and started walking towards the house they both heard a commotion coming from inside. Voices were raised in anger.

'You're a flaming cheat! You owe us the truth as well as the bleeding money!'

'Take that! That's for cheating on us!'

'You can have that as well!'

The sound of punching, hitting, gasping and groaning sailed through the still, early evening air. Graham and Julia stood rigid, transfixed with fear and horror as the sound of hard, flying objects came from inside the house.

A desperate voice yelled: 'for fuck's sake leave me alone! You'll get your bleeding money when I've got it.'

'We're not waiting no longer. You've got it coming to you now.'

There was a shrill, agonising scream as a brick came flying through the window. Julia helped Graham back into the car and drove off as speedily as possible, neither of them saying a word.

Chapter Nineteen

'I've just had some rather splendid news.'

'Oh, yes?' Verity started to get up out of her chair, planning to sit somewhere else. She found Priscilla Prescott most unsettling with her pince-nez and her out-dated diary hanging from a ribbon around her neck. But Miss Prescott had perched on the arm of Verity's chair in such a way that it was impossible for her to get up. Miss Prescott leant forward and spoke in a conspiratorial whisper.

'They came yesterday.'

'They?'

'Yes. They came at last.'

'And they are...?' Verity was no longer surprised by Miss Prescott's confusion.

'Alzheimer's, dear,' Gladys Bates had explained a few days after Verity's arrival at Oaklands. 'Much worse than a broken hip. Broken bones mend but Alzheimer's just gets progressively worse. Sad, isn't it? Miss Prescott obviously had such a brilliant mind. Head of that posh girls' school in Yorkshire. You know the one - near where they make the toffee.'

'Oh, yes?' Verity had sounded vague. At that moment she couldn't quite think of where toffee was made.

'They came yesterday. With such good news,' repeated Miss Prescott.

'I am glad,' said Verity. 'What was the good news?'

'I'm going to be awarded the OBE!' said Priscilla Prescott triumphantly. 'In the Queen's birthday honour's list in August.'

'Congratulations! That's really wonderful news! But the Queen's birthday isn't...' began Verity, and stopped. There was no point really. 'And when are you going to the palace to collect it?'

'In July, after the Queen's birthday.'

'Of course.' There was no point in not agreeing with everything Miss Prescott said. 'Who's going to go with you?'

'Who? My husband of course. I don't see that much of him now. He's in a special home, you see.' Miss Prescott tapped her head. 'Not quite all there, you know. It happens to some people when they get older. It's very sad. We're still devoted of course - quite devoted. But when the mind goes it's difficult to keep closely in touch. Oh, here's Mrs Morrison come to join us.'

'Oh, hello, Elsie,' said Verity, relieved at the prospect of being able to slip away from Miss Prescott unnoticed. 'Miss Prescott has some very good news.'

'Oh, yes,' said Elsie brightly, always ready to listen to gossip. 'And what's the news, Miss Prescott?'

'They came yesterday.'

'They did, did they?' said Elsie, giving Verity a broad wink. 'And who were they?'

'Why, the school governors, of course,' said Miss Prescott, as if she were stating the obvious to a rather dim child.

'Of course,' said Elsie soothingly, slipping into the role of sympathetic listener. 'And what did they have to say?'

'They brought some excellent news.'

'Yes?'

'I shall receive the OBE in the Queen's birthday honour's list.'

'On the Queen's birthday in August,' said Verity soberly.

'Yes, of course,' said Elsie, catching on very quickly. 'That's excellent news, Miss Prescott. I'm delighted.'

'Thank you, dear.' And to the great relief of both Verity and Elsie, Miss Prescott left to spread her good news among the rest of the Oaklands' residents.

Mabel Cooke and Gladys Bates went into the television room together.

'I told you,' said Mabel. 'He's watching the cartoons. I knew he would be.'

'It's all he watches. Although I do wonder how much he sees.'

'Or takes in,' replied Mabel.

They each sat down on one of the Parker Knoll chairs, which formed a semi-circle around the television set. In the middle, with his face so close to the set he almost touched it, sat Victor Bowles. At 97, the oldest Oaklands' resident, Victor was completely bald, extremely deaf and totally blind in one eye. He spent most of the day in the television room, slumped in front of the set, asleep, snoring. He slobbered and dribbled constantly, even in his sleep, and was a most unpopular mealtime neighbour among the other residents. At the moment he was snoring loudly, spittle spotting his chin and dropping onto his very old, well-darned grey jumper.

Gladys picked up the television remote control.

'Excuse me, dear,' she said loudly. 'You don't mind if I switch channels do you, Victor?'

'There's a nice cookery programme on the other side,' said Mabel supportively, straightening up her orange wig.

Victor gave a loud honk and another dribble slid down his chin.

'Did that mean something?' enquired Gladys.

'I don't know, dear.' Mabel got up and leant over Victor. 'All right, Victor? We're going to watch a programme on the other side.'

Victor made no response.

'I'd just flick over, dear,' advised Mabel.

A programme on Indian cooking had already started. Madhur Jaffrey, wearing a beautiful gold-bordered turquoise sari, was explaining how to make a chicken Vindaloo. Surrounded by half the spices of the Orient, she moved elegantly between the working top and the gas hob, chopping, mixing, stirring and tasting; talking all the time in fluent, Oriental-flavoured English.

Victor stopped snoring and moved closer to the television set, watching the programme intently for a few minutes.

'I thought I smelt curry,' he said, and threw up all over the set.

'And she was wearing the exact same necklace as the one I've got,' said Elsie Morrison. 'It was identical. So I thought I'd wear mine the next day, just to see if she'd notice. But do you know, dear,' Elsie leant across the lunch table towards Gladys, 'do you know, when I went to get it out of my drawer, it had gone!'

'What had gone?' asked Brenda Barnes, sitting to right of Hilda Haddock, wearing an impeccably tailored lilac two-piece, more suitable for a wedding than an ordinary weekday lunch in a retirement home.

Elsie put her hand up to her throat. 'My necklace, dear. That Hilda Haddock was wearing exactly the same one as I've got. But mine's missing. I haven't seen it since I last saw Hilda Haddock wearing hers. If it is hers, of course. It could be mine, couldn't it? I wonder? Do you think,' she asked, turning to Mabel Cooke who was sitting on her left, 'do you think there's at thief at Oaklands?'

An embarrassed murmur ran around the table. 'Oh, no!'

'Surely not!'

'What a dreadful thing to say!'

'Where is Hilda Haddock?' enquired Verity. 'I haven't seen her for a few days.'

'She's not too well,' said Mary Mulloy shortly, her uniform rustling stiffly as she got up to clear away the plates.

'Her stomach is it?' asked Gladys.

'Yes,' said Mary.

Mabel straightened up her orange wig before joining in the conversation. 'There must be a bug going around,' she remarked succinctly. 'Poor old Victor threw up all over the telly yesterday. It was quite funny really. Gladys and I were watching one of those cookery programmes, you know, the one with the pretty Indian lady, who was explaining how to make a proper Indian curry. Old Victor was sitting right on top of the set, the way he does, as he can hardly see at all. Suddenly he said: "I smell curry," and was sick all over the place. His vomit smelt really dreadful, I can tell you. Gladys and I got out as quickly as we could and went to find Mary. When the three of us got back to the telly room poor old Victor was lying on the floor. He had to be carried to bed. How is poor Victor, Mary?'

'Poorly,' replied Mary, piling up the plates on the sideboard.

Verity was in the sitting room, comfortably installed in her favourite armchair, absorbed in a Mary Wesley novel, when Gladys came in looking grave. Without any ado she pulled up a chair next to Verity and sat down, dropping her huge handbag on the floor with a dull thud.

'He's dead, dear.'

'Who's dead?' asked Verity in alarm, her heart missing a beat. 'Not James?'

Gladys shot her a funny look. 'No. Oh, God forbid no. Not James. It's old Victor Bowles.'

'Victor!' said Verity, in a voice full of relief. 'But he was old.'

Gladys took her hand. 'Extremely old. Going on ninety-eight, I believe. But it's unsettling, isn't it, dear?'

'What was it?'

'Stomach bug. They say something's going around. Elsie isn't too well either.'

'I thought I hadn't seen her at supper last night.'

'I wonder who we'll get instead of Victor. We could do with another man around this place.'

'And how's Steven?' enquired Verity.

'Oh, very well, I think,' replied Alison, who had been hoping her mother wouldn't ask about Steven.

'You think?'

'It's hard to say. He's still in Morocco.'

'Morocco? I thought he went to Morocco some time ago?'

'Yes. Nearly two months ago.'

Verity gave a rather sardonic laugh. 'He must be enjoying himself.'

'I think he is,' said Alison truthfully.

'I thought Steven's little trips abroad were generally quite short. Just to prospect for future business and see how the land lies, as it were.'

'That's quite right. Usually his trips are quite short.'

'He must have found something of great interest to keep him there for two months.'

Alison didn't reply. She didn't know why Steven was still in Morocco. She didn't want to think about it. The only communication she had received from him was three postcards: one of a long sweep of sandy beach from Agadir, another of a Berber market in the Atlas Mountains and the last one of a water seller in the large main square in Marrakech. The messages were brief. From Agadir he had written: *This is a cold country with hot sun.* From the Atlas Mountains: *Wonderful views.* And from Marrakech: *Anything goes here.*

Alison wondered what Steven had meant by 'anything.'

At the moment she was far more concerned about Kelsey and how she was going to explain the situation to Verity. She knew Verity disapproved of divorce. She also knew that Verity liked and approved of Nigel. 'It's such a nice change to have a professional in the family,' Verity had said, shortly after Kelsey and Nigel's wedding, 'rather than just another businessman.'

Alison had been utterly shocked by Nigel's behaviour. It wasn't just a question of her daughter's word against her son-in-law's. Nigel had actually got his mistress pregnant and the horrid little tart was planning to keep the baby and bring it up on her own, as a single mother.

At least the baby won't be any relative of mine, thought Alison primly. And when Kelsey's divorce comes through, Nigel won't be any relative of mine either. Poor Kelsey! She had been dangerously ill after the miscarriage, so ill she had nearly died and she, Alison, would have lost her only surviving child. Kelsey had cried her heart out. She felt so guilty, she said, as if it had been her fault. But how could it have been her fault? It had been the will of God. But how could there be a God so callous that He let the wrong woman miscarry? And there was that nasty little minx, Susie, more than six months pregnant, walking around as proud as Punch, carrying a man's baby whose wife had lost her own. Was there no justice in this world? And she, Alison, would have to explain the whole sad story to Verity.

'Mother,' she began.

'Yes, dear,' said Verity.

'Mother, I have something to tell you...'

'Something nice, I hope,' said Verity, settling herself more comfortably in her chair.

'Well...' began Alison, but the rest of her words were drowned by an ambulance siren wailing nearer and the screech of brakes as it stopped at the door of Oaklands. Four paramedics dressed in boiler suits the same shade of green as surgeons in an operating theatre, leapt out and ran the few steps up the path to the front door.

'Well,' said Alison, trying again.

'But not so well,' said Verity. 'That's the fourth time an ambulance has called at Oaklands within a week. Someone else must be seriously ill. Apparently there's a bug going around. Two residents have died within the last five days.'

'Died?' said Alison, her eyes widening.

Chapter Twenty

Steven bounced up and down on the diving board a few times to test the spring. Then he took one last big jump and dived gracefully into the pool. He swam a length with a strong crawl, his arms curving in and out powerfully, his legs following in a well-co-ordinated paddle with the minimum of splash.

'Excellent!' called Lars from the poolside, where he lay on a sunbed, tanning his lean, beautifully toned body an even deeper shade of mahogany. Steven swam four more lengths with strong unhurried strokes, looking every inch a professional. He savoured the silky warm water as it lapped around his body and marvelled at the buoyancy keeping him afloat. He felt exhilarated and free. He lay on his back for a few moments to rest, floating, moving his hands and feet just enough to keep his body level with the water. He opened his eyes and gazed in wonder at the brilliant Moroccan sun in a cloudless azure sky, still shining down fiercely, even at five o'clock in the afternoon. He swam to the side and climbed up the small metal ladder. He walked slowly towards the sunbeds, beads of water gleaming brightly on his firm torso, no longer city-white, but slowly deepening each day to a rich chestnut. He picked up his brightly striped towel, wiped his face and briskly rubbed his hair. Lars looked up at him admiringly.

'You're a wonderful swimmer. How did you learn to swim like that?'

'Had lessons when I was a kid.' Steven spread the towel on the sunbed, lay down and closed his eyes.

Lars leant across and proffered some suntan lotion. 'Here. You should use this after swimming.'

'Even after five o'clock?'

'Yes. Even after five o'clock. Skin cancer. It pays to take care. Especially fair-haired people. And you've got blue eyes.'

'Yes. I'm sure you're right.' Steven took the lotion and obediently covered himself with it.

'So you swam a lot as a child?' asked Lars.

'Yes. I did.'

'With any particular goal in mind?'

'No. Not really. It was suggested at one stage that I should take it more seriously but there's not much future in swimming, is there?'

'There's always the Olympics to aim for.'

Steven let out an involuntary sigh. 'Maybe. But there's a lot of swimming up and down to do before then.'

('It's just up and down, up and down, Dad,' Kelsey had said after Kirsty's terrible accident. 'I'm not going to do it any more.')

'Does your daughter swim?' enquired Lars.

'No,' said Steven shortly. 'She doesn't like the water.'

Which was perfectly true. After the accident Kelsey could hardly bear to go into the shower, let alone a swimming pool.

Steven had told Lars very little about his family. So far it hadn't seemed necessary. His family was so far away and he was living such a very different life now. Unbelievably different. Meeting Lars had been nothing short of a miracle. All the more so because it had been totally unexpected. Originally Steven had planned to stay in Morocco for about two weeks. He was at the point where he felt sure that Sun Med could afford to expand a little. After the humiliating sell-out to Verity, business had slowly started to pick up, especially in the last three years. While beginning to feel cautiously optimistic about the future of Sun Med, Steven felt he couldn't afford to be too reckless either. His last expansion into the Far East market had brought nothing but problems, so caution was paramount. But also caution with imagination. Steven knew he was near the point of being able to buy back the business, and he hoped that going into Morocco would help him to turn the corner. He felt sure that the sandy, sun-drenched beaches, (albeit usually full of predatory German tourists,) and the contrast of the cold clear air of the deserted High Atlas Mountains, would appeal to the discerning tastes of his Sun Med clients. Hotel standards were extremely high, which convinced Steven that he could only buy back Sun Med from Verity if he brought Morocco into his business.

The tour Steven had mapped out for himself started in Casablanca and continued to Rabat, Meknes, Fez and then on to Agadir, on the Atlantic coast. At the beginning of the second week, he arrived in Marrakech, where he marvelled at the warm, deep red of the buildings; the constant swirl of traffic, the cars hooting, horse-drawn carriages rattling and clip-clopping, and vendors plying their wares. Tourists were milling around, most of them unsuitably dressed for conservative Islamic tastes, bartering in the souks, photographing forbidden objects or just gawping.

It was in the vast main square, Jemaa el Fna, where Steven had met Lars. Steven was photographing the jugglers, tumblers, drummers, snake charmers, water sellers and dentists, (instant extractions on request,) when he noticed that each time he stopped to take a picture, the same young man seemed to be watching him. The young man was tall and of slight build, with thick, pale straw-coloured hair and a deep tan. His face had delicate bone structure with prominent cheekbones and he had very bright, almost piercing blue eyes. He was neatly dressed in a pale blue open-neck shirt and well-cut beige trousers. He was probably in his mid-thirties. Having apparently been followed by this arresting young man for almost twenty minutes, Steven felt that perhaps he ought to say something. But was the young man English? Steven thought not. Could he be German? Steven spoke no German, or indeed any foreign language, apart from a very little badly accented restaurant French. So he just smiled. The young man smiled back, with a warm, friendly smile, his eyes crinkling up at the corners.

'That looks a good camera.' His English pronunciation was perfect, but there was something definitely un-English about the intonation. His voice had a soft singsong quality, which Steven found most attractive.

'It must take very good pictures.'

'It does.'

'So you take your travelling seriously.'

'Yes. I have to.'

'Have to?'

'Yes.'

'Why is that?'

'I'm a travel agent.' Steven was not generally in the habit of imparting personal information to complete strangers, but this young man somehow seemed diffe-rent. 'This is a marvellous square. The action never seems to stop.'

'Have you taken a photograph from the top?' the young man enquired.

'The top of what?'

'From the roof of that café over there,' said the young man pointing. 'I think in English you say "from the view of a bird's eye." '

Steven laughed. 'You mean a "bird's eye view." '

The young man laughed too. 'My English needs improving. Since I am living in Morocco I speak mostly French, so my English has become, how do you say it? A little more rusty.'

'I think your English is excellent. I don't speak any foreign language.'

'Even though you are a travel agent?'

'That's probably why. I'm too busy being a travel agent to devote much time to anything else.'

'I see. So why don't we go up on the roof of that café so you can take pictures of the square?'

'Yes. Why not? Can we just walk up and photograph? Is it free?'

'All you have to do is buy a drink.'

Steven followed the young man through the ever-thickening crowds towards a rather bleak-looking café in the corner of the square. They mounted two flights of steep, dingy stairs and reached a stark concrete viewing platform, furnished with a few metal tables and chairs. A large fridge stood in a prominent position near the entrance. As the two men walked to the edge to look at the view, an elderly wizened Moroccan got up from his chair and pointed to the fridge.

Steven's companion chuckled. 'We can't get out of the drink. Moroccans are extremely commercial.'

'So I've noticed.'

'But they're also very poor.'

They selected their drinks. But there were no glasses and the 'management' appeared to have run out of straws. They took their cans to a table over-looking the square. Steven sat down and discovered he could no longer see the view. He stood up again.

'The wall's a bit high.'

The young man smiled. 'That's to discourage suicides.'

Steven nodded. 'Of course.' He proffered his hand. 'I'm Steven Hobbs. I'm pleased to meet you.'

The young man stood up. 'And so am I, too. My name is Lars Lindstrom.'

For a moment they sipped their drinks in silence, gazing down at the increasing activity below. More and more street entertainers were arriving and taking up their positions on allotted pitches. Several music groups were performing simultaneously, filling the air with a wild cacophony of sound. Food vendors were taking up their positions along the lines of stalls already erected, each space on the square precisely marked out and numbered in white paint. As the cooking began, the aroma of oils, herbs and spices wafted into the evening air.

Steven took a deep breath. 'Mmm. It smells delicious. Is it safe to eat the food?'

'It depends what kind of a stomach you have. Mine can now handle almost anything. But an American tourist who has just arrived in North Africa would probably die.'

Steven laughed. 'American tourists are ill even in Britain.'

'I believe it.'

'How long have you lived here?' asked Steven, immensely curious.

'Almost three years.'

'What made you decide to come and live in Morocco? I mean - it's very foreign, isn't it. It must have been quite a big step.'

'It was. It's really quite a story. Why don't you come and have dinner at my house? If you think your stomach is strong enough we can have a few little snacks as we walk through the square. Yes?'

A month later Steven was still staying in Lars' house, thoroughly enjoying the privileges and luxuries of the seriously rich. The house, more aptly described as a villa, was built in Moorish style and set in three acres of beautifully landscaped gardens, surrounded by a high wall, an electric fence and guarded by two Dobermans. It was spacious, consisting of a large living room, dining room and five bedrooms, all with en suite bathrooms. There were servants' quarters, including a large kitchen. The interior was lavishly furnished with tiles and *boissérie,* elaborately decorated in intricate Moroccan designs. There were four servants: a cook and a maid in the house and a gardener and gardener's boy, who took care of the grounds and the swimming pool. Steven had nothing to do all day except relax, swim, sunbathe, read a little, and get to know Lars.

Lars was Swedish. His handsome appearance, well-toned body and carefully honed deep tan belied his forty-two years. He was charming, generous, amusing and great fun to be with. He was enormously wealthy, but a little vague as to how he had made his money.

'Various business deals,' he said airily. 'My father was in business so I followed in his footsteps. Not always the right thing to do, but for me it was very good. I was rich by the time I was twenty-five.'

'And now you're very rich,' Steven laughed. 'But what sort of deals were they exactly? I mean, did you have business contacts in Morocco before you came to live here?'

'I have business contacts world-wide,' replied Lars, refusing to be drawn. 'And now to the really important matters: shall we dine in or out tonight? I always like to let Fatima know my evening plans at lunchtime. Then she can make arrangements, one way or the other. I know a really excellent restaurant in the Medina. The owner is American; the chef is French. A combination I find particularly satisfactory. I think I will take you there this evening and then Fatima can have the evening off. Now shall we swim before lunch or just go to my room for a while?'

Steven had become aware of his homosexual tendencies at school. Aged fourteen he had developed a tremendous crush on a prefect called Guy. To his amazement and delight he discovered that his feelings were reciprocated. He and Guy used to meet behind some disused sheds at the bottom of the playing fields. At first they just talked and held hands. Then, as their relationship deepened, they kissed and masturbated each other, but although they never had penetrative sex, Steven often fantasised about it. Then Guy left school and went to university in the North of England. For a term they exchanged passionate letters, but one day Guy wrote to say he was sorry, he had found another lover and wished Steven equal success and happiness. Steven was devastated. There was no other boy at the school who held the same appeal for him as Guy had. After he left school he did everything he could to repress his homosexual desires. He felt there was a certain stigma attached to being gay, which might prevent his advancement in life. He also wanted a son.

So, at the age of twenty-six, he married Alison, a decision that he realised after two or three years of marriage, had been a great mistake.

Chapter Twenty-One

'Hungry?'

James Parker looked across at Verity, calm and poised, safely strapped into the passenger seat of his dark green Peugeot. As always, she was elegantly turned out in a navy pleated skirt, complemented by a navy-and-white spotted blouse.

'Mm, yes. I think so,' replied Verity. 'I'm sure I could manage something light.'

James laughed. 'Something light! I hope we'll find something light on the menu. I've booked at the best restaurant in Westcliff-on-Sea.'

'The best restaurant!' Verity felt flattered. 'I'm sure I'll manage. I've always noticed that the better the restaurant, the smaller the portions.'

'Yes,' agreed James. '*Nouvelle cuisine*. The customer pays top prices just for a nicely decorated plate, then after the meal, he leaves the restaurant hungry.'

'Yes. I remember that kind of restaurant. Hal, my husband, always complained that he hadn't had enough to eat at the end of the meal. He got wise pretty quickly though, and usually enquired when booking the restaurant if they went in for that kind of food.'

'It does look as if it's going out of fashion nowadays, I'm glad to say.'

'Let's hope so. Though just thinking of a decorated plate seems to have given me an appetite.'

'Good. That's splendid. Did you and your husband often eat out?'

'Oh, yes, quite a lot, especially in our younger days. Then it became more of an effort. Booking the restaurant, ordering the cab. In the end even getting dressed up began to be a chore rather than a pleasure.'

'How long is it since your husband died?'

Verity sighed. 'It must be nearly five years now. It was the day after my seventy-fifth birthday. We'd had a wonderful party, with all the family and so many friends as well. Hal was in splendid form. We had a caterer in our house with marvellous food and endless champagne. Hal made such a good speech. He said such kind things about me, in a really witty way. Then at lunch the next day he said he felt a little tired. I said I wasn't surprised after such a big occasion the day before. He was eighty-two after all and even a few extra years can make a difference. After lunch he stood up to help me clear away and he just keeled over, falling flat on his face on the floor. Of course I tried to revive him, but I couldn't remember exactly what to do. It was such a long time since I'd done any first aid. When he didn't respond I phoned for an ambulance. They were ever so good. They arrived in eight minutes. But he was dead on arrival at the hospital. It was so sudden. It took me quite a while to get used to the fact that he was gone. Death is so permanent, isn't it?'

There was a slight sob in her voice and James could feel her trembling.

'Yes,' he replied. 'Death is permanent.'

'It - it leaves such a hole,' she said hesitantly. 'I'd got so used to Hal, you know. He was always there. Dependable and knowledgeable about so many things. Fussy, though. Very particular about how things should be done. He did tend to like things his own way. Don't we all? But Hal seemed to have the knack of persuading people that his way was the best. Of course now it's quite nice having things the way I want them. But compromising doesn't really harm anyone. Hal was such good company.' Verity sighed again. 'I think what I mind most about widowhood is that I have no one to share things with any more.'

James threw her a surreptitious glance. Sharing, he thought.

'Of course,' continued Verity, 'I'm lucky to have such a supportive family. It must be sad not to have a family - to be entirely alone.' She stole a quick glance at James. Did he have a family? He never mentioned them, and she didn't like to ask.

'Tell me about your family,' suggested James. He felt happy and relaxed. It had certainly been a good idea to invite Verity out for the day. It was an excellent opportunity to get to know her better without curious questions from the likes of trying-to-be-glamorous Brenda Barnes and enduring the mad comments of Priscilla Prescott in the middle of a conversation. Even Mabel Cooke and Gladys Bates had their trying moments.

'Alison is the eldest of my children,' began Verity. 'Alison is eminently sensible, perhaps too much so. She does take things so seriously - and too literally. I wonder sometimes if she has enough fun.'

'Is she married?'

'Oh, yes. To a nice man called Steven. I like Steven but he does tend to be a little bit ineffectual.'

'Not good at making decisions?'

'Exactly.'

'What does he do? For a living, I mean.'

'He's a travel agent.'

'Oh! That must be quite interesting. And a lot of fun too.'

'Oh, yes. I think he enjoys it. He travels a lot. He's in Morocco at the moment.'

'A prospecting trip?'

'Yes. Although this trip has lasted for two months, so I'm beginning to wonder if there isn't a bit more to it than just prospecting. Poor Alison.'

James said nothing for a moment. 'Is it a lucrative business?' he enquired at last.

'It certainly was to start with. Then he became too ambitious. At one stage he made some poor decisions, so...' Verity hesitated. She wasn't sure how much she should say. She didn't want to be disloyal to Steven, but talking to James was so comforting.

'About ten years ago he decided to expand too much. You see, his travel firm is called Sun Med and is, naturally, based in Mediterranean countries. But then he went into the Far East with disastrous results.'

'He went bankrupt?'

Verity hesitated again. 'He would have if I hadn't bailed him out.'

'Aah,' said James, not at all surprised. 'And is he recovering?'

'Slowly.'

'But you still have a share in the business.'

'I own the business.'

'Aah,' repeated James.

'And their house and the granny flat.'

'Where you lived until you had the accident?'

'Yes.'

'And now your daughter and son-in-law have a tenant who pays rent?'

'Exactly.'

'And I suppose they are not keen for you to move back into the flat?'

'Not keen at all.'

James was beginning to understand the situation. 'You have another daughter?'

'Yes. Julia.'

'Rather large, with a husband on crutches?'

'You must have seen them visiting me at Oaklands.'

'Yes, quite a few times. What happened to her husband?'

'Poor Graham. He had the most dreadful car accident on the same day that I was knocked into the road. At first it was feared he wouldn't survive. He broke just about everything and suffered massive head injuries as well. He spent three months in hospital. But now he's out he seems to be making good progress, hopefully to a full recovery.'

'What's his profession?'

'I don't know that I'd call it a profession. He's a builder.'

'Doing well?'

'Oh, I think so. Though Julia does ask for money from time to time. They all ask for money.'

James wondered how much money Verity had and if she ever gave any of it away. But he said nothing.

'Do your daughters have children?'

'Oh, yes. Julia and Graham have two: William, who's still at university, and Samantha, who's a model. Alison and Steven have a daughter called Kelsey. There was...' She stopped. It was still too painful to talk about Kirsty's accident. 'Kelsey,' she went on, 'is married to a young barrister called Nigel.' She didn't feel like explaining at this point that Kelsey's marriage was on the point of irrevocable breakdown. There was still hope for reconciliation.

'You certainly have an interesting family.'

'Oh, yes. Interesting, certainly. But I haven't told you about my son.'

'No. Is he the youngest?'

'Yes. He must be...' Verity paused to make some calculations on her fingers. 'Forty-seven, I think.'

'Is he married?'

'No. Russell isn't married and I can't imagine why not. He's so attractive, and of course he has plenty of girl friends.'

'What does he do for a living?'

'He sells antique furniture. He has a shop in a passage in Islington.'

'The Camden Passage. Yes, I know it. Very up-market.'

'But not very profitable at the moment. It seems that Russell sells most of his furniture to foreigners, who don't seem too anxious to buy right now.'

'So he needs your money too?'

'He does. More precisely he wants me to finance a trip to India. He has a most delightful, handsome Indian friend who has asked Russell to go with him to India to help him choose his bride. I think that's charming, don't you?'

James felt Verity had misread certain signals, but he didn't think it was his place to enlighten her. He slowed down for a roundabout.

'Well, here we are, almost in Westcliff-on-Sea. The restaurant is right on the front.'

'How delightful!' Verity felt a sense of mounting excitement.

'There's the sea!' exclaimed James, as he turned a corner. 'Doesn't it look lovely, sparkling in the sun?'

'It certainly does,' agreed Verity. 'Though I wonder what it's like in the winter? Perhaps a bit grey and leaden.'

'I rather like the seaside in the winter. It's so remote - and private.'

James loved the sea at any time of the year. He had always wanted to live by the sea but was never able to persuade his wife of its attractions. Now of course, since Helen's death, he could live wherever he liked. There was such a lot he wanted to tell Verity. The difficulty was knowing how and where to start. Perhaps in the restaurant. If he were to order a full bottle of wine how much would Verity drink? He couldn't afford to go over the limit. But he could suggest a walk along the front after lunch, which would help to sober him up. He found a parking space near the restaurant, squeezing into the small space rather inexpertly on the second attempt. He got out of the car, went round to the passenger side and opened the door for Verity. He offered her his arm.

'Please allow me to escort you into lunch, my dear.'

As they left the restaurant the sun was still sparkling on the sea and James proposed a walk along the front, to which Verity readily agreed. He had thrown caution to the wind and ordered a whole bottle of *Chablis*. He had drunk most of it, hoping the food would absorb a large proportion of the alcohol, but he had to admit to himself that he felt slightly swimmy as they went out into the bright sunshine.

The wine had loosened his tongue and reduced his inhibitions. As he had hoped, Verity had proved a sympathetic listener, although he was slightly ashamed to discover that by the end of the meal he had done most of the talking. He had needed to talk to someone who would understand what it had been like living with Helen for the last five years: five years of drudgery and exhaustion, of glimmers of hope followed by troughs of despair. It was a cathartic experience talking to Verity for almost two hours, as they sat opposite each other in a secluded corner of the quiet seaside restaurant.

At the end of his story, aided by liberal draughts of the chilly, fragrant Burgundy, he had felt drained, but more at peace with himself than he had for a long time.

He took Verity's arm as they strolled along the front.

I hope you don't think I talked too much?

'Not in the least. It's always better to talk, to unburden and share one's problems. I'm sure you feel the better for having talked.'

'Certainly. I feel much happier.'

'Oh, good,' said Verity, as they made their way back to the car.

As James and Verity went in through the front door of Oaklands, they were waylaid in the hall by Gladys Bates on her way to the television room.

'Nice day out?' she enquired, a tinge of acrimony her voice.

'Oh, very nice, thank you, Gladys,' said Verity. 'We had such a good lunch in a cosy little restaurant in Westcliff-on-Sea.'

Gladys's eyebrows shot up. 'A cosy little restaurant, was it? That does sound nice. Must have made a nice change from the usual swill in here.'

Verity was a little surprised by Gladys's tone. She had never thought of her as an envious or embittered person.

'Had a good day here?' she enquired.

'A little dull without our domino game. But we haven't been without incidents.'

'What incidents?'

'There's been another ambulance took someone away,' Gladys lowered her voice confidentially, 'Mabel and me think it was Hilda Haddock.'

Chapter Twenty-Two

'Did your brooch turn up?' asked Gladys Bates, letting her large handbag fall onto the floor with its customary thud as she settled into a chair beside Mabel Cooke.

'Yes, indeed, dear,' replied Mabel, straightening up her orange wig. 'It was found in among her things. It seems it was a veritable Aladdin's cave in there.'

Gladys sighed. 'Yes. So she's gone at last. Poor thing.'

Verity came over to join the two ladies by the window. Placing her stick on the floor, she lowered herself carefully into a comfortable chair. As she did so a large, rather garish brooch on Mabel's cardigan caught her eye.

'That's a pretty brooch, Mabel. I don't think I've seen that before.' What a horrible, tasteless piece of jewellery, she thought, but felt she should make a complimentary comment.

Mabel fingered her brooch to reassure herself it was still there. She had pinned it on so tightly that it puckered up the bright emerald-green cardigan, which clashed with her green and yellow floral skirt.

'Well, you wouldn't have seen it recently. That Hilda Haddock filched it.'

'Filched it?'

'Stole it, dear,' said Gladys, rummaging in her capacious handbag. 'She was a megalomaniac.'

'You mean a kleptomaniac,' said Verity, deadly serious.

'Whatever you say,' said Mabel. 'She was a thief. She'll not be missed.'

'Missed?' said Verity. 'You don't mean...?'

'I certainly do,' said Mabel. 'She died yesterday.'

'Here?' asked Verity.

'No,' replied Mabel. 'In hospital. She was taken there a few days ago.'

'Poor Hilda Haddock,' said Verity thoughtfully.

'But not so poor,' said Gladys. 'Her room was stuffed with the booty she stole from all of us. Cash, wads of notes and small change, rings, bracelets, brooches, nylons, nighties, undies, and belts. And loads of toiletries too. Soap, toothpaste, deodorant, perfume and pills. You name it. It was a right treasure trove in there. Mary couldn't believe it when she and Eileen started clearing out her room out this morning.'

'Well, I never,' said Verity, amazed.

'And look at this!' Gladys continued, taking a lumpy, jangly charm-bracelet out of her handbag, rather as a conjuror takes a rabbit out of a hat. 'This is my bracelet that Hilda Haddock stole some months ago. She was wearing it one day at lunch when I took away her plate. I said it was identical to one I had, but she said it was hers. After lunch I went to check up that mine was still there, but of course it wasn't. There wasn't anything I could do about it. I just had to watch Hilda wearing it every day. Now I'm delighted to have it back. Just as well she died before I did.'

'Well I never,' said Verity again. 'Whatever's going to happen next?'

'I expect it'll be Hilda Haddock's funeral,' said Mabel succinctly. 'I wonder if there'll be any mourners. She never had any visitors, did she? It's quite possible there'll be no one at all to see her into her grave.'

'Who told you?' asked Verity.

'Mary,' replied James, gently guiding Verity towards a bench in the shade. The garden was looking faded and a little over-blown. Early leaves were falling and the trees were tinged with russet and gold that blended uneasily with what remained of the rich dark green of high summer. James felt the familiar sense of sadness and desolation that now overwhelmed him every August. Summer was drawing to a close. There had been another death at Oaklands and soon, in September, he would have to face yet again the anniversary of the deaths of his wife and son, almost five years ago.

'You mean poor old Hilda Haddock will be collected in a council van, taken away in a plain wooden box and buried in an unmarked grave, without any ceremony at all?' Verity was a little shaken.

'Apparently.'

'That's terrible. It seems so - Victorian.'

'Yes. It does, doesn't it?'

Verity heaved a deep sigh. 'And all because she had no money.'

'All because she had no money. Money's a great divider.'

They sat in silence for a few moments, each absorbed in their own thoughts.

'James, we can't let Hilda be buried like that! I mean, after all we've been living in the same house. I can't exactly say she was a friend of mine, but you know what I mean - we ate together at the same table and watched the same television.'

'Yes. I know how you feel.' (How wonderfully sensitive Verity is, thought James). 'What do you think we ought to do?'

'Well, I'm quite prepared to pay for a decent funeral myself.'

(What a gloriously generous person!)

'Of course it needn't be too elaborate,' continued Verity. 'After all, if she has no family or friends there wouldn't be much point in putting on a big show, would there?'

'Of course not.' (And practical as well, thought James). 'I'd be most willing to contribute myself.'

'Perhaps some of the other residents would also like to contribute. Gladys and Mabel are so delighted to have their trinkets back that I'm sure they'd like to show their gratitude in some way. Gladys actually said she was pleased that Hilda had died before she did.'

'Did she really?' James laughed. 'She's certainly forthright! I tell you what: we'll ask the domino group this afternoon if anybody would be prepared to make a contribution towards a decent funeral for Hilda. That'd be a good start.'

Both Verity and James were amazed by the generosity of all the other Oaklands' residents. Mabel was shocked.

'Just shove her into an unmarked grave? That's terrible, dear, isn't it? You can count on £100 from me.'

'Likewise,' said Gladys, rummaging around on the floor for her handbag. I've got my cheque-book right here,'

'But she was a thief,' remonstrated Brenda Barnes, keen to point out the drawbacks of being over-generous.

'Maybe she couldn't help it,' said Mabel. 'Some people get like that as they get older.'

'Yes,' said Gladys, 'like Miss Prescott losing her marbles. It happens to older people'

There was silence as Verity mixed up the dominoes. They were all thinking: older people like us. It could happen to any of us any day.

'I'll give you £110,' said Brenda, never liking to be outdone.

Enough was collected to give Hilda Haddock a really good send-off. James put advertisements in *The Times, The Telegraph* and *The Wanstead and Woodford Gazette* stating the date, time and place of the funeral. As many of the Oaklands' residents as were able went to the funeral. They all gathered in the hall waiting for the *cortège* to arrive at the appointed hour. Precisely at 2.45 pm a sleek black limousine drew up outside the house. Four pallbearers dressed in sombre black suits and holding their black top hats in white-gloved hands, walked slowly beside the hearse. As the owner of Oaklands, Miss Price got into the funeral car first, followed by Mary and Eileen, the two nurses who had cared for Hilda Haddock. The hearse, followed by the funeral car, drove slowly to the end of the road and waited, while James escorted Verity, Gladys and Mabel to his car, strategically parked, facing in the right direction. At the same time Marjorie Grimes and Elsie Morrison were shepherded to Elsie's son's car and Brenda Barnes followed her son-in-law to his. There was a general slamming of doors and buckling on of seatbelts as the little *cortège* made ready to leave. Then one of the pallbearers gave the signal to the driver of the hearse to move off. As the small, sad procession turned the corner, a police car drove up and parked outside Oaklands. Looking in his rear mirror before signalling to pull out, James saw two police officers get out of the car, walk up the short drive and ring the front doorbell. Police! he thought as he followed the funeral car around the corner. What on earth has happened now?

As soon as the funeral was over James suggested to Verity, Mabel and Gladys that they make their way back to his car. He saw no reason to hang about or drive back in a convoy with the other vehicles. They were the first to arrive back at Oaklands, where Verity was surprised to see the police car parked in the road outside.

'It drew up as we left,' explained James. 'I saw it in the rear mirror as we drove off.'

'I wonder what it's doing there,' said Verity, as James helped her out of the car. 'Perhaps it's to do with Hilda's funeral?'

'Or the sudden spate of deaths?' suggested James. 'Maybe our food was poisoned.'

'Goodness gracious!' exclaimed Verity. 'What an idea! Do you think someone is trying to bump off one of us?'

'One of us with money?' said James with a twinkle in his eye, as he guided her solicitously across the road.

'I wonder who that would be,' said Verity in all wide-eyed innocence.

'I wonder,' said James, fumbling in his pocket for his latch-key. (He was one of the few privileged residents to possess one.) As he opened the front door, the two police officers, one of them a young woman, watched from their vantage point. James stepped back to allow Verity to enter the house first and saw the funeral car stop right behind the police car. The two police officers were watching intently in their rear mirror, and as Miss Price stepped out of the black limousine, the two officers got out of the police car and went to speak to her. Miss Price, with her usual prim composure, nodded, said something to Mary and Eileen, and led the two officers around the back of the house to where she had her own private quarters.

'Well, imagine! It's Pricey they came to see,' said James. 'Do you wish to go to your room first to freshen up, Verity, or shall we go straight into tea together?'

'I think I'd like to freshen up first. See you there in five minutes.'

'Right,' said James.

'Julia drove me out to the Queen Anne House near Roydon the other day so I could check on the progress and get a little of feel of working again.'

'I'm delighted to hear that, Graham,' said Verity. 'And how did it feel to be back in harness, as it were?'

Back in harness, thought Julia. Wherever is Mother picking up these new, up-to-date expressions? Oaklands Retirement Home seems to be quite a swinging place. Mother certainly seems to be enjoying it far more than I could ever have imagined.

'It felt quite good really. Of course I didn't do anything too strenuous. Must take things easily for a while yet.'

'Of course,' said Verity.

'Julia just adored the house,' continued Graham, 'didn't you, darling? It's one of the best examples of its period in the whole of the South East.'

'Quite beautiful,' enthused Julia. 'How I would love to live in a house like that. Wouldn't you, Graham?'

Graham was staring out of the window. His eyes had acquired a glazed look.

'Wouldn't you, darling?' repeated Julia.

'What? Yes, of course. Wonderful. We'll do it right away.'

'What do you mean...?'

'That was Ken Spooner outside,' stammered Graham.

'Well, why not?'

'It just seemed rather sudden. He must have made a very quick recovery. I thought he might be dead.'

'Dead!' said Verity. Not another one!'

'No. Well, not dead,' said Graham. 'Maybe just a little unwell. He was rather badly beaten up.'

'Beaten up!' said Verity, completely mystified. 'Whatever do you mean? And who is Ken Spooner anyway? He sounds like a character from a Dickens' novel.'

Graham smiled. 'Yes. He looks like one too.' He wondered whether this wasn't a good moment to tell Verity the whole story, or most of it anyway. If she knew that he had been cheated on by his manager she might feel sympathetic and offer an unconditional loan, or even a gift.

'Well,' he began, 'about two years ago my manager, Ken Spooner, suggested...'

He was interrupted by a light knock on the door.

'Come in!' called Verity.

The door opened and Alison came into the room.

'Oh, hello everyone! I didn't realise it was a party.'

'Do come and join us, dear,' said Verity.

Chapter Twenty-Three

The flames rose high into the air. They crackled, twisted and writhed; a contorted mixture of different hues of red, yellow, mauve, orange, and even shades of blue. They were followed by clouds of belching acrid smoke, billowing out over the stark, barren landscape. As the sparks flew up and landed in all directions, they ignited many little fires in the scrub grass, as dry as tinder. The heat was intense, and considering the large crowd of people who were milling around, the silence was remarkable. They were all local people, who had gathered to pay their last respects to Jalal Banjaree, the Governor of Rajasthan, who had been a figure of immense importance in this vast province of Northern India. He had been both feared and revered by the locals, who, on the one hand appreciated his efforts in trying to improve their thankless and impoverished lives, but on the other, found it difficult to understand their governor's Western educated outlook.

Sudip put another log on the funeral pyre with a heavy heart. His father's sudden death had come as a huge shock. After all, he had been barely sixty-seven years of age, and as far as Sudip knew he had been in perfect health. The telephone call had come out of the blue at 3.00 am.

'Mr Sudip Banjaree?'

'Yes.' Heavy with sleep, Sudip felt confused. 'Yes. Who is it?'

'It's Niteen Gulati. I have bad news. Your father, the Governor of Rajasthan, Mr Banjaree, he is dead.'

'Dead?' Sudip felt as if he had been hit on the head. 'Dead? My father's dead? But he couldn't be! Had he been ill?'

'No. Not ill. But dead now. So sorry. You come here soon?'

'Yes, of course. As soon as possible. But please don't hold the funeral before Thursday at the earliest.'

'Thursday. Funeral Thursday. Will arrange.'

It had been a hectic rush and a scramble, but two days after he had received the phone call, Sudip had managed to rearrange his lectures and book a flight to Delhi and then on to Jaipur. Fortunately, as an Indian citizen, he had no need to apply for a visa. He was met at Jaipur airport by his father's manservant, Ameet, who, weeping quietly, had wrung his hands.

'Oh, Mr Sudip, so sorry! Such bad news! So much shock!'

'How is my mother?' enquired Sudip.

'She remarkable lady. Very quiet. Very composed.'

The calm atmosphere that pervaded in the household had greatly impressed Sudip. His whole family and all the servants were in mourning white and no one spoke above a whisper. Even before he had time to greet his mother, one of the servants had led him to a small room where his father's body, embalmed with many different spices, smelling rich and sweet, lay on an open bier. Sudip's heart felt heavy with sadness as he gazed down at the quiet, still face, whose handsome dark good looks mirrored an older version of his own. He felt over-whelmed with guilt and sadness. Guilt at being absent at the time of his father's death; of being unable to support his mother in her time of grief and of being away from his country for so long. But the guilt went deeper than just his absence from home. It was the guilt manifested by the dichotomy of his life-style: the fact that his Western education had broadened his horizons to such an extent that he now found it impossible to remain for any length of time in his own country.

Although the local people were still piling on logs, the fierce heat was now going out of the fire. The activity was cathartic, a habit synonymous with the Hindu funeral ritual. A soft, soothing murmur could be heard as the holy men recited mantras. Sudip was physically and emotionally exhausted. His conscience told him that he ought to stay here in his homeland, his birthplace, for a while at least, to comfort his family, above all his mother. But reason told him that it would be impossible to stay for long. He was no longer part of his own family. It was almost as though he had been ostracised. After four years of sophisticated London life he had become a different person. He was no longer a Western-educated Indian, but had changed into a dark-skinned European. He knew he couldn't fit in with the set way of life ori-ginally imposed by the Hindu caste system. With new eyes he now saw the enormous social and material gap between the small number of very privileged rich and the vast number of uneducated poor; so disadvantaged in every respect that they could barely scrape enough money together to keep starvation at bay. As if in farewell to his heritage, he threw a last log onto the pyre. The embers would cool during the night and in the morning all that would remain would be a heap of ashes. Then the wind would blow them away and the vultures would arrive in the heat of the day, hoping for some small pickings. A rite of passage. A symbol of India.

'Muslim women look even more repressed than Hindu women.'

'It's the black burqua.'

'And the metal nose piece. I find that quite frightening.'

'I agree. Do Indian Hindu women cover up their heads and faces like that?'

'Oh, no! Their heads are always uncovered. And most of them wear brightly coloured saris, which adds a tremendous splash of colour.'

'Even the poorer ones?'

'Yes. Most Indians are poor. There is a very small, rich upper class.'

'To which you belong?' asked Russell teasingly.

'I suppose so,' replied Sudip cautiously. He hadn't yet told Russell everything.

'I wonder if there are many wealthy Moroccans?'

Russell smiled. 'Well, not here, at any rate. Just look at that sea of donkeys! They're all tied up. It looks as if they've been parked there.'

The coach slowed up and turned right into a car park beside a large fence, which separated it from the donkeys. Sudip referred to his guidebook.

'That's exactly what it is: a donkey park. It says here that this Berber market is the largest in Southern Morocco. The people arrive by donkey and naturally, they have to park them somewhere.'

The two men scrambled out of the coach with the bunch of motley tourists. First came the Germans: large, over-bearing and over-sunburnt, pushing ahead with their heavy cameras acting as battering rams. They spoke loudly, urgently and arrogantly, as if issuing orders, expecting to get exactly what they wanted right away. The English followed in a separate group at a respectful distance. The most unlikely people had struck up friendships, purely out of national solidarity. At the end of the holiday they would exchange addresses, promising to write and perhaps visit each other's homes, or at least meet up in London. But once they had returned home, the residents of Kensington would shake their heads and wonder sadly how they could ever have befriended the couple from Bolton. The Geordies would have similar thoughts about the charming young newly-weds from Petworth. Then the addresses would be thrown away and vows made to make more selective holiday friendships in future.

The small group of French tourists kept themselves even more apart from the rest. They felt rather superior to the other nationalities, mainly because they spoke French, Morocco's second language, still compulsorily taught in schools. After all, they had conquered Morocco - they had experience and inside knowledge of all things Moroccan, which they felt gave them an inestimable advantage.

The Italians made up the noisiest group and stayed together out of sheer self-defence. They spoke no language other than their own and when they discovered that no one else spoke Italian, not even the tour guide, they contented themselves with talking as loudly as possible. They photographed everything in sight, taking care to stand in the way of anyone else who also wished to photograph.

The Americans were the most prominent group of all, probably because of their clothes. All of them, men and women, wore new, snow-white trainers, which they called sneakers. Most of the men wore outsized baseball caps back-to-front, while the majority of the women had immaculate hairdos. Their clothes were brightly coloured, the men's as well as the women's. Garish, shiny anoraks were worn with unco-ordinated plaid trousers or floral skirts. Most of them were over sixty and had never crossed the Atlantic before, so they felt nervous and insecure at being so far away from home. Their main topic of conversation centered on their health: whether their bowels had moved sufficiently or had over-reacted to the change of diet; whether it was wise to try Moroccan food at all, or more prudent to stick to a limited diet of cornflakes and beef-burgers. They agonised over whether their American health care plans were sufficient to cover every emergency and, if the worst came to the worst and they were forced to go into hospital, would they be able cope with the poor hygiene and a foreign language; never mind the medical care, which they were absolutely convinced would be inferior to their customary high standards in the great United States of America.

The tourists walked slowly around the bustling market, keeping strictly in their groups. The harassed tour guide moved from one group to the other trying to explain the historic, religious and cultural background of Morocco in the appropriate language, and also trying to keep the stragglers from lagging too far behind.

'Oh, look, Sharon! What a lovely necklace! I'll get one for me mum - and one for Auntie Agnes as well.'

The guide loomed up behind and started to explain in heavily accented English: 'that is necklace with special Berber pattern. One of most old design...'

Sharon and her friend Julie bought two necklaces each and moved on.

Then, as the guide began showing off his good German to one of the German tourists, his explanation was rudely interrupted by a high-pitched scream coming from the far side of the row of stalls.

'No! No! Give it back! You thief!' screamed an hysterical woman's voice. Stallholders started shouting in guttural Arabic as the woman, now sobbing, tried to run towards the main group of tourists. The guide, anticipating trouble, abruptly stopped his lecture and walked briskly towards the commotion. The woman forced her way through the thickening crowd, sobbing louder, pursued by an elderly Berber brandishing a stick. The woman, unmistakably American, judging by her vermilion T-shirt, green and yellow plaid trousers and snow-white trainers, almost threw herself into the guide's arms.

'Help me, please,' she begged.

The guide asked the elderly Berber in Arabic what was going on, whereby the Berber spat out a tirade of abuse from his cracked and crinkled lips. The guide turned to the American tourist who had begun to calm down. 'I tell you not photograph without permission. The Berber, they proud people. They not like be in photo album in America. You foolish woman. You lucky no worse happen.'

'Tell him to give me my camera back,' said the woman sullenly, without a word of thanks or apology.

By the expression on the guide's face it was quite clear that he felt the woman deserved to forfeit her camera.

Nevertheless, he had his job to think of. He needed the money. If it got around that he supported the locals against the tourists he might find himself unemployed.

'Please give the lady back her camera,' he asked the Berber in Arabic. 'I promise this will not happen again. It's not worth my job,' he added rashly.

The Berber handed the camera over to the guide. A chorus of protest went up from the crowd. The guide gave the camera back to the American. 'Please no do again.'

'No. Thank you.' The lady retrieved her camera and wandered off to commit another blunder.

'Well,' said Russell. 'That was an unpleasant little scene.'

'Yes,' said Sudip. 'How not to behave in a foreign country.'

They both felt relieved that they had kept themselves apart and a little aloof from the other tourists. Neither the tall, pale, middle-aged Englishman nor the slender, dark, handsome Indian felt any affinity with any of the other groups, not even the English one. Sudip felt strangely foreign in Morocco. He felt he didn't belong any more than he belonged in India. He glanced quickly at Russell who was pointing out something about the market.

'This is just like the postcard that Steven sent Alison.'

'Steven?'

'Yes. My brother-in-law. He came to check out Morocco for his travel agency.'

Sudip came back to earth out of his reverie. 'Oh, yes, of course. He came here a couple of months ago, didn't he?'

'Yes.'

'Is he still here?'

'I wouldn't have thought so. From what I gather he just came for a couple of weeks to prospect. Look at these aubergines! Such a beautiful deep purple and a perfect oval shape with the dark green leaves at the end.'

'Yes,' agreed Sudip. 'They'd be delicious lightly fried in batter. How about those peppers? Such a lovely colour contrast between the dark green and the bright red and orange.'

'They'd be good in a ratatouille.'

'Makes me hungry,' Sudip laughed.

'Me too.'

'It'll soon be time for dinner when we get back to the hotel. Shall we eat out in the town?'

'Of course. But maybe a rest first?'

'Oh, I think so. A rest before dinner is always a good idea.'

'Definitely,' said Russell, as he brushed his hand against his friend's hand.

The taxi took them into the centre of Marrakech, through Jemaa el Fna Square. All the brightly lit stalls were occupied by vendors selling their wares and chefs cooked delicious dishes, which the milling crowds queued up to buy. In the centre of the square, in an area free of stalls, a myriad of entertainers were at work: jugglers, dancers and acrobats competing with different bands performing at the same time, creating a wild cacophony of sound. It was dark now, about eight o'clock, and the activity was at its height.

Sudip was enthralled. 'Let's come here tomorrow and have dinner at the stalls.'

Russell was more cautious. 'Is it safe to eat the food?'

'I'm sure it is.'

'There'll be no wine.'

Sudip laughed. It won't hurt us for one night.'

'No. Probably do us good.'

The taxi drove on through the narrow, twisting, scruffy streets of the Medina as fast as the heavy traffic permitted. The streets smelt of urine, sweat and rotting vegetables. Heavily veiled women hurried along trying to look inconspicuous. Children played games and maimed beggars huddled in doorways. Both men were becoming a little apprehensive.

'You're sure this is right?'

'*C'est vraiment ici?*' Russell asked the driver.

'*Oui, monsieur. On est presque arrivé et je vais vous accompagner au restaurant.*'

'He'll take us there?' asked Sudip in surprise.

'So he says.'

The driver parked by a large tree and got out, leaving his car unlocked and the window wide open. The two men followed him across the road and saw an entrance to a narrow unlit passage.

'*Suivez-moi,*' ordered the driver and plunged down the passage. Russell and Sudip looked at each other nervously.

'I wasn't expecting this,' said Russell.

'Nor me,' said Sudip. 'Should we turn back?'

'No. That would be chicken.'

The taxi driver had reached the end of the passage, which finished abruptly. On the right was a huge ornate metal door, a thick bell-rope hanging at the side. The driver pulled on the rope and the bell jangled loudly. They waited for a few moments as slapping footsteps, becoming louder, came along the stone floor. Russell felt his stomach muscles tighten as the door was flung open to reveal a short, squat European in the dimly lit doorway.

'*Bonsoir messieurs! Vous êtes Monsieur Davis?*' he asked Russell, speaking with a strong American accent.

'*Oui,*' replied Russell, his nervousness abating. '*Bonsoir monsieur.*'

The short gentleman opened the door wide. '*Entrez, je vous en prie.*' He proffered his hand. 'I'm Solly Goldstein, owner of the best restaurant in Marrakesh.'

Solly Goldstein led the way along a bare but brightly lit corridor, his floppy footwear making a flapping sound as he walked. He opened a door at the far end and led them through a sumptuous, richly furnished anteroom into the restaurant beyond. It took a few moments for Russell and Sudip to accustom their eyes to the very dim lighting. Russell was beginning to see that there were more than a dozen low oblong tables with deep, wide sofas on either side, scattered with cushions. The tables were laid with snow-white linen, elegant porcelain china, gleaming silver and opulent candelabra. Three of the tables were occupied: one by a middle-aged French couple; another by two Moroccan men, wearing well-cut European suits. At the third table, which they were just about to pass on the way to their own, sat two European men in casual clothes. One was very good-looking, with thick ash-blond hair. The other man, older with thinning hair, looked vaguely familiar to Russell. They sat close together on one of the sofas, their heads turned towards each other, deep in conversation, holding hands. As Russell and Sudip followed Solly Goldstein to the vacant table beyond, the older man looked up He looked straight at Russell, whose eyes had now become accustomed to the dim light.

Russell realised with a shock that the man was his brother-in-law, Steven Hobbs.

Chapter Twenty-Four

Kelsey drew a deep line in the sand with her toe and waited for the next wave to roll in and wash the line away. The sea looked beautiful: an endless expanse of deep sapphire blue, sparkling in the hot Mediterranean sunshine. The waves lapped gently along the curving shoreline, making ripples in the fine white sand as they receded. But although she could appreciate the beauty of the sea, Kelsey was afraid of it. It was, after all, a large expanse of water in which her sister, Kirsty had drowned. She walked slowly along the edge of the shore, watching a large noisy Italian family playing in the sea. There were five children ranging in age from about five to fourteen. The two oldest girls looked incredibly alike. With their rounded bodies, creamy Mediterranean skin, well-developed breasts and long dark hair, they were an attractive lively pair. Kelsey realised they were twins, reminding her poignantly of her own twin sister. They had three lilos and two beach balls between them. The twins were each on a lilo, their hair floating out in the water behind them as they guided the lilos along. The scene brought back memories of the last time Kelsey had seen her sister alive. It had been almost ten years since she had sat by the side of the swimming pool and watched Kirsty drown.

The twins were fourteen. They had grown taller and filled out. And because of all the swimming they both had broad, well-developed shoulders. They had also grown their hair. Shining and wavy, it fell in a thick sheet almost to their waists, their crowning glory, a stunning backdrop to their pretty oval faces and strong shapely bodies. Tim Roche, their coach, disapproved of swimmers with long hair. He felt it was impractical and impeded their speed, despite the regulation swimming cap. He pleaded with both girls to have their hair cut short, but his pleas fell on deaf ears.

Despite the thousands of hours they had put in at the pool swimming up and down, up and down under the eagle eye of Tim Roche, the girls had barely improved their speed in the last year. They had now both become aware of how insanely boring the whole process was. What a waste of their youth! To spend hours in a swimming pool every evening and most of the weekend swimming up and down, just in order to swim a little faster. Of course there were hours in the gym too, but they were equally boring: rowing and cycling on machines; weight lifting to develop muscles they didn't want.

So why did the twins continue on their tedious treadmill?

For one thing, it had become part of their lives. Since they were about seven, a routine had been established, and ever since they could remember, the family timetable had revolved around the girls' swimming. By the time they were eleven, swimming had become the most important thing in their lives: more important than school, mealtimes or even bedtimes. It was the framework of their very existence.

There were other factors too. One was the challenge, the spur of the competition, the drive to do better next time. Each needed to win, to beat not only the other competitors, but each other as well. With each trophy came the urge to gain a more prestigious prize in the next race. There was also another reason. Their swimming had become so time-consuming that the girls had room for little else in their lives. Schoolwork and hobbies had been so neglected that they had been unable to lead normal, well-balanced lives. All they could do was swim up and down. But the hidden motive, the dark secret, which they kept even from each other, was that they were both in love with their coach, Tim Roche. Having recovered from being groped by him three years earlier, Kelsey had begun to fantasise as to what could have happened if she had encouraged him. Then she had been young, raw, ignorant and frightened. Now, nearing fifteen, she had reached sexual maturity and her curiosity was fully aroused. But Tim Roche, now thirty-one, was no longer interested in Kelsey Hobbs or her twin sister, Kirsty. The pretty little mole on Kelsey's thigh held no more attractions for him. Tim Roche was only interested in ten and eleven-year-olds.

Although identical, the twins were not really close. It was as if the closeness in the womb had only served to divide them in life. They resented being identical twins. They hated being compared; they hated being mistaken for each other. It was as if each was being shadowed by an alter ego; a stalking double from whom they could not escape. They were identical in everything they said, thought and did. Even their handwriting was exactly the same. Neither had any way of escaping from the other. Anything achieved by one was mirrored and then eclipsed by the achievement of the other. Any error committed was magnified. As is so often the case with twins, one was usually the leader, the instigator. Born by

Caesarean section, Kirsty had appeared minutes before her sister. This fractional lead into the world seemed to give her the instinctive authority to boss and control her sister, which Kelsey greatly resented.

It was about nine o'clock on a Friday evening. The girls were tired. Even Kirsty had suggested to her sister before their practice session that they should finally pack in the swimming. Neither had shown any improvement lately and the trophies were thin on the ground.

'It's our GCSEs next year, Kel. We'll never get decent grades if we go on spending all this time in the bloody pool. I'm sick of swimming.'

'So am I.'

'I don't want to be an Olympic swimmer.'

'Nor do I'.

'Right. Let's chuck it in.'

'What else'll we do?'

'Have fun. Be normal. Be like everyone else. Have boy friends. Go to discos.'

'Together?'

'Of course. Why not? We've done everything else together so far.'

'Everything else? What else? All we've done, all our lives, is flaming swim.'

'That's why I think we should stop.'

Kelsey sighed. 'Let's discuss it tomorrow. We're here now. We've changed. We're ready. We may as well swim.'

She couldn't help wondering if an even worse alternative to swimming might be going out on double dates. It could end in a double wedding. Perhaps a double mix-up. It was even possible they each might give birth to *more twins*!

All she said was: 'you go first. I'll watch.'

'Okay. Where's Tim?'

'Outside having a fag.'

'He's meant to be in here. We're not supposed to go into the water without him watching. It's the regulation.'

'It'll be okay, Kirsty. We're both quite good enough swimmers to manage without a lifeguard.'

Kelsey never forgot those words. They were the last words she ever spoke to her sister.

As she went to sit at the side, Kirsty dived in and began her crawl; up and down, up and down, counting the lengths as she swam, as she had been taught to do. The crawl finished, she started on her backstroke. Halfway through the second length her cap fell off, and as she went on swimming, her hair worked loose from the rubber band. Now she could feel her hair weaving around her, soft and sensuous, like seaweed. She resisted the urge to take off her costume. She wanted to play around naked in the water like a mermaid. She thought swimming might even be more pleasurable if she were naked and left to her own devices. She abandoned the backstroke routine and wondered how it would feel to loop the loop around one of the ropes marking the swimming lanes. She would be able to watch her hair floating around after her. She started diving over the rope, deftly, gracefully, like a porpoise, her hair flowing behind. Kelsey, watching her from the side, was bemused at first.

'Hey! Kirsty! What on earth...'

Kirsty continued to loop the loop: round and round. At first she felt exhilarated. Then she began to tire. Now her hair had become entangled in the rope. She struggled, but she couldn't pull it free. She tried swimming around the other way, hoping to unwind her hair but it only wound up more tightly. She started thrashing about in the water. She became frightened and began to panic. She tried to shout out, but as her lungs filled up with water, no sound came.

Kelsey went on watching. At first she hadn't understood what Kirsty was trying to do. It had appeared to be a deliberately planned exercise and Kirsty seemed quite in control. There had been no reason for her to interfere. But then Kirsty stopped swimming. She lay in the water, quite still, her long hair entangled in the rope.

'Kirsty!' she called. 'Time to get out!'

But her sister didn't answer. Feeling concerned, Kelsey got up and walked along the side of the pool. At that moment Tim Roche walked in, a bronzed hunk of a he-man in his bathing trunks, smelling of cigarette smoke and Brut For Men.

'What's Kirsty up to?' he enquired.

'I think she's drowned,' replied Kelsey. 'And it's all your fault. You should have been here.'

It was Alison's idea that Emma should accompany Kelsey on holiday to Sardinia. Kelsey had spent five weeks in hospital. After the abortion she had contracted a cervical infection and had become dangerously ill. Alison had been totally distraught by the whole affair. Not only had she lost her prospective first grandchild, but she had nearly lost her only child as well. She had stayed constantly at Kelsey's bedside for several days until the doctors had assured her that her daughter's life was out of danger. Despite this reassurance, she had continued to spend most of each day at the hospital for the remaining four weeks, taking only a couple of hours off each day to see to her affairs. During this time Alison felt totally alone. She had no one to turn to, no one to comfort or advise her. Her mother was in a retirement home, her sister was too preoccupied taking care of her seriously injured husband to spare much time for her niece, and her husband was incommunicado in Morocco.

When she could spare time away from Kelsey's bedside, Alison's first project was to help her headmaster find a temporary replacement for her post as school secretary. Alison loved her job more than almost anything in the world except her daughter. She loved the children, the headmaster and the staff and she had felt part of the building's fabric ever since she had first arrived. She would never willingly have conceded that anyone else could run the school as well as she did. But now that it had become imperative to find a substitute, she felt a tinge of fear that her replacement, albeit a temporary one, might have superior skills to hers.

Alison's second course of action was to find a manager for Sun Med. She interviewed several prospective candidates and finally selected an earnest young man with buckteeth, thick glasses and a rather pimply skin, called Tom Sprockett. She didn't tell Tom Sprockett that the post was temporary. She didn't really know herself whether it was going to be temporary or not. She told Tom that her husband was at present living abroad and had asked her to put in a manager. She had been tempted to invent a story saying that she was widowed, but if Steven should suddenly arrive back from Morocco with little or no notice, there would have been quite a bit of difficult explaining to do.

Despite his initially unattractive appearance, Tom Sprockett turned out to be a great asset. He had a pleasant personality; he was unusually patient with even the most difficult clients and polite on the telephone without being in the least bit servile. He was also extremely efficient and full of ideas for improvements. Alison felt full of hope and began to think that Sun Med might actually run a great deal more smoothly and profitably without Steven in charge.

The temporary school secretary turned out to be a different matter altogether. Her name was Edna Rust. With sandy coloured skin, large blotchy freckles and pale orangey-red hair she looked extremely rusty indeed. She was about forty-five; short, very thin and wore pince-nez. Her studious looks belied her lack of efficiency. She was unpunctual, untidy and mislaid a great deal of documents. She was short-tempered with the children and shouted at the parents on the telephone. In fact, she was a complete disaster. Fortunately, as the headmaster had made the final choice, Alison felt absolved from guilt. After the first week Ronald Spode, the headmaster, started phoning Alison every evening to ask her how soon she would be able to return to work. He would begin by enquiring after Kelsey.

'She's much better,' Alison would reply. 'Her progress is steady, but slow.'

'The deterioration here is steady, but rapid,' Ron would reply snappily almost every evening. 'Any idea when you'll be back?'

'As soon as I can, Ron. I'll come in for a whole morning next week.'

When Kelsey came out of hospital, Alison went back to work. Kelsey went back to live in Emma's flat and Alison gave Emma extended leave for as long as was necessary. Now that Steven was no longer around,

Alison felt it was her sole responsibility to make decisions. As soon as Kelsey was well enough, Alison asked Tom Sprockett to book a fortnight's holiday for the two girls in Sardinia. She would have liked to have gone in Emma's place, but realised that she couldn't ask Ron for more time off and in any case, the two girls would undoubtedly have more fun on their own.

At first Kelsey had objected to a seaside holiday, the first one since Kirsty had drowned.

'Please, Mum,' she said plaintively, 'not the sea. You know I hate the water. Can't we go to the mountains?'

'The sea was Emma's idea, and you do owe her something,' was Alison's reply. 'Besides, mountains are full of rivers and lakes. You can't avoid the water. The world's full of it.'

Secretly she was hoping that two weeks by the sea would restore Kelsey's confidence in the water and might even encourage her to swim again for pleasure.

The first week passed pleasantly enough. Emma lay in the sun until she bubbled and flaked and was finally forced to seek refuge in the shade. She swam, snorkelled and explored rock pools all on her own. Kelsey was altogether more cautious. She still felt tired, drained and rundown. Being fair skinned, she burnt easily and found no pleasure in roasting herself in the sun. Nor did she wish to swim. She equated swimming with danger: the danger of drowning. So she lay in the shade and tried to work out how she should reorganise her life.

Before travelling to Sardinia she had paid a visit to a solicitor who specialised in matrimonial breakdown. Kelsey came straight to the point.

'I want to sue my husband for divorce because he's violent, sadistic and unfaithful.'

'Do you have proof?' enquired Miss Vera Caldicote.

'Yes,' said Kelsey. 'The greatest proof is that he has got his secretary pregnant. She is planning to keep the baby against my husband's wishes. I fell pregnant at almost exactly the same time, but I miscarried through the stress of it all.'

'I'm so sorry,' said Miss Caldicote. 'Can you prove that this woman's baby really is your husband's?'

'I know it is because he's admitted it. But if you don't think there's sufficient proof then we can go for a DNA test.' Kelsey had done her homework.

'Could you prove the violence and the sadism in court?'

'I'm sure I could. Once Nigel's been confronted with the facts in open court he'll confess.'

'What's your husband's profession, Mrs Potter?'

'He's a barrister.'

'A barrister! He could make things very difficult for you indeed.' Miss Caldicote wasn't feeling very optimistic.

'I don't think so. He's not a very good barrister.'

Miss Caldicote raised an eyebrow, but didn't reply directly. Instead she asked: 'do you absolutely insist on going to court?'

'I thought it would the best way to get money out of him.'

'Not necessarily. You could consider a settlement. It will be quicker, cheaper and far less stressful. Court cases can be extremely traumatic.'

Kelsey hadn't thought of the downside of a court case. She had only imagined the pleasure and satisfaction of confronting Nigel: of accusing him of violence, rape and infidelity and being awarded a huge settlement in compensation.

'I do think that before we consider any court case that both you and your husband would be strongly advised to see a marriage guidance counsellor.'

It was Kelsey's turn to be surprised. 'I think it's too late for that.'

'It's never too late to negotiate,' said Miss Caldicote stiffly.

So they arranged to meet again on Kelsey's return from Sardinia.

Now on holiday, Kelsey found it impossible to relax. She felt too tired to do anything, even read a book, and too fraught to rest. There were times when she felt absolutely convinced that she could win a court case. She would imagine facing Nigel in court, feeling exhilarated as she bombarded him with accusations, demolishing him as he stood in the dock, head bowed, looking more and more humiliated. Conversely there were days when she realised she might not win. That Nigel, as a barrister with superior legal knowledge, would demolish her with a fabrication of lies and deceit. She became more and more uncertain of what course of action to take. Should she press ahead for a confrontation in court? Or should she capitulate and go for an out-of-court settlement? She spent many hours weighing up the pros and cons.

Emma tried to rouse her, to inspire a little enthusiasm and galvanise her into action.

'Come for a walk along the beach, Kel. It's glorious paddling at the edge of the water.'

'No. I'm too tired, and you know how I hate the water.'

'Let's go and explore the town.'

'How do we get there?'

'Walk. It's not far.'

'How far?'

'About five miles.'

'You must be joking!'

'No. I'm not. What about taking a boat out? Even a pedalo.'

'That's a really sick joke. We might drown.'

'Of course we won't drown! Kelsey, you're paranoid, and you've become a pain. I wish I'd never come with you on this holiday.'

And Emma really meant it.

By the beginning of the second week Emma was beginning to feel restless. Having burnt and blistered in the sun due to over-exposure without adequate protection, she now carefully rationed herself. She continued to swim at least once a day and went for long walks along the beach wearing a T-shirt, broad-brimmed hat and a liberal amount of high-factor suntan lotion on any exposed parts of her body. But she was always alone. Kelsey, still tired and listless, trying to replan her life, adamantly refused to walk further than the edge of the shore. Emma longed for companionship, male companionship in particular, so one afternoon, well protected against the hottest sun of the day, she set off on her own to walk the five miles to the nearest town.

The walk took Emma nearly an hour and a half and she arrived hot, dusty and thirsty. Before exploring the town, she made straight for the nearest café, found a vacant table in the shade outside on the terrace and ordered a long cold drink. She was surprised to find that the café was quite crowded. Inside a noisy group of Italians was playing cards, cheering loudly each time someone played a good hand. There were several bottles of rough local wine on the tables and each time a bottle was finished, it was quickly replenished by the café owner, beaming delightedly by the fact that he was doing good business on such a hot afternoon. Several of the tables on the terrace were already occupied: one by a middle-aged French couple arguing loudly about money; another by an elderly English couple writing up their holiday diaries, their heads buried studiously in maps and notebooks. At another table sat a noisy American family, their four children constantly making demands, which their parents appeared too weak and tired to resist.

'Momma, I want another chocolate mint chip ice-cream.'

'Yes, Marvin,' said Momma, signalling to the waiter.

'Pop, I don't want this orangeade. It's warm. I want a cold Pepsi.'

'Yes, Chuck,' said Pop obediently.

'Ow! Jasmine bit me!' yelled Mary-Jo, leaning across the table and thumping her younger sister hard. Jasmine tipped up her chair to avoid her sister's blow. The chair fell backwards onto the pavement with a resounding crack, catapulting the little girl into the road. Momma, frightened that her daughter was hurt, stood up too suddenly, knocking over the table. Cutlery, plates and glasses cascaded with a clatter onto the pavement and slid out into the road.

'Oh, Momma! Now look what you've done!' admonished Chuck. There was a deathly hush for a few seconds before Jasmine started screaming. Just as the café owner came out to investigate, a party of six young

English people in their mid-twenties, chatting loudly, sauntered across the street and sat down at a vacant table next to Emma.

'Two more passengers would be ideal,' said a tall, dark young man with a deep suntan.

'But they'd need to know how to sail, Daniel,' objected a slim girl wearing white shorts, her fair hair in a ponytail.

'Not really, Claire,' said another young man with flaming red hair and freckles. 'They could pick it up as they go along. Most of us did.'

'Okay, Fred,' said a short, rather plump young man with thick glasses. 'How do we go about finding these people?'

The fourth man in the group, sitting directly opposite Emma, caught her eye and smiled. Emma's heart missed a beat. They seemed a lively, friendly group of people, English and on holiday. They needed two more people to go out with them in a boat. Well, one of them is sitting right here, she thought.

'I'll come with you,' she said brightly, 'and I'll try and persuade my friend to come as well. She's resting in the hotel. Her name's Kelsey Potter,' she finished lamely.

The group of young people seemed delighted to have solved their problem so quickly and easily. Emma was invited to join their table and overwhelmed with offers of drinks and introductions.

'Have a Coke, an orange juice, a glass of wine. I'm Fred, that's Simon. He's Daniel. She's Claire and that's her friend Lucy. The very tall one is Chris.'

Kelsey was adamant.

'Emma, I will not get into a boat for anyone, not even you.'

Having tried to be her most persuasive, Emma became angry.

'I think you're a rotten old spoilsport. You haven't done a bloody thing ever since we came on this holiday. You lie in the shade and mope and leave me to amuse myself all on my own. You just don't deserve to be on holiday in such a lovely place. I'm utterly sick of you.'

The next day Emma was pleasantly surprised when Kelsey went down with her to the harbour to see them all off. It was a perfect day for sailing. The sun beamed down from a pale blue cloudless sky onto the shimmering, deep sapphire blue sea. There was a light cool breeze, enough to keep a sailing boat scudding along at a comfortable pace. Admiring the view, the two girls walked slowly down to the jetty where the yacht was moored at the far end. She was a small sloop, about thirty feet long, painted white with red-and-white-striped sails. Under the green, white and red Italian flag fluttering from the bow, her name, Miranda, was painted in black.

As Kelsey and Emma approached the Miranda they saw a hive of activity aboard. Two young men were swabbing down the decks; two other young men were passing supplies to two girls in the galley below deck, as they stowed away the goods in lockers and the fridge as speedily and neatly as possible, frantically trying to keep pace with the deliveries from the deck above. When Kelsey and Emma reached the side of the yacht all activity ceased. The deck-swabbers put down their mops and the two stevedores laid down their loads. Wondering why the deliveries had stopped, the two girls in the galley stopped their stowing away and popped their heads through the hatch.

'Hello, Emma,' said Chris, tall, bronzed and fair-haired, extending a hand to help her aboard. 'I'm so pleased your friend has decided to come along too. That'll make us a nice round number.'

Daniel, tall, and as dark as Chris was fair, with an equally deep suntan, extended his hand to help Kelsey onto the Miranda.

'Hello, I'm Daniel.' He smiled, a warm, infectious smile that lit up his wide-set eyes. 'You must be Kelsey. Emma's told me about you. I'm delighted you've decided to join us.'

Kelsey smiled back a little uncertainly, ignoring his outstretched hand. At that moment the two girls swung their way out through the hatch.

'Great!' said the fair-haired one with the ponytail. 'I'm glad you've brought your friend, Emma.' She stood up on the deck. 'Hello, Kelsey, I'm Claire. I'm delighted you've come along. Now we'll have more hands in the galley.'

Kelsey stood on the jetty, arms rigidly by her sides, saying nothing. Daniel looked her up and down, liking what he saw: a pale, slim young woman of twenty-four dressed in white shorts and T-shirt, her dark, shoulder-length hair held loosely back from her face with a white hair-band. She wore flat white sandals, a floppy, wide-brimmed straw hat and sunglasses, which unfortunately prevented him from seeing her eyes. She looked frail and delicate. Emma had mentioned that the reason for the Sardinian holiday was her friend's recent illness, a fact that Daniel found easy to believe.

'It's a very small hop,' he said encouragingly, holding out his hand again.'

'I know,' said Kelsey, not moving.

Daniel wondered what caused her reluctance.

'Not been sailing before?'

'No,' said Kelsey, still not moving.

'You won't have to climb the rigging or anything. The men'll do that. All you'll have to do is help in the galley, the kitchen that is, when the time comes.'

'What happens if the boat capsizes? I can't swim.'

'No problem. Life jackets are compulsory for everyone as soon as we put to sea. Lucy can't swim either.'

'Rubbish!' said Lucy. 'Of course I can. I just can't swim very far. Come on, Kelsey. It's going to be such fun.'

Kelsey hesitated. It would, undoubtedly, be fun. The crew of the Miranda seemed a friendly, lively crowd. Emma was already aboard. If she stayed behind she would have to spend the entire day by herself; afraid to swim, too tired to go for a walk, or even read or sunbathe. She would have to lunch by herself, with only her own gloomy thoughts for company. Emma was right. She had become a mopey, morbid spoilsport. She didn't deserve to be on holiday in this beautiful place. It was time she pulled herself together; time she joined in the activities with people of her own age. She must conquer her water phobia and start swimming again. She must go out on the water in a boat. And here was the boat, all equipped and ready for her to jump aboard, complete with a group of lively young people all her own age. She smiled up at Daniel and held out her hand.

'Yes,' she said. 'I'll come.'

With a light jump Kelsey landed on the deck of the Miranda. Daniel held onto her hand a fraction longer than necessary, putting the other one on her shoulder to steady her. Kelsey felt pleasurable excitement at Daniel's light touch on her shoulder blade and then a stab of fear when she realised what she had done. She had taken the giant leap and jumped onto a boat, which would shortly put to sea for perhaps eight or ten hours. She would be surrounded by water and the boat might sink.

But now it was too late to change her mind.

Chapter Twenty-Five

During the morning they sailed due south for more than two hours along the Sardinian coastline of flat, slivery-white beaches. The monotony was broken up only occasionally by small outcrops of rock forming little coves and the hinterland was equally flat, appearing scrubby and rather dull. They saw no towns or villages, but passed two campsites, with bright tents pitched along by the edge of the beach, making a vivid splash of colour on a shoreline that had hardly changed since they left port. The azure blue sea was as flat as the beaches and as smooth as glass. Only the merest light breeze helped to keep them moving along slowly. The sky mirrored the sea in a paler shade of blue and the water sparkled in the sunshine, which became relentlessly hotter as the day advanced.

Kelsey was beginning to relax. They certainly were a friendly, jolly crowd, who seemed to have known each other for quite a long time. There was plenty of teasing and ribbing about school days, old boy friends and girl friends. At first Kelsey was too nervous to stay up on deck, so she went down to the galley, where she spent the next hour helping Claire and Lucy to store all the provisions.

'Put the breakfast cereal in here, don't you think, Kel?' suggested Claire, falling easily into the familiar version of her name. 'Fits in a treat.'

Fear gripped Kelsey. 'Breakfast cereal! We're not going to spend the night on this thing, are we?'

Lucy sensed Kelsey's nervousness. 'Don't worry, Kel. Chris would have said. These trips are always carefully planned.'

'Not been on a boat before?' asked Claire.

'No,' said Kelsey shortly.

'We'll have to get you along more often, then.'

'Maybe,' said Kelsey, still cautious.

Having stowed away the provisions, they realised there was no need to remain below any longer.

'Come on. Let's go up on deck and see what the others are up to,' suggested Claire.

Kelsey followed the two girls up the steep metal ladder to the deck, where they found Daniel at the tiller. Chris, Fred and Emma were stretched out on sun-beds, sunbathing.

'Good Lord, Fred! You look as if you're on fire!' remarked Lucy. Fred had certainly gone an alarming shade of red. 'Did you put on sun-tan lotion?'

'Loads of it,' replied Fred, surveying himself ruefully.

'What factor?'

Fred held up the plastic bottle. 'Twelve.'

'Twelve! Your skin needs block-out,' said Lucy scornfully.

'Block-out? Then there'd be no point in sun-bathing,' replied Fred.

'Better to be white than burnt,' said Claire firmly. 'And you should be wearing a hat.'

Fred appealed to Kelsey. 'Aren't they bossy?'

'Maybe they're right. I keep in the shade. I find the sun too hot. Emma overdid it last week, didn't you, Em?'

'Yes. I suppose I did a bit.' Emma sat up, and shielding her eyes from the sun, got up and moved into the shade.

Shortly before midday they reached a cove, curving attractively back from the shore, bordered on either side by clumps of rock.

'Anyone hungry?' enquired Chris, who was now at the tiller.

'Yes!' went up the chorus.

'Then I suggest we put ashore.'

'Yes! Hurrah!' went the chorus again.

Chris pulled hard on the tiller and guided the boat towards the shore. When they were about half a mile away from the beach he secured the tiller and threw down the anchor. Kelsey looked puzzled.

'How do we get ashore?' she asked Daniel, who was standing beside her.

'We swim,' he teased.

'But I can't!' said Kelsey, frightened. 'I told you I couldn't before I came on board.'

Daniel patted her shoulder reassuringly. 'Don't worry. You won't have to learn just yet. We've got a rubber dingy. Look over the side.'

Holding tightly onto the rail, Kelsey looked over the side of the boat to where a rubber dingy bobbed up and down in the clear blue water. Looking down made her feel giddy and very apprehensive.

She looked up at Daniel, her eyes fearful. 'How do we get into it?'

'Jump,' teased Fred, coming up behind.

'Oh…!' began Kelsey, feeling Daniel's hand squeezing her shoulder.

'He's teasing you too,' said Daniel. 'We all tease each other. Don't worry. We've got a rope ladder. We shinny down it just like that…'

As they watched, Chris descended the rope ladder expertly and at great speed, followed by Lucy and then Claire. Chris looked up at the remaining group standing together on the boat.

'Who's next? Emma, or Kelsey?'

Fear welled up in Kelsey's stomach. She prayed she wasn't going to be sick. 'You go next, Em,' she mumbled, hoping her knees weren't going to give way. Emma obediently went to the side of the boat, where a gate had been opened to create a small gap in the rail, and holding tightly onto the side, she lowered herself cautiously backwards onto the first rung of the rope ladder. Watched anxiously by the rest of the group, she slowly climbed down the flimsy ladder, hand over hand, one foot at a time. As Chris helped her to land in the dingy, a small cheer went up.

'Well done, Emma! Very good, Emma!'

Kelsey still remained above on the yacht with Daniel, Fred and Simon. Chris looked up at them again. A thought flashed through his mind: what on earth possessed us to invite such a pair of landlubbers on a boating trip? But he dismissed the thought straight away. They were here now and nothing could be done about it. And they did seem nice girls. He thought Daniel rather fancied Kelsey, and he'd taken quite a shine to Emma.

'Who's next?' he enquired again.

Daniel had his arm around Kelsey's shoulders. He could feel her trembling. What on earth's got into her? he thought. She must have had a really traumatic experience to be so afraid of boats.

'I'll go first and you can follow straight away. Okay? Nothing to worry about. Chris'll catch you if you slip. He's very good at that sort of thing.'

He put his head down close to hers and tried to catch what she was saying, as her eyelash brushed his cheek. Kelsey lifted her face to his. Their breaths mingled, just for a second and Kelsey felt a frisson as he squeezed her shoulder harder.

'Yes. You go first.' She barely spoke above a whisper.

Daniel took a few steps forward to the side of the boat, turned around expertly, and holding onto the rail, took a few steps down the rope ladder. When he was half-way he called up: 'Simon, help Kelsey onto the top of the ladder so I can guide her down.'

Simon gently escorted Kelsey to the side of the boat. 'Put your hand here and turn around.'

Trembling, Kelsey did as she was told.

'Now put your foot down and feel for the top rung of the ladder.'

Kelsey obeyed his instructions and, as Daniel took her ankle in his hand, she was aware of another quiver of pleasure. Slowly, step-by-step, Daniel guided each foot down the ladder, as Simon held the top to prevent it from swaying too much. When Daniel had landed in the dingy he called:

'Okay! I've got you!' He reached up, grabbed her by the waist and lifted her down.

Her cheek brushed his lips and he could feel the contours of her breasts, covered in the flimsiest of fabrics, against his bare chest. A rousing cheer went up from the dingy and the boat above.

'Well done Kelsey! Very well done!'

Kelsey sat on a plank in the dingy feeling dazed and relieved. In a moment Simon and Fred joined them and they set off for their picnic lunch on the shore.

'Put a prawn on the barbie, the barbie, the barbie,'
  'Put a prawn on the barbie, dear Lucy, please do!'

Fred sang lustily, although a little tunelessly, to the tune of *'There's a Hole in My Bucket.'*

'Come on, everyone! Join in!' he invited, his blue eyes blazing in his flushed, animated freckled face, his red hair glinting gold and orange in the strong bright sunshine. Lucy got up obediently and put more prawns on the barbeque. Fred began again, conducting this time as everyone joined in enthusiastically.

'Put a prawn on the barbie, the barbie, the barbie…'

The picnic lunch was a great deal more elaborate than either Emma or Kelsey could ever have imagined on a boating party. There was a delicious choice of steaks, chicken drumsticks, pork and lamb chops, sausages and prawns all cooked on a gas barbeque. There were salads of tomato, potato and cucumber. There was bread and cheese and juicy nectarines to complete the feast. There was wine, chilled *Frascati* and full-bodied *Chianti,* sparkling mineral water and orange juice.

Everyone except Kelsey had been for a swim before lunch, so appetites were sharpened all the more. They ate, drank and sang songs until they had all eaten their fill and were not a little drunk. There was nothing for it but to sleep it all off before they made the two-hour trip back to the harbour. Having brought their swimming towels with them and, fortunately, a spare one for Kelsey, they all sought shady places among the rocks and went to sleep.

Fred woke up first. He was shivering with cold and had the most appalling headache. He sat up uncertainly, rubbing his eyes, unsure where he was. He looked around the cove and saw his friends stretched out in various positions, on the sand and in among the rocks.

'Of course,' he said out loud. 'We did have rather an inebriated picnic.'

He stood up unsteadily, his head throbbing, and surveyed the scene. The sun, now quite low on the horizon, had clouded over and a chilly wind was blowing off the sea, making little choppy white-crested waves. He looked at his watch. It was ten minutes to six. Good God! He must have slept for more than two hours! He walked down to the edge of the beach to check up on the dingy, but it was nowhere to be seen. His heart missed a beat as he looked out half a mile beyond the shore for their boat. Yes, thank God, it was still securely anchored in exactly the same position they had left it. But where was the dingy? Had it been carried away by the tide? How would they reach the boat? Would they have to swim? This wouldn't present a problem for any of them except Lucy, who could barely swim, and Kelsey, who seemed terrified of anything to do with boats or water. The dingy would have to be found. As he started walking along the beach he saw Daniel, still asleep beside a clump of rocks.

'Hey, Dan!' he called. 'It's time we made a move. Our dingy's gone.'

Daniel sat up, rubbing his eyes, looking dazed and confused.

Fred walked over to him.

'The weather's changed,' he said briefly, 'and our dingy's disappeared. Come and help me look for it.'

Daniel held out his hand. 'Help me up, please.' Fred pulled him to his feet. 'Oh, God!' exclaimed Daniel, swaying slightly. 'My head!'

'Yes,' agreed Fred. 'Mine too. We had a hell of a lot to drink at lunchtime. But we ought to get moving now. We don't want to be at sea when it begins to get dark.'

'Agreed. What's the problem with the dingy?'

'It's disappeared.'

'Jesus!'

'Yes. We've got to find it, otherwise we won't get our two non-swimmers out to the boat.'

'Or our picnic stuff.'

'Exactly.'

The two young men walked along the shore, hoping to find that the dingy had become trapped somewhere among the rocks. The rest of the party began waking up, most of them feeling dazed and headachy. Emma walked over to where Kelsey lay on the sand, partly covered by a towel.

'God! I feel terrible,' she said.

Kelsey sat up. 'So do I. I had far too much wine.'

They stood up uncertainly, brushed the sand off their clothes and attempted to shake it out of their hair. Kelsey pointed to the shoreline.

'The dingy's gone. That's where we left it.' Fear gripped her. 'How will we get back to the boat?'

Emma tried to sound reassuring. 'Don't worry, Kel. We'll find it.'

They went down to the edge of the sea and were joined in a moment by all the others.

'Where's the dingy?' asked Lucy apprehensively.

'It must have broken its moorings,' said Chris in a factual, casual voice. 'We'll find it. Don't worry.'

They walked along the beach in the same direction that Daniel and Fred had taken. As they turned the corner they saw Daniel a little further on, gesticulating

towards the sea, talking animatedly to Fred. Chris quic-
kened his pace and then broke into a run, followed by
the rest of the group. He reached Daniel, panting, his
head throbbing. 'What's up?'

'The dingy's drifted out to sea. Look!' Daniel pointed
to where a small craft was bobbing up and down in the
choppy sea, moving further and further away from the
shore.

'Are you sure that's the dingy?' asked Chris, his heart
sinking as he thought of how they would get back to the
boat.

'The dingy's not where we moored it so it must be out
there,' said Daniel factually.

'How are we going to get back to the boat?'

'Swim.'

'They can't all swim.'

'We'll tow the two who can't,' said Daniel resolutely.

Chris felt his stomach muscles tighten at the thought
of towing two non-swimmers over half a mile.

'What about our stuff?'

'We'll take what we can and return for the rest
tomorrow.'

By now the others had caught up with them and
stood around uncertainly.

'Where's the dingy?' asked Claire.

'Out there,' said Fred, pointing out to sea.

'Oh,' said Claire. 'So we'll have to swim back to the
boat.'

'I'm afraid so,' said Daniel, relieved that one member
of the group was taking the crisis so calmly.

'In our clothes?' asked Simon.

'No,' said Daniel decisively. 'We'll take off our clothes
and swim with them above our heads to keep them dry.

That way we'll have something dry to wear on the boat.' He looked at Kelsey. 'I'll support you as I swim on my back. I've got a life-saving badge. You'll be quite safe. Chris can help Lucy. We'll go back to the nearest point to the boat and get undressed.'

'What about our stuff?' asked Claire.

'We'll take what we can and come back for the rest tomorrow. Come on. Back to the cove and get undressed.'

Kelsey stood uncertainly on the edge of the shore, watching the rest of the party as they swam out to the boat. They were all good swimmers except Lucy, who was trying valiantly with expert help from Chris. Kelsey felt her stomach churning; her mouth went dry and her palms were sweaty as she clenched and opened her fists. It was now or never. All she was required to do was to swim about half a mile to reach a boat, as there was no other way of getting there. She could no longer conceal the fact that she couldn't swim. She didn't want to swim, but she had no choice. As she watched Chris towing Lucy along, her hair floating out behind her just like Kirsty's, she thought, that's what I should have done. I should have jumped into the pool to save her. I could easily have towed her to the side. It's all my fault she's dead. But I didn't know she was drowning.

Without any further ado she stripped off her clothes, wrapped them in a bundle and walked to the edge of the sea. She stood there for a moment, her silky, milk-white body silhouetted against the darkening sky. Her square shoulders tapered to a slim waist, her breasts stood out round and firm, nipples erect. Below her flat stomach was a perfect triangle of dark pubic hair. Daniel gasped in wonder at her beauty and put out his hand to touch her, but she had already slipped into the sea and was swimming towards the boat with strong, deft strokes.

When they reached the boat they were all exhausted. Even Kelsey, excellent swimmer though she had once been, was totally worn out. Claire lay limp on the deck. 'That's the longest swim I've ever done,' she groaned. 'I hope I don't ever have to swim that far again.'

'Only half a mile.' Chris tried to sound cheerful. He had borne the biggest burden in trying to tow Lucy to safety as well as himself. He felt completely shattered and extremely worried about the journey back to the port that lay ahead. It seemed inevitable that some of it would have to be made in darkness.

'My, you're a good swimmer, Kelsey,' said Simon admiringly. Kelsey could feel all their eyes on her.

'Hiding your light under a bushel, were you?' asked Fred teasingly.

'I wouldn't pretend I couldn't swim if I was that good,' said Lucy, knowing she would be eternally grateful to Chris for giving her such valiant help.

Daniel looked across at Kelsey, who was shivering violently. There must be some good reason why she pretended she couldn't swim, he thought. But this was hardly the time to enquire. We just have to thank God that we all got back to the boat safely and in reasonably good shape. Now we've got the problem of getting back to the harbour before dark, which I think is most unlikely, so we may have an extremely difficult trip. But he refrained from voicing his fears out loud.

They had all piled into the galley and were drinking mugs of steaming hot tea, into which Chris had insisted they put plenty of sugar to build up their energy loss. Clothes had been kept dry during the long swim with varying degrees of success, depending on the aquatic skills and endurance of the individual swimmer. Fortunately, a search through the lockers in the heads revealed an odd assortment of clothing left behind by other holiday-makers who had previously hired the boat. The men went up on deck to change into dry clothes, while the girls did their changing down below. Peals of girlish laughter mingled with male guffaws as they surveyed each other's most unstylish borrowed clothing.

The men remained on deck, getting the boat ready to sail, while the girls prepared a meal in the galley. The copious picnic lunch seemed a long way off and they were all extremely hungry after the exhausting swim. As they had hired the boat for four days they had come well supplied with plenty of dried and tinned food. In less than twenty minutes the girls had produced a hearty hot meal of Heinz tomato soup, frankfurter sausages, baked beans, fried eggs and reheated tinned potatoes. They laid the table as attractively as possible and when everything was ready Claire went up the ladder and called out: 'food's ready! Come and get it!'

Daniel, Fred and Simon went below immediately, leaving Chris at the helm. As Lucy took him up a plateful of hot steamy food, Chris smiled his grateful thanks. The party in the galley became quite merry, despite the self-imposed ban on alcohol. They all realised how important it was to remain alert. Although the sea was a little choppy, the wind was still blowing moderate to fresh. To those sitting comfortably below in the galley the boat's progress seemed quite smooth and effortless.

The situation on deck was quite different. Chris was struggling. As soon as the boat had left the shelter of the cove where they had enjoyed their picnic lunch, he had to pull hard on the tiller with all the force he could muster to steer the boat due north. As soon as he had done so he realised there was a problem: the wind was coming from the north, directly against them. The only course to follow was to tack from side to side, picking up what wind they could to take them in the right direction. The journey back to the harbour would take twice as long as the trip out, all of four hours. Chris looked at his watch. It was after seven o'clock. There was no hope of reaching their destination before eleven. It would be dark by nine, so they would have to spend at least two hours sailing in the dark. His stomach felt hollow as he imagined some of the hazards they might encounter.

At about seven thirty Daniel went up on deck to relieve Chris at the helm. Seeing his friend's tight, set face as he swung the boom from one side to the other, he too, realised the problem. He sat down beside Chris.

'I've come to relieve you.'

'Thanks. I need a bit of relief. See the problem?'

'Yes. We're sailing against the wind.'

'Exactly. It's going to take twice as long to get back as it did to get here.'

Saying nothing, Daniel sat down by his friend and took the tiller. Chris shuffled along the bench seat.

'Won't you go below and join the others?' suggested Daniel. Chris shook his head. 'No. I think it's better if I stay here. Just in case.'

Daniel refrained from asking: in case of what?

They sailed on for another half an hour. As the wind rose, the sails flapped, the jib juddered and tacking became increasingly difficult. The sea was now far more than just choppy: it had become rough. Each time Daniel turned the tiller too sharply a wave slapped into the side of the boat, sending her shooting upwards. As she reached the crest of the wave, a huge trough appeared into which she plunged steeply downwards. Now, despite the cold wind Daniel could feel sweat breaking out on his forehead, the sweat of exertion - and fear.

Fred and Simon appeared on deck.

'Getting a bit choppy up here,' said Fred in his usually jovial way, but his levity died somewhat as the little boat was lifted up on the largest wave so far, held suspended for a moment on the crest and then tossed into a seemingly endless trough.

Fred's jaw dropped. 'Jesus! It's rough, isn't it?'

Grim faced, Daniel hung onto the tiller, saying nothing. Chris said shortly: 'yes - and it's getting rougher.'

'We're going against the wind,' said Simon.

'Yes,' said Chris. 'That's the crux of the problem.'

'I think we'll have to turn around and head south. There's no point in battling against this wind. It'll be blowing a gale force soon. Fred, please go below and ask the girls to organise a search of all the lockers. We need to find shipping charts for the area, a torch and a radio.' He nearly added, 'we'll probably need distress flares as well,' but he thought this could wait until later. There was no point in being too alarmist at this stage.

A thorough search was made below of all the lockers and cupboards. Every nook and cranny of the boat was turned upside down in the hope of finding shipping charts and a radio. It was Kelsey who discovered the flares.

'What are these?' she asked Fred.

'They're flares for sending a Mayday.'

'What's that?'

'It's a distress signal.'

'A distress signal?'

'Yes.'

'In case we get into difficulties?'

'Well, yes. I'm sure we won't need them, but it's good to know we've got them, just in case.'

Fred tried to sound reassuring but he spoke without much confidence. The little boat was now pitching and tossing fiercely, bruising the sea as it landed in the trough of a wave. Up on deck, Chris had taken charge of the tiller again. Although he was undoubtedly the most experienced sailor of the group, he was now frightened. The responsibility rested squarely on him to get them all safely back on dry land. It was useless thinking regretfully of all the navigation courses that he could have taken, but hadn't. He was afraid that his limited experience might prove woefully inadequate. Whatever his qualms, he still felt the only solution was to turn the boat around and sail due south with the wind directly behind them. But this posed two problems: the first one was the sheer physical difficulty of turning the boat a full one-hundred-and-eighty degrees in such a heavy sea. There was the frightening prospect that she could capsize, drowning all on board. Chris hesitated. If the boat did capsize it would be better if everyone was on deck, wearing their life jackets. Then at least they could all get into the dingy.

The dingy. The horrific thought came to him.

There was no dingy. It had drifted out to sea and they had lost it. If they were to capsize they would have to wait to be rescued. They couldn't possibly swim in this sea. With a sinking heart, Chris considered the second, equally daunting problem: by going due south they would be sailing along a coastline unknown to them, unless the charts turned up in one of the lockers. He cursed himself for failing to make a thorough check of the boat before they had set sail that morning. He now realised he had been extremely irresponsible not to have made sure that they had adequate charts and a radio.

Fred came up on deck with a bundle of papers in his hand.

'Charts, Captain,' he said briefly, handing them over.

'Thank God. Well done,' said Chris. 'Take the tiller please, Dan, while I go below and study them.' 'Any radio?' asked Fred.

'No. Just a torch - and flares for a Mayday.'

'Fine,' said Chris, and then voiced his fears out loud for the first time. 'We might need them,'

He went below with the bundle of charts and spread them out on the rectangular table in the galley. He had only been on two navigation courses and was acutely aware of his lack of knowledge. For the purpose of drawing up the charts, the island had been divided into four. Chris picked up the two charts of the northern half and studied them for a moment or two. They were only concerned with the western side of the island, so he put down the chart he didn't need and studied the other one. He ran his finger from the most northerly tip to the cove where they had enjoyed their picnic. Studying it carefully, he could make out the port they had sailed from and the course they had taken to the picnic cove. But there the map finished. The two charts to the southern half of the island were missing. If he stuck to his plan and turned the boat around, they would be forced to sail in the dark in uncharted waters. If they carried on as they were, sailing due north into a gale force wind, they would probably be blown out to sea, or even worse, risk capsizing. Chris knew that their only possibility was to sail due south into the unknown. His next step must be to tell them all to don their life jackets and go up on deck. Then he had to turn the boat around.

Up on deck they made a silent, sombre group: the party of revellers who only six hours earlier had been enjoying an innocent picnic lunch on a sun-drenched beach. In the short time that Chris had been down below studying the charts, the small boat had been blown closer to the shore by the raging wind. Already trussed up in his padded life jacket, Daniel handed the tiller over to Chris and moved along the bench. Chris nodded briefly to the group, still standing, huddled close together by the mast and said: 'please sit down and hold on tight. I'm going to try to turn her around so we'll have the wind behind us. Heaven knows where we'll end up, but I think it's the only solution.'

White-faced and anxious, Chris took the tiller. The sea was now huge: seething and surging around the little craft, resentful and angry. The wind roared and whistled, gusting up to a gale force eight or nine. Suddenly, the largest wave they had yet encountered hit the bow with a terrifying thud, lifting the boat up and up until they were almost vertical. They seem to hang suspended in the air for all eternity. Lucy whimpered, terrified, clinging onto Claire. Kelsey and Emma had their arms around each other. Fred and Simon looked stoically ahead. Daniel stared at Chris, wondering if he should hold onto the tiller as well. Chris hung on with all his force, just trying to keep the tiller straight.

Suddenly there was an enormous crash as the boat fell into the trough. They all felt as if they had left their stomachs in mid-air. The crash was followed by an unearthly silence. It was as if the sea was holding its breath for the next onslaught. Chris seized his chance: it was now or never. He pulled on the tiller with all his force and managed a ninety-degree turn. Sweat broke out on his forehead; his hands were cold and clammy; his heart was thumping loudly. Half-way. They were half-way around now. All he needed was another ninety-degree turn and they would be facing south, ready to sail with the wind behind them. Once more Chris exerted all his strength. But this time he got the timing wrong. Just as the little boat was making its turn, another huge wave hit it broadside on. The boom swung over too quickly with a ferocious crack, breaking the mast in two. The top half of the mast, with the mainsail and jib still attached, flew overboard into the churning sea, taking Lucy with it. There was a horrified silence on board as they all watched Lucy floundering helplessly in the water, her long hair floating out around her, the sail flapping across her face.

Within seconds, without a thought for her own safety, Kelsey dived into the water. She tore frantically at the sail to clear Lucy's face. Then she supported her head with one hand, as she used the other to free her hair from the rigging. Moments later, another huge wave appeared, driving the wrecked boat onto a clump of rocks, dragging Lucy and Kelsey along with it. Claire and Emma were now screaming in terror as Daniel dived into the sea. The three young men remaining on the boat clung on to the small craft in desperation, waiting for a lull in the fierce sea so they could help Daniel to rescue the two girls. The brief lull came and Chris threw a rope.

'Dan! Catch the rope and hold on! Everyone else stay where you are. We've got enough people in the sea already.'

On the second attempt Daniel managed to get hold of the rope. He held on with one hand and put the other arm around Lucy.

'Okay, Kel?' he asked briefly.

'Yes. Okay.'

'You take her feet. I've got her head. Between us we'll get her onto the rocks.'

Slowly and with the utmost difficulty, Daniel and Kelsey towed Lucy onto the rocks, finally managing to get her aboard the capsized craft. She was unconscious, but still breathing. Simon and Chris took turns to give her mouth-to-mouth resuscitation while Fred helped first Kelsey and then Daniel onto the stricken vessel. Lucy stirred, opened her eyes, saw where she was and closed them again.

'She'll be okay,' said Simon, enormously relieved. 'She's concussed.'

'The boom hit her,' said Fred. 'I saw it all happen.'

'So did I,' said Daniel. He put his arm around Kelsey, whose teeth were chattering violently. 'Are you okay? You were incredibly brave.'

'So were you,' said Kelsey, nestling against him for a moment.'

'No dry clothes this time.'

'No. Everything's wet now.'

'Everyone all right?' asked Chris to the frightened, bedraggled little group. 'No one else hurt?'

'No. No. I'm fine. Quite okay,' came the general responses.

'The only good news I can think of right now,' said Fred, with some of his irrepressible optimism returning, 'is that we seem to have landed on a slightly more sheltered spot.'

It was true. The boat had been thrown up on a clump of rocks just out of reach of the whining wind and surging sea.

'Can anyone see what's behind us?' asked Simon.

They all turned and looked towards the shore, straining to make out any shape that might possibly be dry land.

'Wasn't there a torch, Chris?' enquired Fred. 'Or did it fall into the sea along with the sail and the mast?'

Chris groped under the bench seats on what had been the deck. His fingers closed around a torch and a bundle of flares. Switching on the torch, he swung the beam upwards. All eyes followed as he swung it around. Above and behind them was a steep cliff-face, totally unassailable. In front was the raging sea and the howling wind. They were trapped between the two.

Chris tried to sound casual. 'There's not a great deal we can do at the moment. We'll have to wait until we're rescued. Luckily we've got these.'

He set off one of the flares.

'Let's hope we won't have to wait too long.'

Chapter Twenty-Six

'And how long did you have to wait?' Verity was sitting bolt upright, perched on the edge of the seat of her Parker Knoll chair.

'Dawn was rising, wasn't it, Kel?'

'Yes. The most beautiful dawn I'll ever remember. The sky was a rosy pink, flecked with tiny white puffy clouds.'

'I would have thought you would have been far too worried about being rescued to notice the beautiful dawn.'

'Fear focuses the mind,' said Emma, holding out her cup for more tea. 'Thank you, Mrs Davis. It also sharpens the senses and makes one more observant.'

'What did you do while you were waiting? What did you think about?'

Kelsey felt the time had come to tell the shipwreck story from the beginning. The visit to her grandmother was turning out rather better than she had expected. Although the real purpose of the visit had been to ask Verity to lend her some money until her divorce settlement from Nigel came through, Kelsey realised that she had to tell the story of their adventures before she could broach any other subject.

'Shall I start at the beginning, Grandma?'

'Yes do, dear. Would either of you like anything more to eat? These egg mayonnaise sandwiches are particularly tasty, aren't they? And the scones are Cook's speciality. Have another one, Emma?' persuaded Verity.

'Yes, thank you. They're delicious.'

Emma took another scone and looked at Kelsey. She knew her secret now. They had had a long talk in the hotel room in Sardinia before their return to London. Kelsey had confessed to her bulimia and had also told her the heart-rending story of her twin sister's fatal accident in the swimming pool. No wonder Kelsey hated the water so much.

'Well, you see,' began Kelsey, trying to get the events in the correct order. 'Emma met this group of young people in the local town who were looking for two more people to join them on their sailing boat.'

'Which they had hired for the day,' put in Emma.

'Four days, actually,' said Kelsey.

'So you'd planned to go to sea for four days?' said Verity in some surprise.

'No, just one day. They'd planned to return to the harbour that evening and then go out again the following day.'

'I see. So you set off in good weather...'

'Yes. It was brilliant sunshine, really hot and the sea was very calm.'

'We sailed for about two hours and reached a little cove where we anchored the sailing boat and went ashore in a rubber dingy.'

'It must have been quite tricky getting into a small dingy from a sailing boat.'

'It certainly was,' said Kelsey with feeling.

'There were eight of us in the dingy with all the picnic stuff. We were really loaded down.'

'So you had a picnic on the beach?'

'Yes. It was a fantastic picnic. They'd brought along a gas barbeque and we grilled the most delicious food. Steak, chicken...'

'Sausages, lamb chops, prawns...'

'There were salads too...'

'Tomato, cucumber, potato and Waldorf...'

'And lots and lots of wine.'

'So you had quite a picnic.'

'We certainly did.'

'And we had so much to drink that we all fell asleep.'

'Was it dark when you woke up?'

'No. Not quite. But it was after six, wasn't it, Em?'

'Yes. It must have been. And the weather had changed. There was quite a chilly wind blowing up.'

'Then we discovered that our dingy had been blown out to sea.'

'So how did you get back to the boat?'

'We swam.'

'Really! Was it far?'

'At least half a mile.'

So Kelsey has been forced to conquer her water phobia, thought Verity, pleased. But she decided not to say anything.

'Were they all good swimmers?'

'Lucy wasn't. But Chris towed her along.'

'Anyway, you all got back to the boat safely.'

'Yes. Luckily we reached the boat before it got too rough. But the really bad weather didn't start until about an hour later. Once we were out of the shelter of the cove where we'd had our picnic the wind started blowing a gale.'

'It was then that Chris, our unofficial captain...'

'He was marvellous, wasn't he, Kel?'

'Fantastic. He realised that once we'd left the shelter of the cove the wind was actually blowing against us. He tried to tack, which means sailing diagonally from side to side. But he saw it was hopeless.'

'So what did your fantastic captain do?'

'He told us to put on our life-jackets and go up on deck, and then he tried to turn the boat right around, a full one-hundred-and-eighty degrees.'

'But the sea was so rough and the wind was so strong that the boom swung over - that's the bit the sail sits on - and the mast just snapped in half.'

'On its way down it hit Lucy and knocked her overboard.'

'Kelsey jumped in straight away to rescue her. It was an incredibly brave thing to do. They could both have drowned.'

Kelsey looked down at her hands, feeling a bit embarrassed. 'Rubbish. It was the only thing to do. Anyway, Daniel jumped in straight away after me.'

'To rescue Kelsey, who was rescuing Lucy.'

'Then a massive wave came and blew us all onto a clump of rocks. Good job it didn't blow us out to sea, otherwise we'd probably still be there.'

'We thought "hurrah, we're on dry land now," but were we, hell! We all huddled together on the bit of rock, hoping the shore was just behind us.'

'Which in fact, it was. Chris found a torch under one of the seats and he flashed it around. Then we saw the land behind us was such a steep cliff, that it would be impossible to climb...'

'And we had the churning sea in front, so we were trapped.'

'You just had to wait to be rescued.'

'Yes. There was nothing we could do. Absolutely nothing.'

'Chris set off the first flare, as a distress signal. We watched it going up and up. It was very bright. We could see it for miles around.'

'But no one else did. So we sat on in the dark, huddled together, waiting.'

Kelsey's mind went back to that terrifying night, sitting in inky-black darkness, Daniel's arms around her, her cheek brushing against the wet, rough jacket he had found in one of the lockers. He smelt of salt water and seaweed and his hands were stiff with cold. Although their situation was so desperate, Kelsey had felt a certain amount of security being so close to him. She had wondered if she would ever see him again when the holiday was over, assuming of course that they were rescued, or whether this was just a brief encounter, a passing attraction. Emma's voice broke into her thoughts.

'We waited for what seemed an age after the first flare went off. We were all cold and wet, and soon we were hungry too, in spite of the picnic lunch and supper on the boat.'

'Wasn't there still food on the boat?'

'There was, of course. But Chris wouldn't let anyone go below and look. He said there was a danger of being trapped if the boat should turn turtle.'

'So how did you pass the time?'

'We sang songs.'

'Fred led the singing. He was always lively and cheerful. He was terrific.'

'When we couldn't remember any more songs we played games.'

'What kind of games?'

'Guessing games, giving clues to guess famous people.'

'And memory games: describing a room or a person.'

'After about an hour Chris let off another flare.'

'How many flares did you have?'

'Six.'

'It must have been quite tense when the sixth one was let off.'

There was silence in the room. Both girls were remembering the feeling of desperation and despair when Chris had let off the last flare. Everyone had prayed, some out loud, for their rescue. It was their lowest moment. It was still dark. They had been marooned for nearly eight hours and nobody seemed to have noticed. No one even knew where they had sailed to.

Verity broke the silence. 'How long did you have to wait after the last flare had been used?'

'At least an hour, wouldn't you say, Kel?'

'At least. It was still dark when Chris set off the last one. We watched it go high up in the sky, really bright. All our hopes were in it.'

'Then it landed in the sea. That was the worst moment.'

'After a while we heard a helicopter in the distance coming towards us. It flew right overhead.'

'We were so excited we jumped up and down, screaming.'

'We took off anything white that we were wearing and waved it madly.'

'It hovered above us for a second or two, shone down a searchlight and then it disappeared. I thought I was going to cry.'

'Me too,' said Kelsey. 'It seemed an age before the helicopter flew back again. Then it hovered over again us for quite a long time. The captain spoke to us through a megaphone. He said: "we saw your flare and we've come to rescue you. Now listen carefully. I'm going to let down a rope with a harness attached and I want one of you to strap themselves onto the harness. When you're quite secure I'll pull you up into the helicopter." '

Fred volunteered to go first. It was a dangerous operation that none of them had ever undertaken before. The captain lowered the rope with a harness attached to it. Fred clipped himself into it and Chris and Daniel checked that he had secured each clip properly.

'Ready?' called the captain through the megaphone.

Fred waved back in reply.

'I'm going to winch you up slowly. Hold on tight - and don't look down.'

Fred waved. The captain started winching, very slowly at first, then a little faster as he assured himself that Fred was securely fastened and coping adequately. Everyone anxiously followed his progress, wondering how frightened he was, knowing that at any moment they would have to go through the same ordeal themselves. At last Fred reached the helicopter and was hauled in. The captain unclipped the harness and let it and the rope down again onto the rocks. Fred leant out of the helicopter and waved. A big cheer went up from down below.

'Which of the girls wants to go next?' asked Chris.

None of them moved or spoke for a few seconds.

'I will,' said Kelsey.

'Well done,' said Chris quietly. He took the rope, hooked her into the harness and he and Daniel checked that she was safe.

'Good luck,' said Chris, giving her a friendly pat on the shoulder. 'And remember: don't look down.'

Daniel put his hand on top of hers for a few seconds. 'Good luck.'

'Okay?' came the captain's voice through the megaphone. Kelsey waved to him and the captain started winching her up slowly. It was the most terrifying experience she had ever endured. The rope swung wildly, the harness cut into her crotch and chafed the inside of her legs. The ground below seemed miles away; the helicopter seemed very small and insecure as it hovered above, the propellers whirring. Three-quarters of the way up she looked down and nearly fainted with fright.

'Don't look down,' yelled the captain. 'You're nearly there. Look up at me,' he ordered, as he grabbed her and hauled her into the helicopter. Fred gave her a big hug, and then she threw up all over the floor of the helicopter.

It took more than three hours for all of them to be rescued. As there was limited space in the helicopter, the captain was forced to make several journeys. They were taken to the First Aid Post in the local town and from there to the hospital in Cagliari, where they were detained overnight. In the morning everyone except Lucy was discharged. They had all made a good recovery from mild hyperthermia and exhaustion, and with advice to take things quietly, keep out of the sun and not put out to sea for a few days, they were allowed back to their hotels to finish their holiday. Lucy, suffering minor concussion and bruising, was discharged three days later.

'Your grandma's quite special,' said Emma as they walked down the road to the bus stop.

'Yes, she's okay, although she's a bit mean with money.'

'You never got round to asking her for a loan, did you?'

'No, I didn't. But she just loved the shipwreck story.'

'Who wouldn't? It's a frightening tale with a happy ending. Thank God we were rescued in time.'

'So we're having a big reunion next week.'

'Yes, won't that be great, seeing everyone again? Do you think we'll always keep in touch, having shared such a traumatic experience?'

'Only time will tell. It's not long since it happened, is it?' Kelsey contemplated telling Emma about her dinner engagement with Daniel the night before, but changed her mind. It would be better to wait and see how the relationship developed. They reached the end of Olive Grove, turned the corner into Wanstead High Street and walked slowly to the bus stop. As Kelsey saw their bus approaching in the distance, she opened her handbag to get out her bus pass.

'Oh, my God! My wallet's gone!'

'What do you mean: gone? You had it on the way here.'

'Yes, I know. I must have left it at Grandma's.'

'How could you have done that?'

'I wanted to show Grandma the holiday photos, so I took the wallet out of my handbag, as it was easier find the photos. But I must have forgotten to put it back. The photos must be there too. I'll have to go back. I have to have my wallet. It holds everything.'

'I'll come too.'

They let the bus drive on past the stop, walked along Wanstead High Street, turned the corner into Olive Grove and went back to Oaklands.

'I'll go in on my own,' said Kelsey. 'Grandma might be resting. She finds visitors tiring.'

She rang the doorbell, which was soon answered by Mary.

'Back already? she asked.

'I left my wallet in Grandma's room by mistake.'

'Oh, dear. Well, you can go straight in if you like.'

Kelsey walked along the corridor and knocked gently on her grandmother's door, but there was no answer. Supposing her grandmother to be sleeping after their visit, she turned the handle quietly and went in. She almost cried out in amazement at the sight that met her eyes. Her elderly grandmother was standing in the centre of the room in the embrace of a man of similar age. He was smartly dressed in grey flannels and a navy blazer and had a mane of thick grey hair. Her grandmother had her back to the door and Kelsey saw with shock that the gentleman's mouth was fully over hers, as he fondled her breasts through her thin blouse.

Unsure as to whether the elderly gentleman had seen her or not, Kelsey closed the door quietly. She would have to manage without her wallet for the moment.

Chapter Twenty-Seven

'But Dan, she's nearly eighty!'

'What's that got to do with it?'

'People of eighty don't kiss!'

'Why ever not?'

'They're too old!'

'What's age got to do with kissing?'

'Kissing's what young people do.'

'Can't old people kiss too?'

'Well, they can - but just a peck on the cheek. Grandma and her friend were kissing properly.'

'I don't see what's wrong with that.'

'It might lead to sex!'

'So what! There's no rule against old people having sex.'

'N-no. There's no rule, but it doesn't seem right.'

'Rubbish! You can have sex at any age after puberty, perhaps even before.'

'Do you really think so?' Kelsey turned to face him with wide-eyed innocence.

'Of course. The whole point of kissing is to do it properly, and then have sex.'

Daniel took her in his arms. She nestled against him for a moment, savouring the strong smell of his tweed jacket. Then she lifted her face to his. He stroked it gently, smiling at her, tracing the contours of her eyebrows, nose, cheeks and mouth. Then he tightened his grip a little on her shoulders and kissed her, gently at first, then penetrating deeper, his tongue entwining with hers. He felt the excitement mounting in his groin, so he withdrew his tongue, brushed her lips gently and held her close for a moment. A pity he had to stop. But in Epping Forest there weren't many places where one could make love out-of-doors without fear of interruption.

'You've stopped kissing,' she said regretfully.

'It was beginning to lead to sex - the problem being that there's nowhere to have it here.'

'One-track mind,' she teased.

'Why not? With such a gorgeous, receptive girl as you.'

'We could always go back to your flat.'

'I was thinking we might, if we can find the car.'

They walked slowly along the forest path, admiring the sun as it made dappled patterns through the trees. It was now late September, the leaves were already turning, but the mossy ground was still dry, springy and pleasant to walk on.

'Have you visited your grandmother since the kissing episode?'

'Oh, yes. I saw her a few days ago.'

'Do you think either of them noticed that you came into the room?'

'No, I don't think so. They were far too involved in each other. Anyway, Grandma and I had a lot to discuss. I asked her for a loan.'

'A loan! Whatever for?'

'To tide me over until my divorce comes through. At the moment I'm refusing to accept maintenance from Nigel until we're divorced, because I'm holding out for a proper settlement. In the meantime, I've had enough of the travel agency, so I'm planning to pack it in and go on a course.'

'Good for you. What sort of course had you in mind?'

'Beautician. Hairdressing. Herbal medicine. Something not too taxing.'

'Oh!' He sounded disappointed.

Kelsey laughed and squeezed his arm. 'We can't all be clever doctors like you. I left school after GCSEs. And remember, I spent most of my time swimming.'

'Yes, I remember. I'll certainly never forget your swimming. How much has your grandmother lent you?'

'Five thousand pounds.'

'Wow!'

'That's nothing to her. She's seriously rich.'

'Would you like to eat at the same restaurant tomorrow in Westcliff-on-Sea as we did the last time?' asked James, as he and Verity strolled arm-in-arm in the garden at Oaklands.

'Well, yes, that would be very nice, if it's not too expensive.'

James laughed and squeezed her arm. 'No expense is too much for you, my dear.'

What a strange lady, he thought: enormously wealthy and yet not prepared to spend any money. They sat down on the bench and surveyed the garden. The late September sun glinted palely on the autumnal leaves, as they were tossed untidily around the paths and flowerbeds by the light wind. Due to a long dry spell, the grass was full of dull patches. The roses were over-blown and all the flowers were fading and dying except the chrysanthemums. Chrysanthemums. James would never forget the chrysanthemums at the funeral just over five years ago. They were in autumnal colours too: brown, gold and soft dull mauves that contrasted with the brilliant white ones. Many of the mourners had remarked on the beautiful flowers even before they had offered their condolences. He always felt a huge sense of relief when 15 September was over and there was a whole year before the next anniversary, each one dreaded as much the last.

James had been deeply shocked when the doctors had told him nine years ago that his wife, Helen, was suffering from senile dementia.

'But she's only sixty-two, Doctor Barnes!'

'Yes, I know Mr Parker. I'm extremely sorry to be the bearer of such bad news.'

'Is - is there any cure?'

'I'm afraid not. It's an irreversible condition, which mainly affects older people. It's more common in those who have had a history of depression and some emotional instability, which I gather is your wife's case.'

'Yes, that's true. So what can I do to help her?'

'Keep her as calm as possible. Provided you feel able to give her sufficient care, she'll be able to continue living at home. But I'm afraid after a while you may find you have to do most of the housework as well.'

'And if I can't take care of her?'

'She would be better off in a residential home.'

Unfortunately, Helen's condition deteriorated much more quickly than Dr Barnes had predicted. Within a few months James found himself devoting a great deal of time to looking after her, as well as coping with all the household chores. Helen had become increasingly difficult and unco-operative, prone to violence and raging tempers. She became obstinate, refusing to eat, wash, or even get out of bed for days on end. She had nightmares in which she dreamt that devils and ghosts were coming to get her and carry her off to hell. Then there were periods of blissful calm when, after an uneventful, almost normal day, they would have dinner together in the kitchen and then go and sit in the living room. But when James switched on the gas fire Helen started screaming that there were devils in the fire coming to get her. Then James switched off the fire, calmed her down and suggested watching television.

'Good idea,' she would say, but as soon as the television was on she would start screaming again that the evil spirits were now in the television and ghosts had come to haunt her. So James turned off the television and they sat in silence in the dark until he could persuade her to go to bed. This situation continued for more than five years. James's son Robert, and his wife, Jennifer, tried to persuade him to put Helen into a residential home for the elderly and mentally disturbed.

'I can't,' said James. 'Helen's my wife and I love her. She's my responsibility. I can't shove that responsibility onto other people.'

Things had now reached the point where Helen could no longer be left on her own without supervision. If James went out for any length of time a carer had to be found. The carer was usually Robert, Jennifer or one of their daughters. Then the situation went from bad to worse. Helen would rant for as much as an hour at a time. Dr Barnes had supplied James with sedatives for these occasions, but the problem lay in getting Helen to take medication when she was having 'one of her fits', as Robert described them. James would give Helen a sleeping draught at bedtime, but the effect had usually worn off by 3.00 am. Then she was up and out of bed, storming around the house, ranting and complaining that everyone was against her, that devils were knocking at the windows and coming to take her away to hell. After nearly four months of traumatic days and broken nights James was completely exhausted.

'Dad, you must go away for a holiday,' insisted Robert. 'Go and stay with a friend or book into a nice hotel by the sea. Jennifer and I will move in and take care of Mum.'

It was the holiday that ended in a nightmare; a holiday that James would never forget.

Verity noticed James's far away look. She suspected he was thinking of his wife and wondered if he would ever be ready to tell her the end of the tragic story.

James had explained that he had something to show Verity before lunch, so the following morning they left Oaklands soon after breakfast. They arrived in Westcliff-on-Sea just before eleven am feeling in need of refreshment. James parked on the front near an attractive looking café called 'The Cliff.'

'I think we need a cup of coffee before we do anything else, don't you?' he said, holding the door open for Verity to go in first.

'This is nice,' she said as they settled into a corner table. They had a cappuccino each and refused a tempting looking gateau.

'I'm thinking of lunch,' said James.

'I'm thinking of my figure,' said Verity.

'You don't need to.'

'That's because I do,' she smiled.

The coffee break over, they got into the car again and drove a little way along the front. It was a calm, still day. The pale autumn sunshine slanted down obliquely, its rays forming silvery streaks on the blue-grey sea. James drove slowly so that he too could admire the view.

'It's beautiful,' he said. 'I do love being beside the sea.'

By the end of the promenade the road curved around to the left, leading to the main town. James took the second turning on the left and drove along a pleasant tree-lined street. At the bottom of the road was a pair of handsome wrought-iron gates with a sign in large letters reading:

'WELCOME TO WESTCLIFF HOMES.' And underneath in smaller letters: 'Sheltered Housing for Retired People. Homes Still Available. Please Apply Within.'

As James operated the remote control switch, the gates opened.

'Oh,' exclaimed Verity admiringly, as they drove through the gates, which closed automatically behind them. They drove slowly down a long curving drive with small, one-storey brick-built houses on either side. Verity's heart began to thump. Where is he taking me? she thought. Why has he brought me here? Perhaps he's bought one of these bungalows and he's planning to leave Oaklands to come and live here and this is his way of cushioning me from the shock.

James took a right-hand turn and slowed up as they reached a cul-de-sac. At the end stood two double-fronted bungalows slightly larger than the rest. Built of soft, yellow-grey brick, resembling London stock, one had a black front door, the other a white one. James helped Verity out of the car.

'Which colour do you prefer?' he asked. 'Black or white?'

'Oh!' said Verity. 'What a difficult choice.' She wasn't sure whether this was one of James's little jokes.

'You can have either,' he said. 'I have the option of buying whichever house you prefer. Because I'm hoping you will marry me and then we shall move out of Oaklands and come and live here. Which one shall we inspect first?'

Chapter Twenty-Eight

Alison was beginning to enjoy life on her own. It was now more than three months since Steven had left for Morocco on his prospecting tour, which he had said would last only two or three weeks. He had sent three more postcards, all with views of Marrakech, containing brief messages. The first one ran: *This city continues to fascinate.* The second card, arriving about three weeks later, contained the message: *Have not forgotten the real purpose of the visit is to expand Sun Med.* The third one, which had arrived yesterday, had the message: *Have become rather involved. Will write soon.*

Alison put all the postcards on the living room mantelpiece. There were now six of them, but no letter and no real explanation as to why her husband had been away so long. During the first six weeks or so of Steven's absence Alison had felt a little uneasy. It was totally out of character for him to take an extended trip without any explanation. She was used to Steven's trips abroad. Since the early days of their marriage he had travelled frequently around various Mediterranean resorts, prospecting, looking for the right hotels in attractive situations that offered good value for money. Resorts with numerous and varied activities to entertain the punters. In the first year of their marriage, before the twins were born, Alison often accompanied Steven on his trips. She had enjoyed them immensely. It was a life of idle luxury she had never experienced before, in hotels with large, airy, pleasant bedrooms and room service; elegant reception areas; spacious lounges; restaurants with pleasant and efficient waiters serving a multitude of exotic dishes that she had neither tasted nor even heard of. In the first year of their marriage Steven had only wanted the best for his wife. They had been married a mere eighteen months when the twins were born, an event that completely changed their lives. Just a month before the birth Alison was informed that she would become the mother of twins. Neither she nor Steven had any idea of what parenthood involved: neither emotionally nor physically. The twins took over their lives to such an extent that Alison was no longer able to accompany Steven on his Mediterranean excursions.

Alison had never been particularly interested in sex. Unlike most girls nearing puberty, she had rarely examined her changing body. The same lack of interest had prevailed during her pregnancy. She had noticed her swelling stomach with distaste, but avoided feeling her enlarged breasts. Although she had been a virgin when she married Steven, she knew what sex entailed. She had learnt about reproduction in biology lessons at school. But she had no yearning whatsoever to experience sex. To Alison, it was a fact of life; a function performed between a man and a woman in order to create a family. She liked Steven. He was attractive to look at; he was attentive, polite and pleasant to be with. But whether she was in love with him was a question she never asked herself. Alison was not a person who analysed her feelings or studied her emotions. She was not easily aroused, either emotionally or sexually. She knew she had a social obligation to find a husband, marry and have children. Once that had been achieved she felt she could relax into organising her life to suit herself. However, there was one drawback. Although the conception of children had been happily achieved with the minimum of effort on her part, it seemed that sex still had to continue. It was an obligation, an on-going duty. Men needed sex. Her husband needed sex and it was her duty to succumb. So succumb she did, lying passively on their king-size bed while Steven worked himself up into a lather, trying to give her an orgasm before he came inside her. But his timing was invariably wrong. Desperate for sexual release, dimly aware that his wife never seemed to participate fully, or give herself in the sexual act, he usually came too soon. And with muttered apologies: 'Darling I'm so sorry, I'll make it last longer next time,' he would fall asleep on top of her.

As their years of marriage wore on, Steven and Alison inevitably had less and less sex. As Steven's financial worries increased and he started drinking too much, his capabilities diminished. This suited Alison perfectly and she assumed that her husband no longer needed sex. For a while Steven thought so too. Until one night he dreamt about Guy, the prefect at school, and he ejaculated in his sleep. Now with Steven away for more than three months, Alison could sleep peacefully on her own in the large comfortable bed without any guilty feelings of not fulfilling her marital obligations.

With her new-found freedom, Alison was finding that life was enjoyable and very full. She would arrive home from work in the afternoon at about half past four. She would make a cup of tea, put her feet up on the sofa and, as likely as not, doze off for half an hour. On waking, she would tidy away the tea things, have a shower, change and plan her evening. She didn't crave company; she had no fear of silence and no need to fill in the time with any specific activity. She was self-contained, well organised and extremely independent. Usually her first pursuit after the shower was to read *The Daily Telegraph* from cover to cover. Although it arrived on the doormat every morning, she rarely had time to do more than glance at the headlines before she went off to work. She studied the TV listings last, fearing that if she started watching television too early in the evening, the newspaper would remain unread. Having selected the programmes she had decided to watch, she would plan her evening meal. If there was a good film she would watch it while she ate. If the evening consisted of only one or two short programmes of interest, she would slot her dinner in between.

Most evenings she phoned her mother. She still felt guilty that she had managed to persuade Verity to go into Oaklands against her will after the accident. But now that Verity had been happily ensconced for several months, Alison found her pangs of guilt abating. In fact, she was amazed how well her mother had settled in. Verity had always been so proud and independent, refusing help with shopping or cooking, walking to the High Street with her shopping cart. She was also, thought Alison ruefully, a social snob, just as she was herself. Her snobbery had increased with her wealth and little remarks like: 'Such a pity they couldn't have afforded a private education.' 'He was in a public ward in the hospital, poor thing!' and 'He speaks with a terrible cockney accent,' always amused Alison. Her mother had, after all, married the son of a costermonger in Petticoat Lane, making it all the more extraordinary that she had settled so well into the social environment at Oaklands, which earlier she would have felt was beneath her. Alison would smile to herself when Verity described Marjorie Grimes, the chocolate packer, Elsie Morrison, the shop assistant, Brenda Barnes the hairdresser and Mabel Cooke, with her constantly slipping orange wig. Stories of their domino game made Alison laugh and the attitude of Miss Price, as described by Verity, reminded Alison of the senior mistress at her school.

If Steven were ever to return to London and his business, Alison wanted to be sure that everything was in tip-top running order. At this point she was still saying to herself: 'when Steven comes home...' Three and a half months later she was beginning to say to herself: 'if Steven comes home...'

Tom Sprockett, the temporary manager engaged by Alison to run Sun Med in Steven's absence, had turned out extraordinarily well. He had now completely taken charge. He had redecorated the office, redesigned the brochure and had fly-posters printed, which he distributed to all the shops in the High Street, managing to persuade most of the shopkeepers to display them. He advertised in the local press, in three of the dailies and in *The Sunday Times Magazine*. The result was that the punters flocked to Sun Med to book their holidays and the money flowed in. After three months Alison gave Tom a pay rise, and then offered him the post of manager on a permanent basis.

Alison was now back full time in her post as secretary of St Mary's School. The headmaster had been overjoyed to have her back.

'Alison! It's wonderful to have you here again!' he said. 'That Edna Rust was the most terrible woman. Although she was completely disorganised, she managed to rule with a rod of iron. She also insulted the parents and terrorised most of the children.'

Alison had barely finished her first week back at work before Ron went straight to the board of governors and requested them to give Alison a pay rise. 'Mrs Hobbs has been at the school for fourteen years,' he pointed out. 'She's worth her weight in gold.'

An immediate pay rise was granted without question.

It had taken Alison quite some time to come to terms with Kelsey's problems: the matrimonial problem above all. Alison didn't really understand her daughter's attitude to marriage.

'Why does a marriage have to be a partnership, darling?'

'A marriage is for sharing. You shared everything with Dad.'

'I suppose so.' Now that her husband hadn't been around for more than three months, Alison wasn't sure.

'Didn't Nigel share things with you?'

'No. He was a totally selfish bastard.'

'He always helped you with the washing up whenever Daddy and I went around to dinner at your flat.'

'That was a show he put on for you and Dad.'

'Oh!' Alison's eyebrows went up.

'Besides, there's more to marriage than just sharing the washing up.'

'Yes. I suppose there is,' said Alison, thinking of the innumerable times she had lain passively on the bed, with Steven heaving, pushing and blowing on top of her like a randy bull. She looked sideways at her pretty daughter. Kelsey had gained a little weight since recovering from her miscarriage and the resultant illness. She was no longer scraggy and anorexic looking. It never occurred to Alison that perhaps Kelsey had been anorexic, or even worse, bulimic. Kelsey had now managed to control her problem and the result was a gently rounded figure. The contours of her face had softened too, her dark wavy hair shone and her skin glowed, as if it harboured some pleasant secret. Alison didn't like to imagine her daughter in bed with a man. The thought seemed rather distasteful, even obscene. Even so, she couldn't help wondering whether Kelsey shared her dislike of sex, whether perhaps sexual incompatibility hadn't been the main problem between her and Nigel. But it was not for her to ask; and anyway she wouldn't have known how to broach the subject. Little did she know how highly sexed her pretty daughter really was.

'So I'm going on this course,' Kelsey was saying.

'That's nice, dear,' said Alison vaguely, trying to tear herself away from bedroom problems. 'What does the course involve?'

'It's a comprehensive, all-round beauticians' course. It includes diet and massage as well as make-up, manicure and pedicure.'

'That sounds great,' said Alison, trying to be enthusiastic. 'How long does it last?'

'Nine months.'

'And I suppose Nigel's financing it.'

'No. Grandma is.'

'Grandma! Really! You managed to get some money out of Grandma! Was it a gift, or just a loan?'

'A loan.' said Kelsey, hoping her mother wouldn't ask how much.

'Well, I won't ask how much, darling. But well done.' I hope the rest of us will be equally successful, she thought. 'And now about Grandma's eightieth birthday party. I've booked a private room at the Prince of Wales Hotel in Chigwell for Sunday 15 December, at lunchtime...'

When Alison arrived home from school the following day there was an airmail letter on the doormat with an exotic-looking stamp. She picked it up, took it into the kitchen and put it on the table without studying it. I bet it's from Steven, she thought. But I'll make some tea before I open it. She made the tea, put it on a tray with a chocolate wafer biscuit, laid the airmail letter and a letter-opener beside it and carried it all into the living room. She put the tray on the coffee table in front of the sofa, poured herself a cup of tea and picked up the letter. It was postmarked: *Marrakech, Maroc.* She turned the letter over and read the sender's name and address in her husband's familiar handwriting: *From Steven Hobbs, c/o Lars Lindstrom, Villa Bellevue, Marrakech, Morocco.* Alison picked up the letter-knife and slit open the envelope.

Dear Alison,

I feel very guilty for having delayed so long in writing. I wanted to write to you very much but I just didn't know how to express my feelings in words, and I still don't. The longer I put off writing to you the more difficult it has become. I spent the first two weeks here prospecting for hotels for Sun Med. Morocco is a truly beautiful country and there are many excellent opportunities for tourist development by a younger and more energetic person than I am. Sadly, I no longer feel cut out to be a travel agent.

The truth is, Alison, I have met and fallen in love with someone else. I am truly sorry to drop such a bombshell in a letter, but I have no plans to return to England at present. I would like to thank you for twenty-five happy years of marriage and companionship, which I regret have now come to an end. I have found happiness and fulfilment with my new lover, a Swede called Lars Lindstrom. Lars has helped me to be open about my homosexuality and come to terms with what I have known but tried to repress ever since puberty.

I now feel free; free and able to live life openly and honestly as nature intended I should. I regret very much distressing you in this way but there is no alternative other than for us to divorce. I am sorry I do not have much to offer you financially. Your mother owns all I possess, so perhaps she will be able to help you. However, if you should be unsuccessful in approaching your mother, (who is not renowned for her generosity), let me know and I will see what I can do. Lars is extremely wealthy and I feel sure he will want do what he can to cement our new relationship.

When you have thought this over perhaps we can discuss the divorce details on the telephone.

Affectionately, Steven.

Alison stared at the letter in disbelief, crumpled it up and burst into tears.

Chapter Twenty-Nine

'Poor old Ali. Steven's left her.'

'Left her!' Graham put down his newspaper with a sharp rustling sound, letting a sheet fall unnoticed to the floor. 'Did you say Steven has left Alison?'

'That's just what I said.'

'But why?'

'He's met someone else.' Julia lifted the lid off the teapot and inspected the contents. The pot was empty. 'Glad you made yourself some tea.'

'I wondered where you were. I was thirsty, so I decided to go ahead without you.'

Julia heaved her great bulk off the sofa with considerable difficulty.

'Ali rang while you were out and asked me to pop round. But I'd no idea I'd be there two hours.' She picked up the teapot from the tray. 'I'll just freshen this up a bit.'

'Didn't Alison offer you any tea? Especially if you were there two hours.'

'No. She was too upset. Back in a minute.'

Julia took the teapot to the kitchen, put it down on the working top and switched on the electric kettle. The water was still hot, so it didn't take long to come to the boil. The remaining tea in the pot was warm and the tea leaves looked quite fresh. She went to the cupboard, took out

the tea caddy, added another heaped spoonful and poured in the boiling water. She replaced the tea caddy in the
cupboard and looked around for some cake or biscuits.
She took out a tin marked 'Cake' and opened it. It was
empty. She sighed. That was last night, she thought
ruefully. That was the four am raid. She replaced the cake
tin and took out a cylindrically shaped one with a design
of different chocolate biscuits leaping about on it. She
opened it with cautious optimism. She remembered
yesterday it was still half-full, but she could have emptied
that in the night too. She did have a tendency to binge
when practically asleep. Hurrah! The tin was still half-
full. She selected four different types of biscuit, arranged
them on a plate, shut the tin and replaced it in the
cupboard. When she returned to the living room with the
tray she noticed that Graham hadn't picked up the paper
again, but was sitting bolt upright, staring into space. She
put the tray on the coffee table and picked up the teapot.

'Another cup?'

'No thanks.'

'Biscuit?'

'No thanks.'

Julia poured herself a cup of tea and added a little
milk. She took a sweetener out of her handbag and
popped it into the cup. She took the largest chocolate
biscuit off the plate and bit it in half. Graham was
watching her intently all the time.

'Aren't you going to tell me more about Alison?'

'Yes, of course.' Julia put the second half of the biscuit
on her plate. 'It's just that I was rather hungry.'

'So I see. Why has he left her?'

'As I said: he's met someone else.'

'In Morocco?'

'Yes.'

'Someone much younger?'

'It appears so.'

'And is she prettier than Alison?'

'I don't know about prettier. He's a man.'

'A man! A bloke! You mean - Steven's gay!'

'So it seems.'

'Good God! No wonder Alison was too upset to offer you tea! That's appalling!'

'Do you think it's worse that Steven's gone off with a man rather than a woman?'

'Don't you?'

'I hadn't really thought about it.'

'How would you feel if I went off with another man?'

'I'd be much more upset that you'd left me than by the fact that you'd gone off with another man. Would you be really shocked if I went off with another woman?'

'Yes. Far more shocked than if you went off with another man.'

'I don't think the sex makes a great deal of difference. It's the desertion that counts.'

'Which has shocked Alison the most?'

'The desertion.'

'I suppose it would. She's probably more accustomed than I am to having gays in the family. And now we've got two!'

'Graham! I didn't know you were anti-gay!'

'I didn't either. Poor old Alison. What's she going to do? Agree to a divorce?'

'She doesn't have much option, does she?'

'What about money?'

'Well, as you know, Steven is absolutely skint. Don't you remember that Mother bailed them out ten years ago?'

'Yes. Of course I remember. But I thought the business was well on its way to recovery.'

'Apparently not.'

'So what's going to happen to poor Alison?'

'She's asked me to go and see Mother.'

'To ask her for money?'

'Well, yes.'

'So Steven's not offering her anything, although he walked out on her?'

'Yes. He has in a way. Apparently his boyfriend is extremely wealthy and Steven has hinted that he might help Alison financially.'

'Thank God for that.'

'But she won't take it.'

'Why not?'

'She thinks it's dirty money.'

'I see. So she's asked you to go to your mother instead.'

'Exactly.'

Graham picked up his paper from the floor. 'We could all do with a bit of your mother's money.'

'Couldn't we just.' Julia munched her way through the remaining three biscuits.

Sudip slit open the airmail letter carefully. As he read the contents his mouth widened into a huge grin. When he had finished reading he threw the letter into the air and let out a loud: 'Whoopee!'

Russell looked at his friend across the breakfast table with some amusement. Sudip was usually so calm and controlled. Even the news of his father's death hadn't appeared to upset him visibly. He had just become even quieter. This expression of joy was quite unprecedented. Sudip got up from the table and started dancing around the room chanting: 'hooray! Hooray! What a wonderful day!' chanting it at least four times. His happiness was infectious. Russell was smiling broadly now.

'Aren't you going to let me into your wonderful secret?'

Sudip came over and gave him a hug. 'I certainly am. We're rich.'

'That's nice. Shall we go on another holiday?'

'We can go on holiday for the rest of our lives.'

'What do you mean?'

'We can retire. Stop working for ever and go and live wherever we like.'

'How? Why? I mean…'

'I mean we are seriously rich.'

'You mean you are seriously rich.'

'What's mine is yours. You know that.'

Russell felt a warm glow coming over him.

'So, what's happened?'

Sudip retrieved the letter from the floor and waved it in the air. 'This is from the family solicitor in Jaipur.'

'I thought it was from India. What has he written?'

'He's written to say that one of the clauses in my father's will was to authorise the sale of the family jewels.'

'Family jewels? Did you know they existed?'

'Oh, yes. But their value has quite exceeded my expectations. They've been sold for several million.'

'Rupees, or pounds?'

'Pounds.'

'What were they?'

'Sapphires and rubies mainly. Not so many diamonds, which made me feel they were not so valuable.'

'What marvellous news! Who gets all the money?'

'Well, my mother receives half and the rest will be divided between me, my two sisters and my brother.'

'So…?'

'Apparently I'm going to get just over four million.'

'Four million pounds? That's means that altogether there is…' Russell did a quick calculation. 'Thirty-two million pounds. Some jewels. That's amazing! How did such valuable jewels come into your family in the first place?'

'It's a collection going back several generations. Many of the jewels were gifts of gratitude and thanks. You see, my grandfather was a Maharajah.'

'A Maharajah! And you never told me!'

'No. We all have our little secrets. But I would have got around to it some time.'

'I think this calls for a major celebration, don't you?

'Certainly.'

'Frederick's?'

'How about somewhere even more grand?'

'Like?'

'Le Pont de la Tour?'

'They mightn't have a table for tonight.'

'Then we'll go somewhere else tonight and have the real celebration next week. There's plenty of money to spend on celebrating.'

The two men walked along the riverfront from the restaurant, planning to pick up a cab on Tower Bridge.

'Wasn't it an odd coincidence running into your brother-in-law like that in Marrakech?' asked Sudip conversationally.

'It certainly was. I couldn't believe my eyes when I saw him holding hands with a bloke.'

'A nice bloke too, wasn't he?'

'Very nice. I've always liked the fair-haired ones.'

Sudip laughed, his perfect teeth flashing white in his dark face. 'So that's why you picked me.'

'Exactly.'

'Had you any idea he was gay?'

'Absolutely none.'

'What about your sister? Did she have any idea?'

'Oh, I'm sure she didn't have an inkling either. You know, she heard from him the other day.'

'Really? I wondered how long he was going to hang on in silence. Did he ask her for a divorce?'

'He did.'

'I suppose she'll hold out for a substantial settlement. After all, she's the one who's been wronged.'

'She certainly is the injured party. But whether she'll get much of a settlement is very doubtful. It seems that Steven is on his uppers.'

'Uppers?'

'Yes. It's another slang word for broke.'

'Why is he broke? What about the travel firm? I thought he and Alison were business partners.'

'They were until about ten years ago. Then Steven over-stretched himself by expanding into the Far East.'

'So what happened?'

'Mother bailed them out.'

'Your mother rescued the business?'

'Yes. At a price. She insisted on taking over every-thing they possessed - the house, the granny flat, and the business. Everything they owned is on Verity's account, making thousands of pounds a day on the Stock Ex-change. Steven and Alison have nothing to their name except the clothes they stand up in.'

'How dreadful! So what's going to happen to poor Alison?'

'She's forced to go begging to Mother.'

'How terribly undignified.'

'Yes. It is, isn't? She's asked Julia to intercede for her.'

'Poor Alison,' said Sudip feelingly.

'Yes. Poor old Alison. Thank God I don't have to rely on Mother's money any more.'

'Yes. Thank God you don't.'

Sudip squeezed his arm and hailed a taxi.

Chapter Thirty

Gladys Bates couldn't sleep. It was unusual for Gladys to sleep badly. Normally she fell into a deep sleep the moment her head touched the pillow. Of course she had to get up in the night to go to the lavatory. They all did. Old people with old bladders. Gladys wasn't among the luckier, more privileged residents to have her own bathroom. People like Verity Davis, who had so much money she could buy anything she wanted. Gladys didn't dislike Verity. She liked her, and admired her elegance and impeccable sense of style. But even so, there were times when Gladys felt twinges of jealousy at Verity's effortless success and obvious affluence. She envied Verity her beautiful clothes, her elegant bearing, and her stream of visitors bearing gifts of flowers, chocolates and expensive toiletries. Verity always shared her gifts, and was extremely generous with things she didn't want. But there was often that touch of superiority, of the Lady Bountiful about her.

'I don't really need this perfume, dear,' she said, giving a large bottle of Givenchy Amarige to Elsie Morrison, who couldn't believe her luck, even though she had never heard of Amarige or Givenchy. Even so, she felt she ought to protest, just a little.

'I couldn't take it, Verity. Not such a large bottle.'

'Of course you can, dear. Julia, my younger daughter, brought me an equally large bottle of Chanel No. 5 last week. I've already started it so I'd been delighted if you were to accept this one as a little gift. Soon there won't be enough space in my room for all my presents!'

Verity laughed her light infectious laugh, pressing the large bottle of perfume into Elsie's hands. Then there was Verity's string of successes in their domino games. After her first substantial gain, Verity had continued to win more games than anyone else. She never apologised about her success, she was quite matter-of-fact about it.

'It's lucky Alison's dropping by tomorrow,' she said, after she had won £400. She'll be able to bank this for me.'

Gladys was beginning to wonder what proportion of Verity's bank account consisted of her domino winnings. But what Gladys really resented about Verity, what rankled her most, was her friendship with James Parker. James and Verity were making no secret of their friendship. They sat together at lunch and dinner in the dining room, they sat at the same low table in the lounge for afternoon tea and they watched television together. James, always the first to arrive at the domino table, reserved the seat beside him for Verity. After he had said: 'this is Verity's chair,' a few times, everyone accepted it and left the chair vacant. Verity invariably appeared last, a little late, 'making an entrance,' as Mabel had once remarked to Gladys, after a game when Verity had won a lot of money 'to swell her bank account.'

But it was the car drives that Gladys begrudged the most. She had felt quite miffed the first time Verity had mentioned that she had been out for a drive with James. Gladys had just said: 'how nice, dear,' and marched off to the television room. Everyone at Oaklands knew James drove off in his car by himself most afternoons. At first there were various comments. 'You'd think he'd fancy a bit of company, wouldn't you?' or: 'I wouldn't mind going along too.'

But after James had been at Oaklands for more than three years, the residents finally became accustomed to his unaccompanied car drives and had stopped hankering after an invitation. Then bingo! Along comes a new resident who, after a matter of only a few weeks, is invited to go out with him. Gladys couldn't help wondering where they went on their drives: what they actually did and what they said to each other.

Gladys stretched out an arm, switched on the light and looked at the clock on the bedside table. Good heavens! It was twenty minutes past midnight and she had been awake for over two hours! Although there was no 'bedtime rule' at Oaklands, the residents were not encouraged to stay up late. With dinner over by seven pm, most residents found little to do to fill in the time before going to bed, unless they were expecting visitors. Television was the mainstay of their entertainment, television and the domino games, which had now been switched to the evenings after dinner.

'More convenient, don't you think?' said James, after he had suggested the change. 'Fills in the long evenings, especially now that it's getting dark so much earlier.'

And it gives you longer free afternoons on car drives with Verity, thought Gladys at the time. But she said nothing. Unless a game had been planned or one of the members was receiving visitors, the domino group often watched television together after dinner. When the best programmes were over, Brenda Barnes usually drifted off to bed.

'My book always seems to be more gripping in bed,' she would explain. But as she was never seen with a book in her hand, Gladys thought this was just Brenda's excuse for being unable to stay up late. Again, she said nothing. If there were a programme worth watching after nine thirty pm, Gladys and Mabel would sit on and watch with James and Verity. Shortly after ten Miss Price would come in to say 'goodnight' and tell them she was just about to bolt the front door. There was no pressure on anyone to go to bed, but Gladys and Mabel usually took it as a signal that people of their age were expected to retire to bed in order to be fresh for the next day. But fresh for what? When Verity first arrived at Oaklands, she generally followed Gladys's and Mabel's example and also went to her room. But since she had been 'driving out' with James she had also taken to 'sitting on' with him in the evenings and watching television until everyone else was asleep.

Gladys realised she was thirsty. She sat up in bed, slid her legs slowly over the side and reached cautiously for the floor. She fumbled for her slippers, silver with pink pom-poms, stood up slowly and shuffled over to the door where her dressing gown was hanging up. She put it on, struggling a little with the cord, which had come out of its loop. Finally achieving success, she threaded the cord through and tied it in a bow.

She opened the door of her room quietly. She didn't want to wake the sleeping residents, but she was even more anxious not to disturb Miss Price, who was known to have been angry on the occasions when she found residents wandering around the house at night. She crept along the corridor to the bathroom and used the lavatory, appalled by the loud noise the cistern made after she had flushed. She took her tooth-mug down from the shelf above the hand-basin and ran the cold tap. She filled the mug half-way and took a sip. Ugh! Warm water. Disgusting! She decided she would go along the corridor to the kitchen and get a cold drink from the fridge, usually kept well stocked with liberal supplies of chilled tap water, to be served at mealtimes.

The Oaklands' residents all slept on the ground floor and the staff slept upstairs. When the house had been converted into a retirement home more than thirty years ago, two corridor extensions were built, each branching off from the main part of the house in opposite directions. The corridor to the right of the main house, built on land especially purchased at the time, was known as The Field Passage, and the other corridor to the left, extending into the garden, was known as The Garden Passage. Both Gladys and Verity had rooms in The Garden Passage. Gladys's room was right at the end, and although it had a beautiful view of the garden, it was one of the smallest rooms in the house, so Gladys often referred to it as The Box Room.

On her way to the kitchen, Gladys had to pass all the other six rooms along The Garden Passage. Fortunately she had no need to put on any light, for a night-light was always left on. The first five rooms were dark and silent except for muffled snores coming from the direction of Elsie Morrison's room. Verity's room was the last one before the main hallway of the house. As she passed it, shuffling along silently in her silver slippers with the pink pom-poms, Gladys was surprised to see a beam of light shining under the door. I mustn't stumble, she thought, fully aware that Verity had sharper ears than most of the other residents at Oaklands. Suddenly

Gladys heard a low moan coming from Verity's bedroom. She froze. Verity wasn't well! Perhaps she was having a heart attack! Should she knock on the door and ask if she was all right? Gladys paused by the door, her arm uplifted, ready to knock. Then she heard another sound; a low cry of pleasure. Then a man's voice said: 'darling, you were marvellous. Just perfect.'

It was James Parker's voice! James was in Verity's bedroom at half past midnight when all the other residents were fast asleep!

Now Gladys's mouth was extremely dry. Nothing would quench her raging thirst except a glass of really cold water. Realising that Verity and James were probably far too involved in each other to notice any noises in the corridor, she made her way across the hall to the kitchen quarters, pushing open the heavy swing door as quietly as possible. The kitchen was at the side of the house, a large sprawling room with an impractical assembly of ovens, hobs, microwaves, sinks, cupboards and worktops, all haphazardly placed. The light from the street lamp shone in brightly, so there was no need to switch on the electric light. Gladys found a glass in one of the cupboards, so high up on the shelf that she almost dropped it when she took it down. She put the glass on the kitchen table and went across to one of the fridges. Opening it, she discovered that it only contained meat: raw meat and cooked meat. The raw meat was stored on the top two shelves, most of it still wrapped in the paper in which it had been purchased. One of the parcels was slowing dripping blood onto a packet of already opened cooked ham on the shelf below.

'Ugh!' said Gladys out loud, 'what foul unhygienic practice! No wonder three residents have recently died!'

She opened a second fridge, separated from the first one by an old chipped china sink. It contained only vegetables: some fresh and appetising looking, others less so. She looked around the kitchen for a third fridge, feeling sure there must be another one containing milk, fruit juices, and hopefully, plenty of cold water. But there was no third fridge; just two more old chipped china sinks, inconveniently placed, not adjacent to each other. A tall, narrow food cupboard stood next to a very out-dated enamelled gas cooker. Next to the cooker was a door. Gladys opened it cautiously, afraid of hitting the cooker and chipping it even more. The door led into a fairly spacious walk-in larder containing several shelves, well stocked with neatly labelled bottles and jars. In the corner was another fridge, more copiously filled with various types of drinks in bottles and jugs than she could have ever imagined. Gladys burrowed her way into the fridge in search of some really cold liquid, hopefully something a little more interesting than plain chilled tap water. Intent on her search, Gladys hadn't noticed that the larder had an air vent and an open window, set high up, over-looking the entrance to the garage. She found a large jug of gleaming orange juice, lifted it out carefully, carried it into the kitchen and placed it on the table. As she returned to the larder to close the fridge door, she heard voices outside. She stood stock-still, straining to hear what was being said.

'I'm going to put an end to this, Ken,' a woman was saying, her voice shrill with anxiety. 'You're just using my garage as a dump for your stolen goods.'

'My stuff may be stolen but it ain't in there for long. And you owe me,' came a man's voice.

'What do I owe you? I owe you nothing.'

'You know what you owe me. You owe me plenty.'

'What do you mean by that?' The voice increased in pitch.

'I rescued you from sexual frustration. You were so desperate for a man that you stooped low enough to invite the likes of me into your bed.'

There was a moment's silence.

'I wasn't that desperate,' said the woman sulkily. 'You just happened to be the only bloke around at the time.'

'Exactly. So you confided your sad little secret in me. The only person I've ever told, you said. And what a mistake it was too! But of course you didn't know that at the time.'

'What are you getting at now, you scum-bag?'

'I wouldn't advise such dirty language. It doesn't sound nice, coming out of a lady's mouth.'

'What are you implying?' The voice sounded threatening. 'I won't have you holding anything over me.'

'You've no choice. If you refuse me the use of your garidge, I'll make sure everyone knows you're at Oaklands under false pretences. Sister Price! The nerve! You invented your qualifications just so you could take over this home when old Jackson died and left you the house in his will. You've no idea how to run a retirement home! You know nothing about medical care - you don't even know the basic rules of kitchen hygiene! No wonder the old biddies are dying like flies. I don't know how this place has passed any inspection and I don't know what the families of them poor, disintegrating but trusting oldies would say if they knew you was now't but a cheat. If you don't do exactly what I want, I'll tell the whole world you're a lying impostor.'

'You wouldn't ever tell! You wouldn't dare!'

'I'd dare, right enough.'

There was the sound of a heavy door being shut and a car starting up. Then footsteps came along the path by the kitchen window. The side door to Miss Price's private quarters opened and closed and the footsteps faded away into the darkness.

Gladys sat at the kitchen table, rigid with fright; too stunned even to pour herself her much-needed cold drink. Miss Price was an impostor! And her ex-lover a petty criminal! It was all taking place at Oaklands, a retirement home, supposedly a haven for the elderly residents, so they could end their lives in peace and tranquillity.

Suddenly Gladys was overcome with fear and confusion. Her heart thumped loudly, her hands were sweating and her mouth was as dry as a desert. She picked up the heavy jug of orange juice from the table and tried to pour some juice into the glass. As she did so, a fierce pain gripped her chest and shot up her arm. Her hand could no longer hold the heavy jug and it crashed onto the tiled floor with a splash of juice and a loud splintering of glass. Then Gladys slewed sideways, fell off the kitchen chair and landed on the floor in the middle of the mess.

Chapter Thirty-One

Verity followed James down the long hospital ward to the nurses' desk in the centre. The duty nurse looked up and smiled, her casual uniform of loose-fitting grey trousers and pale blue smock making a stark contrast to the smart, stiffly starched white uniform always worn by Miss Price at Oaklands.

'Yes?' asked the nurse, brushing a wisp of stray hair out of her eyes. 'How can I help you?'

'We're looking for a Mrs Bates,' began James, a little anxiously. 'Gladys Bates. I hope she is...?'

The nurse looked at a sheet of paper lying on the desk in front of her, running her finger down a long list of names.

'Yes. Here we are. Bates. Gladys Bates. Bed number 19. She's shown some improvement in the last few days, though you may find her a little bit confused.' She pointed to the bed in the far corner of the ward. 'It's the one over there.'

'Oh, thank you,' said Verity. 'May we just go along and say "hello"? We won't stay long.'

'That's fine,' replied the nurse. 'You can stay as long as you like. I'm sure Gladys will enjoy your visit.'

Verity and James made their way down the long ward. Verity's heart sank at the sight of so many narrow iron beds covered in soulless green counterpanes, some with the curtains drawn round them. The scene rekindled memories of her own stay in hospital after her fall. She no longer admitted to having had a stroke. A stroke sounded so elderly. A fall was more accidental. Anyone could have a fall - at any age. They arrived at the bed in the far corner by the window where Gladys lay, eyes closed, propped up on a mountain of pillows. She was wearing a pink crotched bed-jacket trimmed with white *brodérie anglaise*. Her silver bedroom slippers, complete with pink pom-poms, stood neatly on the floor by the side of the bed. She looked pale and frail and appeared to have shrunk. Verity had a lump in her throat as she sat down in the armchair by the bed and took Gladys's hand.

'Gladys! How are you, dear?'

Gladys stirred and opened her eyes.

'That you, Maureen?'

Verity threw James an anxious glance. 'No. It's not Maureen, dear. It's Verity.'

'Verity,' said Gladys slowly, with a little difficulty. 'Verity. Where's Maureen?'

'I think her daughter's called Maureen,' James murmured in Verity's ear.

'Has Maureen been in to see you?' enquired Verity brightly.

' No, I don't think so.' Gladys didn't seem quite sure.

'Maybe she's away on holiday,' said Verity encoura-gingly.

'Yes, that's it! I remember now!' Gladys tried to sit up by propping herself up on one elbow. 'They've gone to the Bahamas for three weeks. They left on 3 October so they'll be back soon, won't they?'

She slumped back against the pillows, worn out by the sudden exertion.

'They will, of course,' said Verity soothingly. 'Meanwhile, we thought we'd come along in Maureen's place, didn't we James?'

'James?' Gladys opened her eyes again. Her voice brightened. 'Hello, James, how are you?'

'I'm fine, Gladys, thank you. How are *you*?'

'I'm thirsty.'

'Shall I pour you a glass of water?' asked James.

'Is there any orange juice?'

James looked on top of the tiny bedside locker. 'No. I don't see any.'

'Look inside the locker,' suggested Verity, helpfully.

James got up and opened the bedside locker. It was empty, apart from a small packet of Kleenex.

'No orange juice.'

'We'll bring you some tomorrow,' said Verity, reassuringly.

'Thank you,' said Gladys.

James picked up the jug and half filled the tumbler, which stood beside it. Gladys began to giggle.

'You know, the jug was so heavy I couldn't lift it off the table.'

'Which table was that?' asked Verity, knowing full well that Gladys had been in the kitchen at the time of her stroke. The staff had found her early the next morning, sprawled on the floor in a pool of orange juice, lying among shards of broken glass. Everyone at Oaklands knew what had happened. Verity was just curious to hear Gladys's own version, and discover why she had gone to the kitchen in the first place.

James passed the half filled tumbler to Gladys.

'Thank you, dear.' Gladys drank most of the water and handed the glass back to James.

'You were thirsty.'

'Yes. It was a hot night,' said Gladys. 'I decided I needed a really cold drink so I went along to the kitchen. There were lots of fridges, five or six I think. I looked in about three before I found anything to drink. You know, some of the fridges were quite disgusting. One held rotten vegetables. Another one had raw meat dripping onto slices of unwrapped ham. No wonder people were dying!'

James and Verity looked at each other in some bewilderment. Was her story to be believed?

'At last I found the fridge full of milk, water and orange juice.' Gladys continued. 'I took this enormous jug out of the fridge and put it on the kitchen table. When I went back to close the fridge, I heard voices outside by the garage. I realised it was Miss Price talking to a man. She was saying... she was saying...' Gladys closed her eyes. All the talking had exhausted her.

'What was Miss Price saying?' asked Verity, feeling it was important that Gladys should continue her story before she completely lost her train of thought.

Gladys frowned, trying to concentrate. 'She was angry.'

'Angry?'

'With the man.'

'Why was that?'

'He'd been dumping stolen goods in her garage. She wanted them out of it, but for some reason - for some reason the man had a hold on her. He was threatening her.'

'What sort of hold.'

Gladys wrinkled up her nose. I'm not sure. I think it had something to do with sex.'

'Sex!' Verity and James exchanged another glance.

'Or maybe I'm just confused,' said Gladys. 'You see, on my way to the kitchen, along The Garden Passage, I passed all those rooms. Bedrooms, I suppose. Most of the rooms were in darkness. I could hear snoring coming from one of them, but another had a light on under the door. I heard little grunts and moans. At first I thought the occupant was having a heart attack and I felt I should go in and see if she was okay. But then I heard another voice in the room. It seemed as if there was a man in there as well. It crossed my mind that they might be having sex. But I don't think they could've been, do you? Not in a retirement home. It wouldn't be right, would it?'

Verity felt a constriction in her chest and dryness in her throat. She hoped James wouldn't look at her.

'I'm sure you were mistaken, dear,' she said briskly.

'I think I'm getting mixed up,' said Gladys. 'Maureen will get me sorted out when she gets back from her holiday.'

'Of course she will,' said James, not knowing quite what to think or say.

'The man Miss Price was talking to was called Ken,' said Gladys, and worn out with so much talking and trying to remember, she went straight off to sleep.

Since Gladys's sudden departure by ambulance to the local hospital just over a week ago, Mabel Cooke was feeling strangely bereft. She had no idea she would miss Gladys so much. She hadn't consciously realised how much of the day they usually spent together; watching television, strolling in the garden, or just sitting in companionable silence in the lounge. Mabel had received a great shock when Mary came into her room the following morning to tell her that Gladys had been taken to hospital during the night.

'What happened, Mary?'

'Mrs Bates had a stroke, dear.'

'Where? In her bed?'

'No, she wasn't in her bed. She was found early in the morning lying on the kitchen floor in a pool of orange juice and a heap of broken glass.'

'What was Gladys doing in the kitchen?'

'We don't know yet. She's drifting in and out of consciousness.'

'Will she pull through?'

Mary didn't want to raise false hopes. But she didn't want to be unkind either. 'It's hard to say at the moment. She may rally.'

'I'll miss Gladys if she dies.' Mabel got out of bed and walked slowly into the bathroom.

A few days later Mabel sat in the lounge, slumped in a chair, her head lolling sideways, her orange wig slightly askew over one eye. A copy of *Hello* magazine lay open on her lap and she was fast asleep. As James sat down in a chair opposite, Mabel stirred, sat up and straightened her wig, as the copy of *Hello* slid off her lap onto the floor. James leant forward and retrieved it.

'I didn't mean to disturb you, Mabel,' came James's reassuring voice. ' But we thought you'd like to know how Gladys is getting along.'

'We?' said Mabel in some confusion, looking around for a third person.

'Verity and I have just been to visit Gladys this afternoon.'

'How is she?'

'Making quite good progress, I'd say. Oh! Here's Verity. I'm sure she'd love to tell you all the news herself.'

Verity came across the room to join them, tall, straight and dignified, no longer needing her stick. She smiled down at Mabel.

'Has James told you? We've just been to see Gladys.'

'How is she?'

'A bit confused.'

'I suppose that's to be expected. What was she doing in the kitchen?'

'She says she was looking for a cold drink.'

'What's wrong with a drink from the bathroom tap?'

'She didn't say.'

'Do you think she'll survive?'

'I'd say so. By the end of our visit she was almost her usual self. She had quite a lot to tell us, too.'

'Oh, yes. Such as?'

'Well...' began Verity, and stopped. She wasn't sure how much she ought to say. Not yet. The name Ken had rung a bell. She somehow connected the name Ken with Graham, her son-in-law. She was pleased that Julia and Graham were coming to see her tomorrow. She would tell them all about the conversation that Gladys had overheard outside the garage during the night she had suffered her stroke. Perhaps they would be able to make more sense of it than either she or James had been able to do.

'No, Verity, I really had no idea.' Graham realised the statement made him sound rather inefficient, even a bit pathetic.

'You mean to say the man had been working for you for almost ten years and you had no idea that he was stealing your materials and selling them off elsewhere! And he was actually your manager for several months.'

'Self-appointed, Mother,' Julia interceded. 'Graham had no choice or say in the matter. He was, at the time, lying on his back in hospital, in traction,' she added for good effect. It was important the story didn't make Graham look weak. The true purpose of telling Verity everything in such detail was to enlist her financial support. Ken Spooner's lying, cheating and stealing had almost bankrupted Brookes Builder's and Julia and Graham were looking to Verity for *a very big rescue*.

'So at first it seemed that this Spooner was trying to help,' said Verity, trying to get the sequence right in her mind.

'Yes,' said Graham. 'When the recession started to bite after the bank crisis, Ken suggested that to save a bit of money we should get our supplies from a mate of his instead of from Travis Perkins, as we had always done in the past. And the mate wouldn't charge VAT either.'

'So at the beginning, his suggestion worked.'

'Yes, but then the recession worsened and we needed to save even more money.'

'Oh, dear!' said Verity. 'You should have come to me for some financial assistance.'

'We did, Mother,' said Julia. 'But you said that your finances weren't up to it at that particular time. After all, you had recently helped Steven and Alison quite considerably.'

Oh, dear, thought Julia. I haven't told her about Alison's latest plight. We'll have to finish the Brookes Builders' saga now and I'll come back tomorrow on my own and tell her about poor Ali.

'I see,' said Verity, thinking: all they ever want is my money. But all she said was: 'so what's the connection between your Ken Spooner and Pamela Price?'

'Apparently they were former lovers and he managed to blackmail her because of her past indiscretions. So she had no choice except to receive all his stolen goods and keep them in her garage.'

So there was some mention of sex in the conversation that Gladys overheard, thought Verity. I wonder if she really heard noises as she passed my bedroom? Or did she imagine it? Instead she asked: 'here at Oaklands? It's quite a small garage. There isn't much room to store any bulky building materials.'

'Quite right,' said Graham. 'But that was only the first stop. The main distribution depot was the Queen Anne House near Roydon that Brookes Builders was renovating. Ironic, don't you think, that the property I was working on was being used as a depository for stolen goods? Much of which had been stolen from us in the first place.'

'Yes. That is ironic,' said Verity. 'And I suppose the day you called round there to have a look at the place a few months ago, they were handling the stuff.'

'Yes. We were pretty sure it was Ken because we saw the red car outside. The car that followed me the day I had that dreadful accident.'

'And was it Spooner's car?'

'No. Unbeknown to me, Ken had already sold the car to my chippie, Mick Kelly.'

'And it was Mick Kelly who followed Graham on the day of the accident,' explained Julia.

'Why was he following you, Graham?'

'He said he wanted to return my mobile phone, which I had left in Spooner's office.'

'How did the carpenter get into the office if Spooner wasn't there? Presumably Spooner had locked his office before he went off?'

'He had locked it. But Mick had a key.'

'So Mick's involved with the thefts too?'

'Yes. They're all involved.'

'So who made the call on your mobile from the scene of the accident?'

'Mick Kelly.'

'Will he be prosecuted for leaving the scene of a serious accident?'

'Not at the moment. He's in hospital with severe injuries.'

'How did he get them?'

'He was badly beaten up by two men called Eddie and George on the very day that Julia and I called at the Queen Anne House.'

'Are they employees of yours?'

'They were. But now they're facing charges for theft. And an additional one of inflicting grievous bodily harm.'

'So what's happened to Ken Spooner?'

'He's in prison, on remand, awaiting trial for theft and embezzlement.'

'And Miss Price? Come to think of it, I haven't seen her around lately.'

'Then she's probably helping police with their enquiries.'

'In which case she may well end up in prison too.'

'Exactly.'

Chapter Thirty-Two

Susie threw herself onto the sofa and burst into tears.

'Whatever's the matter, Sue?' asked Nigel in a voice full of concern.

'It's twins! I had an X-ray today and it's been confirmed. I'm going to have twins! Bloody hell!'

'But that's terrific news! It'll all be over in one go. We've got a two-in-one bargain.'

'What do you mean?'

'Well, we'll have our ready-made family all in one delivery. Two for the price of one.'

'You make it sound like a special offer.'

'That's just what it is.'

Now more than eight months pregnant, Susie was so huge that she could barely walk. She felt tired, listless, miserable and extremely apprehensive at the thought of how much work twins would entail. And she couldn't make Nigel understand that they shouldn't have sex.

'Nigel, no!' she exhorted in bed.

'But I want to!' he protested. 'You see, you want it too. There!' murmured Nigel, putting in his leg across, in preparation for mounting her.

'No, no! Stop, Nigel. Please stop! It's bad for the babies!'

'Who said sex was bad for babies?'

'My doctor.'

'Why should making love be bad for babies?'

'They might get an infection.'

'Why should they get an infection from making love? That's how they were created in the first place.'

'It's just a sensible precaution.'

'To hell with your sensible precaution! I'm overdue for sex! I haven't had any for almost a month.'

Susie went into labour early the following morning. Nigel called an ambulance and went with her to the hospital. Twenty-eight painful hours later she gave birth to twin boys, born three weeks prematurely and weighing only four and a half pounds each. They were immediately placed in an incubator. Susie was distraught.

'It's all your fault they're premature. If you hadn't been so selfish and demanded sex at the wrong time I would have given birth to full-term babies. On top of it all we're not even married. It's about time you got on the blower to that precious Kelsey of yours and demanded a divorce. One child born out of wedlock would have been bad enough. Now we've got two.'

Nigel went home and called his solicitor.

'Nigel's floozy's had twins,' said Julia, filling up Graham's teacup.

'Really? And when did this great event take place?'

Graham took a delicate cucumber sandwich from the paper doily-covered silver salver, which Julia still used for afternoon tea. Graham thought it out-dated and horribly pretentious, but as it had been, along with several others, a wedding present from Julia's parents, he held his counsel and said nothing.

'Just a few days ago.'

'Who told you?'

'Kelsey.'

'Good Lord! How did she hear?'

'From Nigel.'

'Nigel told Kelsey his girlfriend has had twins! Bit tactless, wasn't it?'

'I don't think Nigel has ever been renowned for his tact.'

'No. But I suspect he had an ulterior motive.'

'You're right, of course. Now that he's the father of twins he wants to speed up the divorce proceedings.'

'Understandably. What's stopping him?'

'Money.'

'Money again.'

'Yes.'

'Who's asking for the money this time?'

'Kelsey.'

'Of course. Even though she walked out on Nigel she had every reason to.'

'Exactly. Nigel cheated on her badly.'

'So what's the problem?'

'I gather from Kelsey that Nigel is pleading poverty and not offering to make any maintenance arrangements.'

'That doesn't really surprise me. Nigel's as mean as he's unfaithful.' Graham took another delicate cucumber sandwich. 'These are particularly delicious, darling.'

'Yes, they are, aren't they?' Julia took two and popped them into her mouth together.

'So what is Kelsey planning to do? Will she sit and wait until Nigel pays up? Will she take him to court, or will she simply go to your mother with her begging bowl?'

'Apparently she's already been to Mother to ask for a loan to finance this course she's planning to do.'

'And did your mother oblige?'

'Oh, yes. Kelsey said Grandma had been quite generous.'

'Excellent! That augers well for the rest of us.'

Julia laughed, filled their cups and helped herself to two more cucumber sandwiches. She picked up a leaflet from the coffee table beside the sofa.

'I found some information about language courses.'

'Oh, yes. Where are they?'

'Quite close by.'

'Good. Which language have you picked out?'

'French and Spanish.'

'French *and* Spanish. I don't think my brain could cope with learning two foreign languages at once.'

'I wasn't suggesting that we'd learn two. It's a choice of one or the other, depending on whether you want to go and live in France or Spain.'

'I don't know anything about living in either country until we go there and have a look.'

'Which we'd enjoy more if we spoke the language.'

'It sounds like a chicken and egg situation.'

'It does, doesn't it? When are you planning to put Brookes Builders on the Market?'

'I already have.'

'Any offers?'

'Not yet. But it's still early days.'

'How would you like to go away for a two week holiday?'

'I'd love it.'

'France or Spain?'

'I'll leave that to you, Julia darling. You love making the decisions.

Kelsey sat bolt upright on the slippery, unfriendly leather-seated straight-backed mahogany chair, clenching and unclenching her hands.

'So you see, Mrs Potter,' Miss Caldecott was saying, 'a court case would not only be expensive, but very stressful as well. Also, what weakens your case somewhat is the fact that you actually walked out on your husband.'

'Wouldn't you have done the same thing if you'd discovered your husband had made his secretary pregnant?' asked Kelsey rather resentfully.

'We are discussing your marriage, not mine,' replied Miss Caldecott loftily. 'In fact, I am as yet unmarried.'

Not surprising, thought Kelsey, disliking Miss Caldecott more by the minute. 'So what do you suggest?' she asked.

'I suggest we go for a substantial settlement.'

'Nigel has practically no money. I told you he wasn't a good barrister. We lived mostly on what I earned in my father's travel agency.'

'Is there any possibility his skills might improve? That he might become a better barrister in time?'

'I've no idea.' Kelsey couldn't see the point of the question.

'You see, Mrs Potter, if you feel your husband has prospects, we could put in a maintenance claim based on his future earnings. On the other hand, if you don't feel optimistic about his career at the bar, we would be better advised to base our claim on his present earnings...'

'Which are hardly sufficient to support one wife and a child. And now they've just had twins.'

'Exactly, Mrs Potter. On the other hand, if you are not in a hurry to obtain a divorce, we could keep your husband waiting and see if his prospects start to improve. How does that idea strike you?'

Kelsey thought of Daniel. 'How long are you suggesting I should wait?'

'A couple of years. Three at the most.'

Obviously Miss Caldecott had never been in love.

'I'm not prepared to wait that long,' said Kelsey. 'And I don't think Nigel would be either.'

'In that case I'll have further discussions with your husband's solicitors and see if we can speed things up.' Miss Caldicott stood up and extended her hand. 'Goodbye, Mrs Potter. I don't think I need delay you further.'

Daniel waited at the bus stop with Kelsey to see her onto the bus, which would take her back to Emma's flat in Wanstead.

'Well, I made a bit of progress today with that dreadful Miss Caldecott. She's going to have further discussions with Nigel's solicitor to see if she can speed up the whole process.'

Daniel squeezed her arm. 'Excellent news. I'm sure it won't be long now.'

'It's really just a question of money.'

Daniel gave her a quizzical look. 'Why money?'

'I want Nigel to pay for cheating on me so badly. I want him to pay for each free screw he had while my back was turned.'

'I understand. But don't string it along for too long. Here's your bus! May I take you out to dinner tonight?'

'Of course. Thank you. I'd love that.'

'Good. I'll pick you up from Emma's flat at seven thirty.'

Kelsey stuck out her arm out as the bus approached the stop. It was only a request stop and the driver was obviously in a hurry. The bus screeched to a halt and swerved slightly, as Daniel gave her a lingering kiss on the lips and helped her onto the platform. The conductor gave them a hostile glare.

'You young people are far too busy kissing to watch out for a bus,' he grumbled. 'Nearly hit the pavement, we did.'

Kelsey ignored him and squeezed herself onto the edge of a seat beside a very fat lady tightly encased in lilac satin, smelling of stale boiled cabbage. As the bus moved off with a roar and a jerk, she waved to Daniel out of the window.

A bottle of champagne stood in an ice bucket at the side of the table. The wine waiter appeared, lifted the bottle out of the ice bucket, glistening coldly, and showed it to Daniel.

'*Dom Perignon 2004*, sir? Is that what you ordered?'

'Yes, thank you. That's excellent.'

'Shall I open it now, sir?'

'Yes. Please do.'

The waiter unwound the wire surrounding the cork and dropped it into the bucket. He eased the cork slowly upwards, allowing it to make its final exit with a resounding 'pop'. He poured a little into Daniel's glass and waited for him to taste it.

'Is it all right, sir?'

'Yes, thank you. It's delicious.'

The waiter filled both their glasses, pausing to let the bubbles subside just before the glasses overflowed. He replaced the bottle in the ice bucket.

'Thank you, sir. Enjoy your evening.' And he backed away.

'Daniel! A whole bottle! We'll never drink all that!'

'Yes, we will. It's a very special occasion.' He lifted his glass. 'Here's to us!'

Kelsey sat still and said nothing.

Daniel put his hand in his pocket, drew out a very small box and laid it on the snow-white tablecloth. He reached out for Kelsey's left hand. Guessing what was to come, her heart thumped loudly and she held out her hand timidly in return. Daniel opened the box, took out a huge diamond solitaire ring and placed on her ring finger. He looked straight into her eyes.

'Kelsey. I love you and I hope you'll marry me.'

Two large tears coursed down Kelsey's cheeks.

'I love you too,' was all she managed to say.

Chapter Thirty-Three

'Are we going to make an announcement or just slope off?' James asked Verity as they walked arm in arm in the garden at Oaklands. It was a bright day in mid-November. There had been a frost during the night, but now, at almost midday, a pale sun shone down obliquely, the air was crisp and still and there wasn't a breath of wind.

'Let's go and sit on the bench over there and discuss it,' replied Verity. They walked over to the bench and James settled her onto it as if she were something extremely precious and fragile.

'Are you sure you won't be cold, my darling?' he enquired solicitously.

'Oh, I don't think so. Not for the short time we shall be here. We'll have to go into lunch shortly, won't we?'

'Yes,' said James, tucking the plaid rug, which he had been carrying over his arm, around Verity's legs.

'Oh, you do think of everything! You're such an angel!'

'I do think of this bench as ours, don't you?'

'I certainly do. This is where we sat and talked the first day I came out into the garden on my own last summer. Do you remember that day?'

'Of course. As vividly as if it were happening now. I was quite captivated but by your charm and elegance and by your beauty. Do let's get married soon. Then we can leave this depressing place, with all its problems and its dull inhabitants'

Verity took James's hand and put it under the rug between both of hers. 'This is what we are about to discuss; sitting here in this pretty garden on our bench, warm and snug under a rug.'

'Well, are we going to make an announcement, or just slope off and tell them all afterwards?' asked James, repeating his question.

'Before we come to any final decision I would like you to tell me the end of your story,' pleaded Verity. 'You promised me that when the autumn was over and you were no longer feeling so sad, you would tell me the rest of what happened and why you came to live in Oaklands. I would like to know more about your wife, your first wife, that is…'

James withdrew his right hand from under the rug, replaced it with his left one and put his right arm around Verity's slight shoulders.

'Before you become my second wife?' he asked teasingly.

Verity felt a twinge of apprehension at his bantering tone. 'I hope you don't think I'm being too curious…'

James laughed and kissed her cheek gently. 'No, of course not. I think you have a right to know what happened before you marry me. I'm sure it will bring us even closer together. It's just … just that it's still painful to talk about, even though it's over five years ago now since it all happened.'

James hadn't slept properly for nearly four months. Helen had become so impossible to control, particularly during the night, that he had even stopped getting undressed at bedtime. Every evening around nine thirty he helped Helen into her nightclothes. It was a routine fraught with difficulties. If he took a nightie out of the drawer she insisted on wearing pyjamas; if he produced pyjamas, she demanded a nightie.

'I was cold in the night,' she would say. So although the central heating was now on twenty-four hours a day, James warmed up the bedroom with a blow-heater about an hour before he took Helen upstairs.

'It's too hot in here,' she complained, lying naked on the bed, spread-eagled across the counterpane in a pro-vocative pose. At that moment she looked beautiful. She had kept her slim figure and she looked at peace with her eyes closed and her hair fluffed out around her head like a grey halo. James loved her then and he want-ed to make love to her. A few times he contemplated making overtures. Once he actually started to stroke her thigh, but she became violent and angry and bit his hand.

'Stop molesting me, you sex-craved monster!' she screamed. So after that he didn't dare risk any closer physical contact other than a brief peck on the cheek.

Helen was perverse about everything. The rooms were too hot or too cold. The light was too dim or too bright. If the door was open, she wanted it closed. When it was closed, she wanted it open. It was the same with the television, or the gas fire. She would ask James to put on one of them, then after less than a minute she would order him to switch it off again. Meal-times were torture. She would say she was hungry and demand a meal at a most unreasonable hour, insisting that James cook some-thing very elaborate. This preparation might take well over half an hour and when James finally served the meal, Helen complained it had taken too long to arrive and she was no longer hungry. Sometimes she would say it wasn't what she had asked for and scream: 'it's looks like shit!' and fling it on the floor. But James was forced to continue the struggle of preparing meals, which his wife consumed with increasing reluctance.

Washing was a different matter altogether. Although James thought unwashed people were in no physical danger, either to themselves or any one else, he found that if he didn't try to give Helen a bath at least once a month, he became aware of a lingering odour round the house, especially in the bedroom. He never announced bath-time. That would have been courting trouble before the procedure had even started. At the appropriate moment, usually when Helen was dozing in an armchair in the living room, he would slip upstairs and run a bath; neither too hot nor too cold; too deep nor too shallow. He would return to the living room and make a subtle noise so Helen would wake up naturally. Then they would play a game.

'You won't guess what I've got upstairs.'

'A surprise?'

'Yes.'

'A nice surprise?'

'Oh, I think you'd like it.'

'What is it?'

'Try and guess.'

And Helen would make several wild guesses: 'It's a dress, a hat, a scarf, jewellery, perfume, soap.'

'Soap. Now you're getting near.'

'Soap? Special soap? A present?'

'Yes. That's right. There's a present of special soap upstairs in the bathroom.'

Interest flickered in Helen's still pretty, but expressionless face. 'I'll go and take a look. Will you come too?'

'Of course.' James helped her out of her chair and together they went upstairs, hand in hand, to the bathroom. Their arrival at the bathroom door, always left open on these occasions, was the moment that James dreaded the most. There was no way of anticipating Helen's reaction to the half filled bath. Sometimes she would just stand there motionless, saying nothing. Sometimes she would say, in a flat expressionless voice: 'what's that?' or 'there's water in there' or 'are you going to have a bath?'

If James said: 'no, the bath is for you,' she could react in many different ways. She might say: 'oh, how nice,' and get in straight away, fully clothed. Or she might say: 'I'll have it later,' go into the bedroom, take off all her clothes and lie naked on the bed. On the day of her last bath, the very last bath that James would ever give her, she had expressed delight at the idea of getting into the water. She allowed James to undress her and stood naked in front of the bathroom mirror, examining her body and caressing it, with murmuring noises of approval. Before getting into the bath, she put her arms around James and kissed him properly for the first time in well over a year. Once in the bath, she lay there motionless for at least five minutes.

'The water's nice and warm,' she said. 'Not too hot. Just right.'

James sat on the stool by the side of the bath and watched her. 'That's good. I always try to get the temperature right.'

'You have - and it is.' She let the water run through her fingers. 'It's smooth and silky. You can see through it.'

'Yes. You can always see through water. It's transparent. Unless, of course, it's dirty. You can't see through dirty water.'

'No. But I wouldn't want to bath in dirty water.'

'No, of course not,' said James, thinking: if someone told me two years ago that I would have a conversation like this with Helen, I just wouldn't have believed them.

'Shall I wash you?' he asked, at length, picking up the soap.

'Yes, please. Is that my special soap? My present?'

'Yes. That's your special soap. Your present.'

'It smells nice.'

'Yes. That's why it's special.'

James began to rub her all over with the bar of soap: neck, shoulders, back, arms and feet. 'If you'd like to stand up I'll wash your legs and - the other places.'

Helen stood up obediently and James gently soaped her thighs and her calves, studiously avoiding the pubic area. Helen let James soap her for several minutes, standing quietly and submissively. Then suddenly she became agitated, muttering under her breath: 'no! I won't stand for it! I can't let him do this!' She started jumping up and down in the bath, shouting: 'go away! Leave me alone, you monster!'

James stopped soaping her and tried to calm her down. 'Don't worry, Helen. It's all over now. All finished. You've had a lovely bath. I'll get you out now and dry you and then we can have a cup of coffee together.'

Helen started hitting him, shouting louder: 'go away! I hate you! You're a sex-craved monster!'

Then she leapt out of the bath and rushed downstairs, leaving a trail of water in her wake. James followed her down the stairs into the living room, where she jumped on and off the sofa and the armchairs. She ran into the kitchen, opened and closed the oven and fridge doors several times, and then, without any warning, she ran out through the back door - unfortunately left unlocked - down the passage at the side of the house, out of the garden gate and into the road. James trundled after her, a heavily built man in his early seventies, struggling to keep up with a woman eight years his junior. But it was the fear that the neighbours would see his demented wife in all her nakedness, or worse still, that she would run into the road and get knocked down by a passing car, that kept him going. Helen ran swiftly along the pavement, her naked body moving freely, unimpeded by clothing, her bare feet oblivious to the pebbles and the rubbish. Sweating and gasping for breath, James finally caught up with her at the corner, where their quiet residential road joined a bus route. He took her arm gently.

'Helen,' he pleaded, almost in tears, 'please don't do this. Come home now and get dressed, then we can have a nice cup of coffee.'

Helen looked at him uncomprehendingly. 'Who are you? Where am I?' Then she took his hand and let him lead her home, as quiet and docile as a lamb.

'Dad, you can't go on like this. You'll have to have her sectioned. Otherwise you'll be the one who ends up in a mental home.'

'Robert, I couldn't do that. She's my wife - and your mother. I can't have her put away in an asylum indefinitely.'

'It needn't be indefinitely, Dad. It could be just as long as it takes to get some more effective medication sorted out. Something that'll calm her down and make her more rational. You can't go on living with her in her present state.'

'No. I'll have to think of something better.'

'Where is she now?'

'In bed, fast asleep.'

'At eleven thirty in the morning?'

'Well, yes. She sleeps a lot. During the day, that is. She's up half the night, you see.'

'Look, Dad. I'm going to make a suggestion.'

'Yes? What is it?'

'I think you should go away for a holiday. You need a break, a complete rest. Jennifer and I will come in and take care of Mother.'

'That's very thoughtful of you, Robert. But I don't know how your mother would react if I went away and left her. She's used to me. I'm the only one who's cared for her during the last year. She could become unsettled, even difficult.'

'Dad, she's difficult now. She's bloody impossible by the sound of it. And you say there are times when she doesn't even recognise you. She'll get used to Jennifer and me. She won't have any alternative. You just go and book a nice holiday. A fortnight in the sun would do you the world of good.'

'A fortnight! I can't go away for two whole weeks and leave your mother!'

'A week then.'

'A long weekend.'

'A week, Dad.'

James booked himself into a small hotel in Brighton for a week. It was early September and the weather was gloriously warm and sunny. He went for walks along the front, enjoying the sight and sound of the sea he had always loved, relishing the clean, bracing air. He went for drives in the Sussex Downs, along narrow country lanes, exploring small towns and villages. Every evening he spoke to his son, Robert, on the phone.

'Don't worry, Dad,' came Robert's reassuring voice along the line. 'Everything's going very smoothly. Mother's just fine. She and Jennifer are getting along splendidly. I suggest you stay on another week. Or go somewhere else, if you feel you've exhausted the delights of Brighton.'

James said he'd think it over.

Saturday 15 September dawned dull and misty, so James decided it would be a good morning to do some shopping in the town. There wasn't much point in taking a walk along the front, or going for a drive if there was nothing to see. He decided he would buy Helen some new clothes. Robert's progress reports on the telephone had been most encouraging. It sounded as if his wife had come out of the dark wood of madness and despair and turned a corner into the brighter world of sanity and hope. James enjoyed his morning shopping. He bought Helen a new dressing gown, pyjamas and a nightie, two skirts with co-ordinating knitwear and a dress. He decided they would try to buy the shoes together when he returned home on Monday. He bought himself a pair of shoes, a jacket, two pairs of trousers and three shirts. More than satisfied with his purchases, he returned, heavily laden, to deposit his bags and boxes at his hotel before going out to lunch. He was greeted at the hotel entrance by the proprietor, in a state of extreme agitation.

'Mr Parker?'

'Yes.'

'Mr Parker, there's a police officer in my office waiting to interview you. I hope it's nothing irregular. Any hint of scandal would give my hotel a very bad name.'

Completely mystified, James went into the office, put his parcels on the floor and closed the door. Robert's soothing reports on the telephone of Helen's improved condition had merely signalled the calm before the storm. Both Robert and Jennifer were so relieved and encouraged by Helen's calmer and more rational behaviour, that on the night of 14 September they drank almost two bottles of wine between them. Unaccustomed to such a large quantity of alcohol, they both fell into a deep and dreamless sleep and failed to hear Helen rampaging around the house during the night, ranting at the top of her voice against everyone and everything. For her part, Helen was incensed that her exhibition was going unnoticed. It wasn't a conscious realisation, but she wasn't used to being ignored. In the last year and a half she had become accustomed to James helping her with the smallest problems. Now she felt the whole world was closing in on her and darkness engulfed her like a blanket. She was suffocating. She felt she didn't have long to live. Maybe if she could get out of the house she could be free again? Free to live life in her own way instead of being trapped with this woman called Jennifer, who kept smothering her in platitudes. She tried the front door, but it wouldn't open. (James had warned Robert and Jennifer to keep all the doors to the outside securely locked at all times and remove the keys.) She went into the kitchen and tried the back door, but she was unable to open that either. She was locked into her own house. Suddenly, an unearthly sense of calm descended upon her. She couldn't get out, so she would have to stay in. But there was no point in going back to bed, as she knew she would be unable to sleep. (She had, after all, slept for most of the day.) So, what do people do when they can't sleep? They read a book, or watch television. Helen hadn't read a book in more than three years and didn't know how she would go about selecting one, so the only other choice was television. She went into the living room, picked up the remote control and switched on the set. It was a porn movie, but it made no impression on Helen whatsoever. Nevertheless, she continued to watch it for about a quarter of an hour. Then she began to feel cold. She dimly remembered it was possible to light a fire in the room, but a certain requirement was necessary which escaped her for a moment. Then she remembered. Matches. There was a box on the table beside the television set. She picked up the box, took out a match and lit it. The head flew off, landed on the carpet and started to smoulder. Helen watched, fascinated, as the smouldering became a small flame and crept along the carpet towards the curtain. The curtains were dark gold brocade velvet, with hand-made pinch-pleats, falling gracefully to the floor, chosen with care and pride by James and Helen more than ten years ago. Helen sat motionless, watching as the flames licked their way up one curtain, across the box pelmet to the curtain on the other side. After that it was a question of only a few minutes before the sofa caught fire, followed by an armchair. As the flames crackled and spread, and the room filled with acrid smoke, Helen was overcome with fumes and slowly suffocated. At the inquest the coroner estimated her time of death as being between three and four am. Upstairs, Robert and Jennifer slept on, their bodies closely entwined, blissfully unaware of the disaster taking place in the house around them. As their lungs filled with poisonous smoke, they died together, shortly after Helen.

When James had finished his story there was a long pause. Verity sat absolutely still, unable to speak. Tears coursed down James's cheeks, as he tried with difficulty to pull himself together.

'You see, I had to come in here,' he said at last. 'I had nowhere else to go.'

'The house…?'

'…Was gutted. Everything gone. I had nothing left except what I had taken with me to Brighton. Fortunately, if it's possible to use that word in such tragic circumstances… fortunately I had taken most of my photograph albums along with me. I had some idea that I might be able to recapture the happiness of the past by looking at the photographs. Helen, Robert, Jennifer and our home. All gone.'

James looked at his watch. It was half past one.

'I'm afraid we've missed lunch,' he said.

Chapter Thirty-Four

'Another cup, Ali?'

'Yes, please.' Alison passed her cup over to Julia for a refill. 'Delicious cucumber sandwiches.'

'Yes. Thank you. I make them most days. They're Graham's favourite.'

'Most days? You mean to say that most days you and Graham have afternoon tea!'

'Every day. We like it. It's our favourite meal.'

'But not on this scale, surely.' Alison surveyed the huge spread of delicacies, as usual elegantly arranged on doily-covered silver salvers. There were egg mayonnaise sandwiches, smoked salmon canapés, caviar in puff pastry and asparagus wrapped in thin slivers of ham. There was a variety of biscuits: shortbread, ginger snaps, abbey crunch and chocolate. There was cake: Madeira, chocolate and fruit. And there were pastries: three cream cornets, three cream doughnuts and six chocolate éclairs.

'We're hardly going to eat all this,' said Alison primly, sucking in her gaunt cheeks, pursing up her thin lips and tucking her legs, like two stick-insects, firmly against the sofa.

Julia laughed, a light tinkling sound. 'Oh, no, it's not obligatory.' Alison marvelled at how such a large woman could have such a little laugh. 'Graham will be in later. We must leave him a few of the cream pastries.'

Alison hadn't seen Graham recently and she wondered if he had swelled up as huge as his wife. Perhaps they had a competition going.

'What's Graham up to this afternoon?' she enquired conversationally.

'He's with the solicitor for the closure of the sale of Brookes Builders.'

Alison's eyebrows shot up. 'He's sold Brookes Builders! Why on earth has he done that?'

'He's retired, Ali. He's had enough. He wants out and he's had an offer he couldn't refuse.'

'Excellent! I'm delighted. But I'd no idea Graham was planning to retire.'

'No? I suppose we haven't seen much of each other recently. Then there was also the question of the manager's embezzlement. Do you remember?'

'No, not really. But I've also had a few things on my mind.'

'Yes. I'm dreadfully sorry. Poor Ali. Such a terrible shock. Are things progressing satisfactorily?'

'If you mean is the divorce going ahead, the answer is "yes." But it's hardly a satisfactory situation being deserted by one's husband for another man.'

'No, of course not. That's not what I was implying. I meant rather - well - is Steven going to pay alimony?'

'Yes. The rat has finally coughed up. He's settled for a substantial lump sum and an allowance for life, provided I don't remarry.'

'Well, you wouldn't, would you?'

'I wouldn't say that. I might well remarry if a hunk of a sexy he-man comes along. It would make a change to be married to a real man.'

Julia's eyebrows rose. 'Did you suspect that Steven was gay?'

'Yes, I did, after a few years. But then it was too late to leave him. We'd had the twins.'

'Yes, of course.'

Alison took a smoked salmon canapé and popped it in her mouth. 'You see, the more I watched Russell, the more I saw the similarities between him and Steven.'

'Such as?'

'Little gestures. The way they use their hands; the slight shrug of the shoulders. The voice too; the unmistakable timbre that most gays have.'

'Yes, I know. Did you ever suspect he was two-timing you?'

'I had my suspicions. He had plenty of opportunity, didn't he? All those trips abroad. Places like Ibiza and Majorca must be crawling with gays, I should imagine.'

'Could be.' Julia wasn't quite sure what she should say.

'But I closed my mind completely to the possibility that Steven was two-timing me. Otherwise I wouldn't have been able to cope with everything: Kirsty's death; Steven's bankruptcy; Mother's predatory rescue; then Mother moving into that lovely flat we'd built onto the house to make money.' Alison gave a deep sigh. 'It's been a real belly-full.'

'Poor Ali. You've had it really hard.'

'You haven't had it that easy either, with Graham's terrible accident and his awful manager nearly bankrupting him. Tell me more about that.'

'Well, the manager, Ken Spooner, is now on remand in prison awaiting trial.'

'Did Graham report him to the police?' asked Alison.

'He was considering it when the law was taken out of his hands.'

'By whom?'

'By Pamela Price: Sister Price, who used to run Oaklands.'

'On what basis?'

'Apparently Sister Price was hoarding Ken Spooner's stolen goods. But she complained that he wasn't paying her enough for his services, so when he refused to pay her more, she went to the police.'

'So they both ended up in prison on remand?'

'Yes.'

'How ironic. So what do you think will happen?'

'We don't know yet. Presumably it will all come out in court.'

'Do you know the date of the trial?' enquired Alison.

'Not yet. But we'll be informed. But you've had much worse problems to face than I have.'

'Yes. Kirsty's death was the worst of all. But I'd - I'd rather not talk about it.'

'No, of course not. How is Steven financing the alimony? Has Mother given him back the business or is his friend helping out?'

'His friend's helping out. Mother's not conceding a thing. She wouldn't budge when you went to see her and it was "no change" when I asked her.'

'Mean old bitch. I bet her account's overflowing. Any idea how Steven's friend has made his money?'

'Steven was a bit vague. "International distribution," was all he said,' explained Alison, rather uncertainly.

'It could be anything, couldn't it?'

'I'd rather not think about it.'

'Quite right. But I'm delighted you've decided to accept the money. Steven does owe it to you, you know, wherever he gets it from.'

Alison sighed again. 'I know. I just didn't want to accept it at first. It seemed like dirty money.'

'I can understand that.'

'But then, when Mother refused to budge, telling both of us that she wouldn't give the business back, or the house, or the flat - well, I didn't have much choice, did I?'

'No, you didn't. What excuse did Mother give you?'

'Old age. Expected longevity. Expenses in the retirement home. All that sort of thing.'

'She told me the same story too,' agreed Julia.

'Thank goodness neither of us needs her money now.'

'Thank goodness.' Julia passed Alison the plate of cream cakes. 'Go on. Have one. Be a devil. You can afford to - and you're so thin.'

Alison took a chocolate éclair and put it on her plate. 'Kelsey told me that Mother had given her some money for her course.'

'Oh, good! Did she say how much?'

'No. And I didn't like to ask.'

'No, of course not. Kelsey was always Mother's favourite.'

'Yes.'

'She's had a bad time too, hasn't she? And so young, poor child.'

'Yes. She's had a dreadful time. I had no idea that awful Nigel was such a bastard,' Alison agreed. 'And now his "little piece" has had twins.'

'Any movement on their divorce? I would have thought his "little piece" would want to be married, wouldn't you?'

'Kelsey did say the other day that things were moving towards a conclusion.'

'Oh, good. I suppose it's a question of money again.'

'It certainly is. Apparently Nigel's pleading poverty.'

'So he's as mean as he's dishonest.'

'Yes. It often goes together, doesn't it?' remarked Alison.

'I suppose Kelsey doesn't want to ask her grandma for more money.'

'Oh, no! She thinks it should come from Nigel. And quite right too. He owes her everything.'

'Yes. Has Kelsey got other prospects? Any new boy friend around?'

'She hasn't said.'

'She won't have any problem finding a new man. She's very pretty.'

'She is, but she's still a bit too thin.'

'Not nearly as thin as she was.' Julia picked up a cream cornet and bit into it. Castor sugar and flakes of pastry flew everywhere. 'Mm, delicious. My favourite. Have one. Ali.'

'I couldn't. Honestly. I'm FTB. I don't know how your body can absorb so much cream.'

'It can't.' Julia patted her huge stomach. 'That's the problem. They're my weakness. An addiction really.'

Alison said nothing.

'You know,' said Julia. 'You came here so we could discuss Mother's eightieth birthday party and we haven't even mentioned it yet.'

'No, we haven't. But we've had a good sisterly chat, which I feel was rather over-due. I've booked a room for twelve thirty lunch at the Prince of Wales Hotel in Chigwell.'

'Who's coming? Just the family?'

'Mother mentioned that she'd like to invite some of her friends from Oaklands. Would that be okay?'

'I don't see why not. How much is this knees-up going to cost?'

'About a thousand pounds.'

'A thousand pounds!'

'Yes. It could even be more. It depends which menu we go for. And how much we decide to pay for the wine.'

'Who's going to pay for it?'

'We could have a whip around the family. What do you think?'

'We could,' said Julia doubtfully.

Chapter Thirty-Five

'Shall we try this one?' suggested Sudip.

Russell stopped outside a bow-fronted shop window with small bottle-glass panes, each one diagonally half-covered in artificial snow. A sign saying 'Ye Olde Tea Shoppe' swung creakily above the door. Sudip looked in through the window, noticing the high-backed cane-seated chairs set around tables covered with blue-and-white chequered tablecloths, laid with china of a similar colour. The small tearoom was almost full. Only two tables near the back were free.

'A bit twee,' said Russell. 'What do you think?'

Sudip laughed. 'Twee. I love that word. My dear Russell, everything here is twee. Stow-in-the-Wold is one of the most twee places I've ever been to.'

'Mm. I suppose you're right. However, if you think all the tearooms will be twee, let's go in here. I could murder a cup of tea.'

Russell led the way into the teashop, the sudden rush of hot air misting up Sudip's glasses so much he could hardly see. They were shown to a table at the back, beside the door to the lavatories.

'Parked by the loos again,' said Russell, taking the worst seat.

Almost immediately a young waitress arrived, tottering in unsuitably high, uncomfortable-looking platform-sole shoes and a miniscule skin-tight mini-skirt. She took their order, scribbling left-handed on a note-pad.

'Just a pot of tea and some buttered scones, sir? No cakes or pastries?'

Russell hesitated and glanced at Sudip, who shook his head.

'No, thank you,' said Russell to the waitress, who clomped off noisily towards the kitchen, her platform-sole shoes making pitiful squeaks on the lino floor tiles.

Sudip shook his head and smiled. 'What the young will wear nowadays just to keep up with the fashion.'

'I don't think anything's changed. The young have always worn absurd fashions.'

'Did you?'

'Probably. I don't remember what I wore in my twenties. Though I do remember what my sisters wore.'

'Yes?'

'The shortest of mini-skirts, almost as short as the waitress, and the thinnest of high heels.'

'Didn't they look ridiculous?'

'No, not at all. They would probably have looked ridiculous if they hadn't worn them.'

'That's a problem Indian women don't have: keeping up with the fashion. It never changes.'

'No. I suppose not. Though there must be competition for the best sari.'

'I think it's more a question of wealth rather than competition.'

Sudip looked around the tearoom. 'This place is full of Americans. It's a real tourist trap.'

'It is, isn't it? How are we going to like living here?'

Sudip delayed replying as the waitress stomped back with their order. He helped himself to a toasted scone, dripping with butter, while Russell poured the tea.

'The countryside is very pretty,' said Sudip thought-fully, as he finished his first bite. 'Delicious scones. Do take one while they're hot.'

They munched in contended silence for a moment as Russell took a cautious sip of steaming tea.

'Yes. The countryside is pretty,' he agreed. 'It's the towns and villages I find less appealing. They're too neat and tidy. Almost artificial.'

'Twee.'

'Yes. Twee.'

'What gave us the idea of moving here in the first place? I can't remember exactly why we decided to look in Gloucestershire, can you?'

'Yes, more or less. Pretty countryside. Plenty of old properties. Full of well-established residents and well-connected people such as the royal family...'

Sudip hooted with laughter. 'I've never heard you talk such rubbish. You, of all people, wanting to live near the royal family! Why! You're a rip-roaring republican!'

'Well - I think the real reason was that we thought living in the country would make a change from London.'

'It would certainly make a change. But whether it would be a change for the better, I'm not sure. Are you?'

'No. Not any more. I think selling my shop in The Camden Passage was so painful I just wanted to move out of Islington as soon as possible.'

'Of course. Quite understandable. But now...'

'Now that I'm getting over the shock, I'm beginning to see certain advantages...'

'In not having to work any more.'

'Yes. And living off my lover.'

Sudip laughed. 'I hope you're enjoying living off your lover.'

'Yes, of course. From the material point of view, but my sense of pride is still not fully accustomed to the idea.'

'Yes. I understand. But would your sense of pride feel any more comfortable living in Gloucestershire rather than in London?'

'Probably more comfortable in London.'

'Good. I hoped you'd say that. I think we'd miss out on too much if we came to live here.'

'Such as?'

'Theatres, concerts, cinemas, restaurants…'

'Ah, yes. Restaurants. In London they're not twee.'

'No. Thank goodness. Then there's my family in London.'

'Would you miss your family if we moved out here?' Sudip wasn't sure whether to take his friend seriously.

'No. I was only joking. But there's always the odd family "do" to go to.'

'We could always stay in a hotel for your family "dos".' Sudip was smiling broadly.

'Like the Prince of Wales.'

'Where's that?'

'Chigwell. It's where my Mother's eightieth birthday party is being held in less than two weeks time. Mother doesn't know about it yet. Alison is hoping that the family will make a financial contribution.'

Chapter Thirty-Six

'This one sounds promising.' Graham picked up a sheet of paper from the pile in front of him on the coffee table beside the tea tray, which was less heavily laden than usual.

'Listen while I read you the details.'

Julia put down the sheaf of papers she had been studying and lay back among the luxuriantly soft sofa cushions. She considered taking another biscuit, but finally resisted the idea. She had been to see her doctor last week with a painful sore throat. She was hardly ever ill, so visits to the doctor were rare. She had barely closed her mouth after the brief throat examination when Dr Phillips remarked, as he tapped her prescription into the computer:

'Julia, my dear,'(he was an old family friend.) 'I haven't seen you recently, which is an encouraging indication that your health still remains good. However, it does appear to me that you have gained a considerable amount of weight since I last saw you, which should not be allowed to continue unchecked.' He finished typing the prescription and handed her the printout. 'Now if you would just slip off your shoes, and perhaps your cardigan, I would like you to hop onto the scales.'

To her shame, Julia weighed in at fourteen stone, eleven pounds. Dr Phillips made a disapproving clicking noise. 'Let's just check you height, shall we?'

She measured just less than five feet two inches. Dr Phillips took her blood pressure, which was normal, and returned to his computer to type out another prescription.

'Take three of these a day. They'll suppress your appetite. Here is a diet sheet. Stick to it as rigidly as possible, especially avoiding all foods with an asterisk. Come and see me in two weeks, by which time, hopefully, you will have lost half a stone.'

Julia left the surgery feeling rather chastened and extremely embarrassed. That was three weeks ago and she had already lost a stone. But she had at least four more to loose.

'With a vaulted cellar, standing on an *hectare* of land, having stunning views of the Burgundy countryside,' Graham was saying.

Julia came to with a start. 'Sounds wonderful,' she said, automatically. 'Where is it?'

Graham referred back to the sheet of paper. 'Thirty kilometres south west of Beaune in a village called - I don't know how to pronounce it.'

'How do you spell it?'

'P E R R E U I L.'

'Oh!' Julia hadn't the faintest idea how to pronounce it either, but she liked to think her French was better than Graham's. 'Pearool, I should think. How many bedrooms are there?'

'None at all yet. There's just a huge loft waiting for conversion. It has a vaulted cellar, four good-sized ground-floor rooms and a barn, a courtyard, two fields dotted with cows...'

'You're making it up!'

'Only the bit about the cows. Look. You can read the rest for yourself.' He passed over the sheet of paper.

Julia studied it carefully for a moment. 'It gives no indication of the size of the village. It could contain less than a thousand people.'

'Would that matter?'

'N-no. But I don't want to live anywhere too remote.'

A vision flashed through Julia's mind's-eye of rain-swept fields dotted with cows, deserted vineyards and derelict farmhouses. Perhaps interesting to visit on a fine summer's day, but in bad winter weather it could be gloomy, and very lonely. What would they do in the winter, just the two of them? There would be no theatres, cinemas or shops. Even the restaurants might be miles away. They wouldn't even have English television. Julia could imagine becoming so lonely and depressed that her only solace would be very large quantities of all the wrong food. Why had Graham suddenly formed this obsession for living in rural France? He had never lived in the country before and knew only a few words of French.

'So I was thinking,' Graham was saying, 'that we would make a list of all the possible properties and ask the estate agent to arrange a tour. We could leave next weekend. I know it's December, but they always say it's better to see a house on a gloomy day. Then it can only improve.'

'Graham! Not next weekend! You've forgotten! It's Mother's eightieth birthday party!'

'Oh, yes! Of course! At the Prince of Wales Hotel in Chigwell. How absurdly bourgeois.'

'Do you think so? Oh, by the way, Mother still doesn't know about it, and Ali's hoping for contributions.

'Contributions? Whatever for?'

'To pay for the party.'

Brr-brr. Brr-brr. Oh, hell, thought Kelsey, sticking her arm out of the warm cosy duvet and switching off the alarm. Seven thirty. Time to get up and go to college. She wasn't finding her beautician's course nearly as interesting as she had hoped. In fact, most days she was bored. But she tried to console herself with the fact that it was better than working in her father's travel agency.

Her father! Panic gripped her suddenly. She had no father. Her father had gone. She had no father and no sister. A wave of self-pity overwhelmed her. The backs of her eyes prickled and a sob rose up from the pit of her stomach. She felt bereft, truncated, for the second time in her short life. She had found it extremely painful coming to terms with the fact that her father was gay. It was the last thing she had ever imagined. She recalled again the terrible evening she had spent with her mother. Alison had phoned her one evening when she happened to be at home, still living in Emma's flat.

'Hello, Kelsey, darling.'

'Hello, Mum.'

'Am I interrupting anything?'

'No, of course not.'

'Are you doing anything this evening?'

'No, I'm not, as a matter of fact.'

'Would you like to come around here for a bit of supper?'

'Well, yes. Thank you. That would be very nice.'

'I'll see you in about half an hour, then.'

'Well, yes, of course.'

There was something in her mother's voice that made Kelsey feel that she had something rather urgent to tell her.

They had finished their simple supper and were well into a bottle of wine.

'It's about Daddy, darling. I think you ought to know what's happened.'

'What's happened to Dad?' Kelsey felt her stomach seize up. 'I mean - where is he?'

'Your father is still in Morocco,' said Alison in a tight voice. 'And as far as I can understand he has no plans to return.'

'He's not coming back?' Kelsey could hardly believe what she was hearing. 'You mean he's left you!'

'Yes. He's left me.'

'For another woman?'

'No. It's even worse than that. Your father has left me for another man. He's gay. Your father is a homosexual.'

Kelsey wrapped the duvet around her head for protection. The tears pricked harder behind her eyes and two large drops coursed down her cheeks. Her stomach heaved and turned over. Suddenly she felt sick. She leapt out of bed and just made it to the bathroom in time. She vomited violently and noisily into the loo. Then she crept back to bed and slept heavily for more than two hours.

Brr-brr. Brr-brr. This time it was the telephone. Cursing Emma for not having a telephone point in the spare bedroom, Kelsey struggled out of bed and padded, naked and barefoot, into the living room.

'Hello.'

'Mrs Potter?'

'Yes. Speaking.'

'Mrs Potter, this is Miss Caldecott.'

Kelsey's heart sank. 'Yes, Miss Caldecott.'

'Mrs Potter, I have some very good news for you. Your husband has finally agreed to give you a substantial lump sum. I think you will be pleased with the amount. If you could spare the time to call round to my office some time this afternoon we can finalise the details of your divorce. Are you free this afternoon?

'Yes, of course.'

'Then shall we say three o'clock? Would that be convenient?'

'Certainly. I'll be there at three o'clock, Miss Caldecott.'

Thank God, for some good news, thought Kelsey, rushing off to the loo to be sick again. And thank goodness Nigel has decided to be sensible at last.

'So that's really good news, isn't it, Dan?' said Kelsey, snuggling up to Daniel on the large comfortable sofa in his attractive flat.

He gave her a kiss. 'That's wonderful news. As soon as the divorce is through we can plan our wedding.'

'The sooner the better. Dan, would you like to be a father?'

'Of course. I've always wanted a child.'

'Good. Because I think I'm pregnant.'

Daniel kissed her again. 'That's even better news! Shall we announce it at your grandmother's party along with our wedding plans?'

Kelsey giggled. 'I don't see why not. It would certainly cause a stir.'

Chapter Thirty-Seven

'It's so nice having Gladys back with us, isn't it, James?' said Verity, sitting down beside him and watching him mix up the two domino sets on the table.

'It certainly is,' he replied. 'She looks well, doesn't she?'

'Remarkably well, considering she's just spent six weeks in that dreadful hospital. I know just what it's like in there.' Verity shuddered at the memory.

'Yes. You've also experienced the horrors of Whipps Cross.'

'Gladys seems to have lost quite a bit of weight, hasn't she?'

'Definitely. But it won't have done her any harm. And it'll give her daughter-in-law the pleasure of knitting her some more lurid cardigans.'

Verity laughed. 'Oh, James! You are naughty!'

James laughed too. 'Naughty but nice?'

'Very nice!' Verity wanted to kiss him, but restrained herself. They hadn't made any announcement yet of their imminent wedding.

James looked at his watch. 'It's a quarter past two already! Everyone's late! I hope we'll get in our seven games before tea.'

Verity loved his attention to every little detail. 'I'm sure we shall,' she said soothingly. 'Have you told them it's the last game?'

'No. I thought I'd wait until the end. It might distract them if they knew it was the last one.'

'Are we going to tell them today about - about us?'

'Let's wait and announce it at your birthday party. It's only just over a week away now.'

'Here comes Brenda. And there's Mabel and Gladys. Good afternoon, ladies.'

The atmosphere around the domino table had become extremely tense. They had played five games. Gladys had won the first one, leaving the stakes at £80. Although no money had yet changed hands, everyone was genuinely delighted that she had won the first game. James won the second game, doubling the stakes to £160. Verity won the third, also doubling the stakes. Mabel won the fourth game, leaving the stakes as they were at £320. James won the fifth game, doubling the stakes again to £640. There were two games left to play. James looked at his watch. It was almost twenty past three. The tea trolley was always wheeled in promptly at a quarter to four. They had to finish by then and have the table cleared. Brenda won the sixth game and doubled the stakes again to £1,280. Brenda always tried hard. She hated losing and needed to win. Mabel started to protest about the large stakes, but James stopped her, saying this was a special game, so Mabel shuffled the dominoes for the last round. No one spoke and the tension was becoming unbearable.

Verity knocked first. 'Double six.' She placed her domino in the middle of the table. Mabel went next. Then it was James's turn. He put down a double five and went again in quick succession. Brenda went next and Verity's turn followed. She put her second last piece on the table. Gladys and Mabel each had three pieces left. James and Brenda had two apiece. Brenda was really nervous now and desperate to win. She placed her second last piece on the table. James went with another double and followed on quickly with his last piece.

'You've won!' shrieked Brenda, in a voice bitter with disappointment.

'Yes, but only because this game is going to be...' James began when the door opened and a tall, gaunt figure with bright red hair, wearing a stiffly starched nursing sister's uniform, strode into the room.

'Good afternoon, ladies and gentlemen. I'm Stacey Struthers. Sister Struthers. I'm the new owner of Oaklands Retirement Home. I hope you will welcome me with a warm round of applause.'

There was deathly silence.

'So what's Sister Struthers like, Mother?' asked Julia, as they sat chatting in Verity's room.

'The worst combination of a headmistress at a girls' public school and a hospital matron,' replied Verity. 'This place is now full of unnecessary new rules.'

'Such as?'

'Punctuality for meals. Limited use of the public telephone. Restricted visiting hours. All very petty.'

'Yes,' agreed Julia. 'Perhaps Alison and I should start looking around for somewhere else?'

'I wouldn't worry,' said Verity smoothly. 'I may make other arrangements.'

Julia's eyebrows shot up. 'Other arrangements?'

'Yes.'

'What sort of other arrangements?'

'I'll let you know in due course.'

Steven stirred, stretched out straight and lay on his back for a few moments before looking at the bedside clock. Good heavens! A quarter to five already! He must have slept for nearly two hours! He was certainly living the life of luxury: a kept man, housed in the palace of a prince. It was almost too good to be true. But it was true. He now had been living with Lars on the outskirts of Marrakech for nearly seven months, with nothing to do all day except swim, read and rest; with the prospect of gourmet dinners followed by long amorous nights. He felt it was time to get up, shower and shave and have the cocktails ready when Lars arrived home. Then they would dine out on exquisite food in one of Marrakech's most renowned restaurants. But suddenly he remembered that Lars was away. He had been away now for almost two weeks. Would he dine out by himself in a restaurant? Almost certainly not.

'My business needs take me abroad,' Lars had explained. 'It's unfortunate but necessary. Don't worry, I'll call you when I can.'

But he hadn't called.

Steven got out of bed and padded, naked and barefoot to the window. Whenever he got out of bed he always looked out of the window. For six amazing months the sun had shone down, faithfully and relentlessly, every day. Although the rays had become gradually lower, they were still full of warmth and suffused the garden with a golden glow. Then, as Lars had warned him, at the beginning of December all had changed.

'The Moroccan winter is short, but it comes. From the beginning of December into early February there will be little sun. Instead we have rain, and on most days, grey sky. That is why, if I can, I go always to the

Caribbean. We go there after the Christmas parties. You will like the Caribbean.'

Steven wondered how there could be many Christmas parties in a Muslim country like Morocco, but decided not to ask any questions. He would wait to be surprised. He had just reached the bathroom door when the phone rang. Hurrah! It must be Lars, he thought. Normally Steven never answered the phone. Either Lars answered it himself or an answer phone dealt with the calls. Steven hesitated. He didn't want to go downstairs stark naked in case he ran into Fatima, whose working hours were known only to herself. The nearest phone was in Lars's study, a small room next door to the bedroom. Lars didn't believe in bedside phones. He said they interfered with sleep and sex. Steven hardly ever went into Lars's study. Lars had never asked him not to, but he had casually remarked one day that there wouldn't really be any point in Steven doing so. After all, he spoke no French, German or Arabic, so it would be best if he left Lars to answer the telephone, most of which were business calls anyway. The phone continued to ring, shrill and insistent, so Steven decided he would answer it after all.

'Hello.'

'Hello, Steven!' said a very familiar voice. Steven felt shock waves running through him.

'Alison! What on earth?'

'You sound surprised, Steven, dear.'

'Well - yes. I suppose I am a little surprised. I - I thought everything was settled.'

'Very nearly,' said Alison smoothly. 'But you forgot to sign one document. Does your friend have a fax?' (Alison never referred to Lars by name.)

'Yes, of course. Lars has everything like that. He needs it for his business.'

'Do you think you could give me the fax number? Then I can send it through right away.'

'Yes. Certainly. Are you sure the divorce courts will accept a fax?'

'We can try. I'm keen to get this whole thing settled as soon as possible.'

'Of course,' said Steven, and he read out the fax number, which was clearly listed beside the telephone.

'If you replace the receiver now, please, the fax will arrive in about a minute.'

Business over, Steven now had to decide how he should fill in the evening. He wondered where Lars was and what was keeping him away for so long. Had he gone abroad? Had he returned to Sweden, which was, after all, his native country? And why hadn't he called? Had he, Steven, been wise to leave Alison and his family to come and live in a completely foreign country? His original plan had been just to 'source' Morocco as another possible option to expand Sun Med. He had no plans to remain here indefinitely. He knew no one, except Lars. He wasn't part of the culture or the religion and he spoke very little French, Morocco's second language. And what about money? Now that he had no job, he was completely dependent on Lars financially. Was that wise? Had he thought it all through really thoroughly? The answer was 'no.' A great deal of rethinking and reorganising was essential if the remainder of his life was to go anywhere at all. Perhaps a swim would help him to think things through. He went into the bedroom and changed into his swimming trunks. Throwing a towel over his shoulder, he walked down the stairs and onto the patio. In front of him stretched the magical pool. He placed his towel on a chair and dived in. With his elegant crawl, he began to swim up and down, up and down.

Chapter Thirty-Eight

Kelsey threw another skirt onto the heap of clothes mounting up on the bed. 'That's too tight as well!' she muttered between clenched teeth. 'And it's one of my favourites! What am I going to wear to Grandma's birthday party?'

Daniel appeared in the doorway and laughed. 'Do I see a heap of abandoned clothing?' he asked, a little mockingly.

'It's all very well for you to laugh, but women have all the problems. Not only do we have to suffer morning sickness and carry the baby around for nine months, but we also have to endure growing obscenely large around the girth into the bargain.'

Daniel sat down on the edge of the bed, taking care not to sit on any clothing.

'I'm sorry. I shouldn't have laughed. Of course it's more difficult for women. It must be hell going through all those bodily changes and then finding you can't even fit into your clothes. Look, I've got the afternoon off. Let's go up to London and I'll buy you a gorgeous new baggy dress.'

'You mean a maternity dress?'

'Yes.'

'Where? Mothercare?'

'I was thinking more of Harrods or Harvey Nicks.'

'Harrods. I doubt if Harvey Nicks sells maternity wear.'

Julia was going through her wardrobe for the umpteenth time. She had lost more than a stone and a half, and four inches around her waist in less than two months. It gave her quite a thrill to find that her voluminous sacks no longer fitted. She was beginning to go in a very little at the waist, but noticeable enough to her. Her behind no longer stuck out like a large protruding shelf, and even her breasts, formally huge and floppy, seemed to have reduced a little. Unfortunately her skin hadn't shrunk quite as much as she had hoped. Her flesh hung down in loose folds, limp and flabby, sagging a little more with each pound she shed. But she refused to let this worry her. When she had decided what weight she was going to stabilise at, and when she was back on a normal diet, she could always resort to liposuction, or, better still, a few deft surgical tucks.

The more immediate problem was what to wear to her mother's birthday party, less than a week away. A shopping trip was imminent. Julia decided she would go to Harrods and buy herself an entirely new outfit, including handbag and shoes, not so much for the party, but as a reward for her abstinence.

What a bore, thought Graham: Verity's bloody birthday party. And just before Christmas, too. We could have fitted in a house-hunting trip to France if it weren't for this party. Julia is looking a bit peaky. I think she's lost too much weight too quickly. She's beginning to resemble a scarecrow hung around with spare flesh. However, I won't say anything. She has shown enormous self-control in cutting out all those pernicious cream cakes. I'll go out tomorrow and buy her a dress as a surprise. Maybe at Harrods.

'Shall we come out at Mother's birthday party?'

'You mean - tell them we're a couple?' asked Sudip, a little uncertainly.

'Yes, darling. Let's tell them we're gay. They'll have to know we've bought the house in Vincent Terrace in Islington and we're moving in together.' Russell sounded happy and confident.

'I suppose so. We'll have to tell your family sometime. About the house, I mean.'

'And about us. I wonder if any more bombshells will be dropped at this party?'

'We'll know in a week, won't we? What are you planning to wear?'

Alison had borne the brunt of organising Verity's party. She enjoyed organising and she was good at it. But she did feel that Julia - and perhaps even Russell too - could have offered her some practical help. After all, Verity was also their mother. Then there was the question of how the party would be financed. The family donations had been lamentably small. Of course everyone knew Verity was rolling in money and they complained endlessly about how mean she was, but Alison felt that perhaps this once, for a lady who was about to be eighty, there could have been some substantial donations from her own family. Alison was beginning to wonder if she would be forced to pay most of the cost herself when the manager of The Prince of Wales Hotel came up with the perfect solution.

'Shall I charge the bill to Mrs Davis's account?' he had asked smoothly.

'My mother's account? What account?'

'Your mother has an account with us,' explained the manager. 'Your father opened an account more than thirty years ago when he used to do a lot of entertaining here. Your mother never closed it on his death. I mean,' he sounded a little embarrassed, 'it just seems a practical solution.'

'Of course,' said Alison. 'It's an excellent idea. Put it on Verity's account. It's her party.'

On the morning of Sunday 15 December Gladys awoke feeling pleasantly excited. Today a party was being held at a smart hotel in Chigwell to celebrate Verity's eightieth birthday, and she, Gladys Bates, had been invited. She glanced at her bedside clock. It was seven am. Was it too early to wake Mabel? She didn't think so, so she got out of bed, feeling around on the floor for her bedroom slippers, (still the silver ones with the pink pom-poms,) slid her feet into them and took her bright green dressing gown with the purple braid off the back of the bedroom door. She slipped it on and opened the door quietly. She was anxious not to wake the other residents, a totally unnecessary precaution, as the house was already humming and rattling with early morning preparations. She walked along the corridor and knocked on Mabel's door.

'Come in,' said Mabel.

Gladys went in and gave a little gasp of surprise. Mabel was sitting in a chair near the window, fully dressed in a suit of harsh mauve *moiré* satin. She was wearing shiny gold shoes and there was a matching handbag on the dressing table.

'Mabel!' exclaimed Gladys, quite thrown. 'You're dressed already!'

'Yes. I'm dressed. I didn't want to be late and keep James waiting. Do I look all right?'

'You look - perfect.'

Even Gladys was a little overwhelmed by the bright colour and shiny texture of her friend's outfit.

'What are you wearing, dear?' enquired Mabel.

Gladys felt unable to compete. 'I haven't made up my mind yet.'

Verity awoke with a headache, feeling stiff and tired. For a moment she wasn't sure where she was. Surely not in the hospital, in that little side room? No. The bed was far too comfortable for a hospital bed. But she wasn't back in Alison's granny annexe either. So where was she? Was she already living with James in the new bungalow? She remembered they had got married yesterday. She and James had decided they would invite no one: neither family nor any friends from Oaklands. The registrar had arranged for two witnesses to be present, so there were only five people there. Verity had felt quite emotional when the registrar had asked: 'will you, Verity Louise Primrose, take this man, James Donald Frederick, to be your wedded husband?'

Verity answered: 'I do,' in a voice barely above a whisper.

When the short formality was over, and oh, what a contrast it was to the huge, extravagant church wedding she had had the first time around, the registrar invited James to kiss the bride. He gave her a long lingering kiss, a proper kiss, he always called it, the first time he had kissed her with anyone else present. Verity felt the registrar's gaze boring into her back, as if to express his disapproval of such a carry-on between two elderly people. Then James had taken her out to lunch at a beautiful new Italian restaurant in Wanstead.

That was yesterday, a most eventful day.

But today promised to be eventful too. Slowly Verity began to remember: today was her eightieth birthday and to celebrate the occasion Alison had arranged a family lunch party at The Prince of Wales Hotel in Chigwell. Of course she had invited James, he was now her husband; and also Gladys and Mabel, a fact she was already beginning to regret. It meant there would be even more people present to hear the announcement of their marriage. Verity realised too, with mixed feelings of relief and regret, that she had just spent her last night at Oaklands Retirement Home. Tonight, after the party, she and James would move into their new bungalow in Westcliff-on-Sea. Everything was fully prepared. All they had to do was drive Gladys and Mabel to the Prince of Wales Hotel and drive them back to Oaklands when the party was over. Now it was time to get up and prepare for another big day. Verity got out of bed, feeling a little sluggish. She walked over to her clothes cupboard, opened the doors, and was trying to decide what to wear when Mary came in with her cup of morning tea.

Alison had asked the family to arrive punctually at the hotel at twelve thirty pm, in order to greet Verity when she arrived with her friends at one o'clock. We're not a big family, she thought sadly, as everyone arrived in their pairs at different times. The first to arrive after Alison was her nephew, William, proud of his first class degree in business studies. He was accompanied by his *fiancée,*

Charlotte, a petite and pretty blonde, whose good looks belied the fact that she had graduated from King's College Cambridge with a first in chemical engineering. A few minutes later William's sister, Samantha, arrived, tall, willowy, expensively and elegantly dressed in a black *crêpe-de-chine* trouser suit, bubbling with the news that she had recently been voted top model of the year. Her 'partner' of the moment was in tow, a small mousy man, much older than she, who said he was 'something' in television.

Kelsey arrived next, looking enchantingly pretty and in the full bloom of health. She was accompanied by a tall, dark, good-looking young man whom Alison had not met before. Kelsey greeted her mother warmly and introduced her escort. 'Mum, this is Daniel.'

Daniel shook hands formally, saying: 'how-do-you-do, Mrs Hobbs.'

As Kelsey turned away to greet her cousins, showing her profile, Alison noticed with a shock that her daughter, although not yet divorced, was most definitely pregnant.

Julia and Graham arrived next, Graham looking tanned and healthy after their recent holiday in Spain. Although Julia had lost a lot of weight, Alison didn't think she looked healthy, despite a light tan. She may have shed pounds, thought Alison, but she's not in good shape. Her skin is loose and baggy, especially under her chin and around her neck, but I suppose in this day and age cosmetic surgery could do wonders.

The arrival of Russell and Sudip completed the family gathering, Russell looking debonair in a navy blazer and grey trousers. Alison found herself staring at Sudip, incredibly handsome, in a suit of mid-grey, worn with an apricot shirt and co-ordinating tie. His perfect teeth gleamed whitely in his dark face, his liquid eyes shone with light and warmth. But, thought Alison, this handsome man is my brother's lover. They perform sexual acts together that normally take place between a man and a woman. This is what my husband now does with another man. She repressed a shudder and tried to remind herself that she was not yet divorced.

The family was chatting together and introducing new partners. Alison mingled, accepting a glass of warm white wine of indifferent quality from one of the waiters. Russell came towards her, closely followed by Sudip.

'Alison, darling! How wonderful to see you looking so well! And in such a stunning dress!' He kissed her effusively on both cheeks. 'Alison, this is Sudip Banjaree.'

Sudip bowed gravely and kissed her outstretched hand. 'Alison, it is such an enormous pleasure to meet you at last. Russell has told me so much about you and I feel honoured to be included in such an important family occasion.'

A car drew up outside. The driver got out and opened the rear door. A cry went up from the assembled guests: 'here they are! Mother's arrived!'

'That's Grandma!'

'No. Not the one in the dreadful purple dress, silly. The slim, elegant lady in the grey suit.'

'Should we sing happy birthday?'

'Look! Grandma's got a man with her and they're holding hands!'

Verity and James led the way in through the open hotel door, followed by Mabel and Gladys. A waiter opened the door of the private room, where the family was lined up to greet the guest of honour. Alison struck up 'happy birthday' in her high, shrill soprano. Finding the key too high, the other members of the family joined in at their own varying pitch.

Verity took a few steps into the room, holding tightly onto James's arm. She wasn't sure where she was. Everything seemed very far away. Her heart was thumping loudly and her breath was coming in short, harsh gasps; her head felt as if a steel band was being tightened around it, her hands felt clammy and her mouth dry. But she was happy, very happy. She was married to James and they were going to live together in their bungalow. And at this very moment her whole family had assembled to wish her happy birthday.

Family and friends all mingled well and the party was a great success. At about three thirty, as the guests slowly began to leave, Gladys approached James.

'James, I know you and Verity have now left Oaklands, but I wonder if you could spare the time to drive Mabel and me back? You see, I forgot to order a cab.'

'But of course, Gladys! I'd be delighted to drive you both back to Oaklands. It'll be just like old times.'

'And probably the last time too,' said Gladys, a lump rising in her throat.

'Let's wait until all the guests have left, then I'll drive the car around to the front.'

'Thank you *so* much, James. You always were kindness itself.'

It was only a fifteen-minute drive to Oaklands. James stopped directly opposite the entrance gate, looking up at the house with a twinge of sadness, but also of relief. Then he noticed that a small change had occurred in the lettering above the front door. The 'S' at the end of

Oaklands had disappeared. He wondered if it had been removed, or had just fallen off. He hoped that the ladies, particularly Gladys and Mabel, wouldn't notice. He opened the driver's door and walked around to the passenger side, to escort Gladys and Mabel back into their home.